The Book Feud

Previously published as The Ghostwriter
of Christmas Past
Amber Eve

Copyright © 2022 by Amber Eve

All rights reserved. No part of this publication may be reproduced, stored or transmitted in any form or by any means, electronic, mechanical, photocopying, recording, scanning, or otherwise without written permission from the publisher. It is illegal to copy this book, post it to a website, or distribute it by any other means without permission. This novel is entirely a work of fiction. The names, characters and incidents portrayed in it are the work of the author's imagination. Any resemblance to actual persons, living or dead, events or localities is entirely coincidental.

1

It's my 15th fake Christmas, and my first as a ghost.

Writer, I mean. It's my first Christmas as a ghost*writer*. I should probably have made that clear from the start, shouldn't I? Honestly, this is the kind of thing that's probably going to get me fired one day. Okay, let me try this again...

It's my 15th fake Christmas here in Bramblebury — a village obsessed with two things:

> 1. Christmas itself.
>
> 2. My ex-boyfriend, Elliot Sinclair, who once wrote a bestselling book — which then became a blockbuster movie — set right here in the village, and based heavily on our 23-day relationship, which ended ten years ago: on Christmas Eve, no less.

No wonder I hate Christmas, rom-com movies, and Elliot Sinclair — although not necessarily in that order — right? It would be hard *not* to hate all of those things when they're practically forced down your throat every December, when Bramblebury is transformed from just your averagely picturesque village into The Most Christmassy Place on Earth.

(Yes, our village is really called 'Bramblebury', by the way, as if it's in Middle Earth, rather than the middle of England. Sickening, isn't it? Then again, my parents named me Holly Hart, like a plucky Victorian orphan who might one day get a job as a governess, so I can't really talk...)

Bramblebury might *look* adorably festive, though, but, like I say, it's all fake.

The snow on the window of the bookstore my dad owns, for instance, is fake; it's this weird foamy stuff that comes in a spray can, and it'll be absolute hell to scrape it off again in January, but Dad's been on a mission to make the place look like a shop (or a 'shoppe' rather...) from Charles Dickens' times, and the tourists have been lapping it up like Oliver Twist finally getting that second bowl of watery gruel, so who am I to argue?

I'm just the resident ghost — *writer* — who haunts the bookstore, desperately trying to divide her time between managing the shop and writing 'motivational' self-help books for people whose lives are even *more* of a mess than mine is.

And trust me, that's really saying something.

"They'll be putting up the Christmas tree soon. And the snow globe."

My assistant manager, Paris, appears from the storeroom — which also doubles as my office — balancing a large stack of paperbacks on one hip, and doing her best to sound like she's too cool to be excited by the news she's just shared, even though I know perfectly well she's had a countdown to today on her phone for weeks now, and is planning to livestream most of it to her 18,000 followers on Bookstagram.

Although she's technically supposed to be my assistant, Paris has been basically running the show ever since I started my ghostwriting side-gig, and had to take a step back. Even Edgar Allan Paw, our shop cat, treats her with something vaguely approaching respect, and Ed once pooped on Oscar Wilde — well, on one of his *books*, anyway — so we all tend to do what she says.

"The globe? Is it here yet?" Levis' head snaps up from his phone so quickly it's a miracle he doesn't have whiplash. It's the quickest I've seen him move since the time Paris said she thought she'd seen J.D Salinger outside the shop, but it turned out to just be Billie the postman, who has a wild ginger beard and is — crucially — still alive: unlike Salinger, say, who is *not*. Levis' disappointment was palpable, because Levi is locked in a perpetual battle to get more views on his Booktok than Paris gets on Instagram, and an appearance by a reclusive — albeit *dead* — author would've definitely done it for him.

Now, however, he's found the next best thing.

"Can we go out and get a photo in the snow globe once it's up, Holly?" he says pleadingly. "Just you and me? Please?"

Paris rolls her eyes and tosses her braids over her shoulder. I'm about to copy her, then I remember that self-help book I wrote for a client last year, packed with top tips on how to be a more effective manager, and I twist my mouth into a reluctant smile instead.

"I'm not sure that would be appropriate, Levi," I say, my jaw aching from the unfamiliar facial expression. "I'm your boss, remember?"

"Yeah, but you're *also* the inspiration for *The Snow Globe*," Levi points out, shrugging. "Which is only the best romantic movie of all time. Of *all time*, Holly. You're basically famous."

"Book," says Paris instantly. "*The Snow Globe* was a book before it was a movie. The book was better. *Obviously*. And we don't know *for sure* the character of Evie is based on Holly. Elliot Sinclair has always refused to confirm whether the story is true or not. He probably just made it all up."

She looks at me through narrowed eyes, as if she suspects some trickery is at play here, because it's impossible to believe that someone like me could inspire anything *at all*, let alone a bestselling novel and the subsequent blockbuster movie based on it. Which it blatantly, incontrovertibly *is*. You can't argue with obvious.

"*Duh*," says Levi, who actually *can* argue with obvious, and does it at every possible opportunity. "Eve Snow is *obviously* her. I know Holly doesn't look anything like Violet King in the movie version, but that's because Violet is a famous actress — and, like, *super* hot — and Holly is... the exact opposite of 'hot'. Sorry, Holly. No offense."

I tug self-consciously at my cardigan, which I convinced myself had a 'sexy librarian' vibe when I put it on this morning, but which Paris — who actually *does* look like a sexy librarian, but in that completely effortless way women in their twenties have — informs me is 'giving Coastal Grandmother'. Whatever that means.

"But the character is *so* based on her," goes on Levi, who has no interest in either secretaries *or* grandmothers. "Everyone knows that. *Everyone*. Well, everyone in Bramblebury, anyway. Or 'Hollybrooke', as Sinclair called it. See! He even named the *village* after her! How many more clues do you need, *Paris*?"

I wince; and not just because of the unfair comparison between me and one of the most beautiful actresses in the world, but because I still can't believe Elliot named the town in his novel after me; as if basing the female love interest on me wasn't bad enough.

I can't believe Elliot did a lot of things, though. Putting a fictional version of me — and him — into his book is the very least of my issues with the guy. Giving her a prickly, 'difficult' personality that everyone would assume was mine ... well, that wasn't exactly *great*, obviously, but he didn't *know* it would be a bestseller when he wrote it, did he? Or that it would be turned into a movie.

He didn't know tourists would come flocking to Bramblebury, desperate to see all the landmarks from the story, and he *definitely* didn't know that, every year after that, the town council would erect a large plastic 'snow globe' in the village square, right next to the equally oversized Christmas tree, so that people could have their photo taken inside it — ideally while standing on tiptoe to kiss their partners through flurries of polystyrene 'foam'.

No one could have known that. Especially not anyone who knows me, Holly Hart: 34-year-old book nerd, recently single cat lover, and 'the exact opposite of hot', as Levi puts it.

"So, *can* we?" demands Levi, from his position next to the coffee machine. "Can we take a photo in the globe?"

I take a deep breath as I try to figure out how to let him down gently.

I have never had my photo taken inside the globe. I hate the stupid globe almost as much as I hate Christmas, cinnamon, and people who think it's acceptable to 'pop in' unexpectedly for a visit, as if they were raised by savages.

Levi, however, has been coming to Bramblebury every year since he was 17, just to pose inside the damn thing, and this year he finally talked us into giving him a job in the bookstore, claiming it was his lifelong dream to work in the town that inspired his favorite book and movie. He's only 20, so it can't have been *that* long a dream, but he was so persistent that Dad ended up buying a coffee machine, so Levi could serve up gingerbread lattes and other sickly sweet drinks to the customers, while also flogging them a range of Christmas candles with names like 'Jingle Smells' and 'Scenta Claus'. (We called it the 'Coffee Corner', after a lengthy stand-off with Levi himself, who wanted it to be 'Koffee Korner', and would have had his way if Paris hadn't threatened to resign over it, saying she couldn't work with people who didn't respect the English language...)

Levi bats his eyes hopefully. He's wearing a bright red Christmas jumper with the slogan 'Jingle My Bells' on the front, and his bleached blond hair is extra spiky today. He looks like a member of a 90s boy band, who are about to record their upcoming Christmas single, and between him and Paris, with her low key glamour, it's no wonder customers to the shop sometimes don't even notice me hiding in the background.

"I'm not 'famous', Levi," I say instead. "And I'm not a character in a book, either. I'm a real person. I am not Evie Snow. This is not 'Hollybrooke'. And Elliot Sinclair isn't—"

I trail off, thinking again about the 'effective management' book, and all of that stuff I put in it about keeping your private life separate from your professional life. Which is honestly pretty difficult when you run a bookstore, and the number one Christmas bestseller every year just so happens to be based on a month-long romance you had when you were 24. *'Boss Babe 101: How to Slay as a Manager'* didn't cover that particular scenario, though, strangely enough — the client didn't seem to think it would be relatable to anyone other than me —

so it looks like I'm just going to have to figure out how to 'slay' on my own here.

"I don't want to be associated with *The Snow Globe*, Levi," I tell him firmly. "Not on social media, and not in real life either, if I can possibly help it. Okay?"

As if on cue, the shop door swings open, admitting a blast of frosty air and a small gaggle of shoppers, who enter the store to the tinny refrain of 'Deck the Halls' from the musical motion sensor Dad installed on the door last year.

Ignoring my carefully curated table of indie authors and new releases, the customers flock to the *Snow Globe* book display by the window, all cooing in unison over how 'cute' the store is, with its squishy velvet sofas arranged around a log fire (a roaring one, naturally), and floor-to-ceiling shelves crammed with every kind of book imaginable.

There's only one book that anyone's interested in, though.

I brace myself as one of the shoppers approaches me, holding her copy of *The Snow Globe* in front of her like a talisman. I know exactly what she's going to say, and, sure enough...

"It's you!" says the woman in an American accent. "Sorry," she goes on, with a self-conscious giggle. "I've always wanted to say that in a bookstore. It makes me cry when he says it in the movie."

I smile weakly, trying to pretend I haven't heard this a dozen times already today, and approximately a millionty-one times in the decade since the book came out.

"This *is* the bookstore from the story, isn't it?" the customer goes on as Paris rings up her purchase and slides it into a bag. "The one where they met?"

I hesitate for just long enough for Levi to come pushing forward, puffed up with importance.

"It sure is," he says, beaming. "Hart Books is, indeed, The Book Nook in *The Snow Globe*. They actually used some exterior shots in the movie. The one where Evie and Luke meet for the first time, and he says that line? That's the door of our shop you see him walk through. The interiors were all filmed on a soundstage, though."

The woman gives an excited little squeal, then hands her phone to one of her friends, so she can have her photo taken standing in the doorway in question.

Levi follows them, offering up more tidbits of information about the making of the movie, while I stand there biting my tongue and trying not to scream, *that's not how it happened.*

Because it isn't.

In real life, Elliot and I didn't meet in the bookstore. In real life, we didn't do a lot of the things he put into his book.

But books aren't real life. I should know; I've written enough of them for my ghostwriting clients, churning out tens of thousands of words on subjects I know absolutely nothing about (It might surprise you to know this, but I am not, in fact, a 'Boss Babe'. And I've never 'slayed' at *anything*...), but which I somehow manage to convince my readers I'm an expert on.

See? *Fake.*

It's all fake; just like the snow on the windows, and the book on the shelf, which claims to tell a true love story, but which actually tells a completely false one.

The one saving grace is that most of the tourists who come here to buy a copy of the book don't know I'm the girl in the story when they repeat that famous "it's you" line to me (or to Paris, or to Dad, or to whoever happens to be within earshot when they walk in). They don't know it was my life before it was a book or a movie. They don't know I'm the real-life 'Eve Snow' — and everyone who *does* know has been sworn to secrecy. (On pain of death, in Levi's case).

It's because I'm not *hot*, obviously, to quote Levi once again.

No one ever looks at me and pictures me as a main character. Most people don't really look at me at all, actually; they just look right through me, as if I'm an *actual* ghost, rather than simply a ghost*writer*.

And sometimes I *feel* like one, too.

The day drags on. I retreat back to the safety of my office to work on my latest ghostwriting project — *Nine-to-Thrive: How to Build Your Side Hustle Empire*. Paris and Levi serve coffee and books, and bicker quietly between themselves about whether Booktok is better than Bookstagram. At some point, a group of men from the council arrive in a van with the snow globe and Christmas tree, both of which they erect in the village square, directly opposite the shop door. There's a brief lull in the steady stream of customers as they start work, so the three of us stand with our noses pressed against the window, watching as the men inflate the giant plastic bubble, then fill it with polystyrene 'snow', which will be blown around by a wind machine for the photos.

"Is it just me, or is this weird?" I ask, as a small crowd gathers to watch them do it.

"It's just you," Levi and Paris chorus, in a rare display of unity.

On the other side of the window, a group of kids squabble over who should be first to have their photo taken inside the globe. In the end, they all go in together, and their proud parents snap photos of them throwing the fake snow around, until someone gets a fistful of the stuff in their face, and it all ends in tears.

"I love this time of year," Levi sighs happily. "It's just so *wholesome*."

We watch silently as a small girl punches her brother in the face, and is dragged out of the globe by her frazzled mother, who yells that Father Christmas won't be coming to their house now.

So wholesome.

So heartwarming.

I watch idly as the little family walks away, and it's just as they reach the center of the village square that I see the ghost.

Or what I *think* is a ghost, at least.

Elliot Sinclair is standing in front of the Christmas tree, one hand shading his eyes against the low winter sun as he looks up at lights, which will be officially switched on in a short ceremony later this week.

But no, he *isn't* standing in front of the Christmas tree.

Because it can't be him.

It just *can't* be.

I press my forehead against the window, my breath misting the glass as I try to get a better look.

I know the man in the square cannot possibly be my onetime boyfriend, and long-time nemesis, Elliot Sinclair: bestselling author of *The Snow Globe*, and professional breaker of hearts.

And yet, he looks so like him; his dark hair curling out from under the edges of a beanie hat pulled down over his ears, his tall frame slightly stooped against the December chill.

I reach up to wipe the window clean with the sleeve of my sweater, firmly reminding myself that there's no such thing as ghosts. And sure enough, by the time the window's clear, and I'm looking out across the square again, the figure by the tree is gone — if he was even there at all — and I'm not totally sure whether I'm relieved or disappointed. (Or, you know, just plain *terrified* that I've apparently started hallucinating. Because that's not exactly great news either, is it?)

I shake my head firmly to get rid of the image of Elliot that's taken up residence there, and go back to what I was doing, telling myself it's totally normal to sometimes think you see your ex lurking around your village, even though it's been over a decade since you last saw him, and he lives at least 4,000 miles away.

It *is* totally normal, isn't it?

Customers come and go. At least half of them say the "It's you!" line as they walk through the door. All of them think they're the first one to do it. Most of them buy snow globes.

"There's just one thing I want to know," says the final customer of the day, handing her copy of Elliot's book to Paris. "How does it end? *Really*, I mean? I know in the movie it ends with her standing him up, so he's forced to go back to America without her. But what happened next? Did he come back? Did she follow him? I can't believe Elliot Sinclair just left us all hanging like that. It's so cruel of him! He really should have given us a sequel."

The woman laughs, her question already forgotten, because she knows — *everyone* knows — there is no answer to it. There was never a sequel to *The Snow Globe*. There were no more books at all from Elliot Sinclair after that, much to the dismay of his legions of fans. That famous cliffhanger ending was never resolved; leaving everyone to forever wonder what happened next, and if the couple in the story got to live happily ever after.

But I *know* what happened.

I know he didn't come back.

I know she didn't follow him.

And that's how I know all of this is fake: the snow on the window, the plastic globe in the village square, and even the story in the book everyone comes here to buy.

Not all stories have a sequel.

Some of them just end.

And that's why there are no happy endings; not in the book, not in the movie, not in real life.

But, once upon a time, I really thought there could be...

2

December, 10 YEARS AGO

It's my fifth fake Christmas.

It's not as bad as the first one. The year Mum died, Dad and I did our best to pretend nothing had changed, as if cheerfully playing host to all of the ghosts of Christmas past would somehow help make the reality of Christmas present a little less scary. As if all we had to do was remember the exact order Mum used to hang the Christmas baubles on the tree, and we'd pass the test. Then people would stop touching me sympathetically on the hand, while asking how I was "bearing up". Dad would be able to open the bookstore for more than half a day without breaking down in tears somewhere in the sci-fi section. Neither of us would ever again be faced with the impossible task of coming up with a non-violent response to the diabolical phrase "Everything happens for a reason."

Christmas was the boss level in the surreal video game my life had become, basically, and I approached it the same way I'd approached every other vaguely pointless test someone had deemed it essential that I pass (GCSE Maths, the school talent show Mum persuaded me to enter in Year 7, despite my startling lack of any discernible 'talent'...);

by briefly making it my entire personality, and preparing for it like an Olympic athlete with a solid shot of winning the gold.

I made lists. I checked them twice. I checked them a third time, and sometimes a fourth. I spent hours reading articles about how to make Christmas wreaths out of old socks, and scoured the cooking section of the bookstore until I found a recipe book called *Mistletoe Munchies*, which I smuggled home in order to surprise Dad with my mince pies and pigs-in-blankets.

Mum would have loved it. But Mum wasn't here. It was down to me now to make Christmas magical; and while Mum had done it apparently effortlessly, and with the same joie de vivre she applied to everything else she ever did, *I* decided to do it by baking a Christmas pudding with so much cinnamon in it that my lips swelled up like Mick Jagger's, and Dad couldn't stop sneezing. Finally, on Christmas Eve, I found Dad crying over an old Christmas card I'd made for him and Mum when I was 6, and too young to know that a happy Christmas was not, in fact, guaranteed, and I think that was the moment I realized there are some things you just can't prepare for. It didn't matter how hard I tried — and trust me, I tried really, *really* hard — Christmas was always going to feel fake from now on, and no amount of mistletoe *or* 'munchies' would change that.

So the Christmas pudding went into the bin. My lips went back to normal (although Dad *does* still call me 'Mick' from time to time...). I swore off cinnamon for life. Then Dad and I ordered takeaway for dinner, and told each other that next year would be better.

But it wasn't.

"I'm just not much of a Christmas Person," I'd started saying by Fake Christmas Number 2. It seemed like an easier thing for people to have to deal with than hitting them with the whole 'dead mum' thing at what's supposed to be the most magical time of year; so I just kept repeating it until it had become as much a part of my personality as my love of books, and my habit of over-planning everything.

And now here we are, on year number 5. I'm 24 years old. It snowed last night; not the pretty, fluffy kind of snow you see on Christmas cards and in romcom movies, but the gray, wet kind that turns to slush as soon as it hits the ground, and seems to worm its way inside your soul. It soaks my boots as I trudge through the village square on my way back to the bookstore, doing my best to avoid the small group of market stalls which are huddled apologetically together against the wind, the stallholders grouped around them with hands thrust in pockets; breath misting the frigid air as they complain about the cold.

The Bramblebury Christmas Fayre has been a village tradition since 1903, with visitors coming from miles around to eat roasted chestnuts and buy things like ugly handmade ceramic elves, and Christmas baubles with 'World's Best Mum!' carved on the front.

As a Non-Christmas Person, it goes without saying that I'd rather go on a date with Martin Baxter, the nerd next door, than visit a Christmas market; and Martin could bore for Britain, so that's saying something. But the fact that the stalls are set up almost directly outside our shop makes it hard to avoid it — especially on days like today, when I have a package to drop off at the post office, and the only way to get to it is by walking through the square. So I run my errand, and am almost back at the shop when something on one of the stalls catches my eye, and I find myself walking towards it to take a closer look.

The snow globe is tucked away at the back of a stall selling second-hand bric-à-brac; almost hidden between a stack of old vinyl records and a teapot the color of snot. It's absolutely *not* my kind of thing. I can't stand clutter; not even the 'vintage' kind, which this appears to be. It disrupts the orderliness of my carefully organized little world, and makes me feel like I can't think clearly. So I have no idea what it is about *this* piece of 'clutter' that makes me stop in my tracks.

Plus, I'm Not a Christmas Person, remember? What would I want with a *snow globe*, of all things?

Later, I will wonder if the globe was somehow bewitched; because that's the only explanation that will make any kind of sense to me once this ordinary-looking ornament has proceeded to wreak havoc upon the course of my entire life, like some kind of enchanted object in a fairy-tale, which the princess was always destined to touch. For now, though, it's still just a snow globe, and I find myself reaching for it in spite of myself, curious to know if the little scene inside the domed glass really is what I think it is.

Just as my fingers brush the dome, though, another hand appears from nowhere, reaching for the globe at the same time. Our fingers collide, and I snatch my hand back, as if it's been burnt.

"Oops! Sorry," I say, looking up and into a pair of deep blue-gray eyes that are staring right back at me, a little too intently to be totally comfortable.

The owner of the intense eyes is very tall, with dark hair that curls slightly at the ends, a nose that's started to turn red from the cold, and cheeks that are either naturally rosy, or just absolutely freezing. He's wearing a pair of dark-rimmed glasses that he reaches up to adjust as I stare at him, and he looks exactly how I've always imagined Gilbert Blythe in Anne of Green Gables: only if Gilbert was around my age, and much better looking than Lucy Maud Montgomery gave us reason to believe.

His lips are turned up at the ends in a slightly bemused smile, and just as he opens them to say something, a fat white snowflake — so perfectly fluffy as to make it almost look fake — descends from the heavens and lands right on the tip of his nose.

I kid you not. A snowflake. An actual *snowflake*. Followed by another, then another still. Within seconds, the gray sludge on the streets has disappeared beneath a blanket of white, and everyone around us has paused to stare at the heavens, as if they're witnessing an actual Christmas miracle. It's almost as if Bramblebury has abruptly decided to give up on being an ordinary little village in the middle of England, and turn itself into the setting of a Hallmark Christmas movie instead — with me and Mr Rosy Cheeks here as the unsuspecting main characters.

The stranger laughs, and reaches up to wipe the snowflake away, his eyes meeting mine in a way that suggests he knows what I'm thinking and totally agrees.

I know beyond doubt that I have never seen this man in my life before, and yet he's somehow instantly familiar to me, as if I knew him in another life, and have been just waiting to bump into him in this one. Which is absolute *nonsense*, of course; right up there with 'everything happens for a reason' and all of those other trite, meaningless phrases so beloved by people whose mums didn't die indecently young. And yet...

"It's you!" I say, in a strange, breathy voice that doesn't sound anything like mine, and which will make me do a full-body cringe every time I remember it from now until the day I die. "*Yours*, I mean!"

I quickly correct myself, my cheeks suddenly hot enough to melt the snow that's still landing on them. "It's *yours*. Here."

I snatch the snow globe off the table and thrust it towards him, embarrassed by my reaction to this total stranger. Not to mention my sudden inability to speak like a normal person.

The stranger's eyes do a thing I can only describe as "twinkling."

I've always wondered what that meant. Well, I guess now I know.

"Oh, no, you take it," he says in an American accent, the exact provenance of which I can't place. South Carolina? Louisiana? Somewhere else where the men sound like they've stepped right out of a movie? "I'll find something else. I'm spoiled for choice here."

He nods in the direction of the stalls closest to us, on which are laid out a selection of Christmas jumpers, and some singing cactus toys, all wearing light-up Santa hats. His eyes do that 'twinkling' thing again as one of the toys starts tunelessly singing 'Deck the Halls'. It's impossible to tell whether he's being sarcastic or not with the 'spoiled for choice' thing. I mean, he doesn't *look* like the kind of guy who'd wear a mustard yellow jumper with 'Santa's Favorite' on the front, but if I've if learned anything from a lifetime spent with books as best friends, it's that a man as seemingly perfect as this one has to have a fatal flaw — maybe his is a love of tacky Christmas gifts and things that smell like cinnamon?

(A man as good looking as him would *definitely* be Santa's favorite, though. So that much is certainly true.)

He hands the snow globe back to me, and I'm so flustered I almost drop the thing.

"No, no, it's yours, seriously," I tell him, poking him in the chest with it again, then instantly wondering why I did that. "I don't actually want it. I was just curious about it."

I glance down at the ornament in my hand. Just as I'd thought, the scene inside is a miniature version of the very square we're standing in right now, minus the market stalls and, well, the *awkwardness*. At its center, two people stand locked in a passionate embrace, the snow swirling around their heads in a way that's oddly mirroring our current reality.

It's romantic *and* festive, and it makes me feel a bit like I've stepped into an alternate reality; one where Bramblebury is beautiful, and Christmas has a shot at being magical again.

No, this is crazy. It's a snow globe, not a portal to an alternate universe.

"Here," I insist, passing it back to the American, who has no option but to accept it this time, unless he wants to make this interaction even more uncomfortable. "All yours."

Before he can say anything else, I turn and walk quickly away through the snow, which is falling faster now, camouflaging all the village's imperfections with its pristine whiteness. I leave a trail of footprints as I go, my mind already replaying that moment in the square when it saw fit to blurt "It's you," at a tourist, instead of "It's *yours*," which I *swear* is what I was going for.

Not that it matters, though. It's not like I'm ever going to see him again, is it?

The thought makes me feel sadder than it should do, given that absolutely nothing really happened. Two people reached for the same object at the same time. It started to snow. That's it. That's literally *it*.

Any connection I thought I felt between me and the man in the square was entirely imagined. It has to have been. This isn't some schmaltzy romance novel: it's my life — and right now my life involves opening up the store, and trying my best to sell some books, so we can afford to pay the rent this month.

Which is exactly what I'm going to do.

Tucking the memory of the man with the sparkling eyes carefully into a corner of my mind, where I can pull it out later, I let myself into the shop, and switch on the electric heater to warm the place up, before selecting a book from the shelves and settling down to read while I wait for the first customers of the day.

I'm a few chapters in, and have just reached the bit where the handsome-but-surly stranger on the plane turns out to be staying in the room next door to the heroine at her hotel, when the shop door creaks reluctantly open with a blast of frigid air.

I quickly stash my book under the counter, annoyed to be so rudely torn out of its fictional world, in which it's sunny and warm, and anything is possible.

So, the exact opposite of the *real* world, basically.

"I'll be right with you," I call out to the customer from under the counter. "Feel free to take a look around."

"Sure," says a voice with a familiar American accent. "Take your time."

I straighten up so quickly I bang my head hard on the underside of the counter, and almost go flying right off my seat.

"Hey! It's you!" says the American, when I finally re-emerge.

And that was when our story started.

3

Of course, in his book, it was Elliot (Or Luke, as he called himself...) who said the now-famous "*It's you*" line first, not me / Evie. And it wasn't just a stupid slip of the tongue, either, like it was when I said it in real life. No, in Elliot's book, it really *was* love at first sight between the two main characters; and when Luke Saunders looks into Evie Snow's eyes and says, "It's you," he means it's *her* — the one he's spent his entire life searching for.

What a crock of shit, right?

That's just *one* of the ways Elliot re-wrote our story, though. Another is the fact that he set that first meeting in the bookstore, rather than at the Christmas market; one tiny change, which was to completely alter the course of our little shop's history, and force us to start stocking shelves full of snow globes, just like the store in the book.

But I'm not thinking about Elliot this morning; by which I mean I'm very deliberately *not* thinking about him, as I leave the little cottage I bought a few years ago, when the bookstore's success finally meant there was money to spare, and walk to The Brew to pick up a coffee before I start work.

I'm not thinking about Elliot Sinclair *at all*. And I'm definitely not buying my coffee from here just because that's where we went on our first 'date'. No, I *always* get my coffee from The Brew — because the stuff Levi serves at the bookstore tastes like boiled socks, let's be honest — and I'm not going to let the ghost of Elliot Sinclair stand between me and my routine. Routine is important. It's one of the few things that stands between me and utter chaos, and so I cling onto it, like Rose clinging to that door in *Titanic*.

The Christmas market is already in full swing, even though it's still early. There's no snow this year (It hasn't snowed *properly* in Bramblebury for ten years now, to the eternal disappointment of the tourists, who come here expecting it to look like it does in the movie ...) but the village is still looking chocolate-box pretty, with fairy lights strung across the square, and a brass band playing Christmas carols off to one side.

It is, as Levi will later observe in the caption of his next TikTok video, "Festive AF".

It's just a shame the same can't be said about me.

"Drink up Holly; you look like you could be doing with some color in those cheeks of yours."

Maisie Poole, Bramblebury's chief librarian and gossip monger, appears as if by magic and slides into the seat opposite mine without waiting for an invitation.

This is the very last thing I need right now.

"Ooh, she does look a bit peaky, doesn't she?" says her sister, Elsie, joining us, as if to prove that, no matter how bad things are, they can always get worse. "I said you're looking a bit peaky, Holly," she repeats loudly for my benefit. "I hope you're not coming down with something?"

"No, it's just the time of year, isn't it?" replies Maisie on my behalf. "Always a hard one for her. And she spends so much time in that bookshop she's even starting to smell like books. Maybe you should give her one of those cake pop thingummys you ordered, Elsie? The young ones love those. They're all the rage, trust me."

The Poole sisters aren't twins, but they look like they could be; both of them small and bird-like, with 'harmless little old lady' vibes about them which totally belie the fact that they have two of the sharpest tongues in town. They're well past retirement age, but they've both been lying about their ages for as long as I can remember, while insisting they're very much 'down with the kids', so their actual age is anyone's guess.

"Holly might love the cake pops, but the cake pops certainly don't love a lady's figure, do they?" says Elise, smiling sweetly as she covers the confectionery on her tray with both hands, as if I might pounce on it without warning. "And she has to be careful, Maisie. She's not really a 'young one' anymore, is she? Not everyone has a metabolism like ours, remember?"

"No. And she's lost one man already this year," agrees Maisie, speaking about me as if I'm not there. "You're right, Elsie. Best not."

I glance down at my figure, currently clad in my favorite dress, which Paris once described as "dark academia, with a twist". She didn't say what the 'twist' was, but now I'm worried it's that it makes me look like Jane Eyre; who she's *also* compared me to lately.

"I didn't 'lose' Martin," I point out, deciding to address the blatant body-shaming another time. "We broke up. It was mutual. He just... wasn't the right man for me. And I *like* the smell of books. It's comforting. What could be better than the smell of books?"

"If you say so," shrugs Maisie, looking slightly put-out. "What are you writing, dear?" she goes on, perking up at the sight of my notebook lying open on the table. "Christmas shopping list, is it? I've had mine done since the start of November. You've left it a bit late, Holly, I must say."

She purses her lips disapprovingly, and I bravely resist the impulse to point out that there's still over a week until Christmas, and I only have Dad and Ed the cat to buy for; one of the upsides of leaving your long-term relationship before the festive season kicks in, I guess.

"It's just some notes for my latest ghostwriting project, Maisie," I tell her instead. "Remember I told you I was doing some freelancing?"

"Ghostwriting?" Elsie's pink cat-eye glasses slide down her nose as she frowns. "Is that books about ghosts, then?"

"Don't be silly, Elsie," says Maisie sharply. "Don't you think Holly has enough ghosts to deal with? I'm talking about the ghosts of the *past*, dear," she continues, leaning forward and lowering her voice dramatically. "Like your poor mother. And that Elliot —"

"Ghostwriting is when you write something for someone else," I interject quickly, wanting to head this line of conversation off at the pass. "Like when a celebrity claims to have written a book, but it's really someone else who wrote it for them. Only I don't write for celebrities: it's just regular people who have an idea for a book, but don't know how to put it into words. So they hire a ghostwriter to do it for them."

"So, you do all the work and they take the credit?" says Elsie, scandalized. "Well, I never. I don't think that seems fair, do you, Maisie? Why not just write the books yourself, Holly? Cut out the middle-man, so to speak. That's what I'd do."

Her eyes narrow thoughtfully, as if she's thinking of trying her hand at it herself; the Poole sisters never miss a business opportunity if they can help it.

"I don't have any ideas," I admit reluctantly. "It's like... I can *write* a book just fine, as long as someone else has come up with the plot. But I don't have any stories of my own. I really wish I did."

This is a hard thing for me to admit, even after all this time. It's one of my greatest failings in life; that and my inability to drive on the motorway at night, or maintain a romantic relationship for longer than ten months.

"Anyway, that's why ghostwriting is perfect for me," I go on, shaking off the melancholy mood that always descends when I start listing my failings. "I get some writing experience, but I don't have to come up with the idea for the book, or figure out how to market it. And I don't really care about not getting credit for it. It's not like I'm writing great works of literature, you know? They're self-help books for people who don't know how to use Google. So it's fine that I don't get my name on the cover."

"Well, it's nice to have a hobby, I suppose," says Elsie doubtfully. "You should ask that Elliot Sinclair for advice, though, Holly. He's a *proper* author. He writes *real* books. He'd be able to tell you how to come up with a story."

"He wrote *one* book a decade ago," I point out, churlishly. "Which makes him a one-hit wonder, if anything. He only had one story in him; and it wasn't even his."

This is pretty rich — and also kind of mean, really — coming from me, the girl who has so far failed to find any stories in her *at all*. That's why I'm a ghostwriter, not a famous author, like Elliot.

"Oh, I don't know," says Elsie. "I'm sure someone told me there was a rumor he was writing another one. Now, who was it who told me that? Was it you, Maisie?"

She looks at her sister thoughtfully, then snaps her fingers as the answer comes to her.

"I remember now!" she says, pleased. "It was young Jimmy, who drives the Amazon van. He heard it from Nora, in the florists, and *she* heard it from Matteo, from that new restaurant. You know the one on Bridge Street?"

"No, Matteo's restaurant is on Castle Walk, Elsie," replies Maisie. "You're thinking of young Mason. His people have the tapas bar. You know, the one with the red and white awning on the front? *Not* the one with the blue door; that belongs to the Smiths. Or is it the Powells?"

The sisters eagerly launch into a quick who's who of Bramblebury, and I do my best to tune out. These rumors about Elliot and a new book start doing the rounds at least once a year, and so far, the 'new book' he's allegedly working on has failed to materialize. I'm at least 74% sure it's just his publisher's way of drumming up more publicity for *The Snow Globe* by allowing people to hope there might one day be a sequel to it, but that doesn't stop my heart doing a fast-paced anxiety dance every time someone mentions it.

The Snow Globe itself was bad enough; I'm not sure I'd cope with a sequel. Not that there would be any chance of me being in it, obviously, seeing as I haven't seen Elliot since before it was published.

"Anyway," I say, clearing my throat to interrupt the sisters, who are now deeply embroiled in a discussion involving who used to run the greengrocers before it was turned into a health food shop. "Elliot couldn't help me with my writing even if I wanted him to, because he and I aren't in touch. I don't know the guy anymore. And he definitely doesn't know me. He never really did."

I glance across at the corner Elliot and I sat in on our first date, as if he might still be sitting there all these years later, listening in to this conversation about himself. But the shabby little booth with the peeling leather seats is long gone; replaced by a huge, glass-fronted fridge containing expensive bottled water and low-cal smoothies. There are no ghosts here. If there were, they'd probably leave, just to get away from the squabbling Poole sisters.

"Evie Snow wasn't much like you in the movie," Elsie agrees. "But I do like the bit where she gives the doctor a piece of her mind. That was very *you*, Holly."

"No, it wasn't," I protest, stung. "That never happened, Elsie. You know that. I'll never forgive Elliot for writing that book of his. It changed everything; and not for the better."

Elsie exchanges a glance with her sister that makes me wish it was more acceptable to argue with elderly people.

"Now, now," begins Maisie. "If it wasn't for 'that book', as you put it, none of us would be here. Well, I mean, we *would* probably be *here*, in The Brew; but it wouldn't look like this. Until 'that book' came out, The Brew was dying on its feet. They could barely afford to keep the lights on. And now look at it."

We all dutifully look around us at the interior of the shop, which bears absolutely no resemblance to the chintzy little tea room it used to be when Elliot and I had our first 'date' here over a decade ago. That's the only reason I can bring myself to keep coming here.

"It's the *Snow Globe* effect," agrees her sister. "It's like magic. It makes everything better."

"Not *everything*," I reply, knowing I sound petulant, but not really caring. "Not everything's been better since *The Snow Globe* came out. And not everything needs to change, anyway. Maybe some things were better the way they were."

Like my heart, say. And the way I used to be able to pick up a book without worrying that there might be a photo of my ex on the back cover. Just the simple things, you know?

"That's the wrong attitude, Holly," Maisie tells me firmly. "You have to move with the times. Get with the program."

"You've got to catch the vibe," Elsie joins in eagerly. "Is that how you say it, Maisie?"

"You have to glow-up," Maisie finishes, ignoring her. "You have to *flex*. Like Elsie and me. We *flex*."

I gape at her, dumbfounded. It's like she's swallowed Urban Dictionary whole.

"Oh, that's a good one," her sister agrees, sipping her tea primly. "We do like to flex, don't we?"

"The question is," says Maisie, leaning forward and fixing me with a gimlet stare. "Do *you*, Holly?"

"Do I... *flex*?" I pick up my coffee mug and take a long gulp in a bid to hide the laughter that's bubbling up inside me. "I ... I'm not sure. I do a pilates workout on YouTube sometimes. Does that count?"

"Do you want to move with the times, I mean?" says Maisie impatiently. "Do you want to glow-up, like the rest of us, or are you just going to keep on complaining about your boring little life, and how Martin left you because you were frigid?"

"Hang on," I reply. "That's a bit harsh, Maisie. I wasn't complaining. And Martin *didn't* say that. Wait: *did* Martin say that?"

"He said you had a heart as cold as ice," Elsie pipes up importantly. "He said not even dragon fire would melt it. He does like dragons, young Martin."

"That's what I said," replies her sister, irritated. "She's frigid."

"Freezing," nods Elsie.

"Maybe a make-over?" suggests Maisie, frowning in concentration as she looks me up and down again critically. "That couldn't hurt, could it? Remember that time you went into the bookstore and walked right past her, because she'd blended in with one of the shelves?"

"Ooh, I know! She could have a Main Character Moment," says Elsie, excitedly. "Remember we read about that on the Internet, Maisie? Everyone was having one. I think *I* had a bit of one this morning, actually."

"You did not," retorts Maisie, who hates being outdone by her sister. "That was just one of your migraines, Elsie. And Holly's already had her Main Character Moment when she was in *The Snow Globe*. She can't have two. That would just be greedy, wouldn't it?"

"I don't need a make-over," I explode, suddenly sounding very like Evie Snow after all. "*Or* a main character moment. I'm quite happy staying in the background, thanks. And I don't have a heart of ice. I can't believe Martin said that. I'm not *cold*."

I *am* actually quite cold right now, to be honest. But my *heart* is a completely normal temperature, and I'm just about to tell them that when I happen to glance at the window of the shop.

And there he is.

Again.

Elliot Sinclair is standing outside The Brew, wearing the same beanie hat I thought I saw him in yesterday, and looking in at us, almost as if I've conjured him into existence just by speaking about him. What's that saying again? Speak of the devil, and he might appear?

I let out a strange, high-pitched squeak of shock, and the mug in my hand suddenly slips through my fingers, hot coffee spilling onto the table in front of me, and dripping onto my lap.

I squeak again, this time in pain.

"Oh, my goodness! Quick, Holly, take this!"

Maisie and Elsie flutter around me like birds, offering paper napkins and words of advice on how to get coffee stains out of clothes (Baking soda and white vinegar, apparently), and by the time they're done fussing, and my view of the window is clear once more, there's no one there.

Of course there isn't.

Which means that I'm either, a) seeing things, b) going insane, or, c) Elliot Sinclair really *is* skulking around a town he hasn't visited in a decade, somehow managing to disappear the split second I lay eyes on him.

I'm honestly not sure which of those three options is the least appealing.

(Okay, I'm lying; it's the last one. I'd much rather be seeing 'things' than seeing Elliot Sinclair right now, trust me...)

"Did you see him?" I ask, looking wildly from one sister to the other. "At the window. Did you see him too?"

They stare back at me with identical expressions of bemusement mixed with concern on their faces. I know I must sound crazy right now, but I *have* to know if I actually *am*. Because that would definitely be helpful.

"Did we see who, dear?" asks Elsie cautiously. "I don't see anyone at the window; did you, Maisie?"

Maisie shakes her head.

"It's just this time of year," she says kindly. "It always sends poor Holly a bit loopy, doesn't it? Remember how she shouted at her poor father that time, Elsie?"

"That wasn't *me*," I exclaim, aghast. "That was Evie Snow in *The Snow Globe*. You see what I mean?" I'm horrified to notice that my voice is starting to sound kind of wobbly now. "Everyone thinks it's true. Everyone thinks I'm *her*, and that I did all those things in the book, but that's not true. It's really not. I—"

But it's no use; Elsie and Maisie might be nodding along as if they completely agree with everything I'm saying, but I can tell that I've lost them. And now I really *am* starting to sound every bit as irrational as Elliot made me — I mean *Evie* — sound in his book; which means it's time for me to go.

"Thanks for the chat," I say, giving them both a smile which I know they'll later describe to each other as "brave. "I best be going."

So I go; leaving quickly, just in case the man I thought was Elliot is still somewhere around; maybe coming out of the gourmet food store, or browsing the market stalls in the village square, hoping to bump into some other unsuspecting woman he can use as 'inspiration' for a book.

But he isn't there. The entire village is conspicuously lacking in anyone who looks even remotely like a bestselling author; or even an American ex-boyfriend.

I'm starting to think I should get my eyes tested.

That would be a perfectly reasonable explanation for all of this. Well, that and the fact that I live in a town that's absolutely obsessed with my ex.

I guess *anyone* would start to think they were seeing him under those circumstances.

Wouldn't they?

Elliot Sinclair isn't the only thing that's stuck in my mind, though, as I make my way to the bookstore. Maisie and Elsie's words are in there too, circling and repeating like a record with a scratch.

I hate to say it, but maybe Maisie is right? Maybe I *could* be doing with making a few changes? Maybe not a 'makeover' exactly, but *something* to get me out of this decade-long rut I've been stuck in? A confidence boost. A goal of some kind. An opportunity to feel like the main character in my own life, for once.

Maybe if I did that, I'd stop imagining Elliot Sinclair around every corner. Because, call me crazy, but I think it's long past time to start banishing that particular ghost of Christmas past.

4

DECEMBER, 10 YEARS AGO

The American is standing by the door, with the collar of his coat turned up against the cold, and he's so distractingly good-looking that I'm in danger of falling off my seat yet again at the sight of him.

"It's me," I agree, pleased to find that I'm managing to sound perfectly normal this time around. "And it's ... you."

On second thoughts, scratch that.

"I'm really glad I bumped into you again." He grins widely, then comes striding across the room until he's standing right in front of me. "Because I think *this* is you, too. Or someone who looks very like you, anyway."

He reaches into his coat pocket, then pulls something out, which he holds up to the light to show me.

It's the old snow globe I picked up at the market earlier; which, now I have the chance to see it up close, is definitely supposed to be Bramblebury village square in miniature. I can even see a tiny version of the building that would one day become Hart Books in the background, snow piled on its roof like the icing on a cake.

It's not the bookstore that the American wants me to look at, though: it's the little couple standing kissing in front of it — her in a red winter coat that's vaguely similar to the one I was wearing this morning; him in what seems to be an Army uniform, but with thick dark hair, and .... is that a pair of glasses he's wearing?

The woman doesn't really look like me at all: it's just the color of the hair and coat that's the same. The man, however, bears more than a passing resemblance to the one currently standing in front of me; and, judging by the way he's smiling down at me, it looks like I'm not the only one who's noticed.

"Here," he says, handing the ornament to me before I can object. "I really think you should have it. It was obviously destined for you."

"Uh-uh. We're not doing this again," I reply, passing it back with a smile. "It's definitely yours. You bought it; you can't just give it away. And I don't believe in destiny, anyway."

"It was only £5," he says, looking amazed at his good fortune. "I felt a bit like I'd robbed the woman who sold it to me, if I'm honest. So you'd be doing me a favor if you'd just take it. It would help assuage my guilt."

He hands it to me again, and I instantly pass it back, as if we're playing Hot Potato.

"Seriously," I tell him. "I don't want it. I... I don't even *like* snow globes."

"You don't? But who doesn't like *snow globes*?" he asks, feigning amazement.

"I'm ... not much of a Christmas person," I tell him, trotting out my old faithful excuse.

"A Christmas person?" His eyes crinkle with amusement. "I'm imagining some kind of giant human here, with, like, a Christmas tree on their head, and cookies for eyes."

"And fairy lights wound around their legs," I join in. "Flashing ones."

"In that case, I don't want to be a Christmas person either," he says firmly. "Because that sounds terrifying. Cute store you have here, by the way. Is it yours?"

He turns and looks around at the empty store, which is more messy than it is 'cute', with dust lining the bookshelves, and a log fire we can't risk lighting until we can afford to have the chimney swept. Which will be never, at this rate.

"Sort of," I tell him, hoping he hasn't noticed the giant cobweb near the door, which I'd have taken down by now if the thought of destroying it didn't make me feel bad for the spider, who I've named Shelob. "It belongs to my dad."

"Family business, huh? You're lucky. I'd love to spend my days surrounded by books."

I consider telling him I'd much rather be writing books than selling them, but everyone I've ever admitted this to in the past has smiled indulgently, the way you do when a little kid tells you they're going to be an astronaut when they grow up, so I just nod as he plucks a book from one of the shelves at random and starts flicking through it.

"Any recommendations for me?" he asks. "I thought I saw you putting a book away when I walked in earlier?"

This is a very generous way to describe what I was doing under the counter, but I can't think of a way to deny I was reading anything without effectively calling him a liar, so I pull out the book and shame-facedly show him the cover, which is one of those illustrated ones, with a bright pink background, and a cartoon couple on the front.

"It's just a trashy romance," I mutter, embarrassed. "It's not the kind of thing I usually read, it was just... it was just the first thing that came to hand."

The hundreds of books that line the walls of the store look on accusingly as the lie leaves my lips. I can almost hear them sigh in despair.

"Oh, I wouldn't call romance 'trashy'" says the American, surprising me. "It's just another type of story, isn't it? I don't think you could claim it's any less worthy than anything else. I doubt Jane Austen would call her work 'trashy', do you?"

I look down at the book in my hand, which is definitely no *Pride and Prejudice*. But, then again...

"I like it because I know there's nothing in it that's going to hurt me," I say in a rush. "No one's going to die, or even suffer, particularly. There's always going to be a happy ending. I ... I appreciate that."

I don't tell him that books with happy endings are the only kind I've been able to read since Mum died. That when I pick up something new, I always flick quickly to the end to make sure there are no dead mothers, abandoned children, or other unbearable plot twists waiting to ambush me. And it doesn't *have* to be a trashy romcom, but it *does* have to be a book that won't hurt me; which can be surprisingly difficult to find. Whoever it was who started that rhyme about how sticks and stones can break your bones, but words can never hurt you had obviously never read the scene in *Black Beauty* where Ginger dies, had they?

I don't tell him any of this, but he's watching me as if he already knows — or at least suspects — that there's more to this than I'm telling him.

"Well, I think we can all appreciate a happy ending," he says softly. "Don't we...?"

"Holly," I tell him, answering his unspoken question. "Holly Hart."

"Holly?" His eyes do the twinkly thing again. It's very distracting. "That's quite a name for someone who is definitely not a scary Christmas Person."

"My Mum loved Christmas," I find myself telling him. "It was her favorite time of year. So she named me Holly, even though I was born in July."

"Was? She's not around anymore?" The smiley eyes crinkle with concern, but for some reason his sympathy doesn't make my barriers instantly go up, the way it does with other people. Somehow, I feel like I can talk to him about Mum without wanting to cry.

"She died," I say quietly. "When I was 19. She had cancer."

He absorbs this fact silently, giving it time to sink in.

"And that's why you want to read books with happy endings," he says matter-of-factly. "Makes sense."

I nod silently, because it does, and he's the first person who's understood that without trying to make me feel stupid or uneducated because I refuse to read *The Boy in the Striped Pajamas*, and will never forgive Louisa May Alcott for killing off Beth March.

"Well, Holly, I'm very pleased to meet you," the American says now, holding out his hand for me to shake. It's warm and soft, and it wraps around mine for just a little longer than is strictly necessary, making me momentarily forget everything else.

"I'm Elliot, by the way," he adds, letting go at last. "Elliot Sinclair. My mom likes Christmas, too, but not enough to give me a festive name, unfortunately. I kind of wish she had, actually. I could really see myself as a Gabriel, say. Or maybe a Rudolph."

Our eyes meet, and we both burst out laughing. I can still feel the touch of his hand on mine, even though his are tucked safely back in his pockets by now.

"So, do you live near here?" he asks, suddenly shy. "I guess you must do if your family owns this place?"

"Very near," I tell him, my heart doing a little dance of excitement. "Right above the shop, actually. With my Dad."

"Right. So I guess that means I might see you around?" he says casually. "I'm staying at The Rose Tavern. Do you know it? What am I saying? Of course you know it. You live here!"

"It *is* the only hotel in the village," I confirm, charmed by how adorably flustered he is. "Although I only know it as a pub. I don't know anyone who's actually stayed there."

"Oh, you're missing out," he grins, recovering himself. "There's at least three rooms for hire upstairs. Only one bathroom, though. That was ... unexpected."

He smiles good-naturedly, not remotely troubled by the spartan accommodation at The Rose, which is the kind of place where you wipe your feet on the way *out*, rather than on the way in. My disappointment at the confirmation that he definitely isn't from around here is tempered slightly by the knowledge that he's almost definitely trying to ask if he can see me again.

Or I *think* he is, anyway.

Is he?

"So, do you ever go to that pub?" Elliot asks hopefully.

"Not really," I admit. "I do go to the café next door most days, though, on my lunch break. They do a really nice ploughman's lunch. Or sometimes I'll have a jacket potato, or a toastie. Those are nice, too."

I stop, realizing I'm rambling. I don't think Elliot's interested in the toasties at The Brew, somehow — which, to be honest, aren't even *that* good.

"Right!" Elliot's face brightens. "Funnily enough, I was just thinking it'd been a while since I had a decent ploughman's lunch." He pauses. "What exactly *is* a ploughman's lunch, again?"

I chuckle.

"You'll have to order one to find out," I say teasingly.

"Maybe I will," he replies, smiling back at me. "And maybe I'll bump into you when I'm doing it? I feel like we owe it to these guys to at least get to know each other."

He indicates the little couple in the snow globe, who are still locked in their eternal embrace. I can't help but laugh at the earnest look on his face.

"Oh, come on," he says, undaunted. "You can't deny that they look just like us. And the fact that we both tried to pick them up at the same time ..."

I hold my breath, convinced he's about to tell me everything happens for a reason; in which case I'll already have identified his fatal flaw.

"It's a sign," he finishes. "Don't you think?"

"I don't believe in signs," I reply firmly, wishing for the first time in my life that I did. "It's a coincidence, that's all. Coincidences happen much more often than people realize. That's why so many people believe in things like fate. They..."

I stop, realizing I'm about to ruin this near-perfect moment with my unfortunate habit of regurgitating information I once read in a book. And I really don't want to ruin this moment; or spoil my chances of seeing Elliot Sinclair again.

"I have lunch around one," I say instead, my voice strangely squeaky.

"Well, great. I guess I'll see you there, then."

Elliot smiles with relief. Even though he looks like someone who smiles often, the effect is no less devastating every time he does it, and it's virtually impossible not to smile back at him; which isn't something I'm particularly used to doing these days, it has to be said.

He pauses, as if he's about to say something else, but then the shop door bursts open and a young couple come in, chattering loudly, and breaking the spell.

I have never resented anyone more in my life.

"I'd better get going," says Elliot apologetically, as the man approaches the counter, ready to ask for help with something." It's been nice meeting you, Holly Hart."

"You too."

I smile in a way that I hope makes it clear I'm not just being polite, and that I really, genuinely mean it, but he's already gone, the shop door slamming behind him as a gust of wind catches it.

I go to help the customers at the counter, and it's only later, when I'm tidying up at the end of the day, that I notice the snow globe still sitting on the counter, next to the cash register.

He left me the snow globe.

And tomorrow, I'm going to see him again.

5

I arrive at the bookstore just in time to intercept Dad, who's attempting to force a large box filled with books through the door, his glasses steamed up with the effort.

"Here, let me take that," I tell him, glad of the distraction as I grab one corner of the box and help him carry it inside. "What are these, anyway? Not more copies of *The Snow Globe*?"

I pull a face, but Dad's too busy moping his brow with the handkerchief he keeps in his jacket pocket to notice.

"No," he says, turning back to the box. "No, it's the latest Vivienne Faulkner, Holly. Here, take a look."

He pulls a hardback out of the box and hands it to me. It's called *A Season for Second Chances*, and the picture on the front shows a couple walking hand in hand down a snowy street, both wrapped up in gigantic scarves and beaming at each other, presumably delighted by their 'second chance'. On the back cover, Vivienne Faulkner herself flashes an unnaturally white smile as she sits on a chair that looks like a throne, wearing a sharp, Barbie-pink trouser suit, and looking like she's about to try to sell us something from the Avon catalog.

"Looks like the same old tripe she always churns out," says Dad, cheerfully. "Should sell well, though; she always does. Let's try to clear some space near the front of the shop for these, shall we?"

I nod, although I'm secretly planning to read the new book as soon as I get a chance; because Vivienne Faulkner may be the queen of trashy romance, but every single one of her books comes with a guaranteed happy ever after — and normally a dashing billionaire, who falls for a really quite ordinary girl, into the bargain — and she writes so many of them that you have to admire her, really; even though admitting that would be a bit like saying you'd rather have a Big Mac than a nice, juicy steak.

Sometimes you just want a Big Mac, though.

Don't you?

I've just finished unpacking the books, determinedly keeping my back to the window as I do it, so there's no opportunity to imagine any ex-boyfriends looking through it, when my phone pings with a message alert. I swipe to open it, expecting it to be either confirmation of my last book order for the store, or possibly some foreign prince who desperately needs to temporarily transfer several million dollars to my account as a favor — because those are the only two types of email I seem to get these days, and even *I* know the second one is just spam.

For once, though, it's neither.

It's a message from the ghostwriting agency I do all of my work through, and the contents of it do absolutely nothing to reassure me that I'm not either going mad or imagining things.

"Everything okay?" says Dad, seeing me sit down suddenly on one of the squishy sofas in front of the fire. "You look like you've seen a ghost."

"No," I reply, feeling the blood rush to my head as I look up from the screen in amazement. "Well, I mean, yes, I think I have. But it's *me*, Dad. *I'm* the ghost. Or I *will* be, anyway. I've just been offered a fiction-writing job."

The commotion that breaks out following my latest job offer lasts all day, and is still raging as we prepare to close the store for the night.

"Look, it's fine," I tell the room at large, during a brief gap in customers. "I haven't said I'll take it yet; I don't even know anything about this project, other than that it's a novel, rather than a self-help book, and it's urgent, apparently."

"But why would someone ask *you* to write a novel for them, Holly?" says Dad, puzzled. "I thought it was just non-fiction you'd been writing for this 'agency'?"

He says the word 'agency' as if he fully suspects there *is* no 'agency', and it's all just an elaborate cover for something far more nefarious.

"I think the person they'd originally hired for it must have dropped out at the last minute or something," I tell him. "That's the only reason I can think of that they'd ask me to do it instead. It's not like I have any novel-writing experience that might have won them over.

Everything I've done for them so far has been non-fiction. So, you know, it might not go anywhere."

"Probably not," agrees Levi, cheering up. "Are you sure it's not just another one of those phishing emails? You do get a lot of those, Holly."

"Shut up, Levi," says Paris firmly. "Of *course* Holly can write fiction. She won that creative writing contest, didn't she?"

I smile at her gratefully, even though I know she's just saying this because she wants my job. And also because she'd say anything to contradict Levi.

"That was in high school," I admit. "It was before..."

It was before Mum died, is what I'm about to say, but don't, stopping myself at the last second because I don't want to upset Dad any more than I have already. Before Mum died, I still planned to go to university; to study creative writing, and to maybe one day be a writer myself. Before Mum died, I planned to travel the world, live somewhere hot and sunny, and fall in love. Before Mum died, I planned to do a lot of things.

But then everything fell apart; me and Dad most of all.

There was no way I could leave him after that; no possible way I could leave home — not for college, not for love, not for anything. So, instead, I stayed; to help with the bookstore and everything else. I didn't go to university. I didn't see the world. And okay, I technically *did* end up with a writing career of sorts; but titles like *Unfollow Anxiety: Breaking Up With Your Fears*, and *Hashtag Hustle: Turning Your Passion into Your Paycheck* aren't exactly the kind of thing I was thinking of when I said I wanted to be an author.

But this latest project could be. And, okay, I won't get to have my name on the cover of whatever novel I end up writing, but, even so, it's a start. And wasn't I just thinking about how much I needed a change? A 'glow-up' as the Poole sisters called it?

I was. And now here's the very opportunity I was looking for, arriving with absolutely impeccable timing. All I have to do is say yes to it; which is exactly what I'm going to do. Before I can change my mind, I hurry into my office, where I pull out my phone, and call Harper Grant, the woman whose name is on the bottom of the email from the agency, with a signature explaining that she's a commissioning editor, responsible for connecting ghostwriters with clients.

"No, it's right enough; the job's yours if you want it," Harper confirms, once I've sheepishly explained that I think she might have messaged the wrong person by mistake. She has a soft, maternal-sounding voice, which is immediately reassuring, and makes me picture her sitting at a desk covered with family photos, with a purring cat on her lap.

"Really?" I know from my research for my last writing project — *'Glow Up: the Guide to Faking It Til You're Making It'* — that I should be trying to project my 'best self' here, in order to convince this woman I know my own worth, and am a fully competent adult who she can trust to do the job. It's just... well, I don't really *feel* like a fully competent adult who she can trust to do the job. Or even an averagely competent one, if we're being brutally honest.

"Yup, really." Harper sounds amused by my surprise. "The client's seen some of your previous work, and they really liked it. They're offering more than your usual rate, too, seeing as it's such short notice."

She names a figure that's almost twice what I've been making for my self-help stuff, and makes me wonder again if I'm imagining all of this.

"That's... that's amazing," I say croakily. "Really... amazing."

"Look, I'll get all the details over to you along with the contract and the non-disclosure," Harper goes on, kindly pretending not to notice I've apparently lost the power of speech. "I don't have everything to hand right now, but I can tell you it's a fiction project; a Christmas romance."

"Oh."

My excitement at being picked for this project goes down a notch. The whole time I've been thinking about this job, it never once occurred to me that the book they'd ask me to write might be a romance — and a Christmas one, at that. And as much as I love *reading* romance, I haven't exactly been *living* it; not even when Martin and I were still together. No, with the exception of the books I squirrel away to read in secret, my life is a romance-free zone. And a Christmas-free zone, too. All of which makes me the least-qualified person on the agency's books — and maybe even in the entire world — to attempt to write a Christmas-themed romance novel. It's like asking a snowman to write a book about saunas. Or a vampire to write a cookbook.

What if you make a complete mess of it, and it all goes tits up? says Levi's voice from the back of my mind.

He's right, though, isn't he? Harsh ... but right. Me writing a Christmas romance would be a recipe for total disaster. It would almost definitely all go "tits up". I should say no. I'm going to say no.

"Holly? Are you still there?" Harper sounds worried. "Is there a problem?"

"Um, no, no problem," I reply, not wanting to let this nice-sounding woman down. "It's just... can I think about it? Just for a bit?"

There's a short pause, during which I cross my fingers tightly, willing her not to hate me for my indecisiveness.

"Sure," she says, her voice reassuringly warm. "I can give you until tomorrow morning. Will that be long enough?"

"Of course," I say quickly, not at all sure it will be. "That'll be just fine."

"I can't do it. I absolutely *cannot* write a Christmas romance. I'm going to have to say no."

It's a few hours later, and I'm standing in the main room of the village hall, watching my Aunt Lorraine issue directions to a group of volunteers who're all busily hanging up Christmas decorations. The hall is festooned with fairy lights, like most of the other buildings in town at this time of year, but the interior hasn't changed in decades, and the magnolia walls and faint 'gym hall' scent are the only clues I'm not living in a simulation here in Bramblebury, which was looking almost sickeningly festive on the way here.

"Don't be silly, Holly, of course you can write a whatever-it-is," says Lorraine, looking at me sternly over the top of her glasses. "You can write anything you like. You can *do* anything you like. Never forget that, okay?"

Lorraine is Mum's sister, and while Mum was soft and nurturing, like a hug in human form, Lorraine is what would probably be best described as a 'force of nature'; which is why she's the perfect person to head up the village community association — the reason we're here on this cold December night.

"I appreciate the vote of confidence," I tell her, as she hands me a large cardboard box filled with what I'm assuming are more decorations. "It's just ... a Christmas book? It's not me, Lorraine. I'm not..."

"You're not a Christmas person," Lorraine finishes for me, in the tone of someone who's heard all of this before. Which she has, to be fair. "But maybe you should be. Have you ever thought about that?"

"What, opening up my cold, hard heart to the wonder of the season?" I say, going for sarcasm as my first line of defense, as usual.

"I wouldn't put it quite that way," says Lorraine, who, true enough, isn't exactly known for her way with words. "But it was your mum's favorite time of year, Holly. You know that. She'd hate to think she'd ruined it for you."

"She didn't ruin it for me," I reply shortly. "It's not like she died on purpose. And anyway, it's not just Mum. It's everything. This place, and its weird obsession with Christmas. Its obsession with—"

"Elliot?" suggests Lorraine shrewdly. "Is that what this is about? Elliot and his book? Still?"

I shrug, feeling like a sulky teenager again as I put the box of decorations on the floor at my feet. As I straighten back up, I notice I'm standing right next to a small brass plaque that's set into the wooden floor.

"*This is the exact spot where Evie kissed Luke for the first time in The Snow Globe*", it says, in swirly letters. I close my eyes in an attempt to fend off the memory the sight of the plaque always triggers, but it slams into me anyway, almost knocking me off my feet with the force of it.

This place.

Seriously.

"I thought I saw him earlier," I confess, shaking off the memory like a dog shaking the rain out of its fur. "Elliot. At The Brew. And yesterday, too, outside the shop. I thought I was going mad for a second."

I glance around the hall, suddenly worried I might see him again. If his ghost was planning to appear anywhere, it would be here; right on this *exact spot*, in fact, to quote the writing on the floor.

But the room is reassuringly ordinary.

It's just *me* who's haunted.

"Do *you* think I'm going mad?" I ask Lorraine, knowing I sound stupid, but feeling the need to put the possibility out there, anyway. My aunt frowns.

"I think this is just a difficult time of year for you," she says, unconsciously echoing Maisie's words from earlier. "And all of this probably isn't helping, is it?"

She indicates the box at my feet.

"What, Christmas decorations? Well, no, I guess not. I'm pretty used to them by now, though. I—"

I pause, noticing that one corner of the box is torn, with something that doesn't look much like a Christmas decoration peeking through the gap.

"Wait. What *is* this stuff, anyway?"

I bend down and pull the lid off the box, somehow knowing already what I'm going to find.

And yup: there it is. Approximately 20 copies of *The Snow Globe*, all staring up at me smugly, as if to say "I told you so".

"What are these doing here?" I ask, straightening up and turning back to Lorraine, who has the grace to look sheepish. "I thought I was here to help you set up for the Over 60s Christmas Dance?"

"Oh, you are," she assures me, not quite meeting me in the eye. "But ... that's not until next week. First, it's the book festival. Remember?"

I groan, slapping my hand across my forehead in frustration.

The book festival — or 'fayre' as I believe it's styled here in good ol' Bramblebury. How could I have forgotten about the book festival? It's not like Paris and Levi haven't been talking about it every day for the last month. I'm pretty sure Dad's even booked a table at it for the shop, actually; didn't he mention something about that just the other day?

"I've been so busy trying to finish my latest ghostwriting commission before Christmas," I tell Lorraine, in an attempt at an explanation. "It completely slipped my mind."

"Is that the book about learning how to communicate with your cat?" asks Lorraine, who's the only person who even feigns interest in the books I produce for the agency.

"No," I reply gloomily. "They said there wasn't enough of a demand for that one. It's the one about side hustles."

Which brings us neatly back to the subject of my *own* side hustle: and the Christmas romance novel I've just been asked to write for it.

"I just don't think I can say yes to this one, Lorraine," I say, perching on the end of one of the trestle tables. "What do I know about romance? I'm 34 and single. My last serious relationship ended with me threatening to report him for stalking."

"That reminds me," says Lorraine. "Martin was in here earlier, looking for you. Had a face like a wet weekend on him."

"See?" I reply. "That's not romance, Lorraine; it's just plain creepy, the way he follows me around. And Martin was the longest relationship I've ever had. What does that say about me?"

"Oh, come on, Holly," says Lorraine. "So you've had a bit of bad luck with men. It doesn't mean you can't write about romance. Here."

She stoops down and rummages through the box on the floor, before holding up one of the books inside it, as if she's proving a point.

"This," she says, prodding the front cover with a neon pink nail. "This is one of the greatest romances of all time. Or so everyone says, anyway. And it's literally about *you*. *You're* Evie Snow. So I'd say you probably know a bit more about romance than you think you do."

"*The Snow Globe* isn't a romance book," I reply, sounding a lot like Paris. "Romance has to have a happy ending. This doesn't. *We didn't*. You could call it a love story — if you were being generous — but you can't call it a romance. And, anyway, it's not even true. Well, hardly any of it's true. And the bits that *are* ... they're just Elliot's side of the story, aren't they?"

"So maybe it's time to tell your side of it?" Lorraine says, shrugging. "Why not? Write your own book. Take control of the narrative for once. At least it would stop everyone asking how it ended all the time."

She picks up the box of books and starts laying them out on the table, and I stand there for a moment watching her, my mind whirring.

It's true to say that, ever since *The Snow Globe* came out, with its cliffhanger ending, readers have been clamoring for a sequel.

It's also true to say, however, that I can't be the one to write it. Not just because there *is* no 'part two' to the story — Elliot and I just *ended*, and that was that — but because publicly associating myself with *The Snow Globe* is the very *last* thing I'd want. It's bad enough that everyone here in town knows that Evie Snow was based on me; I don't think I'd cope if everyone else in the book's fandom knew too.

Maybe I could do it anonymously, though? Like, under a pen-name, say.

Or as a ghostwriter.

"Thanks, Lorraine," I say, giving her a quick peck on the cheek as I get ready to leave. "I'll let you know what I decide to do about the romance book."

I leave the hall, and step straight into what appears to be some kind of festive theme park that's been set up in the village square.

There are fairy lights. There are lanterns. There's food trucks and Christmas music, and a surprisingly large crowd of people, all gathered around the Christmas tree, with rosy cheeks and giant churros in their hands.

Of course; the tree. They're all here for the annual spectacle that is the switching on of the lights. I completely forget that was tonight.

I'm just passing the tree itself — which I see has been hung with dozens of miniature snow globes this year — when the countdown starts.

"Three!" yells the crowd. "Two!"

I quicken my step in a bid to get out of the way, but the crowd is so large and excitable that I end up stumbling; the heel of my boot sticking on one of those infernal cobblestones, and sending me over on my ankle. For just a second, my hands clutch at thin air, looking for something to grab onto, and then, just as I'm about to lose my balance, an arm appears on my elbow, holding me steady as I wrench my foot free and stand up straight.

"ONE!" yells the crowd.

Fireworks explode above the square as the Christmas tree lights flash on, shimmering against the dark sky.

"Thanks," I say gratefully, turning to look up into the eyes of the man who's still holding me upright; dark blue eyes that twinkle with the reflection of Christmas lights and fireworks, and a hundred and one memories. Eyes I would know anywhere. Eyes that are definitely not those of a ghost, or a mirage, or even the product of my over-active imagination, but the familiar blue eyes of the man I once thought was the love of my life. It's Elliot Sinclair.

6

DECEMBER, 10 YEARS AGO

Things like this don't happen to me.

I don't usually bump into handsome strangers in snowy village squares, for instance.

And, if I did, I'd be willing to bet they wouldn't look at me the way Elliot Sinclair is looking at me now: as if we're not actually strangers at all, and he can see something in me that no one else ever has.

And yet here we are, tucked into a corner booth at The Brew, on what even I have to acknowledge is most definitely A Date; and a pretty damn good one, too.

He stood up when I arrived. He pulled out my chair for me. He blushed when our fingers touched over the coffeepot, but he didn't move his hand, and neither did I, so now we're sitting here across from one another, *almost* touching but not quite, and I think it might just be the best thing that's ever happened to me.

And, okay, the ploughman's lunch is a crushing disappointment — pity the poor ploughman who had to go to work on a single slice of soggy lettuce alongside some pre-packed ham and plasticky cheese — but Elliot politely pretends not to notice, and I'm too nervous/excited to eat much anyway, so it's all good.

It's better than just *good*, actually. From the moment we sit down, being with Elliot feels a bit like finding the missing piece of that puzzle you've been trying to solve for years now, and discovering it was in your pocket the entire time. We talk and talk; the words tumbling and overlapping as we attempt to bring each other up to speed on the events of our entire respective lives up until this shared moment, in a quiet little cafe with snowy footprints slowly melting onto the cheap lino floor and sticky tables covered with plastic cloths.

Elliot is 26, he tells me, and his family is from Florida, although he's just graduated from law school in California. He's spending a few weeks in England before going home to join the family business at some point in the presumably not-too-distant future — although that's one topic of conversation I'm determined to avoid for as long as possible.

"But why Bramblebury?" I ask, puzzled, as a bored-looking waitress appears to pour us some more coffee. "It's not exactly a tourist hot-spot; especially not compared to America or California." I sigh, thinking of blue skies and palm trees; azure seas and golden sunsets. The America of my imagination is probably nothing like the reality of the place, but I refuse to believe it's not significantly better than *here*.

And I've always thought reality was overrated, anyway.

"No, it's not," Elliot agrees, grinning. "Believe it or not, though, as soon as I saw it, it was love at first sight. And that was even *before* I bumped into you."

He smiles shyly, and my stomach does a not-unpleasant little flip-flop as his words sink in.

"But why? What does Bramblebury have to offer that Venice doesn't?" I ask, trying to sound like it's completely normal for me to be flirted with by men with beautiful eyes and bewitching smiles. "Snow globes aside, I mean?"

"Oh, I totally came for the snow globes," he assures me. "Which were one hundred percent worth it. But I also have a family connection to the area that I wanted to check out."

I blink rapidly, suddenly convinced he's about to do that very American thing, where they claim to be one-forty-eighth English, and descended from one of Henry VIII's lesser-known mistresses.

"My great-grandfather was stationed near here during the war," Elliot goes on, to my relief. "He died before I was born, but he used to talk about the place a lot, apparently, so I kind of grew up hearing about it. He said it was like a village from a story."

"A horror story, maybe." I smile, to show I'm joking, even though I'm not really, and fully believe Bramblebury to be the very armpit of England. "I guess it might have looked a bit better back then, though."

"It looks pretty good from where I'm sitting," Elliot says softly, making me blush. "But no, not a horror story. Maybe a biography, though? I was... " He pauses, as if he's trying to decide something. "I was thinking of maybe having a go at writing it, actually," he says in a rush. "My great-grandfather's story."

He shrugs dismissively, as if this is no big deal. But he's wrong. What he's just said is a very big deal indeed. Or, at least, it is to me.

"Wait: so you're a writer?" I say, leaning forward in excitement. "But I thought you said you studied law?"

"Oh, I did," he replies. "But only because it was what my family expected, and... well, they were the ones who were paying." He shrugs again, his cheerful expression faltering slightly. "But I've always wanted to write. I'm not sure I'd call myself a 'writer'" he goes on, making scare quotes with his fingers around the word. "But, yeah; it's something I've always done. Something I've always wanted to do more of." He looks at me across the table, a lock of dark hair falling across his eyes, which are exactly the same shade of blue as the thick sweater he's wearing, and currently filled with something that might be hope.

"I've never actually told anyone that," he says, bashfully. "I always worry it'll just sound stupid."

"It doesn't," I assure him, a little too eagerly. "It really doesn't. I've always wanted to write, too. It's my biggest dream."

"Really? So why haven't you?" He reaches up and pushes the hair out of his eyes, which are fixed on mine, as if my answer to this question is of the utmost importance. I don't remember the last time I was this interesting to someone.

"I've tried," I confess. "Plenty of times. But it just never seems to work. I think... well, you know how everyone tells you to write what you know?"

Elliot nods.

"Well, I don't know very much," I tell him bluntly. "I don't know anything *at all*, really. Or nothing anyone would want to read about, anyway. I've spent my entire life in a bookshop, in a small town. I haven't traveled, like you have. I haven't been to Europe — or America. I haven't been anywhere, really. I've just kind of stood still, in the place I've always been. I don't have a story."

"I don't believe that for a second, Holly Hart," Elliot replies immediately, his dancing eyes serious for once. "Everyone has a story. You just don't know what yours is yet. And that's fine. I'm not sure what mine is, either." He shrugs, self-deprecatingly. "But I do know you're not necessarily going to find it in Paris, or Rome, or any of those places you think you need to go to 'find yourself', or whatever it is you're looking for. Maybe your story is right here."

"In Bramblebury?" I laugh lightly, already feeling embarrassed by my little 'poor me' outburst. "God, I hope not!"

"Why not? My great granddad said he had a helluva time here, apparently. I bet if he was writing his story, he'd set it here."

"Is that what you want to do, then?" I ask, trying to steer the conversation back into territory that makes me sound a little less unhinged. "You want to write his story for him?"

"Sort of. I don't really have a lot to go on," he says. "But I'd kinda like to give it a shot. And I can already see what he liked about the place."

He gives me one of those smiles of his, and it feels like the first signs of spring, after a long, long winter.

"Is it the snow globes or the ploughman's lunches?" I ask teasingly.

"Both. It's mostly the beautiful booksellers with the awesome accents. I like those the most."

It takes approximately three seconds for my cheeks to turn as red as my coat; the one Elliot said reminded him of the woman in the snow globe.

"Sorry," he says. "That was super cheesy, wasn't it? Maybe I should be trying to write a trashy romance instead of a biography."

"I liked it," I confess, blushing some more. "No one's ever called me beautiful before. It was nice. You're nice."

I bite my lip, wishing I'd come up with something better than the faint praise that is 'nice' — the most lukewarm compliment in all the world. But Elliot's face lights up as if I've just told him he's won the lottery of life *and* been nominated for a Pulitzer.

"Well, I think you're very nice too, Holly Hart," he tells me sincerely. "And I'm very glad we both reached for that snow globe at the same time yesterday."

"Oh, that reminds me," I say, reluctantly breaking the spell our conversation seems to have cast. "You forgot this."

I pull the snow globe out of my bag and place it carefully on the table between us. Tiny snowflakes float to the surface, stirred up by the sudden movement, then float softly down over the heads of the tiny couple who I'm starting to agree do look a bit like us.

"No I didn't." He grins easily. "I wanted you to have it, remember? And I still do."

I had, of course, suspected as much when I put it in my bag earlier. I just wanted to be absolutely sure.

"Seriously," Elliot says, seeing me hesitate. "Keep it. It'll probably get broken if I try to put it in my suitcase, anyway."

I pick up the globe and pretend to examine it again, so I don't have to look him in the eye. I don't want to think about his suitcase, or when he might start packing it. And, in any case, I have to admit, the snow globe is growing on me. I'm starting to quite like it. Or maybe I just feel grateful to it for its role in my meeting with Elliot Sinclair, who thinks I'm beautiful. Elliot Sinclair, who wants to be a writer, like me. Elliot Sinclair, who reaches across the table and takes my hand in his, and who somehow makes it feel like the most natural thing in the world.

"Would you like to go for a walk?" he asks hopefully. "Maybe show me some more of this town of yours? I should probably get to know it a bit better if I'm going to set my book here."

I glance guiltily at my watch. I really should be getting back to the shop by now. My lunch break technically ended 20 minutes ago, which means Dad's left manning the place on his own.

Not that there's much to 'man', though. I served a grand total of two customers this morning — and one of those had only wandered in because she thought we might have a bathroom she could use. (I really hope she enjoys the copy of *Rebecca* I talked her into buying, though; I might only have spoken to her for a few minutes, but there was a definite air of the second Mrs. de Winter in the timid way she asked to use the facilities...)

Besides, isn't Dad always telling me I should stop worrying about him and the store, and let myself live a little?

And isn't he right?

Maybe I could live a little. Maybe I could do it right now, with this lovely man, who's watching me with so much hope in his eyes that there's absolutely no way I can bring myself to disappoint him. Or myself, even.

"I'd really like that," I say, reluctantly letting go of his hand so I can pull my phone out of my bag. "Let me just send my Dad a quick message to let him know I'll be late, then I'll be right with you."

The snow has started to fall again as we leave the cafe and crunch our way across the square. The stalls that make up the Christmas market are still selling exactly the same tat they had yesterday, but today it doesn't look quite as sad to me. I try my best to see the village through Elliot's eyes as we wander through the twisty, cobbled streets, past buildings that have stood here for probably hundreds of years, their thick walls and lopsided windows hiding lord knows how many secrets.

I can see how, to someone more familiar with the sun-bleached streets of Florida or palm-fringed California boulevards, Bramblebury might look charmingly quaint, even in its current, slightly dilapidated state; like the kind of place you might read about in one of those paperbacks which have titles like 'A Christmas to Remember' or 'Susan's Festive Wish' written in a swirly script. I can see why Elliot might want to set his book here, too, I guess, and as we wander through the streets, me pointing out 'landmarks' he's probably already seen, but pretends to be amazed by, it's impossible not to be pulled along by his enthusiasm.

We stop in front of the town hall — a Victorian building with a single, square clock tower in the front. It's normally hired out for things like aerobics classes, and AA meetings, but today it's busier than usual, with old-fashioned swing music cascading out through the open doors and onto the snowy street. Through the large windows, a small group of elderly folks can be seen jiving and jitterbugging along to the music, their white heads bobbing like dandelions in a stiff breeze as they circle the main hall, which is being used as a dance floor.

If it wasn't for the advanced age of most of the dancers, the scene would look like it had come straight out of a World War 2 movie; a fact which is explained only when I see a laminated sign on the noticeboard in the entrance to the building, advertising the Bramblebury Over 60s Christmas Dance, which is taking place here this afternoon.

"Is it a dance hall?" asks Elliot, watching as the band strikes up a jaunty new tune. "It looks like a fun place."

"It's just the town hall," I explain, trying to see this, too, through his eyes. "Although I think it might have been a dance hall at some point, back in the day. I'm sure I remember Dad saying something about that. Hey, maybe your great-grandfather came here when he was in town?"

"Maybe he did." The thought makes his face light up. "Let's pretend he did," he says, grinning down at me. "Let's pretend he stood on this exact spot, with a cute English girl he'd just bumped into in the village, and then they went inside to dance."

"And then they lived happily ever after?" I say, my heart keeping time with the fast pace of the music as I wonder where he's going with this.

"Well, no, I guess not," he says apologetically. "I don't think my great-grandmother would've appreciated that somehow, and she was from Boca Raton, so..."

"Ah. Maybe not, then."

I stuff my hands into my coat pockets, trying not to be too disappointed at the idea of this completely fictional mini-romance not ending well. Elliot, however, is undaunted.

"Let's do it," he says, his eyes shining as he holds out his hand. "Let's go inside and dance."

I'm about to say I don't really dance; which is true, as it happens — not to mention the fact that I don't think either of us will pass as over 60s, somehow. But it strikes me now, as I stand next to him, that there are a lot of things I don't do these days; like laughing, for instance, or falling asleep without spending at least 20 minutes worrying about imaginary scenarios that are unlikely to ever come to pass. I don't ever really let go, and allow myself to enjoy something, without worrying about losing it.

But maybe I should.

"Sure," I say, returning his smile as I slip my hand into his. "Why not?"

Why not indeed?

Laughing at the sheer ridiculousness of the situation, we walk hand-in-hand into the hall, and join the crowd of old folks on the floor, none of whom seem particularly perturbed by our presence among them.

Almost as soon as Elliot and I set foot on the dance floor, though, the music changes from a fast-paced foxtrot — or, at least, I think that's what it is — to a slow waltz; the kind that requires you to stand close to your partner and put your arms around them.

Okay, this is definitely not how I imagined my afternoon going.
Not that I'm complaining.

"I should warn you, I'm not much of a dancer," Elliot says softly, reaching out and pulling me towards him. I nestle easily into his arms, surprised to find that it doesn't feel awkward at all.

It feels quite perfect, actually.

"It's okay," I reply, tilting my head to look up at him. "I'm not either. I guess we'll just have to make it up as we go along."

And so that's what we do.

I put my hand on his shoulder, he winds his arm round my waist, and we sway together to the music, slightly out of time, but not remotely caring.

The scene is not particularly romantic. The lights in the hall are far too bright — probably due to some kind of health and safety red tape to make sure no one sues the council if they trip and fall — and Elliot and I are both still bundled up in our winter coats; me with my bag slung awkwardly across my shoulders, and him still with that tomato-red scarf of his wrapped around his neck.

It might not be romantic, but it *is* absolutely perfect; and when the song comes to an end, and he leans forward and kisses me, his lips soft and warm against my snow-chilled skin, I know beyond doubt that this is one of those moments that I won't need to redraft in my mind when I think about it later; because it's absolutely perfect the way it is.

The kiss goes on and on; my body molding to his, and his hands coming up to gently cup my face, until the dancers around us notice the young couple kissing in their midst, and burst into a spontaneous round of applause: which still doesn't convince us that it's time to stop kissing.

I don't think it'll *ever* be time to stop kissing.

I *do* think I'm going to remember this moment for the rest of my life.

What I *don't* know — but am destined to find out — is that pretty much everyone I know, plus a few hundred thousand people I *don't* know, is going to remember this moment too; but ever so slightly differently, when Elliot puts it into his book, turning the 40s-themed dance into the actual 1940s, and me into a local woman with a faintly ridiculous name.

On this cold December night on my 24th year on earth, though, I have absolutely no idea that none of this is real. All I know is that I've just met someone who makes me feel like this Christmas might not be so bad after all. And so I reach up to wind my arms around Elliot Sinclair's neck, and I kiss him back as if this is the start of something that might last forever.

Because I really think that it might be.

7

I'd be lying if I said I hadn't imagined this scenario a few times in the years since I last saw Elliot Sinclair.

Not this *exact* scenario, obviously. No, any time I've allowed myself to imagine what it would be like to bump into him again, I've been poised and elegant, and really quite jaw-droppingly beautiful; not staggering around on the cobbles like a very drunk baby elephant, like I am now.

"Holly?" says Elliot, making it sound like a statement of disappointed fact, rather than a question.

This, of course, isn't right either. The Elliot of my imaginings is always pathetically grateful to be in my presence once more; desperately begging my forgiveness as soon as he lays eyes on me. This Elliot, however, lets go of my arm as soon as I'm upright again, looking like he's already planning his exit.

Which he probably is, knowing him.

He's good at planning exits, after all.

Still, at least he didn't say 'It's you'. That would've been too much, even for him.

"I knew it," I gasp, wincing with pain as I put my weight onto the foot I've just released from the pavement. "I knew it was you outside the cafe this morning. And yesterday, in the square! I thought I was going mad at first, but I wasn't. You're ... you're really here."

The look on Elliot's face confirms that I'm babbling. I close my mouth quickly, before I can depart any further from the imaginary script in which Elliot and I meet for the first time in a decade, and I pretend not to recognize him.

"*Why* are you here, though?" I burst out, instantly failing in my resolve to be cool and distant, and not to say anything else. "Why now?"

Elliot looks down at me, as if I'm a problem he's trying to figure out how to solve. The lights of the Christmas tree illuminate his face, which is sharper and more angular than I remember. He's not wearing his glasses. His hair is shorter and neater, although still with that slight curl to it that suggests it might spring back into its familiar, slightly disheveled state at any second.

He looks older, of course — I expect I do too — but the biggest difference is in his eyes.

There's no twinkle in those dark navy eyes now; just wariness and distrust — two emotions I can't help but think he has absolutely no right to direct at *me*, when he's the one who's well and truly proven he can't be trusted.

How *dare* he act like *he's* the one who got ghosted, when we both know it was *me*?

"My publishers asked me to come," he says in a 'stating the obvious tone'. "It wasn't my choice, trust me."

Trust me.

Famous last words.

"Right," I say, with as much dignity as I can muster, given that my ankle feels like it's on fire, and my most significant ex is looking at me as if he only barely recognizes me. "Your publisher. Of course."

I'm not going to ask *why* his publishers wanted him to come to Bramblebury.

I'm *definitely* not going to ask if it's got anything to do with the sequel to *The Snow Globe* he's permanently rumored to be writing.

I'm not going to ask him anything at all, actually. This is the new Holly Hart he's looking at. The one with the fresh new start, and a publishing deal of her own, albeit as a ghostwriter, rather than a 'real' author, like Elliot.

"So, why's that, then?" I blurt out, proving once again that my willpower is less than stellar. "Why'd your publisher want you to come here? You're not writing another book, are you?"

Elliot's cheeks darken slightly, as if he's embarrassed .

Well, good. He *should* be embarrassed if he really has come to my hometown to celebrate the publication of the book he wrote about our relationship; the one that broke my heart all over again. He *should* be begging my forgiveness, just like he does in my imagination.

Instead, he just shuffles his feet awkwardly, then reaches up to adjust his glasses, remembering at the last second that he's not actually wearing them anymore.

"I'm here for the book festival, actually," he replies at last. "The publishers have booked a stall at it. Like I say, it wasn't my idea, I promise."

My eyes narrow with suspicion. We have the book festival in Bramblebury every year; it's been more popular than ever since *The Snow Globe* put the village on the literary map. Elliot's never felt the need to come to it before, though; which makes it strange that he'd decide to rock up here after all this time, even if his publisher was putting pressure on him. Unless...

"I'm not just here for the festival," he adds, confirming my suspicions. "There's... well, some other stuff, too."

"Right," I say, biting back the urge to ask what the 'other stuff' might be, and if it has anything to do with me. I feel like I've used up my daily quota of stupid questions now — and some of tomorrow's too, for good measure. "Well. I guess I'll be going, then."

I can't quite figure out how to end this interaction gracefully. I'm not going to lie and say it was nice to see him, and I really hope I *don't* see him around, so I stand there for a moment, before turning on my heel in an attempt at walking away, with my head held high; the way I *should* have walked away from him years ago, when we met.

Instead, though, I find myself stumbling yet again, the ankle of the foot that got trapped between the cobblestones buckling under me, and almost tripping me up for a second time.

Shit. This is the last thing I need when I'm trying to pull off a suitably dramatic exit.

"Holly, wait."

Before I can figure out what to do, Elliot's beside me, his arm around my waist this time, a whiff of the cologne he always used to wear sending me whizzing back through the years, like some kind of lovelorn time-traveler.

"Is it your ankle?" he asks, apparently oblivious to the cocktail of conflicting emotions that's making me feel dizzy. "Can you stand on it?"

"Yup," I reply brightly, almost shrieking in pain when I put my weight on my foot to test this theory. "I'll be absolutely fine. You can let me go now."

I look pointedly down at his arm, and he springs back as if he's been stung. I immediately wobble dangerously on my one reliable leg, like an Edwardian lady having an attack of the vapors. Or a very drunk person.

*No, this is **definitely** not how I pictured our first meeting going.*

Elliot looks at me doubtfully.

"Look," he says, after what appears to be a short but spirited internal tussle. "I'll just help you into the shop. We're almost there, anyway. I can't leave you like this."

He looks over my shoulder, to where the light above the door is illuminating the Hart Books sign just across the square. The shop itself, though, is in darkness; everyone's gone home for the night, and now a new problem has just occurred to me.

"I don't live above the shop anymore," I tell him, wishing briefly that I did; it would be much easier to hobble across the square on one leg than to make it all the way to the cottage, on the very outskirts of the village.

"You don't?" His tone is surprised, and a tiny jolt of indignation joins the other ingredients of my emotion cocktail.

"No, Elliot," I reply shortly. "I haven't lived there for years. Dad doesn't, either. Did you seriously think nothing would've changed since you were last here? That I'd still be living with my dad and working in a shop, while you were off being a famous author, and … whatever else you've been doing. I wouldn't know, obviously. You didn't exactly stay in touch."

"No. No, of course I didn't think everything would be the same," he's saying now, a small crease of annoyance appearing between his lowered brows. "Of course I didn't."

He doesn't bother trying to explain what he *did* think, though. Or if he even thought about me *at all*. Instead, he just stands there, as if he doesn't know what to do next.

Well, I guess that makes two of us.

"Holly?"

Another voice suddenly breaks the strained silence that's fallen between me and Elliot, and I look up to see my ex-boyfriend — my *other* ex-boyfriend, I mean — Martin coming towards us through the crowd, clutching a particularly large churro he's just bought from one of the food trucks.

I've never been so pleased to see him in my life.

"Everything okay here?" Martin asks, stopping next to me, and looking at Elliot with suspicion. "Oh." His face falls as he recognizes the man beside me. "It's you."

Elliot and I both visibly flinch at this casual use of *that* line. Martin, however, appears to be completely unaware of the significance of what he's just said. I'm sure he's heard the line — it's too ingrained in popular culture at this point for him *not* to have heard it. But, then again, Martin takes great pride in being one of the few people in Bramblebury never to have read or watched *The Snow Globe*. It's like a badge of honor for him; and one of the main reasons I finally agreed to go out with him, after years of turning him down. (The fact that not liking *The Snow Globe* is the most interesting thing about him, meanwhile, is one of the main reasons we broke up...)

Elliot nods stiffly in Martin's direction, in a manner that makes it impossible to tell whether he's recognized him or not. To be fair, Martin has gained some weight and lost some hair since they last met; plus, there's a thin crust of sugar around his lips from the churro he's been eating. But his sandy hair and affable expression are unchanged, so I'm certain he must know he's face-to-face with his onetime rival.

I'm just not sure he cares.

"Um, Elliot was just leaving," I say, somehow managing to resist adding the words *he's good at that,* even though I desperately want to. "Martin, I don't suppose you'd walk me home, would you? I've hurt my ankle."

I hold it aloft to show him, regretting this morning's decision to wear the high-heeled leather boots which looked fabulous in the mirror, but which just seem frivolous and silly now they've quite literally been my downfall. You can't even *see* my ankle underneath them, obviously, but Martin makes some appropriately concerned noises, before straightening up and offering me his arm, which is reassuringly steady. Leaning on it feels a bit like pulling on a favorite old sweater, and makes me feel briefly guilty for having spent the last few weeks desperately trying to avoid him.

He might not be the most exciting man I've ever dated, but at least he's always been there when I needed him. And he's never tried to write a book about me, either.

There's that, too.

"Come on," he says, clearly relishing the opportunity to take charge of a situation. Martin is very good at taking charge of situations.. "Let's get you home. I left the car parked just around the corner. You know that place on Morrison Street? It was the closest I could get it; I can't believe how many people turned out to see the lights."

I squeeze his arm gently to get him to stop talking; the difficulty of finding a parking space in Bramblebury at Christmas time is one of Martin's favorite topics, and once he gets started on it, we could be here all night.

"Well, nice seeing you again," he says politely, turning to Elliot, who hasn't spoken since Martin arrived on the scene, like a churro-weilding knight in a shining puffer coat. "We'd, er, best be getting off home, then."

He says this in a way that strongly implies that the 'home' we're going to belongs to both of us, and I don't bother to correct him. Why *shouldn't* Elliot think I've moved on? I mean, I have, haven't I? And, okay, it's not actually with Martin — right now it's not with *anyone* — but that doesn't mean I'm some kind of modern-day Miss Havisham, still sitting among the ruins of my youth, in my Dad's dusty old bookshop, does it? There have been other men since Elliot. I've done things with my life. I've even written books; and, okay, they might not be bestsellers, like *his* book, but at least they're true. (Well, most of them are. I still have doubts about the usefulness of *How to Manifest Your Dreams Using Your Moon Sign*, but that doesn't mean the information in it wasn't meticulously researched, to the best of my ability.)

"What's he doing here, then?" Martin asks, as I hobble on his arm towards the street he's parked his car in ("A real gift of a space, Holly; I couldn't believe it when I saw it was empty!"). "It's not something to do with this book he's supposed to be writing, is it?"

I glance up at him, surprised. Martin is one of the few non-bookish people in my life. In fact, other than *Lord of the Rings* (Which is a given, really), and *A Game of Thrones* (Which he claims to have read, having only seen the TV show), I'm not sure he's finished an entire book in his life. He's the last person in the world to have his finger on the pulse of the publishing industry; which means he's either been talking to the Poole sisters, or this rumor about Elliot and a new book really has grown legs.

"Where did you hear about that?" I ask casually. "Did Elsie tell you?"

"No, Levi did," Martin replies, holding onto me a little tighter than is necessary. "When I popped into the bookstore earlier, looking for you. He was all excited about it — more than usual, I mean. Said he'd seen something about it on TikTok, so he was sure it must be really happening this time."

"Oh. Right."

We walk on — or hop on, in my case — and I try to ignore the creeping sensation of doom that's prickling the back of my neck. I often feel a sensation of doom. It's one of my defining characteristics; the way I always anticipate the worst, as if expecting bad things to happen will somehow rob them of their power to hurt me.

But this is different. *This* feeling of doom is very real; and I'm 100% sure it's connected to Elliot Sinclair. Well, who else has the ability to make me feel like my world's been turned upside down with just a few short-sentences? Not Martin, that's for sure. Not *anyone*, actually.

Only Elliot.

"So, is he?" says Martin, blissfully unaware of my uncharitable thoughts about him. "Is he here to write another book? Is that what you were talking about just now? Or did he want to talk about something else?"

His hand tightens on my elbow, and I feel a flicker of sympathy for him. It can't have been much fun for him, either, living in the shadow of *The Snow Globe*, and constantly having to field questions about a decade-ago relationship his girlfriend had with someone else. And I may be his ex-girlfriend now, but that doesn't mean I don't care how he feels.

"No," I tell him truthfully. "No, he didn't mention a new book. We didn't really talk much at all, really. I just tripped right in front of him, and he stopped to help me. That was it."

And that *was* it. Someone tripped. Someone else caught them. End of story. Not even Elliot Sinclair could turn that briefest of interactions into the opening scenes of his sequel.

But what if he *does*?

Or *tries* to, at least?

The thought rolls around my head all the way back to the car (Which is, as Martin promised, parked in a *really* great space). And, by the time we pull up outside the gate of my house, and Martin finally accepts my assurances that no, I don't need him to come in and 'look after me', the bouncing thought is creating so much noise in there that the only way to silence it is to pull out my phone and open up the email from the agency.

"*Hi Harper,*" I type, collapsing onto the sofa and propping my foot up on the coffee table in front of me. "*Hope you're well. Just wanted to thank you again for the ghostwriting offer, and let you know that I'm happy to accept. Let me know when you'd like me to start!*"

Then I hit send.

If Elliot can write a book, then so can I. But if he thinks he can use me as material for his plot this time... well, let's just say he has another think coming.

8

DECEMBER, 10 YEARS AGO

When I wake up next to Elliot Sinclair the morning after our first date, and first dance, I have three thoughts in quick succession.

The first is that I never, ever do things like this. I do not crash pensioner dance parties with virtual strangers, no matter how handsome they are, or how much their accent makes me feel like the leading lady in the movie of my life. I do not spontaneously agree to go back with them to their slightly dodgy hotel room, above a pub. And I definitely do not sleep with them on the first date. Nuh-uh.

The second thought is that I really hope Dad hasn't called the police and reported me missing, because, well, see above: I never do things like this. No, really: I don't. I'm good ol' sensible, reliable Holly: the daughter you never have to worry about, because she's so scared of seeing that look on your face again — the one you didn't know you were making when we realized Mum was dying and we were going to have to spend the rest of our lives without her — that she never puts a single foot wrong.

The third thought, though, is different. The third thought is *I bet this is the first **and** last time this ever happens*, and it's quickly followed by a fourth thought, which is *I don't want it to be.*

(There is a fifth thought, too, and it's that The Rose Tavern is every bit as grim on the inside as it looks from the outside. Elliot's room has a rusty old sink in the corner — presumably to make up for the lack of an en suite — and the tobacco-yellow walls have been painted only three-quarters of the way up, as if whoever did the job couldn't find a ladder high enough to reach all the way to the ceiling. But, right now, I don't care about any of that.)

"Good morning."

Elliot smiles up at me sleepily from the pillow, his arms already reaching for me. Thanks to him, I don't have any more thoughts for quite some time. Later, though, once I've texted Dad to let him know I'm fine, and he's not to worry about me, another thought occurs to me.

"Tell me more about this book you're thinking of writing," I say, propping my chin on my hands as I look at Elliot across the slightly threadbare pillows. "Do you think you'll actually do it?"

By way of answer, he jumps up and crosses the room to where a battered leather holdall is sitting on top of the equally battered wooden dresser. He rummages inside the bag, then leaps back onto the bed, hanging me a thick cardboard folio stuffed with loose leaf paper.

"*Chapter One...* "I read, pulling out the first page, then lowering it so I can look at him over the top. "Oh my God, Elliot," I squeal, scanning the closely typed words. "You're not just thinking about it; you've actually done it!"

"Well, not quite." He chuckles self-deprecatingly. "I've made a start on it. What you're holding there is the first four chapters. I wrote most of it when I was back home, but I wanted to bring it with me, so I could read over it. There's quite a few things I need to check. And it's —"

He frowns, a small crease appearing between his dark eyebrows.

"I feel like there's something missing with it," he tells me. "I'm just not sure what it is, yet. I was hoping coming here, to Bramblebury, would help me figure out what it is. This is where it's set, you know? I figured I should probably see the place if I'm going to write about it."

"Sure." I lie back down, snuggling into his side again as I scan the pages in my hand. "And it's about your great-grandfather?"

"Yeah. Well, it's based on what I know about his time here during the war," he replies. "Which isn't a lot, to be fair. So it's mostly fiction, really. I liked the idea of it, though; you know, the American in England, the fish out of water. Which I assume he must have been; at least at first. Although he did make friends here. I have photos of some of them, actually..."

He throws the covers back and bounds out of bed again, rummaging through the bag until he finds what he's looking for; a small leather wallet, from which he produces a handful of photos.

"Here you go," he says, rejoining me. "Most of these seem to have been taken at the army base, but there's one or two I think might have been taken here..."

I flick carefully through the photos, which are fragile and yellowed with age. Elliot's great-grandfather looks back at me; a solemn-eyed young man with Elliot's curly dark hair, who looks impossibly young to have been sent away from home to serve in some faraway war.

My heart contracts with pity for him.

"It's okay," says Elliot, watching me. "He came home. He was almost 90 when he died."

"That's good to know," I reply, grateful to him for having read my mind. "You know how much I appreciate a happy ending."

The next photo is the one Elliot thought might have been taken here in Bramblebury. I recognize the village square right away, although there's no war memorial — obviously — and the sepia-tinted streets surrounding the square look oddly bare without the various trees and shrubs that have grown up since this was taken.

The photo is one of those ones taken by a street photographer. I remember Mum showing me some similar shots of her own relatives. Most people couldn't afford cameras in those days, she'd explained. So professional photographers would hang out in busy streets and snap photos of the passers-by, which they'd then try to sell to them. Most of them probably bought them, too; for some, they might have been some of the only photos they had of themselves.

In the photo in my hand, Elliot's great-grandfather is striding through the square, wearing a US Army uniform (Or I assume that's what it is), and with a huge smile on his face. And no wonder he's smiling, because on one arm, there's a young woman, her head tilted back as she looks up at him, as if she's hanging on his every word.

The woman is in uniform too, although I don't know enough about the era to know what kind. But she wears a smart skirt and matching jacket, with sensible looking shoes and a peaked hat. The photo is so old and faded that a lot of the detail has been lost, but she has a pretty, heart-shaped face, and dark, arched eyebrows, like a movie star.

"I'm guessing this isn't the great-grandma from Boca Raton, then?" I say, passing the photo back to Elliot, and moving on to the next one, in which the same woman poses in front of a Christmas tree, wearing a thick wool coat with a swishy skirt, which makes me wonder why people stopped dressing so well.

"Nope. They didn't meet until after the war. I don't know who this woman is, actually. As far as I can gather, he never mentioned a girlfriend — if that's what she was."

"Oh, I'd say that's definitely what she was," I reply, my curiosity piqued by the young couple who look so happy in their photo together, but who were doomed to spend the rest of their lives apart. "I wonder who she was? And what happened to her after the war?"

I wonder what happened to her after he left her, is what I really want to say here. Because he must have done, given the little Elliot knows about the man in the photo. We know he went back to America. We know he married someone else. And now Elliot wants to write his story, but all I can think about is *hers*.

I flick quickly through the rest of the photos, finding two more of the movie star woman tucked in among shots of the village. She's beautiful, whoever she is.

I wonder what her story is?

"Can I read this?" I ask, picking up Elliot's manuscript and leafing through the pages.

"I thought you'd never ask," he says with a grin. "Of course you can. I'd be honored. Maybe you can help me figure out where I'm going wrong with it. That missing piece of the puzzle."

"Oh, I'm not sure about that," I reply. "I just read books. Well, and sell them. I don't know anything about writing them."

"Well, that makes two of us, then," he says lightly, taking the pages from me and throwing them onto the table by the bed. "Anyway, we can talk about the book later. Right now, I've got other plans for us…"

We spend the rest of the morning lying curled around each other in the lumpy little hotel bed, watching the snow fall lazily outside the window.

"This is so nice," I say, as the light starts to fade, and we still haven't left the room. "*You're* so nice."

"Okay," Elliot replies, propping himself up on one elbow to look me in the eye. "That's the second time you've called me 'nice' now. I'm going to have to beg you to stop."

He leans forward and kisses me lightly on the lips, to show me he's not being entirely serious.

"Why? What's wrong with being nice?" I ask, after the kiss has gone on for much longer than he probably intended. "Don't you want to be nice?"

"Nope," he says firmly, shaking his head. "Nuh-uh. 'Nice' is one of the most insipid words in the English language. I'd rather be almost anything else. I want to be... brave. Stupid. Crazy. Magnificent. But not 'nice'. No one ever remembers 'nice'. And, anyway, the nice guy is never the one that gets the girl, is he?"

"I don't know about that," I reply, grinning. "You seem to be doing okay so far. But I get what you mean. For me it's 'sensible'. Or 'hard worker'. People are always telling me I 'try really hard' or I'm 'such a hard worker'. Which is *fine*, but... well, it's not the same as saying I'm *good* at whatever it is I'm 'trying hard' at, is it? And no one ever remembers the person who *tried hard*, either — they just remember the one who succeeded. Or who failed spectacularly. No one remembers ordinary."

"You're anything but 'ordinary', Holly Hart," Elliot says softly, tracing the contours of my lips softly with his finger. "I know I'll remember you."

And there it is: the subject we've yet to broach. The one we've been carefully avoiding ever since we met. The one where he goes back to America — soon, maybe? — and all of this becomes just another memory.

Until now, we've avoided talking about it at all. But now he's put it out there; which means there's no point continuing to pretend we're at the start of something when we're already at the end.

"I'll remember you too," I reply, swallowing down the lump that's risen in my throat. "When you go home. When *do* you go home?"

"My flight leaves the day before Christmas," he says, not looking at me. "My Mom made me promise I'd be back for Christmas Day."

I nod, mentally adding another reason to hate Christmas to my already long list.

"But look," he says, brushing the hair back from my face so he can look into my eyes. "Let's not think about that for now, okay? Let's just enjoy each other's company. Let's just ... well, live for the moment, I suppose." He grins. "What d'you say?"

I hesitate.

I should say no to this. I should get up and leave, with my heart still intact. Because I know beyond doubt now that this isn't going anywhere. No matter how much I like him, there's no future for me and Elliot Sinclair; and the knowledge of that already hurts more than it should, given the short time we've known each other. If I spend more time with him, though, it's only going to make it worse.

I should protect myself from the hurt I know is in store if I let this go on. I should say goodbye now, and let the last 24 hours just be a beautiful memory that will fade with time, until I'm not totally sure it even happened, or if I just dreamed it.

But then I think of Mum.

I think about how you never really know when it's going to be the last time you do something — or say something, or see someone. You don't know until it's too late, and there's no time left to do all the things you planned when you thought you still had time.

But with Elliot, I *do* know. I know exactly how much time we're going to have. I know exactly when it will end. And the fact that this ... whatever this is ... between us now has an end date — December 24th, to be exact — makes it feel all the more important that we try to make the most of what little time we have.

The thought is an oddly exciting one. Because, the fact is, I'm not the kind of person to seize the day, or take risks. No, I'm the kind of person who reads the ends of books before the start, to make sure they're not going to hurt her. The kind of person who recently started arranging the books on the shelves in the store by color, rather than alphabetically, after seeing someone do it like that online. Dad says it's "an absolute nonsense" which makes it impossible to find anything, but something about it makes me feel calm and in control, as if I really am making order out of chaos. And if I can do that; if I can just control the chaos, and make everything around me feel *perfect*, then maybe I can finally feel safe.

But I'm *not* safe, am I?

Losing Mum showed me that.

And although I've never been the type to take risks, I'm starting to think maybe I should take a risk with Elliot Sinclair. That maybe it would be worth it. That I'm 24 years old, and have spent my entire life standing still; and maybe it's time to change that? To do exactly as Elliot says, and 'live for the moment' for once, as cheesy as that sounds.

Ever since Mum died, I've always dreaded winter; the season we lost her. But maybe this winter could be different. Better. Warmer. Maybe things could change. Maybe *I* could change; or I could *try*, anyway. And if I fail, I could at least fail spectacularly.

"Christmas Eve," I say thoughtfully, snuggling back into Elliot's arms. "That gives us almost 23 days. It's not a lot of time, really."

"Oh, you can do a lot in 23 days," Elliot assures me, dropping a kiss on top of my head. "Trust me."

I tilt my head back to look up and into those beautiful blue eyes of his.

"Okay," I tell him, a sudden rush of adrenaline making me feel like this might just be the best idea I've ever had. "Okay, I trust you. "

And I did.

But I really shouldn't have, should I?

9

The cottage I bought when I finally moved out of the apartment above the bookstore has a pretty, white-brick exterior, and roses around the door from late spring to early autumn. It looks like it's been created just for Instagram, but its location, on the outskirts of the village, and at the top of a steep hill, means the tourists haven't discovered it yet, so it remains a haven of peace and quiet, even when the rest of the place is busier than a city-center supermarket a few minutes before closing on Christmas Eve.

The morning after my encounter with Elliot, I wake up early and get gingerly out of bed, sighing with relief when I put my foot cautiously to the ground and discover it's not nearly as painful as I thought it would be. I guess that bag of frozen peas I put on it last night must have worked.

I wander through to the kitchen to make some breakfast, checking my phone first to find that Harper Grant hasn't replied to my email yet, but I do have three new WhatsApp messages from Martin, suggesting that we get together later 'to talk', plus one from Levi, which says simply "OMFG", with a link underneath it.

I click the link while I'm waiting for the kettle to boil, hoping it's not going to be another one of those TikTok videos he keeps sending me, in which people lip sync 'hilariously' along to some of the key dialogue from *The Snow Globe*, as the movie plays in the background.

But it's not a TikTok video.

I almost drop the phone into my cereal bowl as the page opens to reveal a photo of Elliot — Current Elliot, not Past Elliot — above a headline declaring that the 'reclusive author' is set to return to the setting of his award-winning novel and movie for an event sponsored by his publisher. The website I'm looking at appears to be a book blog, and it goes on to breathlessly report the rumor that a big announcement will be made at the upcoming book festival, before ending with some speculation that the long-awaited *Snow Globe* sequel might be in the works.

Fantastic.

I push the cereal bowl aside, my appetite suddenly gone.

So it's true, then.

I don't mean the bit about Elliot being back in town, obviously: I already *know* that's true. But the photo of him on this website is a new one, with a little copyright symbol in one corner, followed by the name of his publisher, Saturday Lane. As far as I know, this is the first new photo of Elliot that's been released since the book was published, so to call him 'reclusive' would be like saying Steven King is quite popular, really.

If he's agreed to have new publicity photos taken, it must mean he has something to publicize. And I don't even need to read any of the follow-up messages from Levi which suddenly start blowing up my phone to take a wild guess what it could be.

I pull my dressing gown tightly around me, as if it's a piece of fluffy armor that might protect me from whatever Elliot has to say about me in his next book; or whatever he *doesn't* have to say about me, as the case may be. Because, as I stand there, sipping my coffee at the kitchen window, it occurs to me that I don't know which is worse; having your ex-lover write an entire book based on your relationship, or having him write a sequel to it that doesn't include you at all.

Why would he, when I'm no longer even a side-character in his life?

I'm in the process of untangling this thought — and gently chastising myself for thinking it at all, because even *I* can see how unreasonable it is to be annoyed at him for writing about me, and *also* annoyed when he doesn't — when the phone in my hand pings again, and I glance down to see Harper Grant's name on the screen.

"*Good morning Holly!*" begins the email she's sent me. "*So great to have you on board with this project! Contract and NDA are attached; if you could sign them and send them back to me ASAP, that would be great!*"

I rub my eyes, dazzled by all the exclamation marks, and wondering how on earth she manages to sound so perky at such an early hour. Then again, a glance at the time in the corner of the screen tells me it's not quite as early as I thought it was, so I hurry myself into the shower, and, before long, I'm in the car, choosing to drive the short distance to the bookstore rather than risk my ankle again by attempting to walk it.

I've forgotten, however, that it's December in Bramblebury. Although it's still early, the streets are packed with people all making their way to the Christmas market and the snow globe, so I end up stop-starting my way through the village, thanking my stars that, as the manager of the store, at least I can't get in trouble for being late.

I've almost reached the high street, when I'm forced to stop again, for a set of temporary traffic lights the council has set up in an attempt to control the flow of traffic heading towards the square. I prop one elbow against the side window and rest my head on my hand, watching as Christmas shoppers wander by, each of them wrapped up like parcels against the chill; and this time when I catch sight of a familiar figure among them, I know for sure I'm not seeing a ghost.

No, this time I know the man in the wool coat is definitely Elliot Sinclair. I'm not seeing things. I'm not going mad. He really is here in Bramblebury, coming out of a house with a pale pink exterior and a shiny black front door. He really is stopping just outside it, and looking back to say something to a woman who stands in the doorway; a woman with long dark hair piled elegantly on top of her head, and a winter tan that she definitely didn't get anywhere in England. A woman who's wearing a very short silk dressing gown and smiling at Elliot in a way that makes my elbow suddenly slip from its position against the window and come crashing down on the car horn, which immediately bursts into life, startling passers-by, and making a little boy burst into tears.

"Patience, love," yells the man in the car in front of mine. "We're not going anywhere until the light changes, you know!"

I do know. And so it is that I'm forced to sit there, hemmed in by the traffic on each side of me, as Elliot comes down the path of the house, and lets himself out through the front gate, which is — naturally — a white wooden one, to match the little picket fence around the garden.

I slide down in the driver's seat until only the top of my head is showing above the steering wheel.

Please don't let him have seen that. Please don't let him have noticed me.

"Holly?"

Elliot raps sharply on the car window, peering in with a frown that confirms that yes, he did, in fact, 'see that'.

Elliot starts to mouth something at me through the window, gesturing for me to wind it down. Before I can do it, though, the light suddenly turns green, and the car in front of me pulls away, moving so slowly it feels like time briefly starts to go backwards.

"Sorry," I mouth back insincerely. "Got to go."

And then I put my foot down and pull away, leaving a surprised-looking Elliot Sinclair in my rear-view mirror.

Which is exactly where he's going to stay.

I walk through the shop door a few minutes later to find the place in uproar.

"An email," Levi shrieks, coming barreling towards me and sounding like he's had too much of his own coffee. "We've had an email! From Saturday Lane. Read it to her! Read it!"

He looks at Dad, whose hair is standing on end as if he's been raking his hands through it.

"It *is* rather exciting, Holly," he begins, beaming at me. "It says—"

"It's about Elliot Sinclair," interrupts Levi, who I'm starting to think missed his calling as an actor, if his current level of drama is anything to go by. "Did you know? Did you know about this?"

"I'll read it out," says Dad, patting the pockets of his cardigan in a state of agitation. "Now, where did I put my spectacles? I was sure I had them with me."

"Could someone just tell me what's going on?" I beg, as he wanders over to the register and starts rummaging underneath it. "Please, put me out of my misery here."

Paris steps forward. She's carrying Ed the cat like he's a baby, and although she's trying to project an air of calm, as befits her assistant-manager-who-secretly-wants-to-be-the-*actual*-manager status, her eyes are shining as if she, too, has recently overdosed on Levis's Elf Eggnog Espresso.

"We had an email from Elliot Sinclair's publicist," she says importantly. "It wasn't the *publisher*, Levi. It was the *publicist*. There's a difference, you know."

She shoots Levi a 'so there' kind of look, then turns back to me.

"You know how I've been keen for us to start hosting more author visits and signings?" she says. I nod, knowing what's coming, but hoping against hope that I might be wrong.

For once, though, I am not wrong.

"Well," says Paris, squeezing Ed so hard that he jumps out of her arms and stalks off, disgusted. "It turns out that Elliot Sinclair wants to do a signing while he's here in town. And he wants to do it here. At Hart Books."

I step behind the counter and hang up my coat and bag, silently trying to process this information.

"I'm surprised you're on board with this," I say to Dad, speaking low enough that only he can hear me. "I thought you hated Elliot?"

Dad freezes in the act of polishing his glasses, which he's finally realized he was wearing the entire time.

"Oh, I wouldn't say *that*," he says casually, not looking at me. "I didn't *hate* him. I didn't think he was the right man for *you*, is all."

I raise my eyebrows in disbelief.

"He's very much turned out to be the right man for the *store*," though, says Dad, unable to hide his excitement at this. "For the whole town, really. Just think of how many of his books we'll sell with him here to sign them! I wonder what people would be prepared to pay for a signed copy, plus a chance to meet the man himself?"

"I'd pay a *lot*," confirms Levi, who's been blatantly listening in. "Like, I already have a copy of every edition they've ever released, obviously, but a signed one trumps them all. D'you think he'll do a Q&A?"

"I wonder if he'd take a selfie with me?" says Paris, forgetting to look bored for once. "Will you ask him for me, Holly?"

"Oh, stop it, all of you," I burst out, unable to listen to this for one more second. They all stop what they're doing and look at me, surprised.

"Elliot Sinclair isn't going to be taking selfies with anyone," I begin. "Or TikToks, or ... or whatever it is I can see you planning, Levi. He's not doing a Q&A. Honestly, if it was up to me, he wouldn't even be allowed to cross the threshold of this store. I wouldn't let him. "

The bell above the door suddenly bursts into life, interrupting me with a loud blast of *Deck the Halls* as the door swings open.

"Hello," says Elliot Sinclair, stepping across the threshold in exactly the way I just said I wouldn't allow him to. "I hope I'm not interrupting anything?"

"Look, I'm sorry to barge in like this," Elliot says a few minutes later, once the excitement caused by his arrival has died down a smidge, and Dad, Paris, and Levi have all been banished to the Coffee Corner. "I just wanted to check if you were okay after last night. And, well, this morning. What *was* that this morning, by the way? With the car horn?"

He smiles; a ghost of his old smile, but a smile nonetheless.

"I don't know, Elliot," I say frostily. "You tell me. What *was* that this morning?"

"Uh, that's... that's what I just asked you?" he points out, not unreasonably. "Or did I just imagine that? I was asking what you were doing, honking your car horn at me?"

"I wasn't honking it *at* you," I reply indignantly. "I was honking it *because* of you. I, um, just happened to see you, that's all. Coming out of that house. With that woman. First thing in the morning."

There's a good chance I could go on like this forever, in short, staccato sentences that come out sounding more like accusations than statements.

Luckily, though, Elliot steps in to stop me.

"Katie," he says, his ghost smile fading. "Her name's Katie. Katie Hunter."

He looks at me as if this should mean something to me, but it doesn't, so I simply nod, not knowing what else to do with this information. He's not denying that he was coming out of this 'Katie' woman's house so early that it suggests he must have spent the night there. Then again, I don't want him to think I *care* about who he spends the night with. Because I don't. I definitely don't. It's nothing to me. It's...

"How's your ankle, by the way?" Elliot asks, in a change of subject so abrupt that it almost gives me whiplash. "That's the main reason I came in."

"It's fine, thanks," I reply. "It was just a sprain. I put frozen peas on it."

"Peas. Right."

Elliot isn't listening. He's stepping a little further inside the store now, gazing around and ignoring the three musketeers over there, who are lined up on the sofa gaping at us over their giant mugs of coffee.

"This place is looking great," he says, sounding like he means it. "Really. It's different, but the same."

"We have you to thank for that," says Dad, ignoring the warning glance I shoot at him and getting up to join us. "This is still our biggest seller."

He reaches out and picks up a copy of *The Snow Globe* from one of the displays. There's a long and very painful silence as we all stand there looking at it.

This moment should have come with a trigger warning.

Elliot Sinclair should come with a trigger warning.

"Well, great," says Elliot unconvincingly. "I'm glad it's helped."

"Oh, it's *helped* alright," I hiss, unable to stop myself. "If by that you mean it's helped me become the village laughingstock."

Elliot's head jerks backwards as if he's been slapped. Dad silently places the book he's holding back on top of the pile and backs away slowly.

"A laughingstock?" Elliot says, frowning. "How so?"

I stare at him incredulously.

"You wrote a book about me?" I tell him slowly, amazed I'm having to explain our personal history to him. "About us? It got turned into a movie?"

There's a moment when it occurs to me that I might have got it wrong; that maybe he based the love story in his book on some *other* English girl he met in some *other* small town, in some other December. But then he nods, and I'm an annoyed mixture of emotions once more.

"I did," he confirms solemnly. "I did do that."

We hold each other's gaze; me wondering how it can possibly be the case that he looks so the same, when everything else about him is so different.

"I knew it," I hear Levi mutter from position on the sofa, followed by a soft *whump*, which I imagine is probably Paris hitting him with a cushion.

I don't look around to confirm it, though. I'm too busy watching Elliot and wondering what he's going to say. How he's going to defend himself.

"You didn't like the book, then, I take it?" he says, shrugging in an 'aw, shucks' kind of way that fails to mask the hurt I can see in his eyes.

I open my mouth and then close it again. In the imaginary versions of this conversation — and there's been quite a few of them, over the years — I've always known exactly what to say to Elliot on the subject of his book. But now that the opportunity has finally presented itself, I find myself suddenly struck dumb.

It's stupid, but I don't want to hurt him.

Even after all this time, I can't bring myself to hurt him.

"It's not so much the *book* I didn't like," I mutter, even though it definitely is the book. "It's more... well, the attention I've had because of it. I don't like the attention. You know I don't like attention."

"The attention?" Elliot's blue eyes scan the store, which is, of course, currently empty of customers, for what has to be the first time in days. "I saw the globe thing, outside," he goes on. "Is that what you mean?"

I look at him wordlessly. It's crazy to me that this man, who I once thought knew me better than anyone, even despite the short amount of time I'd known him, can be so completely unaware of what my life has been like since he last saw me.

Then again, how *would* he know? It's not like we stayed in touch.

"That's one part of it," I say evenly. "But then there's also..."

The lies you told about me. The fact that you ghosted me, then made it sound like it was my fault. The way you broke my heart.

"I don't think I'm really cut out to be the main character in a book," I say. "Or a movie-based-on-a-book, even. I think I was always destined to just have a supporting role. It's ... it's strange, is all. It's been strange."

The silence that follows this statement is so acute I can almost hear Levi and Paris exchange disappointed glances, having expected more drama from me. Elliot, meanwhile, just stands there, shoulders slumped slightly, looking like I've just told him his baby's ugly.

Which I guess I have, in a way.

"You were always the main character for me, Holly," he says at last. "Always."

Across the room, Paris lets out a gasp of delight.

"Oh my *God*," says Levi, in a stage whisper.

Drama delivered.

And now I guess the next line is mine.

I just have no idea what it should actually *be*.

To hide my discomfort, I reach for the laptop that's sitting open on the counter in front of me, and start tapping away at it importantly, my fingers moving on auto-pilot as I stare determinedly at the screen.

You were always the main character for me.

Why did he say that when we both know it's not true?

"Okay," says Elliot, when it becomes clear that I'm not going to give him whatever answer it is he wants from me, because this is Holly he's talking to — not Evie Snow, whose lines he can dictate. "Right. Well. I guess I'll be going, then. How's Martin, by the way? I was ... surprised to see him with you last night."

The email from Harper Grant is on the screen. I open it, just to make myself look busy, then click again to open the contract attached to it, for good measure.

"Martin? Martin's fine," I reply vaguely, distracted by the contract, which is several pages long and written in the kind of legal jargon I'll probably need a translator for. "He took me home."

Elliot opens the door (*Deck the Halls* sounds very out of place when you're in the middle of a stand-off with the ex who once wrote a book about you, just in case you were wondering...) and stands there for a moment, as if he thinks he might still be able to rescue this scene if he just gives me a chance to try to stop him from leaving.

I don't, though.

Because, as I scan the document in front of me, one eye still on Elliot in the doorway, a familiar name catches my eye.

I scroll back up, now fully focused on the screen in front of me.

No. That can't be right. I must have misread it, surely?

But I haven't.

There it is, in fourteen-point Times New Roman:

This agreement is made and entered into on [Date], between **Vivienne Faulkne**r ('Author') and **Holly Har**t ('Ghostwriter'), collectively referred to as the 'Parties,' for the purpose of writing and developing the work [Title TBC]...

I blink several times and read it again, the words starting to swim before my eyes. I feel like I've just had a double-shot of Levis' extra-strong espresso, shortly followed by a ride on a particularly twisty roller-coaster.

Vivienne Faulkner.

The author I've agreed to ghostwrite for is none other than Vivienne Faulkner; queen of romance, and the person responsible for a large percentage of our non-Snow Globe related book sales every month.

It doesn't seem real. It *can't* be real.

I, Holly Hart, have somehow managed to land the ghostwriting gig of a lifetime.

It's an *actual* Christmas miracle.

And I'm not allowed to tell anyone about it.

Which is just fine, as it happens: because when I finally look up from the computer screen, my fingers still trembling on the keyboard, I find that Elliot Sinclair has already gone.

10

DECEMBER, 10 YEARS AGO

As it turns out, I'm not particularly good at living 'in the moment'.

For most people, living each day as if it's your last means living with gay abandon, and little regard for the consequences. And good for them. I wish they could teach me their ways, because, in reality, it's kind of exhausting, really, living each day as if it's your last. Always worrying if you're enjoying things enough; if you're truly experiencing life to its *absolute* fullest, or if there's perhaps something more you could be doing to ensure you're appreciating it all appropriately.

Or maybe that's just me?

I think it *has* to be just me, because I'm just over a week into 'living for the moment' with Elliot, and if my life was a movie, I guess this would be the montage scene.

The snow keeps falling, turning the village into a scene from a Christmas card. We go for walks in it, our hands linked, even though our fingers feel like they're about to fall off from the cold by the time we head back indoors. We drink mugs of hot chocolate in cozy pubs, with log fires and Christmas carols playing in the background. (I draw the line at mulled wine, but I can't deny the vibes are still the same…) We spend long afternoons curled up in Elliot's sagging double bed in his hotel room; me reading, him writing, both of us just marking time until we can reasonably forget everything else and fall into each other's arms again.

It's amazing. It's perfect, actually. Even the days when I have to work at the bookstore, and Elliot comes and sits at the counter with me, while Dad glares at us from between the bookshelves like a soap opera spy, have a slightly surreal, dreamlike feeling to them, which has me constantly questioning when I'm going to wake up.

And the entire time it's happening, the knowledge that there's a time-limit to it all hangs above us like a noose. I try my best to ignore it, because I know perfectly well that's not how this is supposed to work; that over-thinking everything doesn't exactly meet the criteria of 'living in the moment'. That we're having a fling, not falling in love. But then, every time I meet Elliot's eye, and he gives me one of those smiles of his, I realize this doesn't feel like 'just a fling' at all; and the thought of his imminent departure becomes a rogue full-stop in the middle of a sentence I wanted to read to the end.

I don't tell Elliot any of this, though. There isn't much point. He's leaving, and there's nothing either of us can do about it; so I just smile back, and kiss him as if I haven't realized there's an upper limit on the number of times we'll do this.

But there is.

I don't know what the exact number is, but from the moment we met, Elliot and I were destined to have only a set number of kisses, a certain amount of walks in the snow, and only a handful of days together.

One day soon, all of this will end. And it won't be anything like losing Mum, because Elliot will still be somewhere out there in the world, but it will still hurt — which is why, I tell myself I'm *living in the moment*, but, the entire time I'm holding a little of myself back. Telling myself this isn't serious. That we're just having fun; or *enjoying each other's company*, as Elliot put it.

I tell myself I can do this. That some people are just meant to be a single chapter of your life; even the ones who seem like they're going to be one of the main characters. That's how it is for me and Elliot. We're a short story, nothing more. A one-season romance that will end along with the winter.

And that's why I can never let him know that, in my head, I've been secretly imagining a different ending."

"So? What do you think?"

We're lying in Elliot's bed again, our feet intertwined as I finish reading the latest pages of his manuscript. I put them down beside me and turn to face him.

"I like it," I say carefully. "I think the characterization is amazing. Your great-grandfather — Luke — especially. I feel like I know him."

"But...?" Elliot looks at me anxiously. "I'm not wrong, am I? There's something missing?"

I prop myself up on one elbow and rummage through the piles of paper scattered on the bed until I find what I'm looking for.

"I think it needs something more," I tell him, holding up the photo of the couple in the square, so he can see it. "I think it needs this. *Her*. Or someone like her, anyway."

"Her?" He looks at the photo, then back at me. "The woman in the photo? You think I should turn it into a love story?"

He pulls a face, as if the thought doesn't exactly appeal to him.

"Not exactly," I say, smiling as I place the photo back down on top of the others. "It doesn't have to be the whole story. But maybe a sub plot? Something to, I don't know, kind of pull people through it? Give them something to hope for — other than that he makes it through the war alive, I mean? I don't know. It's just an idea. You're the writer, here; I just read."

"Hey. Don't do that," Elliot says seriously. "Don't put yourself down. I asked you to take a look at it because I value your opinion. I wouldn't have asked if I didn't."

I force a smile, stoically resisting the ever-present impulse to say something self-deprecating, and completely spoil the moment. Because that's not what 'live for the moment' Holly would do, and that's the Holly I'm currently pretending to be.

"You're smart, Holly," Elliot insists, refusing to let me off the hook. "I don't understand why you seem to think you're not. Did someone tell you that? Is that why you doubt yourself so much?"

He sits up, as if he's prepared to leap out of bed and fight them, if I say they did. This time, my smile is genuine.

"No one said that," I assure him, giggling at the fierce look on his face. "It's just... well, *me*, I guess. *I* tell myself that. Look, I didn't go to college like you did. Or like all of my friends did. I just stayed at the bookshop. And then the people I grew up with all graduated and moved away, and I'm still here; still in that bookshop, still doing exactly what I've always done."

I do my best to keep my tone light, but Elliot isn't fooled.

"Well, for one thing, there's nothing wrong with the bookstore," he says firmly. "I think it's pretty cool, actually. And, for another—" he reaches out and threads his fingers through mine — "Just because you're here right now, it doesn't mean this is where you'll always be. There's a big old world out there, you know. Maybe it's time to think about seeing some of it?"

The words hang in the air between us. I think about Florida, with its orange groves and theme parks; about California palm trees swaying in the sun. I think about sunshine; the kind of heat that feels like a physical presence — a wall of warmth that hits you as you step off the plane.

Then I think about Dad, trying to manage the bookstore alone; going home each night to an empty flat; getting a little older, and a whole lot lonelier with every year that passes.

The sunshine and the six-lane highways abruptly disappear, like the mirage that they are.

"Maybe I will one day," I say, as if the thought of leaving doesn't occupy my every waking thought. "Right now, though, we have this book of yours to think about."

I pick up the pages again, signaling that this part of the conversation is at an end. Elliot watches me for a few moments longer, then gives the tiniest of shrugs, before reaching out and picking up the photo from the pile on the bed.

"Okay," he says thoughtfully. "So, what are we thinking? Who is she? How does he meet her?"

I rest my head on his shoulder so I can look at it with him.

"I don't suppose we'll ever know who she was in real life," I say. "But it doesn't really matter if it's fiction you're writing. You can just make something up."

"It wasn't *going* to be fiction," Elliot says, still looking at the photo. "I had it in my head that it would essentially be a biography. But I get what you mean about it needing a sub-plot. I guess it's a bit dry without one. And I kind of like the idea of turning real life into a story. That could be fun."

"Real life *is* a story," I protest. "But you could still make this a true one, if you really want to. You could still write it as a biography, I mean. You'd just need to find out who she was, first. If that's even possible."

"Oh, it'll be possible," he says. "Maybe not *easy*, granted, but still. It's not *that* long ago, really. I found tons of records going back to the war when I visited Fort Stafford — that's the military base he was stationed at. It's a museum now, though, so that made it easier."

I nod, remembering visiting Fort Stafford on a class outing when I was a kid. It's just a couple of miles from Bramblebury, and the soldiers would apparently frequent the village pubs and dance hall on their time off. It's strange to think Elliot's great-grandfather was one of them; that he might even have sat at the bar below us at some point, or visited the bookstore — or whatever it was back then. To Elliot and me, it *is* just a story, but to him — to the man this book is about — it was very real. It was his life, and he was the main character; just as we all are, in our own stories.

"I like that way of thinking about it," Elliot says, when I share this thought with him. "I like the idea that we're all busy writing the story of our life, even if we never put pen to paper. And he never did;

which makes me all the more determined to do it for him. Find out the truth. Tell the full story. And I guess that means starting with Mystery Woman here."

Our heads touch as we peer together at the photo, but the woman in it remains frustratingly indistinct, almost as if she's a ghost who got caught in the act of disappearing.

"And you're *sure* he didn't leave any letters or diaries?" I ask again, thinking longingly of how amazing it would be to solve the mystery of the woman in the photo by poring over some decades old journals, found in a musty old attic. Like one of those old adventure stories I used to love so much as a child, brought to life.

But Elliot shakes his head.

"Nope. Or, if he did, no one bothered to save them. Like I said, his house was sold years ago; these photos are all that were left. I guess I could go back to the military base and see if there's anything I missed," he goes on. "But I doubt there'd be anything useful. They kept records of the men who stayed there, sure. But there's nothing about their actual lives."

"No, I guess there wouldn't be," I reply, saddened by the thought of all those lives being reduced to simply the known facts: that all that's left is a start date and an end date, and none of the really important stuff that happened in between.

"I suppose we could try the library?" I go on, not feeling particularly hopeful. "I haven't gone in there in years, but I guess they might have a local history section. Or I can ask Dad if he has any ideas; he's pretty into anything involving the war."

"Maybe his parents knew my great-grandpa?" Elliot says, his eyes lighting up. "Or his lady friend? Shit!" He slaps a hand over his mouth, a look of horror on his face. "What if she's your great-grandma?"

"Relax," I reply, laughing. "Neither of my parents were from here. Mum's family moved down from Scotland when she and Lorraine were just toddlers, and Dad grew up in London. He met Mum at university. So it's okay; we're definitely not related."

"Well, thank God for that." He pulls me closer. "I'm still not sure you should ask your dad about this, though. I'm pretty sure he hates me."

I glance up at him. He's smiling, but his eyes are serious. Also: he's not exactly wrong.

"He doesn't *hate* you," I tell him, struggling to find a way to explain the hard looks and endless questions Dad fires at Elliot every time he comes into the shop with me. "He's just a bit over-protective, is all."

He's just scared I'm going to run off to America with Elliot and never come back, would be closer to the truth here, but I don't want to have to admit that this is a possibility that's so much as entered my head, even in the context of Dad and his paranoia about it, so I let it go.

"I guess that makes sense," Elliot says, kissing me softly on the top of the head. "You're all he's got. I can't blame the guy for being afraid of losing you. You would be a very hard person to lose, Holly Hart."

Is it just my imagination, or is there a wistfulness to his tone that suggests it's not just Dad he's talking about now?

For a split-second, I consider asking him; of breaking the unspoken promise that we're not going to talk about anything as serious as 'us'

— because there *is* no 'us'. Not really. Not after Christmas Eve, when he'll fly back home to Florida and his family, and that'll be that.

So, I just reach up to kiss him, and I don't think about how every single kiss takes us one step closer than the one that will be our last.

I don't think about that at all.

Instead, in the days that follow, I pour all of my energy into helping Elliot try to figure out the identity of the woman in the photo.

We visit the library and the war memorial. We go back to the barracks, and even wander among the graves in the snowy churchyard, holding hands and feeling like characters in a movie who're about to stumble upon the answer to a decades-old mystery.

But, of course, we don't.

The village library does, indeed, have a local history section and a selection of old newspapers, which are accessible via an ancient microfiche reader. But none of the books and pamphlets hold any clues for us, and we don't know what to even search for in the newspapers ("Local woman photographed with U.S. soldier" being an unlikely kind of headline, even for a time without rolling news media...), so we leave empty-handed. The war memorial, of course, contains only the names of the village men lost to the war, and the barracks, as Elliot predicted, can tell us nothing other than that his grandfather was, indeed, stationed there for a while. As for the graveyard, meanwhile ... I have no idea what we thought we were looking for in the graveyard. We're probably not going to be starting new careers as detectives after this, let's put it that way.

And so the mystery woman remains elusive. But instead of being discouraged by this, Elliot becomes even more determined to find her.

"You know you don't have to know the truth about her," I remind him one morning, a few days into the search. "You can just make it up. Turn it into fiction. At least that way, the mystery woman can be whoever you want her to be."

We're sitting together on a bench at the top of the hill just outside the village. It's not a steep hill, or even a very interesting one, but it has a view out over the village itself and the surrounding countryside, which makes it a popular place to come for a stroll.

"I know," replies Elliot, handing me one of the paper cups filled with hot chocolate which we bought on the way here. "But I don't want to make it up. I need to know who she was, and what happened to her. I want what I write to be real."

"She's really got under your skin, hasn't she?" I comment, sipping my drink and trying not to feel jealous of a woman who's either long dead, or almost as old as the hill we're sitting on.

"It just bothers me," he replies, taking my hand in his. "I hate the thought that she existed, and then she was gone, and no one seems to know what happened in between. You know that thing about how you're never really dead until your name's spoken for the last time? I don't think that should be just for famous people, or one's who've lived dramatic lives. It should be for everyone. Everyone's story deserves to be told."

He turns and smiles at me self-consciously, as if he thinks I might make fun of him for the slightly schmaltzy sentiment. Instead, I just squeeze his hand through my mittens.

"You want to keep her memory alive," I say simply. "And his, too. I get that. I really get that."

"You feel the same about your mom, I guess," Elliot replies. It's not a question, so there's no need to answer it, but I give his hand another squeeze, grateful to be understood without having to explain just how hard it is to think Mum could have been here — that she could have lived an entire life, fallen in love, given birth, *mattered* — and then just suddenly be gone, as if she was never here at all.

I really, really get it.

"You were right, though," says Elliot. "About the story, I mean. This is exactly what it needs. It needs that element of... well, romance, I guess. A human connection. I like that."

"That's what all the best stories are about, aren't they?" I reply, watching as he sips his hot chocolate, leaving a tiny spec of froth on his upper lip, which I would very much like to lick off. "People. Connections."

"Exactly," says Elliot, nodding so enthusiastically he almost spills his drink. "Because what else is there, really? When all's said and done?"

It's the kind of thing I've always thought, but never actually said, too worried that I'd sound pretentious, or just plain stupid. But Elliot never seems to think about things like that; or, if he does, he doesn't let it stop him. He just says what he thinks, truthfully, and from the heart. It's one of the things I admire most about him.

"Are you even real?" I ask, chuckling. "Or am I just imagining you? Because I feel like you must have a flaw of some kind. Maybe not a *fatal* one, exactly, but still; no one can be *this* nice and not have a flaw."

"Oh, now, we agreed you wouldn't use that word," he grins, dropping a kiss on the tip of my frozen nose. "Anything but nice, remember?"

He kisses me again, and then he wraps an arm around me, and we sit there and finish our drinks, looking down at the winding streets, and the little snow covered-rooftops. From this distance, and under its unaccustomed blanket of white, Bramblebury actually looks quite pretty. Snow has a way of doing that, though; of tricking you into thinking things are better than they are, by briefly hiding all the imperfections.

That's why I don't trust it.

And I shouldn't trust Elliot, either.

I don't know that yet, though. So I just sit there, snuggled into his chest, completely unaware that the man beside me does have a flaw.

I just haven't found out what it is, yet.

11

In *The Snow Globe*, Evie Snow is a spy. It's the reason people in the village are always coming up to me with a conspiratorial wink, as if I'm *actually* the character from the book, and my job at the bookstore is merely a cover for the secret double life I've been living all along.

Yeah, right. *I wish.*

Then again, as I sit in my office in the back of the shop on the evening of Elliot's book signing, it occurs to me that, for the first time ever, I actually *do* have something in common with Evie, because I, too, have a secret double life right now; only mine is as a ghostwriter, rather than as a spy.

Okay, so it's not *exactly* the same thing. I *do* feel a *bit* like a spy, though, as I pull up a fresh browser window on my laptop and type in Elliot's name, glancing over my shoulder first, to make sure Levi or Paris aren't about to burst through the door and catch me in the act of Googling my ex.

Not that there's anything much to find; a fact I know all too well from all the *other* times I've tried typing Elliot's name into a search engine over the years. This is a guy who didn't even attend the premiere of the movie his book was based on — or any of the award shows it was nominated at — so I guess it's no surprise that he's not on social media, either; not even an ancient Facebook account or a comment on someone else's Instagram.

He is un-stalkable. (Which, as Levi says, is just plain *rude* of him, really...) And even though this morning's search results are now filled with links to articles about his rumored new book, and his upcoming appearances at the Bramblebury book fair, there's still nothing to tell me what he's been doing with himself for the past decade — or how Katie Hunter comes into whatever that is — so, after a few frustrating minutes, I give up, and type in Vivienne Faulkner's name instead.

This time, I have much better luck. Faulkner's been in the business for a long time now, and has a website complete with photos of her posing in what looks like a seafront mansion, plus links to interviews she's done with various bookish publications. From these, I learn that she's married, lives in California, and writes romance books "to put a little bit of love into the world".

Yuck.

At a guess, I'd say Vivienne's probably in her sixties, and she's beautiful, in a very sleek, glamorous kind of way that makes me wish I hadn't looked her up, because it's just making me feel even more intimidated by her, and completely out of my depth with this commission.

Then I remember the phone-call I had with Harper Grant this morning; the one in which she told me the reason Vivienne is having to use a ghostwriter for this project is because she's been too unwell to write it herself; and, in an instant, the polished facade of Vivienne's carefully curated website is revealed for what it is — just another way to hide the truth that lies beneath.

"We've pushed the deadline back three times now already," said Harper, sounding uncharacteristically anxious. "We just can't do it again. The readers will be expecting another Christmas novel from her for next year, you know? And Vivienne doesn't want to let them down. She's very dedicated to her fans."

I'd murmured reassuringly down the phone, pretending I knew what it was like to have 'fans' already waiting for your *next* book to come out, even though your current one has only just been released.

"So, as you know, the book doesn't have a title yet," Harper goes on. "But it's about a woman who essentially reinvents herself by having a whirlwind romance one Christmas. It's empowering for her. It allows her to take charge of her life, and become the person she's always wanted to be. Do you know what I mean?"

"I ... yes, I do," I reply, a vague feeling of déjà vu making the hairs on the back of my neck stand up. "Got it."

"We're hoping Vivienne will at least be able to get a fuller idea of the plot over to you soon," Harper told me. "But in the meantime, if you have any ideas of your own, Holly, well, it wouldn't hurt to jot them down, and I can pass them on to her. Just ... well, just in case."

Just in case WHAT? I wanted to ask, but didn't, remembering just in time the advice I wrote into *Glow Up: The Guide to Faking It 'Til You're Making It* about believing in yourself, so everyone else believes in you too.

Maybe I shouldn't have believed in myself *quite* as much when I assured Harper I'd come up with some ideas for the plot of this book and send them over to her, though? Because now here I am feeling a bit like I'm a toddler who's been entrusted with transporting a 10-tier wedding cake across town, such is my lack of experience on the romance front.

Then again, I may not know much about romance, but I *do* have some form with 'whirlwind' Christmas flings, don't I? Well, *one* whirlwind Christmas fling.

Maybe one is all I need, though?

I stare at the blank screen, wondering if I can really do this; if I can use Elliot, and our 'live for the moment' relationship as inspiration for Vivienne's book. It's what *he* would do, after all.

That doesn't mean it's the *right* thing to do, though.

This dilemma, however, is going to have to wait to be solved. For now, I can hear a low buzz of voices on the other side of the door, which tells me the store is starting to fill up already for Elliot's book signing, so I close the computer with a sigh and go out to help.

"Oh, Holly, there you are," says Dad, as I emerge from the office. He's carrying a tray filled with champagne glasses, and the tie he's wearing has been tossed over one shoulder: a sure sign that he's feeling stressed. "Look, you really don't have to be here, you know," he goes on, reaching out to pat me on the arm, and making the champagne glasses wobble dangerously. "We all know how... well, *difficult* this time of year is for you. And that's even without Elliot being back in the picture."

I nod, noticing that he's 'Elliot' now, and not 'your young American' or even 'that gormless wazzock" as he once called him. How the times have changed. They clearly haven't changed so much that people haven't stopped giving me sympathetic looks and talking about my 'difficult time of year', though, and, all of a sudden, I've had enough. I'm tired of being poor Holly, who has to be tiptoed around every

Christmas, in case she bursts into tears. I'm 34 years old, and a ... a boss babe. And I think it's time to take my own advice; to 'unfollow anxiety', and to 'glow up,' as it were.

Starting with this book signing.

"It's fine, Dad," I tell him, taking the tray before he can spill any more of the drinks. "I can see how busy the place is. You need all hands on deck."

This is true. The little shop is the most crowded I've ever seen it, with people milling around, sipping champagne and chattering excitedly about the 'reclusive' author they're about to meet. I spot Levi holding court over in the Coffee Corner, which has been turned into a makeshift bar for the evening, while Paris stands next to a table piled with copies of *The Snow Globe*, looking like she might start a fight with anyone who dares to take one before Elliot arrives to sign them.

The sofas and squashy armchairs have all been pulled back to the edges of the room to make way for rows of wooden chairs, which are already almost full. Maisie Poole sits front and center, holding a glass of champagne in each hand, and, to my horror, I spot Martin near the back, sweating slightly in his thick puffer jacket, which he's refusing to take off, even though the room is hotter than Hades.

With the exception of Maisie, the front two rows are filled with what I'm assuming are members of the press — Elliot Sinclair's first ever public appearance is a big deal in the book world — but there's no sign of Elliot himself, so I start cautiously circling the room, handing out drinks, and occasionally stopping to sip on one myself, in a bid to steady my nerves.

My plan is to just stay out of his way; which shouldn't be difficult given that he's the big, famous author guy, and I'm just the girl serving the drinks. Just as long as no one mentions my secret identity as Evie Snow (Which they shouldn't do, after the lecture I gave Levi and Paris this afternoon...), it should be no different from any of the other author events we've hosted since Paris stepped in as assistant manager.

Well, other than the huge amount of people in attendance, obviously. Under normal circumstances, these things tend to attract a handful of people at most, but this event is different; as evidenced by the flurry of excitement that ripples through the room as Elliot finally steps through the shop door.

Conversations stop mid-sentence as everyone pauses to watch him shake hands with a flustered-looking Dad, then make his way to the table that's been set up at the back of the store. Today, he's wearing a pair of dark-rimmed glasses, which aren't identical to the ones he used to wear, but which are close enough to take me instantly back to the first time he walked into this store. With his thick hair combed neatly back from his face, and just a hint of stubble on his jaw, he looks every inch the distinguished author, and I instantly start to regret my own choice of outfit, which, Paris informs me, is 'giving modern-day Jo March,' whatever that means.

Not that it matters. It's not like he's going to see me in this crowd.

Just to make sure of that, I move to the side of the room furthest away from Elliot, who's accompanied by a glossy-looking woman in a tight black dress, who I'm assuming is his publicist, or assistant, or someone else from the publishing house. She isn't the woman whose house I saw him come out of the other morning, but I still have to fight back a totally unreasonable twinge of jealously as she lays a proprietorial hand on his arm, showing him where to stand.

"Well, um, good evening, everyone," says Dad, wringing his hands together anxiously as he steps up to introduce Elliot. "Thank you all for coming. I'm sure the gentleman next to me needs no introduction, so I'll let him get on with it, shall I?"

He peers around the room, as if asking permission to leave, and the audience applauds politely, everyone's eyes locked expectantly on Elliot, who has his hands in his pockets, as if this is a completely normal way for him to be spending a December evening.

This is new too. The Elliot I knew would've burst out laughing at the idea of speaking in front of a crowd. I always assumed that was why he refused to do any publicity for his book when it came out; because he just wasn't serious enough to do something as grown-up as making a speech. But now here he is, looking suave and sophisticated, and totally at home as he smiles around at us all from his position in front of the audience.

I wonder if this is who he was all along? If the bashful, self-effacing Elliot I met by the market stall was just an act, and the whole time he was hiding this heart-breakingly handsome stranger behind his sweet smile and sparkling eyes?

Was it all just pretend?

"Thank you, Alan," he says to Dad, sounding very American, somehow, in the confines of the little bookshop. "I'm so happy to be back here in Bramblebury. This is where it all started for me, and I can't think of a better place to celebrate the 10th anniversary of *The Snow Globe*."

The audience applauds again, with the exception of Levi, who gives a small shriek of excitement, before being elbowed in the side by Paris.

"I think the plan is to take some questions before I start signing; is that right?" Elliot asks, turning to the woman in the black dress, who nods her confirmation. Instantly, a small forest of hands springs up as the members of the audience all compete for his attention. Elliot leans back, perching casually on the edge of the table behind him as he scans the audience, before selecting a woman in the front row, who's carrying an expensive-looking camera and a notebook.

"Is it true that you're also here to announce your next book?" she asks breathlessly. "And that it'll be a sequel to *The Snow Globe*?"

Before Elliot can answer, little black dress woman steps forward.

"Mr. Sinclair will only be answering questions about *The Snow Globe* at this time," she says, sounding like she's reading a statement that's been prepared in advance. "His focus is very much on the anniversary for now, and we really appreciate your understanding on that."

A small sigh of disappointment ripples through the audience — started, no doubt, by Levi. But they soon recover themselves, and within a few seconds the hands are in the air once more, and Elliot's answering questions ranging from the banal ("How long did it take you to write the book?") to the really quite ridiculous ("If you were a cat, what would your cat name be?").

Elliot answers every question with the same care and attention, no matter how stupid it is, pausing to consider his answers (His cat name would be 'Jay Catsby', he says...), and looking each questioner in the eye as he responds, as if they're uniquely important to him. He's funny, self-deprecating and clever, and as I stand at the back of the room, watching him, I can't help but smile along with everyone else, caught up in the spell he's casting over the room.

Finally, Elliot's glance lands on Levi, who's been straining so hard to get his attention that he's almost lifted himself right off the ground.

"My question is about inspiration," says Levi innocently, his eyes flicking over to me, before re-focusing on Elliot. "I wondered if there was anything in particular that inspired you to write this particular book? Or any*one*, even?"

I clench my hands so hard I almost drop the tray I'm holding.

I *knew* I shouldn't have just taken his word that he wouldn't mention me. I *knew* he'd somehow find a way around it.

Levi keeps his eyes fixed on Elliot, knowing perfectly well that if he were to turn *my* way, my glare would probably turn him to stone. Elliot, however, looks out at the audience, his familiar blue eyes searching the room until he finds me.

"Yes," he says, holding my gaze in a way that makes it impossible for me to look away. "Yes, there was someone, as it happens. Someone very special."

The entire room seems to hold its breath; or maybe it's just me. I'm definitely the only one whose hands are shaking right now as I wait for the answer that has the potential to turn my life upside down for a second time, as well as confirming that I, Holly Hart, am 'someone special'.

So, a bit of a double-edge sword, really. To say the least.

"His name was Luke Sinclair," Elliot says. "And he was my great-grandfather. I named the main male character in the book after him, in fact, although I changed his surname, to make the connection less obvious."

The crowd murmurs with interest, but the tray in my hands doesn't stop shaking. This time, though, the tension I'm feeling is from anger rather than apprehension.

He's not going to mention me at all, then? Not even a single acknowledgment of how I helped him come up with the main plot line?

Elliot continues talking, addressing Levi now, instead of me. He talks some more about his great-grandfather, and his connection to Bramblebury. Behind him, his assistant/publicist/whatever she is glows with excitement. This is the first time anyone's ever heard the story behind the book — or the part of the story Elliot's willing to tell them, anyway — and it's absolute gold, as far as book sales are concerned. I can practically see the dollar signs in the woman's eyes as she thinks about how all of this will play out in the book press tomorrow; how excited readers of *The Snow Globe* will be to find out it's a true story.

They won't know the *whole* truth, though, will they?

"We have time for just one more question," says Little Black Dress, glancing at her watch. "And then we'll have to get on with the signing."

A slightly smaller selection of hands go up this time, but it's Paris who Elliot selects for the final question.

"I was wondering about the snow globe," she asks, twirling a braid around her finger. "The one the book's named after, I mean, not the book itself. I just wondered ... given that you've just told us the story was based on a real one, does that mean the snow globe was real, too? Was there ever an *actual* snow globe? And do you still have it, if so?"

For the first time, Elliot's confidence seems to falter.

"I... um..." he begins, sounding more like the man I used to know. "I... yes. Yes, there was, actually. I bought it here in Bramblebury; at a

Christmas market very like the one I passed on the way here, actually. But no. No, I don't still have it. I don't know what happened to it. I wish I did."

Once again, his eyes find mine in the crowd, but this time his gaze seems to hold a challenge of some sort.

I think I've had enough now.

I place the tray of champagne carefully down on top of a pile of Vivienne Faulkner books — the sight of which does absolutely nothing to calm me down — then turn abruptly on my heel and march into my office at the back of the shop, closing the door firmly behind me, then collapsing into a chair, my mind an alphabet soup of emotions.

I can't believe he did that.

I can't believe he looked at me as if he was daring me to say something.

I can't believe he wrote me out of the story of The Snow Globe.

And I can't believe I care.

Why *do* I care?

I sit at my desk, rubbing my temples wearily as I try to make sense of this. I've spent 10 years trying to disassociate myself from Elliot and his book. It makes no sense at all that I'd suddenly want to be acknowledged as the woman in the story.

And I don't.

Not by the rest of the world, anyway.

As I sit there, though, the low hum of conversation from behind the door telling me the question-and-answer session has come to an end, and they've moved on to the signing, it occurs to me that I *would* like to be acknowledged by Elliot himself.

And he didn't.

He just pretended I had nothing to do with it; as if I didn't even exist.

And now I guess it's time for me to do the same with him.

12

DECEMBER, 10 YEARS AGO

"Dad, you wouldn't happen to know how I could go about finding out who the woman in this photo is, would you?"

It's later the same day, and I'm working a shift at the bookstore while Elliot goes back to his hotel to do some more work on his book, and call his family back home.

Dad takes the photo from me readily enough — he loves this kind of thing — then looks at me suspiciously as he clocks the U.S. army uniform on the man in the shot.

"This isn't something to do with this Elliot chap, is it?" he asks, his face tight with some repressed emotion.

Dad never refers to Elliot by just his name. He's always "this Elliot chap", or "that American of yours"; a way of referring to him that underlines the temporary nature of Elliot's presence in my life, and reminds me of my promise not to get attached.

"It's his great-grandfather," I reply, knowing I'm going to have to tell him the truth if I want to get anything useful out of him. "He was stationed here during the war."

"At Fort Stafford, I suppose," says Dad, interested in spite of himself. "I remember visiting the museum there when I first moved here with your mum. Interesting place. Caused quite a stir in the village, I believe, back in the day."

"Really? How so?" I lean forward, looking again at the photo of the handsome GI and his ghostly companion.

"Oh, well, not everyone in villages like this welcomed the incomers, Holly," Dad replies, taking his spectacles off and polishing them with the sleeve of his sweater. "Especially not the men, who had to go off to war and leave their women at the mercy of the glamorous American soldiers. You have to remember, it was a different time back then."

I nod. Now that he's put the idea into my mind, I can definitely imagine Elliot's great-grandfather causing 'quite a stir' here, as Dad puts it. His smile reminds me of Elliot's. It's almost identical, actually. And Elliot definitely causes 'a stir' in me, so it figures his great-grandpa might have had a similar effect on the women of the village; including, I suppose, the one on his arm on that long-ago afternoon.

"But what about her?" I ask, going back to the photo. "I know there's not much to go on, but I thought it might be some kind of military uniform she's wearing. What do you think? Could women even join the military back then?"

"Oh, yes," says Dad, holding the photo up to the light. "Not in combat roles, obviously, but they did lots of other things. Radar operators, code breakers, spies..."

He grins at me, and, for just a second, he looks almost like his old self again; the way he was before Mum died.

"You think she could've been a spy?" I ask, already itching to see Elliot and pass on this nugget of information. "That would be amazing for the boo ... for her, I mean. How exciting."

"Hmm, well, I wouldn't get too carried away," says Dad kindly. "It's more likely she was just a clerical worker of some kind. Admin support, that kind of thing. If you look closely, I think there's a badge of some kind on her jacket. Could be ATS, perhaps? There's one on her hat, too, although it's harder to see because it's so blurred."

My disappointment at the thought of the woman being a boring old admin worker rather than a spy is forgotten as I join him at the shop window, both of us peering up at the photo in the weak December daylight.

"ATS?" I ask, looking at the little dark shape on the mystery woman's jacket, which could very well be a badge. "What's that? And how would I find out if she was a member?"

"Auxiliary Territorial Service," replies Dad. "As for how you could know if this woman was involved, though, I'm afraid I have no idea; not without a name, at least. I suppose you could try the library. I bet Maisie would love to get her teeth into a local mystery."

He hands the photo back to me with a grin.

"We already tried there," I reply glumly. "We didn't find anything much. Maisie was on her lunch break when we were there, though. I guess we could go back and ask if she has any ideas."

"Oh, I'm sure we can trust Maisie to be full of ideas," says Dad. "Why is this so important to you, though, Holly? Why do you need to find this woman? And why doesn't that American of yours know who she is, if she was connected to his ... who was it? His grandfather?"

"Great-grandfather," I correct him. "And no, she wasn't 'connected' to him as such. He married someone else after the war."

"And left this one behind, I suppose," says Dad, indicating the woman in the photo, and scowling as if her alleged abandonment is a personal affront to him. "Typical of the Americans at that barracks, from what I've heard. Had their fun, then buggered off home again, and to hell with the consequences."

I blink with surprise. It's not like Dad to sound so vehement. He's normally the very definition of 'mild mannered'. Then again, I have a feeling that it's not 'the Americans' in general he has an issue with; it's *one* American in particular. And he's not a visiting GI, either.

"We don't know he 'abandoned' her," I reply, feeling the need to stand up for Elliot's ancestor. "There could be lots of reasons why they didn't end up together. That's what we're trying to find out."

Dad sniffs loudly.

"There could be many different reasons," he agrees. "Not many happy ones, though, I shouldn't think. I wouldn't imagine their story had a happy ending, whatever it was. How could it, if he was always going to be going back to America in the end?"

This time there's no mistaking which American we're talking about. Dad's about as subtle as an elephant trying to disguise itself as an aardvark. That's why he always used to leave this kind of thing to Mum. But, of course, Mum isn't here, which means it falls to him to step in and stop me from having my heart broken.

"I'm just helping him with some ... some family research, Dad," I say reasonably. "That's all. I'm not planning to run off with the guy, if that's what you're thinking."

The look on his face confirms that's exactly what he's been thinking, and my heart contracts with guilt.

"Well, I should think not," he says, in a faux-casual tone. "You hardly even know the chap. It would be very odd indeed if you were thinking of some kind of future with him."

He takes his glasses off and starts polishing them again, awkwardly aware that he's clumsily steered the conversation into territory neither of us is going to be comfortable with.

"I *do* know Elliot," I tell him, staunchly defending myself. "I know him better than anyone, actually. And he knows *me* better than anyone."

I think about the long, meandering conversations Elliot and I have had in the days since we met; the shared confidences, the nights spent whispering in the darkness rather than falling asleep. I'm not lying when I say he knows me better than anyone else; that, in the short time I've known him, I've told him things I've never told anyone in my life. I'm not lying when I say I know *him*.

But I also know Dad's right: there's no more of a future for me and Elliot than there was for his great-grandfather and the woman in the photo. I know that it would be stupid of me to think otherwise.

"Don't worry, Dad," I say lightly, turning to the nearest bookshelf and starting to rearrange it, even though we haven't had any customers to mess it up first. "I'm not going anywhere. You can trust me on that."

Dad clears his throat in gruff acknowledgement and goes shuffling off to the back of the shop to switch the kettle on, leaving me alone with my books and my thoughts.

I'm not going anywhere. That much is obvious.

But, all of a sudden, I think I really want to.

The Bramblebury village library is very old, and it's almost as cold inside as it is out on the street. I wrap my arms around myself to warm myself up as Maisie Poole, the chief — and, indeed, only — librarian, comes bustling over, her eyes lighting up at the sight of Elliot, and the opportunity for fresh gossip he brings with him.

"Holly," she exclaims. "What a treat! Coming to check out the competition, are you? And this must be your American!"

She looks at him speculatively, her little sparrow-eyes taking in every detail so she can report back to her sister Elsie — and the rest of the village — later. It occurs to me that if she ever fancies a change of career, she'd probably make a pretty decent writer herself, with the way she hoards nuggets of information the way a squirrel stores up nuts for the winter. She should give it a try.

"Hi, I'm Elliot," says the American in question, holding out a hand, which Maisie shakes in the manner of a queen granting an audience to one of her grateful subjects. "It's lovely to meet you."

"Oh, he *is* a charmer, isn't he?" says Masie, her tone failing to make it clear whether she means this as a compliment or not. "And what can I do for you two lovebirds, then?"

I explain as briefly as I can that we're looking for information on a woman who might have lived in the village a long time ago.

"This is all we have to go on, I'm afraid," says Elliot, pulling the photograph of his grandfather and the mystery woman out of his wallet. "I know it's not much, but we're really hoping you might be able to help. Anything you can tell us at all would be amazing, really. We're kind of desperate here."

I glance up at him, a little surprised by how seriously he's taking this 'research' of ours.

I thought we were just going to make something up if we couldn't track down the mystery woman? I didn't realize we were 'desperate'?

"Dad thought the uniform might be ATS?" I put in. "I don't suppose you know anything about that, Maisie."

Maisie's lips pucker with annoyance under their frosted-pink lipstick.

"I'm not quite *that* old, Holly," she says, sniffing. "I wasn't even born during the war, you know. Although I suppose anyone over 30 seems ancient to you."

Elliot and I exchange glances.

"Holly tells me if there's something you don't know, it's probably not worth knowing," he says, jumping in smoothly to rescue me. "I'm guessing that's why you're so good at your job."

My muscles tense as I wait for Maisie to figure out that I told him that in relation to gossip, not to her job at the library, but, to my relief, she just reaches up and pats her hair self-consciously.

"Some people have been known to call me the Queen of the Library," she says, trying and failing to sound modest. "I wouldn't say that *myself*, you understand, but, well, there *is* a reason the library is doing so well these days. Not that the bookstore isn't, too," she adds quickly, turning to me. "How *is* your poor father, Holly? It's a difficult time of year for you both, isn't it?"

Maisie tilts her head to the side sympathetically, as if she hasn't spent the last decade pretending the library and bookstore are two rival gangs in a literary turf war, each struggling for dominance over the town of Bramblebury.

Yes, she should definitely be a fiction writer, if she ever quits the library.

"We're fine, Maisie, thank you," I reply, suppressing the urge to square up to her like an extra from *West Side Story* preparing for a dance-off. "But the woman in the photo? Do you think you can help us figure out who she was?"

"Oh, yes," she says, remembering the reason for our visit at last. "The Auxiliary Territorial Service, wasn't it? I think we *might* have something on that somewhere, but I'll have to check when I can find a spare second. I'm rushed off my feet here, as usual."

She indicates the room we're standing in, which is empty but for the three of us, and has a faint aroma of mildew and neglect.

"Leave it with me, though," Maisie adds, with a martyred expression. "I can't promise anything, but I'll do my best. Why do you want to know, though? Who do you think this woman is?"

Her eyes light up at the thought of fresh gossip material.

"We're not sure," Elliot replies, saving me the trouble. "It's a bit of a mystery, unfortunately. This is all I know."

He hands her a piece of paper torn from his notebook, on which he's scribbled down his great-grandfather's name and regiment, along with the approximate dates he arrived in and left England.

"Oh, I love a good mystery," says Maisie, scanning the note greedily. "I've read all the Hercule Poirot books in the library, you know. The Miss Marples, too. Although I always manage to figure out whodunnit before the end, which spoils it a bit."

"This should be no problem for you then," replies Elliot kindly. "I'm sure you'll have the case solved in no time."

"Well, I'll do my best," replies Maisie, blushing slightly. "He's a proper charmer, this one," she says, giving me a glance of approval before turning to go. "Young Martin better watch out; it looks like he's got himself some competition."

"Martin?" asks Elliot, smiling uncertainly as Maisie sweeps off importantly to scare some children who are loitering near the computer terminals. "Who's Martin, and why is he my competition?"

"He isn't," I assure him, taking his arm as we head back into the street. "Martin Baxter is the boy next door. Literally, I mean. His parents own the bakers; you know the shop next to ours?"

"Right. So you guys grew up together, then?"

"Not really. We grew up next to each other," I correct him. "Martin and I never really had anything in common, but he was convinced we did, what with the whole 'parents being shopkeepers' thing. He's ... well, he's always had a bit of a thing for me, I guess. He thinks that us living next door is a sign that we were meant to be together."

"But it never happened?" Elliot asks. "You two never got together? Sorry," he adds quickly, "I know it's none of my business, I just ... well, I guess I'm just worried about the competition now."

He gives a low chuckle, and I squeeze his arm reassuringly.

"You have absolutely nothing to worry about," I tell him firmly. "Martin's not my type. Never has been, never will be. I like tall, handsome Americans, you know. Ones who write books about dead grandfathers, and like to start wild goose chases over mystery women."

"That's very specific of you," Elliot replies, laughing properly now.

"Oh, my requirements are very specific," I assure him. "I'm pretty sure there's only one man who can fill them, actually. I — "

I manage to stop myself from speaking right before I go on to tell him even more clearly that he's the only man for me, even though we're only supposed to be having a fling.

"Speaking of mystery women," I say, abruptly changing the subject. "I really wish we'd been able to find out at least *something* about her today."

"Patience, my angel," Elliot replies, giving me one of those melt-your-heart smiles of his. "Give Maisie a little bit of time. I have a feeling she's a woman who won't give up until she's found out every last little thing."

"That's the thing, though, isn't it?" I reply, the words bursting out of me without my permission. "We don't *have* time. Not even a little bit. Because you're going home."

At first I think Elliot hasn't heard me. He keeps on walking, my hand still tucked into his, and my heart growing heavy as I realize I've done the thing I promised myself I wouldn't do; I've broken the unspoken code by referencing the fact that he's leaving. I've opened Pandora's box, and now I'm going to have a hell of a time trying to get it closed again.

"Come with me, then," Elliot says, stopping so suddenly I almost walk into him. "Not forever," he adds quickly, seeing the look on my face. "Not if you don't want to. But come for ... for a vacation. Come for Christmas. Florida's still warm in December; you'd love it. And my mom makes a mean roast turkey."

I stand there gaping at him in the street as the snow starts to fall, thick and fast, as if to underline his point about the Florida sunshine.

"Okay, you don't have to have the turkey," Elliot says when I still haven't said anything. "I know you don't like Christmas. Forget

Christmas. We'll go to the beach. We'll go to Disney. We'll go anywhere you like. Just... say you'll come with me."

His eyes find mine through the falling snow, and I have to look away to protect myself from the hope I can see in them.

"It's not the turkey," I say at last, feeling like I'm in a movie. "It's... it's everything, Elliot. Dad. The store. I can't just leave. It's not that easy."

I say it, but in my mind I see sunlight glittering on water, and white sandy beaches stretching down to the sea. I see the possibility of something other than a small town and a life lived through other people's words. I see the start of a story of my own.

"I know it's not," Elliot says, crestfallen. "But, like I say, it doesn't have to be forever. You could just come for the holidays. Hell, your dad could come too, if he wants."

"He won't." I smile at the thought of Dad standing on a tropical beach in his sensible cardi, looking like someone's filed him on the wrong shelf. "He wouldn't leave the store."

But *I* could.

The thought starts as a whisper, but it quickly worms its way right to the back of my mind and makes itself at home there.

I have some money saved up from my wages at the store. I could use it to buy a plane ticket. I could visit Elliot in the States, and I could spend Christmas somewhere that wouldn't remind me of Mum every single moment.

"Maybe you could think about it?" Elliot says, somehow sensing me wavering in my decision not to go. "You don't have to decide right away. We have plenty of time."

We don't, obviously. We have hardly any time at all, really.

But now he's suggested we might have more.

"Sure," I say lightly, as if he's asked me to think about what I want for lunch. "I'll think about it."

And that's a promise.

13

I'm still sitting at my desk, staring at the blank screen I'm using to write down my story ideas for Vivienne — or not write them down, as the case may be — thirty minutes later, when the office door opens, and Elliot appears, walking right in without even asking.

Great.

"I brought you a coffee," he says, placing a steaming takeaway mug in front of me. "I figured you could probably use one. Your friend Levi made it for me. No cinnamon, though; I remember how much you hate it."

*At least he remembers **something**, then.*

I bite back the words on the tip of my tongue, and pick up the coffee cup, noticing he's holding one of his own, too. "Your dad said I'd probably find you in here," he says, looking around the tiny room, which he knew only as a storage cupboard. "He said it's your office? Are you writing, then? Is that why you need an office now?"

His eyes land on the laptop, and I snap it quickly closed, even though there's nothing to see.

"No," I say quickly. "It's just bookstore stuff. Invoices, you know. Staff rotas. That kind of thing. The store's been doing much better since ... well, you know. There's a lot more admin to take care of."

There's an awkward silence as the memory of our previous conversation about the bookstore doing better — and why — hovers dangerously above our heads before disappearing again.

"Oh. Right. That's a shame," Elliot says, taking a sip of his drink and wincing slightly as the sugar hits his taste buds. "Not that the store's doing well, obviously," he adds hurriedly. "That's amazing. Seriously. It's just ... I thought you might be working on that novel you always wanted to write. Or something else, maybe?"

"Nope," I reply briskly, turning away and pretending to tidy the already-immaculate desk. "I still have the same problem with that. No stories, remember? Nothing to tell. Although, I guess I could just do what you did, and make something up?"

Elliot shuffles his feet awkwardly, and I briefly consider throwing myself face-first into my coffee: I suspect the scalding heat of it would be marginally less painful than the look on his face right now.

Why did I say that? Why couldn't I just let it go for once?

"Look," he begins, "About that. I didn't know it would affect you so much; what I wrote. I didn't know it would make you a ... what was it you called it? A 'laughingstock'? It didn't cross my mind that it might embarrass you. I didn't even think anyone would read it, if I'm honest. I definitely didn't imagine all of this."

He pulls at the collar of his shirt as if it's in danger of strangling him. He's not sounding nearly as self-confident now that it's just me and him. It makes me like him more.

"No. No, I don't suppose you did," I reply, softening. "It's... quite something."

"I suppose that's one way of describing it."

He gives a wry chuckle that takes him another step closer to the Elliot I remember.

"That plastic globe thing outside," he says. "I was *not* expecting that. And I went by the Rose Tavern, but it's been re-named, apparently? Now it's—"

"The Globe," I confirm, cringing inwardly. "There are a lot of things around here named after snow globes now. I'm amazed they didn't just rename the town Hollybrooke and be done with it. Nice name, by the way."

I'm being sarcastic, which is something the old Elliot would've known right away. This one, however, just grins, as if it's a joke we're both in on.

"I know; it's cheesy as all get-out. But I have a soft spot for the name Holly, for some reason. I really wanted to use it."

He smiles again, and it somehow manages to reverse time, and send him spiraling back an entire decade until he's back to being the aspiring writer in the big scarf, who told me he'd never forget me.

"You didn't say that earlier, though?" I reply evenly. "When Levi asked you if anyone inspired you to write the book? You just said it was about your great-grandfather. You didn't mention me at all."

I try my best not to sound too needy — or just plain whiny — as I say it, but the look of surprise on Elliot's face suggests I haven't succeeded.

"I didn't think you'd want me to," he replies, making it sound like a question. "When I saw you earlier, you seemed so angry about it; about the book, and the attention you'd got from it. I didn't want to make things worse for you by admitting Evie was based on you — especially not in front of the press that were there. Not to mention

Maisie Poole, who made me sign five copies for her. Hey, is it just me, or has she not changed *at all*?"

He blinks rapidly, and I have to bite my tongue not to laugh at the comical expression on his face.

"Rumor has it she has a portrait in the attic," I say, deadpan. "Either that or she's a vampire. It's definitely one of the two. Possibly both, knowing Maisie. She's nothing if not thorough."

This time his smile is one of relief tempered with caution.

"And you?" he asks softly. "What's your secret? Because you look exactly the same, Holly. *Exactly*. I felt like I'd gone back in time when I bumped into you the other day. It was ... yeah."

I really want to know what 'it' was — 'yeah' doesn't really give me much to go on here — but I'm too thrown by the unexpected compliment to ask.

"Oh, I'm definitely a vampire," I reply seriously. "I survive on the blood of the people who've crossed me."

"That would've made one hell of a plot twist," he says, chuckling. "Shoulda used that one for sure. Unless I'm one of the people who've crossed you, obviously. Which I kind of think I am, given your reaction to me not mentioning you earlier. Either that or this coffee's much worse than I thought, and *that's* why you're annoyed with me?"

He takes another sip and pulls a face.

"Oh, the coffee's terrible," I assure him. "And you're not *totally* wrong about me not wanting to be outed as Evie Snow, either. I don't... I don't really know why I was annoyed out there when you didn't mention me. I don't want that. I've never wanted that. I've never wanted to be connected to the book."

"Has it really been that bad for you?" Elliot asks. "Being Evie? I'm sorry, Holly. That's not what I wanted. Really, it's not. I didn't think for a second that the book would make life difficult for you."

"But ... she's so *awful*," I say, before I can stop myself. "I don't even know why he falls for her; she's just... *urgh*."

I almost knock my drink over as I wave my hands expansively to emphasize my point. Whatever my point's supposed to be.

Elliot rubs his jaw thoughtfully, in a way that suggests my feedback is critical to him.

"You don't like Evie?" he says, his tone light. "You think she's awful? Or 'urgh' even?"

"*Everyone* thinks she's awful," I correct him. "*Everyone* thinks she's 'urgh'. That's why everyone laughs at me. Well, everyone who knows she's supposed to *be* me, anyway. And that includes Maisie Poole, so, you know... *everyone*."

Elliot shrugs.

"*I* like her," he says simply. "I like her a lot. And I don't think she's 'awful' at all. I don't think it's strange in the slightest that he falls for her. I think she's feisty. I think she's brave. I think she's hurt, and damaged, and I think sometimes she does things because she doesn't want to be hurt any more than she already is."

I swallow, my mouth suddenly dry.

"Anyway," he goes on, before I can reply. "It's done now. I can't go back and change it, as much as I'd like to. So I'm sorry you hated the book, but trust me; you're not the only one who was disappointed in it."

I swallow again. It seems to be the only thing I'm capable of doing right now. Because one thing's for sure; I have no idea what to say to him. My mind is a blank page; one that I can't help wishing someone else would write on, just to tell me how to feel about everything he's just said

I don't know how I feel anymore.
Not about Elliot, not about his book, not about anything.

And I really thought I did. When I came storming into this office earlier, I had Elliot firmly cast as the villain in this story; the Machiavellian, scheming liar who gas-lit me into thinking he loved me, then wrote a book that guaranteed I'd spend the rest of my life as a joke.

But now I've been completely wrong-footed. The Elliot standing in front of me isn't the two-dimensional character he's been in my head all these years. He's a real, whole person; one with thoughts and feelings that I absolutely haven't taken into account, because it was too easy to just resent him instead.

"I didn't say I *hated* it," I tell him, my voice almost a whisper. "I didn't... I don't *hate* it."

"Oh, yeah? You could've fooled me."

There's an edge to his voice that I've never heard in it before. It reminds me of how much I don't know about him; how I never really did know him. How *can* you know someone in the space of three weeks? Why did I ever think I did?

"I don't hate it," I say carefully, "I just don't understand it, is all. I don't understand why you made so much of it up. You were the one who was so set on figuring out the truth. Remember how hard we tried to find the mystery woman from the photo?"

"I remember. The visit to the library. Maisie and her Hercule Poirot novels. Hey, I walked past the library a couple days ago," he adds, grinning at the memory. "I see it's had a bit of a makeover, too. It didn't smell musty at all. Maisie must be delighted."

"It's the snow globe effect," I tell him, remembering what Elsie said in the coffee shop a few days ago. "It makes everything better — unless you're actually *in* the book, then it just makes everything much, *much* weirder. But don't change the subject. Why'd you spend all that time trying to find her if you were just going to make it all up, anyway?"

Elliot shrugs.

"It was fun," he says at last. "Wasn't it? It gave us something else to focus on. It made us a team."

"And we wouldn't have been one without that? Wait: what am I saying? Of course we wouldn't. You don't become a 'team' in 23 days, do you? You don't really become *anything* in 23 days. We weren't even a couple; not really. It was barely even a relationship."

I put my drink down so quickly the coffee sloshes out of the lid and onto my hand. I think I get it now; why he changed so many of the details that ended up in his book. He did it because the 'mystery woman' was better as a blank slate. She was more useful that way, because if he didn't know who she really was, he could turn her into whoever he wanted her to be. And I guess the same goes for me. Twenty-three days wasn't enough for him to know me, let alone love me. So he had to pretend.

"I don't know what you want me to say to that, Holly," Elliot says, throwing his hands up in exasperation. "Do you want me to argue with you? Do you want me to apologize?"

I want to say yes to this. Yes to all of it. Because I do. I want him to tell me I'm wrong; that we were every bit the 'team' I thought we were, and I want him to apologize for not living up to the imagined version of himself that existed only in my head. Imagination is always better than reality, though, isn't it? And, unfortunately for us, no one's writing this script for us, so we're having to make it up as we go along.

"Holly, are you in there?"

The door swings open and Dad's head appears, his hair now doing a passable impression of Albert Einstein's.

"Oh!" he says, looking surprised to see Elliot standing in the corner of the room, as if he's haunting it. "I thought you'd gone, Elliot? Your publicist has been looking for you."

"Thanks for letting me know," says Elliot, sounding normal again. "Tell her I'm on my way, would you?"

Dad's head disappears again, and Elliot and I face each other, neither of sure what happens next.

"For what it's worth," he says. "I *am* sorry. I didn't mean for the book to ruin your life. I really didn't."

"It didn't. I've had a perfectly nice life, thanks," I say stiffly. "It's been... nice."

"Nice? Is that all?"

Elliot gives a low chuckle.

"I'll leave you to get on with your nice life, then," he says, crossing to the office door, which he tugs open with much more force than it actually requires. Then he stops suddenly and turns back to face me.

"*Do* you still have it?" he asks, framed in the doorway. "The snow globe? I've always wondered."

I look up at him from my position at the desk.

"No," I say quietly. "No, I don't. I got rid of it years ago."

"Right. I should've guessed."

There's nothing I can say to that, so I just sit there at my desk and watch as the door swings closed behind him. Then, once I'm sure he's definitely not coming back, I open the desk drawer beside me and rummage around in it for a minute until I find the thing I'm looking for lurking at the back.

I pull it out and place it on the desk in front of me, checking the door first to make sure it's definitely closed.

The snow globe still looks exactly the same as it did ten years ago. The tiny buildings are still recognizably Bramblebury, the snow still swirls around them, and the little couple still stand there, locked in their eternal kiss.

Everything's the same.

And yet every single thing is different.

14

DECEMBER, 10 YEARS AGO

For the two days that follow Elliot's suggestion that I come to America with him for Christmas, I let myself believe I'm actually going to do it; that I'm going to hop on a plane, and my life is finally going to begin.

They're two of the best days of my adult life, and they are, of course, completely fake. I know it even as I'm looking up the prices of flights during my lunch break and wondering what the temperature's like in Fort Lauderdale in December. I know I can't actually go — and even if I didn't know it, the look on Dad's face every time he sees me head out to meet Elliot would get the message across loud and clear. But imagining Christmas in Florida is a special treat I allow myself to indulge in, just for a little while. It's like a vacation for my brain; and Elliot's right there with me.

"You wouldn't have to leave right after Christmas," he says one frozen afternoon as we sit on our favorite bench at the top of the hill, eating fish and chips wrapped in newspaper. "You could stay for New Year. Or, you know, longer. You could stay as long as you like, really. Your dad could manage the shop on his own for a bit, couldn't he?"

"I'm sure he could," I agree, there being no point in trying to argue otherwise. Even Elliot, who finds everything about England quaint and magical, has noticed that we never seem to have any customers when he comes to meet me at the store. "It's whether he'd *want* to, that worries me."

This isn't really up for debate either. I already know exactly what Dad would have to say about the idea of me spending Christmas in America, and it's not a thought I like to dwell on, because it doesn't really fit with the fiction I've created around the idea.

"What's your parents' house like?" I ask Elliot instead, stuffing another chip in my mouth. "Is it near your apartment?"

"Nowhere's near anywhere in Florida," he says, grinning. "It's not like here. You can't just walk places. You need a car to get anywhere." I snuggle into his side and listen to him talk about the house he grew up in, with its pool and its golf course view, and think about how different it sounds from the life I've known up until now. It seems crazy to me to think that this man I've come to know so well inhabits a world I've never seen; that I know what his voice sounds like when it's rusty from sleep, and what he looks like when he's dreaming, but not what color his bathroom is, or whether he hangs his sweaters or folds them. And I *want* to know. I want to know everything; from what kind of sofa he has, to how he celebrates his birthday. I want to know what his life looks like; and, more than that, I want to see it for myself.

"What are they like?" I ask, my mind seizing on something new to worry about. "Your family, I mean? D'you think they'd like me?"

It takes him so long to answer, I start to panic that he's going to say no.

"They're complicated," he says finally, screwing the wrapper from his fish and chips into a tight paper ball. "Nice, but... complicated."

"How so?"

"Oh, just in the way all families are complicated, I guess. Ours isn't anything out of the ordinary, really. No skeletons in the closet. Well, not that I know of, anyway."

Elliot rolls his paper ball a little tighter and stares out at the landscape in front of us, which is in its finest Christmas-card form after the unusual amount of snow we've had this week.

"You haven't finished researching your great-granddad yet, though," I reply teasingly. "Maybe you'll unearth a few skeletons there."

The arm I'm leaning against suddenly goes tense, making me look up at him in surprise.

"About that," Elliot says slowly. "It's probably best if you don't mention the book when you ... if you see my parents."

"Really? Why? You don't think they'd like it?"

"No," he says shortly. "No, they wouldn't. Oh, not because of the subject matter," he adds, sensing my surprise at this. "My dad was the one who got me into researching the family tree in the first place. It's kind of a passion of his. It's the *writing* part he wouldn't like."

"He ... doesn't like writing?" Now I'm really confused. "How could he not like *writing*?"

"It's not that he doesn't *like* it," Elliot replies, his fist closing tightly around the wrapper in his hand. "It's that he doesn't think it's a good enough career for one of his sons. I don't think he sees it as a career at all, actually; just a hobby. And a distraction. He doesn't want me distracted. He wants me to come back from this trip and go work for the family business, like my brothers. He thinks that's what I'm going to do."

"But you don't want to," I say, understanding. "You want to write, instead."

I squeeze his arm gently, thinking about how similar we are; both of us stuck working for businesses we didn't choose, just because it's what's expected of us.

"It isn't realistic, though, is it?" Elliot replies. "Writing? It's not like it's going to earn me enough to live off. It's probably not going to earn me anything at all, actually. That's what's so frustrating about it. I feel like I'm just chasing some stupid dream that's never going to come true."

"It could, though," I tell him firmly, hating this sudden switch from happy, positive Elliot to someone who sounds more like ... well, *me*, really. "Of course it could. It's not a stupid dream, Elliot. Your book is good. It's going to be even better once we figure out the finer details of the plot. And there are plenty of people who make a living out of writing. Like Stephen King, say. Or... or other people like Stephen King. Why shouldn't you be one of them?"

"I don't think I'm going to be the next Stephen King, somehow," Elliot laughs, his good humor restored. "And those 'finer details of the plot' are kinda important, really. But hey: if I could be one of the people who makes a living from figuring out difficult plot points, then what's stopping you being one of them, too?"

"Oh, everything." I sigh dramatically, resting my head on his shoulder. "My dad isn't exactly thrilled with the idea of me doing anything other than working for the family business either, in case you haven't noticed."

"I guess we'll find out how he feels about that soon," Elliot says. "When you speak to him about our Christmas plans."

He kisses me on the forehead, and we sit there looking out at the view, me turning the idea of 'our Christmas plans' slowly over in my head, marveling at how quickly we've become people with *plans* together.

"The thing is," I say slowly, watching a rise from one of the chimneys below us, in a lazy trail across the winter sky. "This thing ... us. It was just supposed to be a fling, wasn't it? It wasn't supposed to last past Christmas Eve."

"We didn't actually say that," Elliot points out, his voice coming from above my head. "We just said we'd enjoy each other's company while it lasted. So who says we can't make it last longer?"

His tone is deliberately light, but there's an entire subtext to what he's saying, and finding out exactly what it says has just become the most important thing in my life.

"That's just it, though," I reply, sitting up, and pushing my hair out of my face so I can see him properly. "We can't, can we? Not really. Say I do come to Florida. Say I come for Christmas — or even as long as New Year. I'll still have to come home again, eventually. All we'll be doing is delaying the inevitable. All we'll be doing is making it harder when we have to say goodbye. I'm ... I'm just not sure I can do that. I'm not sure I want to."

I stop talking, realizing I've done it now: I've well and truly destroyed the whole 'living for the moment' illusion, and revealed myself as exactly what I am: a girl who's scared of getting hurt.

It's true, though, isn't it? The fact is, I don't want to be just a chapter of Elliot's life. I want to be the whole story. And I know it would be greedy of me to expect a happy ending, but the truth is, I want that too.

"You're not sure you want to spend Christmas with me, or you're not sure you want to say goodbye?" Elliot asks. "I just ... I need to be very clear what you're saying here, Holly, because it kind of sounds like you might be breaking up with me?"

"I'm not," I reply, hating the wary look in his eyes, and the fact that I'm the one who put it there. "Well, not yet, anyway. But, I mean, we've been breaking up since the day we met, Elliot, haven't we? Because we know it can't last. We live on different sides of the world. And me coming to the States with you for a week or two isn't going to change that. We're still going to have to say goodbye."

I chew my bottom lip anxiously, not used to making emotionally charged speeches. Or waiting for a response to them.

Before that response can come, though, there's a sudden flurry of activity as the birds in the surrounding trees all take off at once, the quiet of the hillside shattered by the arrival of Maisie Poole, who comes trudging up the hill towards us.

"Oh, there you both are!" she says brightly, as Elliot and I exchange surprised looks. "I thought I'd find you two here!"

"Maisie? What on earth?" I say, wondering if the rumors are true and she really does have spies working for her — because that's the only explanation I can think of for her certainty that she'd find us on top of this hill.

"Budge up," she says, plonking herself unceremoniously between us, and placing a large leather handbag on her knee. "I have something to show you."

I risk a glance at Elliot over the top of his head as she opens the bag and rummages inside it, but he's too focused on Maisie for me to be able to decode the look on his face, or figure out what he might have been planning to say to me before we were interrupted.

I watch impatiently, willing Maisie to hurry up as she continues to search through the contents of her bag. I'm half expecting her to produce a couple of lamps and a hatstand, like Mary Poppins, but instead she pulls out a brown manila envelope, from which she produces an old, black-and-white photograph.

"Ta-da," she says, smiling triumphantly as Elliot and I lean forward to take a look at it. "The ladies of the Auxiliary Territorial Service, photographed in front of Bramblebury Village Hall, in 1943. Recognize anyone?"

I squint down at the faded photo, which shows around a dozen women standing on the steps of the hall, all of them wearing the same uniform as the mystery woman in Elliot's photo. It takes me a moment to spot her, and then Elliot and I see her at the same time.

"Look! There she is!"

The mystery woman is standing towards the back of the photo, on the very top step. Her smile isn't quite as wide as it is in the photo with Elliot's great-grandfather, but she's still recognizable from her heart-shaped face and distinctive widow's peak.

"Evie Snow," Maisie says, as proudly as if she's just conjured her out of thin air. "It says so on the back. Look."

She flips the photo over and shows us the list of names, written in faded ink, by someone who's presumably long gone by now.

"Evie Snow," breathes Elliot, taking the photo carefully from Maisie. "The mystery woman has a name."

And what a name it is, too.

"Surely that can't have been her real name?" I comment. "She sounds like a character in a book rather than an actual person."

Elliot's eyes meet mine over the top of the photograph, both of us thinking the same thing.

"I'm afraid a name is all she has," Maisie interrupts, clearly relishing her role as messenger. "I had a quick look on one of the library computers — I'm very clued up about the Internet, you know — and there were no Evie Snows in Bramblebury, either on the National Registration that happened in 1939, or the next census, which was in 1951. They didn't bother during the war, you know; too busy trying to stay alive, I expect."

"Right. So how would we go about finding her, then?" Elliot asks, undaunted.

"Oh, you can't," replies Maisie cheerfully. "Well, you could try the usual routes, I suppose: births, marriages, deaths; that kind of thing. But I'd be surprised if you manage to find anything. I know it's a bit of an unusual name, but she wouldn't have been the only Evie, or the only Snow in the country. And that's assuming she never changed it by marriage."

"What about the Ministry of Defense?" suggests Elliot. "They'll have records of members, surely?"

Maisie nods.

"They do," she agrees. "But they'll only supply them to next of kin. *Is* she next of kin, do you think?"

She looks at him eagerly, hoping for some fresh gossip.

"No," Elliot says, sounding as disappointed as Maisie looks at this. "No, she isn't. I don't know who she was. And it doesn't look like I'm going to find out, either."

His shoulders sag in defeat. I really want to hug him, but I have to wait while Maisie flutters around, putting the photo of Evie Snow back into its envelope, and then launching into a long, pointless story about her sister Elsie's next-door neighbor, who she suspects might be 'up to something'.

Finally, though, she says goodbye, and heads off back down the hill, leaving Elliot and I to digest the fact that the search is over, and we're still no further forward.

"Well, I guess that's that," he says, as the top of Maisie's red bobble hat disappears behind the crest of the hill. "It looks like this book is going to have to be fiction, after all."

"Is that such a bad thing?" I ask, puzzled by how seriously he's taking this. "I know you wanted to figure out what really happened — I did, too. But it was always a long shot, Elliot. There was always a chance we'd have to make that part of the story up."

"I know," he says, taking my hand. "I just hate not knowing, is all. I hate loose ends. I hate that someone's entire life can just ... disappear. Like it didn't matter."

"That's not necessarily true," I point out. "Someone must know what happened to her; what her story was. And even if they don't, she was still real. She still mattered. Things don't only become real once someone's written about them."

"Don't they? Do you really think that, Holly?"

Elliot's words are soft, but his eyes, when I finally meet them, hold a challenge which makes me wonder which one of us I'm trying to convince here.

I'm the one who's always felt like things haven't really happened to me until I've written them down, after all. That's why I've never written anything about Mum dying; not even in my diary. I always felt like once it was down on paper, it would make it real; and, as long as it isn't, I can continue to pretend on some level that it didn't happen.

So I'm a fine one to lecture Elliot about writing and reality, when I don't even believe my own words.

"What I think is that you can still write an amazing story about them both," I reply, shrugging off the question. "And I guess the best thing about it is that this way you at least get to decide how it ends."

"And what about us? How does our story end?"

The question is the one that's been circling my mind endlessly, almost since we met, but it still comes as a shock to hear it spoken out loud.

"I'm not sure," I admit, my palms suddenly clammy with nerves despite the chill of the afternoon. "I've been trying not to think about it. I just know it has to."

This time, my words are even less convincing.

"And is that what you want?"

His hand tightens almost imperceptibly around mine, as if he's steeling himself for an answer he knows he's not going to like.

"No. Of course not," I tell him. "It's the very last thing I want. If it was up to me, it would last forever."

My voice catches on that last word. Until now, my feelings about Elliot have been a secret I've been trying to keep even from myself. But now they're out there in the open, and it's a feeling that reminds me of the time I fell off a swing when I was eight years old — or, more specifically, of the moment before I hit the ground, when it felt almost like flying. This, too, could go either way; although, if my past record is anything to go by, I suspect the only way for me is down.

My entire body tenses up, waiting for the moment of impact.

But it doesn't come.

Instead, Elliot takes my face gently in his hands and tilts it up towards his, until I'm forced to look him in the eye.

"That's settled, then," he says simply. "I'm glad we're on the same page."

"Are ... are you making a book pun?" I ask croakily.

Elliot grins.

"Bad time to get cheesy on you, huh?" he says wryly. "Sorry. What I meant to say was that I feel like that too. I don't want to have to say goodbye to you, Holly. Not on Christmas Eve, and not any time after that, either."

We look at each other, both of us intensely aware that everything has just changed between us.

"So, what do we do? There's that whole 'different continents' thing to deal with, remember?"

This time, my voice comes out as a whisper rather than a croak. It's only a marginal improvement, but Elliot doesn't seem to notice.

"So we'll deal with it," he says lightly. "Somehow. I don't know exactly *how* yet, but we'll find a way. It can be one of those plot points we have to figure out."

"You're doing it again with the book puns," I say, laughing. I don't care, though, because, instead of answering, he just leans forward and kisses me, and it's the kind of kiss that makes me feel like he might be right; that we can figure this out.

And maybe our story won't have to end after all.

15

It's called 'insta love' according to Paris. It's her least favorite trope.

"It's love at first sight, basically," she tells me, pausing in the act of shelving a new delivery of romantasy novels the morning after the book signing. "When the two main characters meet and they instantly *know* they're destined to be together. *The Snow Globe* is one example of it, obviously, but there are loads more. It's, like, super popular, for some reason."

She looks at me as if she might be about to hold me personally responsible for this; which honestly wouldn't surprise me.

"Was that what it was like, then?" she asks, curiosity getting the better of her, and forcing her to drop the 'cool girl' act for a second. "With you and Elliot? Was it just like in the book? Did your eyes meet across the bookstore, and then, WHAM! That was it?"

I take the books from her and start organizing them according to the color of their spines, even though I know she'll just put them back into alphabetical order again as soon as I'm safely in my office.

"No, of course not," I reply, my eyes fixed on what I'm doing. "We didn't meet in the bookstore. And I don't believe in love at first sight, anyway. Or 'insta love' or whatever you want to call it. It's definitely not what happened to me and Elliot. Everyone knows how *that* turned out."

"We don't *really*, though," points out Paris bluntly. "No one knows. In the book, he waits for her in front of the Christmas tree in the village square, like they agreed, but she doesn't turn up. We never find out why. It's like he meant to write a sequel at some point, but just never got around to it."

"The thing with the Christmas tree didn't happen," I tell her, still focused on the books. "Elliot just made that bit up."

The question of what *did* happen hangs in the air between us, like a piece of mistletoe on an unsuccessful first date. Strangely, not even Levi has ever dared ask me about the *real* ending of my relationship with Elliot. No one has; not even Dad. Which means Elliot is the only person who knows; because, God knows, it's as much of a mystery to me as it is to anyone else.

"Is it weird?" Paris asks, having allowed a respectful amount of time to pass between this question and her last one. "Him being back here?"

"Yeah," I admit, pulling my hair back and securing it with a pencil I grabbed from my desk earlier. "It's pretty weird. I wish I'd had some time to prepare for it, you know?"

"To, like, get your hair done and stuff?" Paris says, watching as I wrestle with the hair in question, which continues to evade my attempts to wrestle it into submission. "I totally get that. That's what I'd do too, if I was going to be seeing my ex. And I'd make sure I was wearing something, like, *super* hot."

"Um, I just meant time to, you know, *mentally* prepare," I reply, a little taken aback. Now that she's mentioned it, though, I suppose if I'd known I was going to be bumping into Elliot that day, I might have taken a bit more care with my appearance. I probably wouldn't have worn the 'Jane Eyre' dress, for one thing. And maybe I *should* stop using stationery as hair accessories?

"Paris," I say suddenly. "What *would* you wear if you were going to be seeing your ex? If you were me, I mean?"

I add this last bit because Paris is very much a 'Gen Z' dresser, which means she's currently wearing jeans so wide I'm pretty sure I saw Ed the cat hiding under them earlier. She always looks amazing, but I'm not convinced the same would be true of me if I decided to try to 'slay' like Paris.

Paris takes a step back and looks at me critically.

"It depends what kind of direction you want to take, really," she says seriously. "Like, are you thinking clean girl or cottage core? Edgy or party girl?"

"Um, I just want to look like *me*, but better," I reply, making a mental note to look up all the things she just said later, so I can finally start to understand what the hell she's talking about. "Just so I can look him in the eye when I see him at the book festival and not have to feel like he's the only one who's moved on since ... well, you know."

"Okay, so what I'm hearing is that this is as much about confidence as clothes," says Paris. "It's about living your best life. Empowering yourself. Embracing your authentic self."

"That's exactly it," I reply, too relieved by the fact that she hasn't just laughed at me to question what embracing my 'authentic self' might involve. "That's what I'm trying to do. But what do I *wear*, though? To empower myself um, *authentically*?"

Paris bites her lip thoughtfully.

"I'm thinking a kind of crossover," she says. "The dark academia thing *kind* of works for you, but you need to sex it up a bit. You know? Because it's one thing to love books — that's why we all work here — but that doesn't mean you have to dress like a Brontë sister. You know?"

I absolutely do *not* know, but I nod anyway, pretending to know exactly what she's talking about. Paris, however, is not fooled.

"Holly, do you want me to take you shopping?" she asks, with the air of someone offering to do me a huge favor. "Or do you feel like you understand the assignment here?"

I glance over at her. I had *thought* I 'understood the assignment' as she puts it, but it's becoming increasingly clear that I don't understand *anything*, really; and definitely not 'the assignment'.

"Shopping, please," I reply meekly. "That would be amazing, Paris, thank you."

She shrugs, as if it's no big deal, but the corners of her mouth turn up ever so slightly.

"We can go during my lunch break, if you like?" she says. "There's that new boutique on the high street. It's tiny, but it's got a lot of great brands."

By 'a lot of great brands', I know she means 'a lot of incredibly expensive brands'. Post Snow-Globe Bramblebury is filled with shops which would probably be best described as 'chi-chi'. But I don't have time to drive to the nearest big town just to wander around the charity shops I usually buy my clothes from, and I do have some money saved up, thanks to my habit of never actually doing anything with my life, so it's going to have to do.

Plus, if someone as picky as Paris approves, that means it's *got* to be good; which is why, just over an hour later, we find ourselves leaving the store together, both of us being very stiff and polite as we try to acclimatize to this unexpected new turn our working relationship has taken. I'm just starting to entertain the beginnings of a daydream in which we become close friends, who're forever popping in and out of each other's houses, and borrowing each other's clothes (Because I'm at least ten years younger and a hundred times cooler in this vision, obviously), when Paris suddenly says the four words guaranteed to ruin my day.

"Isn't that Elliot Sinclair?"

I look in the direction she's pointing, and, sure enough, there he is; strolling along the main street of the village, looking for all the world like a man who isn't even remotely worried about bumping into his ex while wearing a pencil in his hair. And not just because he doesn't even *have* a pencil in his hair. Actually, he looks like he could easily apply to be in a hair commercial, if the whole 'bestselling author' thing ever starts to get old. It's kind of unfair that he looks so good, while being so ... *him*.

Maybe *he's* the one with the portrait in the attic?

It's not Elliot I'm looking at, though, great hair aside.

No, all of my attention is currently fixed on the woman next to him; a woman who *also* has spectacularly good hair, as well as a face I recognize instantly as the one I last saw waving goodbye to Elliot from the doorway of her cottage a couple of days ago.

It's Katie Hunter: and she's smiling up at Elliot as if he's some kind of tasty treat she's saving for later.

Somewhere in the back of my mind, a memory attempts to fight its way to the surface, before being abruptly drowned out by the wave of inexplicable jealousy that comes after it.

"Holly? Are you okay?"

I tear my eyes away from Elliot and Katie, to find Paris watching me warily, as if she's already deeply regretting her offer to take me clothes shopping.

"I'm fine," I reply brightly, in a tone that sounds unconvincing even to me. "Just ... just looking forward to my makeover, that's all."

"I didn't say anything about a *makeover*," Paris replies, her horrified look casually destroying my vision of our future friendship. "I'm not a miracle worker. But look, here's the place I was telling you about."

She steers me through the doorway of a little boutique, which is about half the size of the bookstore, and decorated entirely in stark white, with items of clothing displayed like works of art. I wander around cautiously, too scared to touch anything, while marveling at the fact that a place like this even exists in Bramblebury; a village which, until recently, boasted an Oxfam shop and a place selling equestrian gear as its only source of 'fashion'.

The Snow Globe effect strikes again, I guess.

Within minutes, Paris is herding me into a changing room with an armful of clothes, which I dutifully try on, waiting for the moment when I'll look in the mirror and think, "Yes, that's it. That's the woman I want to be. My life is now changed."

But the moment doesn't come. The clothes are all beautiful, even to my unpracticed eye, but nothing looks quite right; by which I mean nothing makes me look like Beautiful Katie Hunter — or Bloody

Katie Hunter, rather, who has suddenly become the gold standard of attractiveness to me.

And meanwhile, no matter what I try on, I'm still just Holly.

"This isn't fair," I complain to Paris when I emerge from the changing room a few minutes later, my cheeks red from the mini workout I've just had struggling in and out of a selection of bodycon dresses. "If my life was a movie, this would be the moment where I take off my glasses and basically turn into another person. Like Superman."

"You don't wear glasses," replies Paris, ever the pragmatist. "And your life technically *is* a movie, anyway. It's just not the movie you want it to be."

"Not yet, it isn't," I mutter, feeling like I should apologize to the sleekly sophisticated shop assistant at the door as we leave the store empty-handed. "But I'm working on it."

Paris eyes me curiously, but whatever she's about to say is lost as I step through the doorway of the little boutique and walk straight into something very tall, and very solid.

Something, in fact, very Elliot Sinclair.

"Holly," he says politely, not sounding particularly surprised to find me almost falling over him for the second time in the space of a week. "How are you?"

"I'm great," I reply, quickly scanning the street for any sign of Bloody Katie, and relaxing slightly when she fails to materialize. "Just been doing a bit of shopping with my friend Paris."

Paris's eyebrows almost disappear into her hairline at this, but she doesn't contradict me, and I smile at her gratefully, relieved to be 'showing up as my best self', as she instructed me earlier.

"That's nice," says Elliot. "Is that a pencil in your hair?"

He reaches out and removes it, like a magician performing a trick — only in this case, the only 'trick' he manages to pull off involves my hair rapidly uncoiling itself like one of Medusa's snakes, and absolutely no one is impressed by it.

"Oh, *that's* where it was," I reply, pushing hair out of my eyes and reaching for the pencil. "I was looking for that earlier when I was ... when I was..."

"It was when you were working on your new book, Holly, wasn't it?" says Paris, coming unexpectedly to the rescue. "You were so into it you must've got distracted."

I stare wordlessly at her, not totally on board with the direction she's taking this conversation in, but not quite sure how to turn it around.

"Your new book?" Elliot says, his eyes flickering with an emotion I can't identify. "So you *are* writing again?"

"Oh. Um. Yes. Yes, I am," I reply, feeling Paris's elbow connect sharply with my ribs. "I'm working on a novel, actually. I can't say much about it, it's—" I stop myself just in time, before I can let the fact that I'm just the ghostwriter slip out. "It's still just a very rough idea. You know how it is."

"She has a publisher and everything," says Paris, apparently deciding that now is the moment to be my wing-woman. "So it's a real book. She's not just saying that to make herself look good."

I cringe inwardly, making a mental note never to get on the wrong side of her, if this is what she thinks 'being supportive' is like.

"But Holly, that's great," Elliot says, with what looks like the first genuine smile I've seen from him since he arrived back in town.

"That's *really* great. I always said you should write a novel. So, what's it called? Or can you not say?"

I start to shake my head, before Paris's elbow changes my mind.

"It's called *If This Was a Movie*," I say, blurting out the first thing that comes into my head, then cringing as I realize how stupid it sounds. Then again, Elliot *did* name the town in his book 'Hollybrooke', so maybe it's not the *most* stupid thing he'll have heard.

"I like it," he says, his grin widening. "I really like it. It's very *you*."

There's a tiny window of opportunity for me to ask him what he means by this rather than simply filing it away so I can overthink it later (Which is also *very me*, actually...), but I'm distracted by the way he's looking at me as if we're still close enough to chat about our lives like this — and also by the little white scar just above his left eyebrow, which proves that we aren't, because I know it definitely wasn't there ten years ago. Every time I see him, I notice some little detail about him that's different, and every one of those details provides even more proof of the life he's lived without me, and me without him.

I wonder if Katie Hunter knows how he got that scar?

"Oh! Hello there!"

The door behind us opens and Katie herself emerges from the boutique, laden with shopping bags, and looking from Elliot to me and then back again, almost as if she knows what I was thinking. That rogue memory attempts to surface yet again.

She reminds me of someone. I just can't remember who it is.

"Katie! Um, this is Holly," Elliot says, looking uncomfortable; as well he might, I suppose. "Holly, this is Katie."

"Oh, yes! *Holly*! Of course!"

Katie says my name in a tone that suggests she knows significantly more about me than I know about her. I'm not planning to hang around to find out exactly what Elliot's told her about me, though. I'm not that much of a masochist.

"Right, well, we better be going, Paris," I say briskly, linking arms with my surprised assistant manager. "Books to sell, books to write. No rest for the wicked. Nice to meet you, Katie! Come on, Paris."

I set off down the street at a quick march, dragging Paris along behind me, and feeling quite proud of how... breezy... I managed to be.

Yes. Breezy. That's how I'll be from now. I'll be brisk and breezy, and that way Elliot will never know just how much it hurts me seeing him with someone else, in the place that used to be ours.

"Holly, let me go," Paris squeaks, as I almost knock her off her feet in my haste to get away from them. "You're being *really* weird, by the way," she adds. "Even for you, I mean."

Oh.

So, maybe *not*-so-breezy, then. Maybe I'll just be "really weird" instead.

That sounds more like the old me. I know Paris would agree.

But 'the old me' isn't going to write this book, ignore her ex, and change her life, is she? No, she isn't. Which is why, as soon as we're safely back at the bookstore, I thank Paris again for her shopping help, then head into my office and open up my laptop.

I *will* write the book I just told Elliot about. And, one day, I might even forget the reason I wrote it, or the man who inspired it, the way he seems to have forgotten me.

One day.

"Hi Harper," I type, opening up the email chain I have going with her. "What do you think about this for a plot…"

16

DECEMBER, 10 YEARS AGO

It's one thing for Elliot and I to decide we want to stay together, rather than breaking up on Christmas Eve, like some kind of fairy tale in reverse, but it's a completely different thing trying to figure out exactly how we're going to make that happen. Especially when the clock is ticking down to the date of Elliot's planned departure, and our relationship is about to hit its deadline.

"Okay, so you just moving to America obviously isn't feasible," Elliot says, as we walk hand-in-hand between the two rows of scraggly fir trees that pass for Bramblebury's Christmas tree farm, which is located in a muddy field just outside the village. "Or not right away, anyway. There are visas to think about, work permits ... probably all kinds of other things we don't even know about yet."

I nod, finding it reassuring the way he's speaking about this as if all that's preventing us from being together is a bit of an admin issue, which we'll one day work our way through.

But, of course, it's so much more than that.

There's Dad, for one thing. There's the bookstore for another. And then there's the small matter of my entire life until now having been spent here in the U.K.; a fact that makes the idea of me suddenly moving to America with a man I've only just met seem every bit as ridiculous as I know Dad will say it is if I ever work up the courage to tell him I've been thinking about it.

"You could stay here," I suggest, stopping to inspect a particularly pathetic looking specimen of a tree. "You did say you like England."

"I do like it," agrees Elliot, just as I knew he would. "But you know my visa's about to run out. I'd have to go back, even if my mom wasn't determined to have the usual Sinclair family Christmas, with every single member of the family in attendance."

"So, we do long distance, then," I say, as we move on. "Just for a while. Just until we figure out what our next step should be. We can do that, right?"

I already know Elliot's going to say yes to this, because it's a conversation we've already had at least twice since we decided the end of his trip wasn't going to mean the end of *us*. But I also know that *saying* something isn't the same as actually *doing* it; which is why I'm already starting to worry that we're being hopelessly naïve to think we can keep a relationship alive across two continents and God only knows how many miles.

(4,350, to be exact. I Googled.)

This is not how you keep yourself safe.

This is not how you protect yourself from heartbreak.

"Hey," says Elliot softly, watching the emotions play out across my face. "Don't do that. Don't talk yourself out of it before we've even tried."

I give him a weak smile, wondering how it is that he always seems to know what I'm thinking; and, more importantly, how to *distract* me from what I'm thinking, when what I'm thinking is that we've both obviously lost our minds, and this is never going to work.

"What about this one?"

He gestures to a tree which is oddly lopsided, with more branches on one side than the other.

"I don't even know why you made me come here," I protest, shaking my head. "I don't *want* a Christmas tree, Elliot. Dad and I haven't bothered with one in years now. It's kind of weird, when you really think about it; putting a giant dead tree in your living room. You'd never do that at any other time of year, would you? Plus, they're messy and huge, and you have to spend weeks picking the needles out of the rug once they're gone."

Oh, and they're *dead*, obviously.

There's that, too.

"Why would I want to get attached to something that's already dead?" I ask plaintively. "There's no point. It'll just make me feel sad."

"Because it'll be beautiful while it's here," says Elliot, stopping in front of what must surely be the worst excuse for a 'Christmas tree' in the entire field. "And it'll bring you joy."

But this tree is definitely *not* beautiful. It's like the Christmas tree version of a Charles Dickens' orphan; sickly and weak, with a look about it that suggests it might not live to see Christmas day.

In spite of myself, I kind of love it.

"Not everything has to last forever, Holly," says Elliot gently. "Some things are only meant to be in your life for a little while; it doesn't mean you can't still enjoy them while they last."

I look up at him with what I know is a panicked expression.

"I'm speaking hypothetically, obviously," he says quickly. "And, well, about *trees*. I didn't mean *us*. Don't look at me like that."

"*Hypothetically*," I reply, smiling to let him know he's forgiven, "If I *were* to buy a Christmas tree, this is the one I'd buy."

"Because you feel sorry for it?" he replies, grinning in an 'I knew it' kind of way.

"Yes. Because I feel sorry for it. And because if *I* don't buy it, no one else will. So it'll just have to sit here on its own, and watch all of its tree friends go off to new homes, leaving it behind, all alone. You should never have brought me here, Elliot. Seriously. This won't end well now."

"Um, again, you *do* know it's just a tree, don't you?" Elliot says, looking like he's starting to agree with me. "It's not a metaphor. It doesn't have feelings, like we do."

"Oh, I know," I assure him, smiling to prove how very sane I am. "But it's not 'just a tree'. It's a poor little unwanted tree. And that means I'm going to have to buy it now, aren't I? I suppose we could put it in the shop window, with some fairy lights on it, rather than trying to get it upstairs to the flat. Maybe it'll help persuade some customers to come in."

Given the sorry state of the tree in question, I very much doubt it's capable of persuading anyone to do anything at all. And I'm not sure there are enough fairy lights in all the land to make this thing look festive. But now my mind is made up, and I can't possibly leave it, so Elliot pays Billy the farmer ("I absolutely insist," he says firmly, when I try to object. "It was my idea to get a Christmas tree, so I'm the one who's going to pay for it...") and then carries it to his hire car, where it immediately deposits at least 20% of its needles, before driving it back to the shop, where it loses another 10%.

"What's this?" says Dad, looking at the tree as if he's never seen one before as Elliot and I drag it to a space in front of the window, our cheeks red from the winter chill. "I didn't realize you wanted a Christmas tree, Holly? You should've said. I'd have bought you one myself."

He somehow manages to say this with an inflection that makes it hard to know which one of us has disappointed him more: Elliot for buying me a Christmas tree, or me for wanting one in the first place.

"I didn't," I reassure him quickly. "Elliot and I were just passing the farm — well, it's just a field, really — and we thought it might be fun to take a look. Then I saw this guy, and, well, here we are."

Dad's mouth settles into a thin line of disapproval, although whether it's aimed at me, Elliot, the tree, or all three of us, it's still impossible to tell.

"Um, I'll just pop upstairs and see if I can find some decorations for it," I say, ignoring the pleading look Elliot gives me as he silently begs me not to leave him alone with Dad.

But maybe it'll be good for them.
Maybe it'll give them time to bond?

It takes me at least 15 minutes to find the old box of Christmas decorations which have been stuffed at the very back of a cupboard in the flat above the shop, and when I come back downstairs with it, I find Dad and Elliot standing at opposite sides of the room, with Elsie Poole in between them, as if she's about to referee a boxing match.

"Oh, Holly, there you are," she says, looking relieved to see me. "I just popped in to give you this. It's for a book festival Maisie's been planning; you know, through the library? Well, it seems she's managed to get the community association on board, so it's going to be happening in a few days. I said I'd help with the publicity, and see if we can get your father involved too."

She holds up a home-made 'leaflet' which her sister has obviously made in Paint Shop Pro, with the slogan, "Come for the books, stay for the gossip."

"You'd like to take part in a book fair, now, wouldn't you, Alan?" Elsie says soothingly, speaking to Dad as if he's recovering from a serious brain injury. "It'll be good for the shop. And Christmas is no time for competition, so Maisie says you two should put the hostilities behind you and work together for once. Seeing as it's for charity, you know?"

Dad blinks, as baffled as I am by the idea that he and Maisie are locked in some kind of bookish fight to the death.

"I suppose it could be good for business," he says, coming over and taking the leaflet for me. "Christmas Eve, is it? Bit short notice, Maisie, but I suppose you'll help with this, Holly, won't you?"

Elliot and I exchange looks.

We both know I'm not just going to drop everything and move to America with him, but we have still been talking about the possibility of me going there for Christmas. "Just for a week or so," Elliot said earlier, as we drove back to the store, the tree in the back seat tickling the backs of our necks. "Just to get a feel for the place; see how you like it."

I didn't say yes or no. I need to talk to Dad about it first; make sure he's going to be okay with me leaving him on his own for a few days.

And now it looks like the time to have that conversation has come.

"About that," I begin. "Christmas Eve, I mean. I was thinking ... if it's okay with you, I mean, that I might ... well, I might like to ..."

The shop door opens, and I stop speaking, grateful for the interruption, until I realize it's Martin Baxter from next door, carrying a large brown package and shaking the snow off his boots.

"Holly," he says, beaming at me. "I brought you some mince pies. They're fresh out of the oven. I thought you and your dad might like them."

He holds up the bag, and I smile back weakly, not wanting to tell him I can't stand mince pies.

Across the room, Elliot's eyebrows twitch as he takes in 'the competition'. Then he pulls a book from the shelf closest to him and holds it up, winking at me from over the top of it, and forcing me to suppress a giggle.

"Wonderful, Martin," says Dad, rubbing his hands together with pleasure as he comes forward to take the bag. "How kind of you. You must thank your parents for us."

Like me, Martin still lives in his parents' flat above their shop in the village. It's another example of one of the things he thinks we have in common. Unlike me, though, Martin seems quite content with this state of affairs. I expect he'll be there forever, until *Baxters and Son* bakers is just the 'and son' bit.

I give an involuntary shiver, my life if I stay in Bramblebury flashing rapidly in front of my eyes.

It would be everything I've never wanted. A nice, sensible husband; maybe not Martin himself — I can't bring myself to see him as anything more than the slightly strange guy next door — but certainly someone *like* Martin. A job for life in the bookstore. Christmas with the in-laws. Friday nights in the pub. *Mince pies*.

And there would be nothing wrong with any of that. It would be what most people would describe as 'nice'. But I am not 'most people'. And the more I think about it, the more I think I agree with Elliot about that word. I don't think 'nice' is going to be enough for me. Not any more.

Elliot's eyes meet mine across the top of his book, as if he knows exactly what I'm thinking. Then he gives me a tiny nod, which is all it takes to help me make up my mind.

"Dad, that thing I wanted to talk to you about," I say, speaking with a confidence I don't feel. "It was about Christmas."

"Oh, yes?" says Dad, distractedly. He's fetched a plate from the storeroom at the back of the shop, and is carefully arranging the mince pies on it. He doesn't look up.

"It's just, I know we don't have any plans," I go on, my courage wavering slightly as I notice the label sticking out of the back of his jumper, a reminder that he has no one but me now to look after him.

Elliot smiles at me from behind his book. It's called *Escape to the Sun*, which feels like a sign.

"So I was ... I was wondering if you'd mind me spending it with Elliot," I say in a rush, wishing I'd chosen to do this without the audience of Elsie and Martin, who're both looking on with undisguised interest.

Dad looks up, his glasses slightly askew.

"Oh," he says, surprised. "Right. Well, I suppose he could join us, if he wants to. He'll have to give me his takeaway order, though. You know how early you have to get it in for Christmas."

He makes this idea sound every bit as unpalatable as Martin's cinnamon-laced mince pies.

"I thought he was going to be back in America by then, though?" Dad goes on, sounding disappointed. "Has there been a change of plan?"

There's a silence so loud I start to think I can actually hear the needles dropping off the tree by the window.

"Yes," I say at last. "Yes, there's been a change of plan. Elliot's still going to America, but ... well, that's what I wanted to talk to you about. Because I want to go with him."

17

I start writing Vivienne Faulkner's book the day after my unexpected meeting with Elliot and Katie in town. It's about a woman from a small town in England who flies to America for Christmas — or 'the holidays', as Harper insists I refer to it, for the benefit of Vivienne's U.S. readers — and has a whirlwind romance with a handsome American.

There are no prizes for guessing where the idea came from, needless to say.

I'm writing the life story I never got to have; bringing my winter of missed opportunities to life, one painstaking word at a time. I'm making it real by writing about it, and my imagination makes it wonderful, in the way all completely made-up things are. It's a Christmas fling without the fear; and with absolutely none of the real-life consequences that made my relationship with Elliot end the way it did.

On the page, I do all the things I always wanted to do, but never did, and when I've written a couple of thousand words without stopping, I take my laptop and wander over to The Brew, so I can read it over while Paris and Levi attempt to join forces in decorating the Christmas tree that was delivered to the shop this morning, and which Levi wants to hang *actual books* on, much to Paris's disgust.

At least here I can work in peace, without being interrupted every few seconds.

"Hello, Holly."

Or maybe not.

I reluctantly tear myself away from the world I've been creating on the screen, and look up to see Elliot standing next to my table, carrying a tray filled with a huge bowl of The Brew's famous butternut squash soup, and some crusty bread.

"Mind if I join you?" he asks, with a glance around the busy cafe. "There aren't many spare seats in here."

I *do* mind, as it happens — lunch with my ex is the very last thing I had on my 'to do' list for the day — but I'm too much of a people pleaser to actually voice this, so I simply nod wordlessly and watch as he takes a seat opposite me, shrugging off his coat and making himself comfortable, as if he's planning a nice, long, leisurely lunch.

I pick up my own soup spoon and take a huge gulp, determined to force it down as quickly as I can, even though it tastes like wet socks.

"This place has changed a bit," Elliot says, with a wry smile. "I was hoping the ploughman's lunch might still be on the menu, but it's all artisan breads and dishes with truffle in them now. Not a single pickled onion to be seen."

He picks up his spoon and dips it into his soup, apparently unaware of the door he's just opened to our shared past, and the effect the memory of our first date still has on me.

"They serve avocado on toast for breakfast now," I reply, deciding to stick to safer subjects than the one that's now looming large in my mind, thanks to his mention of that long-ago lunch. "And quinoa porridge."

"Yuck." Elliot pulls a face which I struggle not to laugh at. He's wearing a dark blue turtleneck sweater, and has ditched the glasses again; I'm guessing he must have contact lenses now. Nevertheless, he still looks clever and sophisticated, in addition to being ridiculously handsome.

I reach up and pat my hair self-consciously, relieved to find it pencil-free today.

"Are you working on your novel?" he asks now, nodding at my laptop, which sits open on the table in front of me. "*If This Was a Movie*? Wasn't that it? It's a great title."

I look down at the computer as if I've never seen it before. I feel like now would be the right time to tell him it's not really *my* novel. That although I technically *do* have a publisher, like Paris said, I'm just a ghostwriter, not a *real* author, like him.

Then I remember the look on Katie Hunter's face as she looked up at him in the street yesterday; and the knowing way she said my name, as if she was privy to some kind of inside information on me — the kind of things you might divulge about your ex-girlfriend during pillow talk with your current one, say.

Elliot's long since moved on from me. It's time I moved on, too. And, anyway, the publisher might be Vivienne Faulkner's, rather than mine, but I *am* the one writing the book; and coming up with the plot, actually. Now I come to think of it, Vivienne's had no involvement at all so far, other than the very brief synopsis she gave Harper, about the woman who reinvents herself by having a holiday romance.

I guess her health must be even worse than I thought it was.

"Um, Holly?" Elliot says, breaking into my thoughts. "Are you okay?"

"Sorry," I say, blinking. "I was just ... thinking about the book, that's all."

"It was like watching an entire movie play out on your face," he says with a smile. "It must be a great plot, to get that kind of reaction from you."

"What did you mean yesterday?" I ask suddenly. "When you said the book title was 'very me'?"

Elliot pauses, his spoon poised just above the bowl.

"Well, just what I said, really," he says after a second. "Haven't you spent your entire life comparing everything to fiction? Wishing for the movie version? Or the plot of a book?"

I take a deep breath and push my soup bowl away from me, so I'm not tempted to throw it at him.

"That's a bit rich coming from the guy who literally turned my life into fiction, don't you think?" I say levelly. "And how would you know how I've spent my life, anyway? It's not like you've been here for any of it."

"Sorry," Elliot says, looking stricken. For a second, I think he's about to reach across the table and take my hand, but he changes his mind. "I didn't mean it as a criticism," he says quietly. "I know it sounded like that. I just phrased it badly, that's all. I just meant you live in your imagination, Holly. All writers do, I think. It's how we survive life; by turning it into stories. I guess you already know that about me, though."

He attempts a smile, but it doesn't quite reach his eyes.

"And will you be turning Katie Hunter into a story, do you think?" I reply, unable to stop myself. "Like you did with me?"

"Katie?" Elliot frowns. "No, I don't think so. It's her grandmother I'm interested in."

I'm really glad I've finished eating that soup, because I'm pretty sure I'd have choked on it, otherwise.

"Her... *grandmother*?" I splutter, convinced I must have misheard him. "Are you serious?"

"Sorry, no," Elliot corrects himself. "No, I'm not. It's her *great*-grandmother," he goes on, speaking as if this is a completely normal thing for him to be admitting in public. Or *at all*, even. "Her grandmother would be too young."

"Too *young*?"

It's more of an incredulous shriek than an actual question, but Elliot appears to consider it carefully.

"Well, yes," he says seriously, dipping some bread into his soup. "Her grandmother wouldn't have been alive during the war. So Evie would've been her great-grandmother. I'm sure that's right."

He pops the bread into his mouth.

"This tastes like grated feet," he says, chewing. "It's good to see some things haven't changed around here. The food's still pretty terrible."

"Wait. Evie?" I ask, my mind still struggling to get past the image of Elliot and a 90-year-old. "Do you mean Evie Snow? But I thought your girlfriend's name was Katie?"

"Girlfriend? I don't have a girlfriend," Elliot replies, confused. "I'm very single right now, I can assure you. Katie's Evie's great-granddaughter."

Somewhere in the back of my mind, a memory surfaces. A woman with dark hair and a pale face, laughing up at a handsome American. Katie and Elliot. Or...

"Of course," I breathe. "The woman in the photo. That's who she reminded me of."

"Right," Elliot says. "Who did you think I was talking about?"

"Wait," I reply, leaning forward. "So, Katie Hunter is related to Evie Snow. Your mystery woman."

Elliot nods.

"Uh-huh," he says, his mouth twitching with the ghost of a smile. "Did you really think she was my girlfriend?"

"Doesn't matter," I reply quickly, too relieved to be embarrassed by my mistake. "But... how did you find out, Elliot? I thought it was going to be impossible to track Evie down?"

Elliot stares guiltily down at his food.

"I, um, hired a private detective," he says, still not looking at me. "I just wanted to know, Holly. You know how much it bugged me, not knowing. And it turns out that nothing's impossible if you throw enough money at it. Who knew, huh?"

I take in the expensive wristwatch he's wearing, the designer cologne that keeps wafting over to me, the sweater that looks like cashmere.

I guess being on the bestseller list every Christmas really does pay well.

"But... after all this time?" I reply at last. "You still wanted to find her so badly you paid someone to do it? But why? You already wrote the book. You gave her a story."

He gave her *my* story, is what I mean to say. In the pages of *The Snow Globe*, Evie and Luke became me and Elliot. We didn't know their story, so Elliot gave them ours, instead. And now he's telling me there's *another* story, just waiting to be told.

And suddenly, everything clicks into place.

"Wait," I say, my voice tight with emotion. "Is it true, then? You really are writing the sequel? You finally found the story you were looking for, and now you're getting to write it?"

Elliot doesn't reply, and in the silence, another realization dawns.

Katie Hunter, laughing up at Elliot, the same way her great-grandmother looked up at his great-grandfather; that's who they reminded me of yesterday. Luke and Evie. Katie and Elliot.

She may not be his girlfriend — yet — but I think I know who's going to be the inspiration for Evie Snow in the long-awaited sequel to *The Snow Globe*. Because wouldn't it make sense that the man obsessed with recreating their story on paper might also want to recreate it in real life, too?

I've been well and truly replaced.

"Wow, is that the time?" I say, glancing at the spot on my wrist where my watch would be if I hadn't forgotten to put it on this morning. "I have to go. The bookstore will fall apart without me."

This is blatantly untrue, as anyone who's ever met Paris would testify. I'm 'doing her dirty' here, as she would say herself. Nevertheless, I start gathering my things as if I know everyone's going to be desperately waiting for my return, then rush out of the cafe with the same haste, leaving Elliot at the table behind me.

Okay, so he might not *actually* be dating someone's great-grandmother, and that's definitely a relief, don't get me wrong. But his obsession with the people who inspired his book is only slightly less weird than that, and I think I've heard more than enough about it now. Even watching Levi hang books on a Christmas tree would be better than this.

"Holly, wait."

Elliot catches up with me just in front of the village Christmas tree, which I see has been hung with dozens of miniature snow globes this year.

This place.

I mean, seriously.

The Christmas market is in full swing, and there's a line of people waiting to have their photos taken in the snow globe. They all watch with interest as Elliot grabs the sleeve of my coat, turning me to face him.

"The publisher does want me to write a sequel," he admits, ignoring the onlookers. "They've been putting a huge amount of pressure on me, actually. It's been ... well, it's been really hard."

I shrug, not really caring how 'hard' the life of a world-famous author is. It's kind of hard to feel sympathy for him, all things considered.

"They want to announce it at the book festival," Elliot goes on, looking desperate. "But I don't want to do it. I still don't have the answers. Katie doesn't know anything about Evie and Luke. She'd never even heard of him; I guess that, whatever happened between them, Evie didn't tell anyone. So I still don't know how it ends."

"Elliot, this is insane," I tell him firmly. "You know that, right? You've been chasing this story for over a decade now. You don't *need* to know how it ended for real. You just need to decide how you *want* it to end, then write that. You're an author. I'm sure you can do that."

"That's just it," he says in a strained voice. "I don't think I can, Holly. Not without you to help me, like you did with *The Snow Globe*. That's what I wanted to ask you. That's why I really came here. Will you help me?"

He scans my face for a reaction, his expression suddenly vulnerable in a way that makes me want to reassure him. At the same time, though, I can't quite believe the audacity of the man — to come here and ask me to help him write the sequel to the book that's been the bane of my life ever since it came out.

"Are you for real?" I hiss, trying to keep my voice low enough not to be overheard by all the passers-by, out doing their Christmas shopping. "Do you know what it was like for me when your first book came out, and everyone figured out who it was based on? Do you seriously think I'd want to have anything *at all* to do with the next one?"

Elliot takes a step back, as if I've slapped him.

"No," he says. "No, I should've ... it was stupid of me. I'm sorry. You've been ... very clear how you feel about my book."

His shoulders sag with defeat and I once again find myself fighting the impulse to comfort him, which is ridiculous, really. I know Elliot doesn't need comforting. Elliot's a rich, famous author, whose biggest problem in life is a mild case of writer's block.

All the same, as I stand there in the crowded village square where we first met, I can't quite bring myself to walk away from him.

"What happened to her?" I ask suddenly. "Evie, I mean? You must know that much, if your detective tracked her down?"

"Yeah," he says, shuffling awkwardly from foot to foot. "Yeah, I know that much. I know she survived the war — well, obviously, given that she has great-grand kids. And I know she moved away from here, and got married, and settled down. She had a nice life, from what I can gather."

"Nice?" I reply, raising my eyebrows. "You must hate that for her."

He chuckles softly.

"I'm going to an auction tomorrow," he says. "Katie told me about it. Her parents just finished clearing out some stuff from her grandparents' house, and they're selling it off. She thinks some of Evie's things might be among it."

"Right," I reply, not really sure what to make of this sudden change of subject. "That'll be ... fun."

I imagine a serious-faced Elliot rifling through a pile of old-lady clothes and random pieces of bric-à-brac, and stifle a smile.

"I suspect 'weird' is the word you were going for there." He grins ruefully. "Look, I know I'm not going to find anything significant," he adds. "I'm not *totally* obsessed."

He waits for me to agree with him, but I'm not sure spending years of your life obsessing over a random old photo is a good way to demonstrate how *not obsessed* you are, so I just wait for him to continue.

"I'm really not," he insists, as if he's read my mind. "I haven't spent the last ten years thinking about this, you know. I hadn't been thinking about it at all, actually, until my publisher started leaning on me for a sequel. But once it was back at the front of my mind again it became ... oh, it's just a loose end, I guess. And I figured now was as good a time as any to tie it up."

He shrugs again, and I wonder if he's thought about *me* in the last ten years, or if it's just his return to Bramblebury that's brought me back to the front of his mind, too.

Quite the trip for him, if so.

"Well, I know how much you hate loose ends," I tell him, wondering if I'm one, too, but somehow managing not to ask.

"You could come with me?" Elliot says, proving there's apparently no end to the way he can surprise me. "To the auction? It's not far from here, actually. It's in this big old country house. It looks pretty cool, from the website. I think you'd like it."

I really want to point out that he has no idea what I'd like any more; and no right to be acting like he still knows me. I want to tell him that he has no business asking me to do anything anymore — not helping him write his books, and definitely not tracking down long-lost mystery women, who may or may not have had a role in one of his ancestor's lives.

I want to tell him all of this, but right at that moment, something cold and wet falls out of the sky and flutters past my nose. It's followed by another, then another, and when I tilt my head back to look up at the sky, I realize two things in quick succession.

The first is that it's snowing in Bramblebury, for the first time in almost a decade.

And the second is that, even though I know it's quite possibly the worst idea ever, I want to know how Evie's story ends, too.

18

DECEMBER, 10 YEARS AGO

The shock that follows my declaration that I want to spend Christmas with Elliot in the States is so intense that even Elsie Poole is rendered momentarily speechless by it, which is something I can't remember ever happening before.

Martin mumbles an awkward goodbye, and heads for the door, pausing to hold it open for Elsie, who goes hurrying after him, uncharacteristically keen to leave the scene of a crime. Elliot closes his book and replaces it on the shelf, his eyes still trained on me.

Only Dad continues arranging his mince pies on the plate, as if nothing has happened. If it wasn't for the fact that no one — not even someone as slow and deliberate in his actions as Dad's always been — can possibly take *that* long to set out half a dozen pies, I'd be starting to think nothing *had* happened, and that I'd just imagined my little moment of bravery. Or stupidity. Or whatever it turns out to have been, once Dad finally speaks; which he only does once he's found the absolutely perfect positioning for the mince pies, at which point he straightens up and turns to face me, his cheeks slightly redder than usual.

"Of course, you must do whatever you want, Holly," he says calmly. "For Christmas and for everything else. You're a grown woman, after all. Time for you to start living your own life, I think. You mustn't worry about me. I'm more than capable of looking after myself, you know."

Then he picks up the plate of pies and empties them all abruptly into the rubbish bin next to the counter.

"Well, time we closed up for the day," I think, he announces to no one in particular. "I'm sure there's a tin of tomato soup upstairs that I was planning to have for supper. Yes."

He turns the sign on the shop door to 'closed', then shuffles off towards the stairs that lead to our apartment above the shop, and there's nothing left for me do but stand there and watch him, feeling like I've just done something unforgivable, that no amount of warmed-up tomato soup will help fix.

"You okay?"

Elliot touches me gently on the shoulder, having somehow crossed the room without me even noticing. I nod wordlessly.

"He took it pretty well," he says uncertainly. "He said all the right things."

"Yeah. He did. So why do I feel so bad about it?"

I hand him the box of decorations which I suddenly realize I've been holding this whole time, and sit down in my usual seat behind the counter — the one with the cushion that's so well-worn it's practically molded to my butt, but which I can't bring myself to replace because Mum bought it, just a few months before she died.

Mum.

The thought of her brings a lump to my throat, and I have to duck behind the counter for a moment, pretending to be looking for something, so I have time to compose myself.

When I straighten up again, though, Elliot is still standing there watching me, one of those evil-looking Elf on the Shelf toys peeking its head over the box of decorations he's holding, as if *it's* watching me right along with him.

Mum bought that, too. Dad and I said it was creepy and would probably murder us in our sleep, but she said it would be fun. And then, once she was gone, we stuffed it into a box, and forgot all about it.

"Elliot, I don't think I can do this," I say in a wobbly voice. "I just can't."

"Holly, it's okay," he says softly, putting his arms around me. I wind my arms around his waist and tuck my head into his shoulder, breathing in the strong, clean scent of him.

"Um, just so we're clear," he mumbles into my hair. "What is it you can't do exactly? Is it the tree decorations or the coming-to-America?"

"Both," I reply in a small voice. "Neither. I can't do any of it. But most of all, I can't leave Dad. You saw him, Elliot. You saw the way he looked when I told him I wanted to go. I know he said he was fine with it, but ... he isn't fine. He obviously isn't fine."

I pull back so I can look at him, horrified to realize that I'm having to do it through the tears that are filling my eyes.

Elliot reaches up and carefully brushes them away.

"Hey," he says softly. "It's okay. You don't have to do anything you don't want to."

"That's the thing, though," I say slowly. "I *do*, don't I? I mean, I don't *want* to stay here, but I don't want to leave Dad, either. And I don't want to leave you. Or for you to leave me. I ... just don't like the ... the *leaving*. I wish it wasn't so hard."

I also wish I didn't sound quite so pathetic right now, but if Elliot notices, he's kind enough not to mention it.

"Let's forget about 'the leaving' for now, then," he says, kissing me on the forehead. "Let's just do something fun; take our minds off it."

"Like what?" I ask doubtfully, struggling to imagine what could be 'fun' enough to stop me thinking about the look on Dad's face when I told him I wanted to go to America.

Elliot thinks for a second.

"Ice skating," he says triumphantly. "Sandra at The Rose told me there's a pond near here that's frozen over. Apparently they've turned it into an ice rink."

"Really?" I reply, wondering who 'they' are, and what on earth they were thinking. "That sounds kind of dangerous, don't you think? Remember when Amy fell through the ice in *Little Women*? That's where 'living dangerously' gets you."

"Yes. And Laurie pulled her back out again, didn't he?" says Elliot. "Then they lived happily ever after."

He grins at me in a 'gotchya' kind of way.

"That's just a story, though," I point out, feeling like the killjoy I undoubtedly am. "This isn't one."

"Everything's a story," Elliot replies. "And sometimes living 'dangerously', as you put it, is the only way to really tell it."

"I don't know how to skate, though," I protest, my resolve wavering in the face of his enthusiasm.

"You think I do?" he laughs. "I'm from Florida, remember? But we'll figure it out. And Sandra told me she has some skates we can borrow, before you use that as your next objection. I was going to suggest we go tomorrow, but hey; no time like the present, huh?"

He beams at me, and my final shred of resolve breaks.

"It sounds like you've got it all figured out already," I comment, wishing every other puzzle in our lives could be this easy. "How can I say no?"

A few minutes later, we're bundled up in our winter coats again, and crunching through the snow to the hotel, where Sandra, the normally dour-faced landlady, hands up some skates, her face lighting up at the sight of Elliot, who's obviously added her to the list of people he's charmed in this village.

My skates are slightly too big, and his are a little too small, but we take them anyway, and drive the short distance to the pond, which, as Elliot said, is completely frozen over, its surface glistening with frost. Although Dad closed the shop early today, it's already starting to get dark by the time we arrive, but people have pulled their cars up as close to the pond as they can get them, and switched on the headlights so the ice is illuminated, the handful of skaters on its surface looking ghostly in the dim light.

"I'm really not sure about this," I mutter as Elliot and I wobble our way out to what used to be the edge of the pond. "I'm still thinking about Amy March."

"Think about Laurie instead," Elliot replies, his eyes dancing with amusement. "Come on; I promise I won't let you fall."

I'm not totally sure about that either, given that he's having difficulty remaining upright himself, but after the first few minutes, which we spend looking a lot like cartoon characters about to do the splits, we start to get the hang of it.

"See?" says Elliot triumphantly as we glide somewhat shakily around the ice, sticking carefully to the edges so that if it *does* break, we'll only end up soaked to the knees, rather than one of us being forced to mount a daring rescue operation (Which is what I secretly expect is going to be the outcome of this). "I told you it would be fun."

"You did," I agree breathlessly, holding onto his arm with both hands as we gather speed. "And it is. You were right."

"And just think," he says, attempting to spin me around in a circle that ends up more like a very large square, "You would never have known if you hadn't given it a chance."

"Why do I get the feeling you're trying to tell me something?" I reply, laughing.

"Who? Me?" says Elliot, feigning surprise. "Never!"

He spins me again, and this time it's a little more successful. I hold tightly onto his hand, feeling like I'm flying as we speed across the ice together, the wind rushing past my face, and tying my hair in knots.

It really *is* a lot of fun.

I really should have tried this sooner.

I probably should've tried a lot of things sooner, actually.

We skate until it's almost too dark to see properly, then take one final spin around the lake, congratulating ourselves on how much we've managed to improve in such a short space of time. Just before we leave, though, I pull out my phone to take a selfie of us both, only to realize my fingers are too frozen to hold it properly.

CRASH.

With a sickening crack, the phone slips through my numb fingers and lands face-down on the ice. I scramble instantly to pick it up, but I already have a horrible feeling I know exactly what I'm going to find, and sure enough...

"Oh, shit."

I stare at the cracked screen of the phone, which is now suspiciously blank, then press the on button a few times, without much hope.

"This doesn't look like a phone that wants to work," observes Elliot, taking it and trying the same thing, with exactly the same result.

"It's fine," I say, taking it back and stuffing it into my pocket, not wanting something as stupid as a broken phone to spoil the mood. "I'm sure it can be fixed. Or I'll buy a new one. I might take it to Martin, next door, actually. He's really good with stuff like this. Honestly, it wouldn't surprise me if it turned out he'd actually been working for MI5 this whole time, and the bakery was just a front."

Elliot pouts.

"Don't take it to Martin," he says. "I know I don't know the guy, but I do know he's into you, so, look, I'll take you to get it fixed tomorrow, okay? We'll make a day of it; go into town and have lunch or something. My treat. Anything but meeting up with Weird Martin."

"Okay, okay," I laugh, taking his hand as we make our way back to the car. "I'm not turning down an offer of lunch. I will need to get the phone sorted, though. Otherwise I won't be able to stay in touch with you if ... well, you know."

Elliot just nods, and holds open the car door for me, saying nothing. Once we're inside, though, he produces a flask of hot chocolate he's somehow managed to procure from the surprisingly amendable

Sandra, and we sit together sipping it as our bodies gradually start to thaw.

"That was amazing," I say, watching as the last couple of skaters glide across the lake in front of us. "I'm glad you suggested it now."

"I'm glad you let me talk you into it," Elliot replies. "I know you weren't keen on the idea to start with."

"No. But, like you said, it's good to give things a chance."

We fall silent, both of us thinking the same thing.

"It was brave of you," Elliot says suddenly. "Telling your dad about Florida, earlier. That can't have been easy for you."

"No," I admit, swirling the hot chocolate around in the flask before handing it back to him. "No, it wasn't. I still feel terrible about it."

For a moment, the only sound in the car comes from the heater, which is turned up to full-blast, in an attempt to warm us up again.

"You know, I meant what I said," Elliot says quietly. "You don't have to do anything you don't want to do. But you are going to have to make a decision soon, Holly. I only have a few days left here. If you're going to come back with me, we have to start organizing that. Book you a ticket, let my parents know you're going to be coming with me…"

"I know, I know," I reply, interrupting him. "I've … I've been trying not to think about how long we have left. But I guess it's becoming inescapable, isn't it? There's just five days until Christmas Eve. That's nothing, really."

I think of Dad, sitting alone upstairs in the flat, eating his solitary bowl of tomato soup, probably with the label still sticking out of the back of his sweater and only the creepy elf doll for company, and my eyes fill with tears again.

"It's not his fault, you know," I tell Elliot, blinking them back. "For being so overprotective of me. He's doing his best to let me go. I know he is. It's just ... well, he loves me. That's all."

"But I love you, too."

The words come out of the darkness like a confession. Which I guess is exactly what it is.

"Shit," Elliot mumbles, staring down at his hands on the flask. "That just slipped out. I didn't mean to say it. Well, I mean, I *did* mean what I said, obviously, I just ... I didn't mean it to sound like I was giving you some kind of ultimatum. I—"

"I love you too, Elliot," I say, interrupting him before he can tie himself in any more of a knot. "And I *did* mean to say it. *And* I meant what I said."

"Really?" His smile feels like a warm blanket on a crisp, cold night. And the kiss that comes after it feels like coming home after a long time away. Which isn't something I'd know anything about, ironically enough. But I'm starting to think I might just be brave enough to find out. Honestly, if he keeps on kissing me like this — like his actual life might depend on it — I might just be brave enough for anything.

"I'm not asking you to choose between me and your Dad, Holly," Elliot says seriously, when we pull apart at last. "I'd never do that. I'm just asking you to choose yourself for once. Do what makes *you* happy. I think that's what he'd want you to do, too, if you were to really talk to him about it. And I think you need to do that; don't you?"

I shiver, even though the car heater is still blasting away.

"I know I do," I reply, also knowing that I *really* don't want to. "And I will. I promise. I'll do it soon."

I don't bother adding that I'll *have* to do it soon, because Elliot already knows that.

He knows there's only five days left until Christmas Eve; just five days until both of our lives change.

And now I just need to decide what, exactly, that change is going to be…

19

It snows steadily through the night, and by the time I wake up the next morning, the world outside my bedroom window has been transformed into the kind of winter wonderland that makes me almost glad I told Dad I wouldn't be coming into the bookstore today. Because I might be spending the morning with Elliot Sinclair instead, but, hey: at least I won't have to listen to Levi bang on about how it's the first real snowfall in Bramblebury in ten years, almost as if Elliot's return has fulfilled some kind of ancient prophecy and triggered a second winter.

"I know, I know. I should've said no. I don't know what came over me."

I'm standing in the kitchen at home, speaking to my aunt Lorraine, who I suspect has been sent here by Dad, to make sure I'm still in my right mind, given that this is the first day off I've had in months.

"It's definitely an *unexpected* decision from you," Lorraine says, the expression on her face making it clear that she's going to be reporting back that no, I'm most definitely *not* in my right mind. "I thought you said you didn't want anything more to do with Elliot Sinclair? Or have I been picking you up wrong all these years? Has the complaining just been, I don't know, some strange kind of performance art, and you've been secretly hoping to see him all this time?"

Lorraine looks at me shrewdly, and I turn quickly to check my reflection in the mirror by the door.

"No," I reply miserably. "You're not wrong. I *did* want nothing more to do with him. But then..."

"You saw him again, and it was like no time had passed?" says Lorraine, who's a self-confessed Vivienne Faulkner fan, and is going to *love* my new book for her, seriously. "Your eyes met, and you realized you still loved each other?"

"No, of course not," I reply, before she can get too carried away. "Anything there was between Elliot and I ended years ago, when he left the way he did. It just ... well, it just feels like there's unfinished business between us, that's all."

Like *why* he left the way he did, for instance. That's the main thing I want to know, but have been too afraid to ask.

But all of that's in the past; and, of course, you can't rewrite the past, no matter how much you might want to; or be secretly attempting to, via your latest ghostwriting project.

I sigh, and turn back to Lorraine.

"I don't know why I said I'd go with him," I tell her honestly. "It was a moment of madness, I guess."

It was the snow, starting up right at that minute. It was the way it sent me back in time, and made me remember how it felt when I met him. It was the way he looked at me and laughed at the snowflakes falling on us, and the way it all felt exactly like the first time.

So, actually, I guess I do know why I agreed to go with him after all. I'm just not willing to admit it.

"Speaking of madness," says my aunt. "Have you seen Martin lately? He keeps 'popping in' to ask me how you are."

"I haven't seen him," I reply, not wanting to admit that I've hidden in the office — and, on one occasion, under the counter in the Coffee Corner — every time Martin's 'popped in' to the bookstore for the same reason. "But he's texted me a few times. I wish he wouldn't. I hate having to keep telling him we're not getting back together. It's like kicking a kitten."

"Keep kicking, though," says Lorraine firmly, making me smear the lipstick I'm attempting to apply onto my cheek in shock. She's normally such an animal lover. "Not literally," she adds hastily. "But seriously, Holly, don't go back to Martin. He's not the one for you."

"I wasn't planning to," I reply, surprised by the intensity in her voice. "Why are you so against the idea, though? I thought you liked Martin?"

"I do like Martin," she insists. "He's ... nice. I just think you can do better than just *nice*, that's all."

And there's that word again. 'Nice' is the word everyone uses to describe Martin. Well, everyone except Levi, who once described him as "completely delulu, and not in a good way". 'Nice' might translate to 'boring' in Martin's case, though, but that's the reason we got together after Elliot left. Because 'nice' might mean 'boring', but 'boring' means 'safe'. And sometimes safety feels like the best option.

"I'm not getting back together with Martin," I reassure Lorraine, who finally leaves, taking the first few pages of my Vivienne Faulkner book with her, promising to read them and let me know what she thinks. Once she's gone, I pace anxiously up and down the kitchen floor, watching the snow continue to float lazily down outside the window until a sleek black car pulls up outside, and Elliot climbs out, looking around with interest at the little street perched on top of the hill.

"Nice place," he says, as I open the door to meet him, quickly stepping through it so he doesn't expect me to ask him inside. "I'm sure I recognize these houses. Isn't this the hill we used to...?"

"That's not why I bought the house," I cut in quickly, closing the door behind me. "I just like the view, that's all."

"It's a great view," Elliot agrees, pretending not to notice how defensive I sound.

I cringe inwardly at myself. It's not like he was accusing me of buying a house near the bench we used to sit on just for old time's sake, was it? But now I've made it sound like I *did* do that, which means our trip together is off to a predictably awkward start. Not that there's any way us taking a trip together could be anything other than awkward, I suppose.

Remind me why I agreed to this, again?

"Where are you staying, by the way?" I ask once we're safely cocooned inside Elliot's hire car and driving away from the hill and its memories. "I keep meaning to ask. I'm guessing it's not The Rose this time?"

"The Globe, you mean?" he says, with a chuckle which suggests he's much more comfortable with references to his book than I am. "No, I decided to give it a miss this time. I'm staying in an Airbnb just outside town. My assistant found it for me. It's pretty nice, actually. You'd like it."

There it is again; that casual assumption that he still knows me. It's both infuriating and confusing, because it makes it hard for me to pretend we're just two random strangers who happen to be taking a car ride together; which would be my preference for this situation.

But Elliot continues talking as if we're a couple of old friends who haven't seen each other in a while, and he does it all the way to the house the auction is taking place in; which is, as he said, on a country estate around 10 miles from Bramblebury. By the time we pull into a parking space in front of the old Georgian manor which sits at its center, I know he's living in Sarasota now, in a house near the beach, and that he has three nephews and a niece, all of whom he dotes on. I know he made enough from *The Snow Globe* to not have to join the family law firm after all, and I know his parents discovered they were actually pretty okay with that turn of events after all — presumably once the royalties started rolling in.

"So, what do you actually *do*, though?" I ask, as we get out of the car and crunch our way across the vast, circular driveway towards the house, which looks straight out of a Regency romance. "If you're not writing, I mean? What do you do with your time?"

"Oh, I still write," Elliot replies vaguely. "Just ... nothing like *The Snow Globe*."

His answer only gives me even more questions, but before I have time to ask any of them, we're walking up the steps to the polished front door, where a well-dressed woman greets us and hands us a glossy brochure each, before directing us to the 'great hall' as she calls it, where the auction will be being held.

"Isn't this place amazing?" says Elliot as we make our way down a long hallway lined with oil paintings, our feet sounding unnaturally loud against the tiled floor. "It has a maze in the grounds, apparently. And it looks like it's haunted. Don't you think?"

"Oh, it's *got* to be haunted," I agree, as we pass a particularly creepy painting of one of the previous owners, who looks like he probably sleeps in a coffin and comes out at night to stalk his innocent victims. "I'd be thoroughly disappointed if it wasn't."

"Same," replies Elliot. "I'd be asking for my money back if there wasn't a mysterious lady in white, at the very least; or a creepy little girl, say. Twins, ideally."

I laugh, remembering the night we watched *The Shining* together on the tiny screen of his laptop, and I dropped the entire box of popcorn on the floor when the twin girls appeared.

Elliot smiles down at me as if he's thinking of the same thing, and my laughter abruptly turns into a wave of sadness for the life we could have lived if things had been different. The movies we could've watched together. The books we would've read, and then completely re-written in our heads when we compared notes on them later. The trips we would've taken, and the completely uneventful evenings we'd have spent at home, doing nothing more exciting than simply being together.

"Um, I think it's this way," I say, breaking eye contact before Elliot can figure out what I'm thinking, in that uncanny way he always had of knowing what was on my mind almost before I knew myself. "Either that or this is where all the ghosts are, judging by the noise."

The low murmur of voices guides us to the hall, where rows of chairs have been set up, all facing a makeshift stage, which a man in a tweedy kind of suit — the auctioneer, presumably — is standing on.

"What is it you're hoping to find here, anyway?" I ask as we take our seats near the back of the room, me very aware that this is nothing like the jumble sale I've been imagining ever since Elliot told me about it.

"You said you thought there might be some things that belonged to Evie?"

"One thing in particular," Elliot replies, flicking through the brochure. "Let me try to find it..."

I can't begin to imagine what kind of thing Evie Snow might have left behind that would hold any clues at all to what happened between her and Elliot's great-grandfather, Luke, but the auctioneer is clearing his throat loudly, then banging his gavel on the desk to signal the start of the auction, so I leave Elliot to his brochure, and turn my attention to the front of the room instead.

It's the first time I've ever attended an auction, and I'm pleased to find that it's almost exactly the way it always looks on TV, with the auctioneer talking very fast, and a smattering of people standing at the back of the room with phones clamped to their ears and serious expressions on their face.

The goods on offer, meanwhile, range from the eye-wateringly expensive (A tall and rather ugly vase, which sells for £30,000), to the comparatively affordable (A portrait of a sad-looking dog that only reaches £90, although that's only because I sit on my hands to stop myself putting in a sympathy bid, just to make it feel better), and I look on, fascinated, as all of these little fragments of the past find their way to new owners.

"You really wanted that vintage teddy bear, didn't you?" whispers Elliot during a short gap in the proceedings while a gigantic tapestry with a picture of a frog on it is hauled up to the front of the room. "I saw the look on your face."

"Don't," I groan, holding my hands over my face. "It was the saddest thing ever. Imagine some child having that, and cherishing it, and then it ends up at some auction, unloved. It makes me want to cry. And, well, *buy* it."

Most other people would laugh at this, but Elliot just nods, as if it makes perfect sense to feel sad over the fate of some long-ago child's much-loved toy being auctioned off to the highest bidder — whose bid was actually disappointingly low, as it happens. But the auctioneer is starting up again, so I sit firmly on my hands once more, terrified to move in case I inadvertently buy something, as the frog tapestry sells for more than I paid for my car, and the next lot is carried up onto the stage.

"Lot 32," calls the auctioneer. "Antique snow globe making kit, dating back to the early twentieth century." He continues speaking, but now my attention is focused on Elliot, who sits up a little straighter in his seat, his eyes fixed on the front of the room.

I'm confused. Elliot said the item he was interested in buying belonged to Evie Snow. He didn't mention anything about snow globes.

What does Evie Snow have to do with snow globes?

Surely it can't be...?

"... which would be ideal for collectors of holiday memorabilia," finishes the auctioneer, whose speech I've completely missed. "Can I start the bidding at £100?"

Elliot's hand instantly rises. So does someone else's at the back of the room. There are only two bidders, though, and if I was hoping for a dramatic, to-the-death style bidding war — which I secretly was — I'm doomed to be disappointed, because the other bidder drops out quickly, leaving Elliot the proud owner of the kit, for just £185.

"I'd have paid much more than that," he says, his eyes shining as we gather our things, and get ready to leave, a few minutes later. "Come on, let's go and pick it up."

I pull on my coat and follow him wordlessly to the collection point, which is in a smaller room next to the hall.

"Elliot," I say, watching him hand over his credit card, before carefully taking possession of a sturdy looking polished wooden box with the initials E and S embossed on the lid. "How did you know Evie made snow globes? I'm assuming that's what you're thinking here?"

"I didn't know," he replies, turning to me and looking at the object in his hands as if he can't believe his luck. "I had absolutely no idea until Katie told me some of her things were being sold off, and I looked at the auction listing. I couldn't believe it when I saw it. And I don't suppose it's got any connection to ... well, to our snow globe. But, look, let's go out here and take a look, shall we?"

He nods in the direction of a set of double doors which have been propped open to allow visitors to exit via the back of the house, where there's a wide flight of steps leading down to an ornamental garden, with a little tearoom in a conservatory off to one side. There's even a pond off in the distance, with a pair of swans appearing to float effortlessly on its glass-like surface.

It's really too cold to be sitting outside, but now that the snow's finally stopped, the sky has turned a clear, bright blue, which makes the snow on the ground sparkle in the sun, and there are a few hardy souls sitting at the picnic tables dotted around the terrace, their hands cupped around steaming mugs of something that smells nauseatingly spicy. Elliot and I choose a table close to the garden and sit down, the wooden box in front of us.

"Ready?" asks Elliot, looking exactly like the little boy he must once have been, opening a gift on Christmas morning.

I nod, smiling at his enthusiasm. I know from the auctioneer's description that the kit inside the box is only a partial one, with just enough to make one or two snow globes. It was sold, according to the brochure, as a collector's piece, rather than as something actually usable — I guess most people just buy snow globes in shops, or from market stalls, like we did, rather than making them themselves — so I'm not really expecting much. The fact that the mystery woman in Elliot's photos apparently had a hobby that even tangentially links her to us is a big enough coincidence for me to get my head around, without the contents of the box being actually interesting. But then Elliot reaches out and carefully opens the lid of the box, with the air of a man about to unleash all of Pandora's secrets into the world, and we both lean forward, our heads almost touching as we peer into the velvet-lined interior.

Inside the box is a jumble of items, including tiny houses and other buildings presumably designed to go inside a snow globe, plus a single glass dome.

"It smells funny," I comment, registering the musty scent of the interior. "It reminds me of churches."

Elliot isn't listening, though. Instead, he reaches back into the box, carefully moving the contents aside as he picks up something very small that's lying in one corner.

"Oh, my God," I breathe, all thoughts of churches and their smell forgotten as he holds the item up to show me.

There, on the palm of his hand, stands a tiny couple, locked in an embrace; her in a bright red coat, him in an Army uniform, with dark hair and glasses. The colors are a little faded from all the years that have passed since they were painted, but they're still instantly recognizable.

"It's *them*," I say, my eyes meeting Elliot's over the tops of the little couple's heads. "It's the exact same couple as the one in our globe."

He nods, as if he doesn't quite trust himself to speak.

"Does that mean Evie made our globe, too?" I ask, hardly able to believe this can be the case. "I mean, seriously; what are the odds?"

"I think she might have," Elliot replies, putting the little figures carefully back inside the box. "I guess it's possible she just bought all of this as a kit, and it was mass-produced somewhere, but I don't think so. Look, there are paintbrushes in here too."

There are; plus a couple of tubes of paint, which have long-since dried up.

"I think she at least decorated them herself," he goes on, sifting through the various items. "Which means there's probably a reason she painted them the way she did."

"You mean the army uniform?" I say. "The coat?"

I think of the photo of Evie in her swishy-skirted coat. It's in black and white, so there's no way of telling what color the coat was, but ... I guess it could've been red.

"Yup," says Elliot, grinning so widely that a woman who happens to be walking past our table turns to look at him curiously. "Something must have inspired her to dress them like that, right?"

"Meaning?" I'm pretty sure I know what he's getting at here, but I want to be totally sure.

"Meaning exactly what you said." He leans back in his seat, practically rubbing his hands together with glee. "It's *them*, Holly. It's Evie and Luke. They're the real couple in the snow globe."

Or, to put it another way: it's *us*.

20

DECEMBER, 10 YEARS AGO

I sneak out of Elliot's hotel room before he's even awake, and head back to the flat for a shower and a change of clothes before I start my shift at the bookstore.

When I come downstairs to the shop, though, I find the lights already on, and Dad sitting behind the counter, with two takeaway coffees in front of him, and a paper bag bearing the name of a bakery in the next town, that everyone secretly agrees is much better than Martin's parents' one, next door.

Okay, this is obviously serious. I can tell, not just by the look on Dad's face, but also by the fact that he never buys takeout coffee. He thinks it's a waste of money when we have a perfectly good kettle at home.

But, this morning, he's not only gotten up early, he's also clearly coaxed our ancient Volvo into action, and driven to the nearest bakery to buy me a treat.

I haven't even heard what he has to say yet, but I already want to cry.

"I thought we should probably have a chat," he says, smiling as I pull up a stool to join him. "Here, I got you this. It's one of those fancy ones you like."

The coffee he hands me is actually just a regular latte, but that's what counts as 'fancy' to Dad, so, yes, it would appear that he is definitely about to make me cry, one way or another.

"Holly, I think you should go to America for Christmas," he begins, making me almost fall off my seat in shock — as much at the directness of the statement as at what he's actually saying. This is a man who can sometimes take a good ten minutes to make a point; but here he is, jumping right into a difficult conversation with both feet.

Maybe I'm not the only one who's been desperately in need of a change lately.

"You do? Really?" I pick up the cake bag and peer inside, wondering what's brought this on.

"Yes. I do," Dad says firmly. "Look, I know I didn't react as well as I could've yesterday, when you mentioned it. It was a shock, that's all. But I've been thinking about it all night, and I think you should go with this young man of yours. It'll be good for you. Put some color into those cheeks of yours."

I sip my drink thoughtfully. He's saying much the same thing he did yesterday, but it feels different, somehow. It feels like this time he actually means it.

"I really don't want to leave you on your own, though," I tell him. "I'd worry about you. It's Christmas. You shouldn't be on your own at Christmas. And there's the shop to think about, too."

"Well, I don't think we need to worry about me being overwhelmed with customers, if that's what you're thinking." Dad replies, his eyes crinkling at the edges as he smiles. "And I don't want you worrying about me, either, Holly. I'm a grown-up. It's my job to worry about *you*, and I'm not sure I've been doing enough of that, have I? I've been so wrapped up in my own problems, and trying to make this place work ..."

He glances around at the empty store, which we both know isn't *just* empty because it's not actually open yet.

"Last night, when I was doing all that thinking, it occurred to me that I should probably have spent more time worrying about you," Dad says quietly, staring into his coffee cup, which I notice he hasn't touched. "I should have been worrying about what it would do to you, keeping you cooped up in this old place when you should be out living your life however you want."

"Dad, I love 'this old place,'" I tell him, touching him gently on the hand. "Because it's ours. And you haven't been keeping me 'cooped up' in it, either. It was my decision to come and work here rather than going to uni. It's not like you forced me to do it."

"No. I didn't have to," he replies, smiling sadly. "You've always been such a good girl, Holly. Never caused me or your mum a moment's trouble. Of course you would stay here to help your old dad. Of course you would. But that's not fair on you, is it? And that's why I think we should sell the place."

This time I really do sway dangerously on the high stool, because I did not see this coming.

"Sell?" I say, gripping onto the counter with both hands. "Wh ... what do you mean sell it?" "Exactly that," says Dad mildly. "This has nothing to do with you and your young American," he adds quickly. "I've been thinking about it for a while, actually. Business ... well, it hasn't exactly been booming, has it? You know that. And maybe it's time to just admit that it isn't going to pick back up. There's a season for everything, Holly. But it's important to know when the season's over, so you can move on."

"I don't want to move on," I say fiercely, those tears that have been threatening ever since I walked in finally starting to make their presence felt behind my eyes. "I don't want to sell up."

I say it, and in that moment, I absolutely mean it. The bookstore may not have been my dream, but it was his. It was Mum's. And it's very hard to watch a dream die. I know that as well as anyone. Which is why I don't think I can let him do this.

"Now, now," Dad says in a no-nonsense tone, handing me one of the napkins that was wrapped around the base of our coffee cups. "No tears now. It's not something to cry over. It's a new opportunity, I suppose. A fresh start. And, for you, it's one that can begin with that trip to America. Haven't you always wanted to go there?"

"Yes," I admit reluctantly. "But ... not like this, Dad. Not by leaving you alone. Not if it makes you feel like you have to close the shop. I was only planning to go for Christmas, you know. And then ... well, we said we'd just wait and see what happened after that. I don't know yet.

"And you never will know, either, if you don't give it a go," replies Dad, who I'm starting to think must have put some whiskey in his coffee, because it's unlike him to be so assertive. This is the same man who puts the SatNav on to drive to the supermarket, even though it's the same journey he takes every week. Motivational, "seize the day" style pep talks *really* aren't his thing.

"And anyway," he adds, getting up to tidy away our empty cups. "I won't be on my own. Elsie Poole's asked me to join her and her sister for Christmas dinner."

"Wh ... what?"

Okay, now I'm *certain* he must be drunk. Elsie Poole? And *Dad*?

"Oh yes," he says, adjusting his glasses as if he's preparing for war. "She popped back in after you'd gone, yesterday. Said she'd overheard us talking, and wondered if I'd like to come round and spend the day with them, seeing as you'd be in the States."

"The States? Who's going to the States?"

I look up in surprise to see Martin Baxter hovering near the back of the shop, having somehow managed to materialize there without me seeing him come in.

"Sorry," he says quickly. "Didn't mean to just pop up like that. I let myself in the back door. Your dad gave me a key."

None of this makes Martin's sudden appearance in the still-closed bookstore any less strange to me, but Dad goes forward to greet him as if he's been expecting him; which, it turns out, he *has*.

"Ah, Martin," he says, in a tone that totally belies the fact that he's just been talking about closing down his beloved family business *and* having dinner with the Poole sisters: two things I'd have difficulty ranking in terms of how unlikely they'd have seemed to me a mere five minutes ago. "Thanks for coming. I asked Martin to come round and take a look at the computer, Holly," he says, turning to me. "My email's been playing up again. He's very good with technology, aren't you, Martin?"

"I'm okay, I suppose," says Martin, looking pleased. "What's this about America, though? You planning a little holiday, Holly?"

"Um, sort of. Maybe," I mumble, glancing at Dad, who beams back at me as if this is a jolly little plan that we've cooked up together.

"Holly's thinking of going for Christmas," he says, still in Possibly Drunk Mode. "With her young man. Elliot, he's called. You've met Elliot, Martin, haven't you?"

"Not officially, no," says Martin, stiffly. "I know who he is, though. I've seen you two around, Holly."

He gives me a look which suggests the sight hasn't exactly been a pleasant one, but I'm still too busy thinking about Dad and the bombshell he's just dropped — well, the series of bombshells, rather — to care much about what Martin Baxter thinks of my boyfriend.

"Dad, we need to talk some more about this," I say quietly, surrendering the shop counter to Martin, who slips behind it and switches on the old laptop that sits there. "There's so much to discuss."

I go over to him, wishing Martin hadn't turned up right at this minute. Or at all, even.

"No, Holly," says Dad, with the air of a man who definitely isn't drunk, but who *has* made his mind up about something. "There isn't. I want you to go. I want you to enjoy yourself for once. I've been selfish, stopping you from doing that. And I'll still be here when you get back, you know. I'm not going anywhere. Well, not yet, anyway."

I really want to ask him what his plans are; what he'll do if he does sell the shop, and where he's planning on living if the flat that . But Martin's presence makes the shop feel smaller than ever, so I file the questions away for later, sensing I'm not going to get very far with them for now.

"Why don't you head out for a bit?" Dad says kindly. "Go and get some fresh air. Speak to young Elliot. I can hold the fort here."

We both know the 'fort' really doesn't require much in the way of 'holding' these days, and I do really want to see Elliot, so I can talk all of this over with him, so, after a moment's hesitation, during which Dad reaches out and almost pushes me towards the door, I hold my hands up in surrender

"Okay, okay," I say, going to collect my coat from its hook. "I'm going. But we *will* be talking about this later. And we need to do something about this, too," I add, looking at the little Christmas tree in the window, which looks even sadder than it did yesterday, with the evil elf still peeking out from the box of decorations which have been left next to it. "Maybe I could get some lights for it while I'm out?"

"Do that," says Dad, nodding. "That will be lovely, I'm sure."

I look at him doubtfully, still unconvinced by this positive new persona I'm sure he's putting on. But he's already turning away to speak to Martin about his email, so I wait another few seconds, just to make sure he isn't planning to burst into tears as soon as I'm gone, then I pull on my coat and head out into the snow to find Elliot.

Because if anyone can make me feel better about all of this, Elliot can.

"Maybe you should take him at his word?" Elliot says, a short while later, once I've finally tracked him down at The Brew, where he's busy working on his book. "Maybe he really has been thinking about selling up for a while? Maybe he genuinely does think it would be a good thing for you to come to Florida for Christmas."

He gives me one of his very twinkliest smiles, but I'm too distracted by thoughts of Dad to give it the attention it deserves.

"I don't know," I say, chewing nervously on the end of the pencil he's given me to make some notes on his latest pages. "I'm not sure I can believe him. He seemed ... different."

"Different how?"

Elliot pushes his laptop aside so he can concentrate on me fully. I love the way he does that. I love the way he always makes me feel like everything I have to say to him is of the utmost importance; whether it's my opinion on a TV show we've both watched, or — as in this case — my complicated feelings about my father's abrupt personality transplant.

"I'm not sure. He was being weird," I reply, feeling stupid. "I felt like he was just telling me what he wanted me to hear."

"Maybe he was," Elliot says softly.

I blink up at him, surprised. I'd been expecting him to disagree with me; to reassure me that Dad was 100% on the level when he told me he really wanted me to go to America. But here he is, agreeing with the very thing I wanted him to argue with me about.

"Isn't that what parents do?" he goes on. "Good ones, anyway. They do what they think's best for their kids, even if it's not what's best for them. My mom used to get up at 7 am every Sunday morning to drive me and my brothers to soccer practice. And she once let us raid her makeup bag for our Halloween costumes, even though she was 90% sure Seth would try to eat some of it. And he did. Anyway, it sounds to me like that's probably what your dad's doing right now. Not eating makeup, obviously, just ... trying to put you first."

"But I don't want to be *first*," I wail, making a little girl at the next table look over at me with wide-eyed interest. "I want *everyone* to be first. I want to do what's best for all of us. Wait: you played soccer?"

Yet another thing I didn't know about him. Maybe not a *massively* important one, granted ... but still.

"Yeah. For years. But seriously, Holly; your dad's right. It *would* be selfish of him to try to guilt you into spending the rest of your life in the bookstore, if that's not what you want to do."

"Like your dad trying to guilt you into becoming a lawyer?" I shoot back, feeling like I need to defend dad suddenly.

Elliot scratches his head as if he's thinking.

"Well, yeah," he says, shrugging. "Yeah. You're right. We should be able to live our lives however we like. Sounds to me like your dad just realized that first. Maybe we should follow his lead."

I gnaw at the end of the pencil until it almost falls off.

"I'll do you a deal," I say at last. "I will if you will. I'll stop working for my dad and come to America for Christmas if you tell *your* dad you don't want to work for him, either. That's only fair, right?"

Elliot doesn't answer for so long I start to think I shouldn't have said it. But then he nods, his eyes meeting mine across the table.

"That's only fair," he agrees. "And I guess even if it does all go horribly wrong, and I end up causing a huge scene over Christmas dinner, at least I'll have you there to comfort me afterwards."

"Oh God, I wasn't suggesting you should do it at *dinner*," I reply, my stomach somersaulting at the thought of spending Christmas dinner with Elliot's family. But the corners of his mouth twitch, and I realize he's joking.

"Stop messing with me," I say, punching him lightly on the arm. "This is serious, you know."

"Oh, I know. It's very serious. I'd never mess around with Christmas dinner. Once you've tasted my Mom's mashed potatoes, you'll know why."

I punch him again, and he grins, then takes my hand; possibly to stop the punching.

"So, we're really doing this, huh?" he says, making my heart join my stomach in its acrobatics act as the reality of what we've just decided starts to take hold.

Christmas in America. Dad selling the bookstore. Elliot telling his parents he wants to be an author. Everything changing.

It's absolutely terrifying. But, at the same time, it's everything I've ever wanted. And if I don't do it now, I have a feeling it might never happen.

"Yes," I say firmly, my hand tightening around his as if in a secret handshake. "We're really doing this."

"Then that's settled," says Elliot, getting to his feet and starting to gather his things. "Come on; we've got some plane tickets to buy."

21

It starts snowing again on the way home from the auction; big old flakes that cover the windscreen of Elliot's hire car within seconds, and leave me crossing my fingers and hoping he knows how to drive in this weather.

"I can't believe this," says Elliot for what must be at least the fifth time since we got back into the car. "Seriously, can you believe the same woman we've been trying to find all this time is the person who made our snow globe? Just imagine her making it ... maybe showing it to Luke, and then all these years later, his great-grandson happens to be the one to find it on some market stall? It's crazy."

He slaps one hand down on the steering wheel, just to underline his point.

"It's pretty wild," I agree, trying not to think about the way he keeps talking about us as if we're still a 'we'. "If you'd put it into your book, I'd have put a big red line through it and told you coincidences like that just don't happen in real life. Wait: *are* you going to put it into your book? The next one, I mean? Oh, my God, you are, aren't you?"

I clap my hand over my mouth, pantomiming shock, and Elliot's hands tighten on the wheel, his shoulders rigid with sudden tension.

"I don't know what I'm going to put into the next book," he says at last. "Seriously. If I did, I wouldn't have my agent hounding me for ideas every few minutes. Or it feels like that, anyway."

He slams the brakes on to avoid a snow plow that's just pulled out of a side road in front of us, and I take advantage of the distraction to carefully arrange my face into a more neutral expression than the one it instantly assumed at the mention of his successful-author problems.

Excuse me if I don't feel *too* sorry for the man rumored to have been given one of the biggest advances in his publisher's history.

"That's not why I asked you to come with me today, though," he goes on, pulling in behind the tractor, which is now moving painfully slowly along the little country road. "I wasn't looking for inspiration, or trying to persuade you to help me again. I got the message about that yesterday. Loud and clear. I was just genuinely excited when I realized there might be a connection between Evie and our snow globe. I thought — well, I hoped — you might be too. Or that you might be interested, at least."

This time I'm *definitely* going to object to the casual reference to "our" snow globe; but then I remember how I lied to him about not knowing what happened to it, and I quickly close my mouth on the words.

"I was interested," I tell him reluctantly. "I *am* interested. It's just —"

I'm saved the trouble of figuring out exactly how to finish that sentence by Elliot, who swears loudly as a spray of snow hits the windscreen, thrown up by the snowplow in front of us.

"Um, are you okay over there?" I ask, as the hire car veers dangerously close to the center of the road before righting itself. "You have driven in snow before, haven't you?"

"Of course I haven't driven in snow, Holly," he replies, speaking through gritted teeth. "I'm from Florida. And the last time I was *here* in the snow, the roads were cleared *before* I got on them. I've driven in torrential rain and hurricane-force winds, though. It's the same thing."

"I'm not sure it is, really," I begin, stopping when I see the look on his face. "D'you want me to drive?" I offer reluctantly, not sure I'd do much better, really — especially considering that it only seems to snow when he's here; so, once in a decade, basically. It's not like I have a huge amount of experience with driving in the stuff either.

"No, it's fine," he insists, frowning as another solid wall of snow hits the windscreen. "It's totally fine. I'm in complete control here."

I stifle a giggle as he attempts to indicate to pass the snowplow, and turns the hazard lights on instead.

"Maybe we should pull over?" I suggest. "Just for a few minutes, to let this thing get far enough ahead that it's not going to be constantly trying to bury us all the way home?"

"I told you, it's fine," he repeats, his knuckles white on the steering wheel.

The snow on the windscreen gets thicker, the wiper blades struggling to clear it.

"Elliot, just pull over," I say firmly, feeling the car start to drift to the center of the road again. "I don't think this is going to stop anytime soon. Look!"

Up ahead, the sky is pure white, appearing almost to merge into the road, making the surrounding countryside look surreal and other-worldly. It's not just snowing any more; it's a full-on blizzard, and I feel a twinge of apprehension as I think of the narrow, hilly little road we'll have to navigate to get back to the village.

"Still, I guess it'll give you more material for your book if we get stuck out here," I say when Elliot continues driving. "So, at least that's something."

"Okay," Elliot says, his jaw tight with some suppressed emotion. "That's it."

I look on incredulously as he slams on the brakes, before jamming the car into reverse and starting to execute a three-point turn — only it ends up being more of a 15-point turn thanks to the narrowness of the road and his inability to steer on the slippery surface.

"Um, I was just joking," I say. "You know, trying to break the tension? You don't have to take me at my word and try to throw us into the middle of some thriller plot, you know."

Elliot curses again as the car's wheels spin under us.

"Please tell me we're not at the start of a movie right now," I say pleadingly. "Please tell me I'm not the one who dies first, because she wore the wrong shoes for the snow."

I glance down at my leather boots, chosen this morning because they make my legs look longer, and because Paris deems them to be *almost* acceptable. *Not* chosen for their usefulness in the snow, needless to say; and I've already had one footwear-related incident this week — I'd really prefer not to have another.

Elliot pauses in the act of wrestling with the steering wheel, and his dark blue eyes lock onto mine.

"No, Holly," he says. "I'm not kidnapping you, and we're not in a thriller movie. I'm trying to get us off this road and back to my rental, so we can talk. I think it's time we had this out once and for all; don't you?"

The Airbnb Elliot's staying in turns out to be just off the road we were traveling on, and about half-a-mile back, which explains his decision to take us there, rather than trying to drive the rest of the way into town in the blizzard.

What's slightly less clear to me as we bump our way down the short driveway is what, exactly, he's hoping to achieve by us 'having it out', as he puts it. It's not like I'm going to forgive him for leaving me the way he did; or for using me as material for the dislikeable 'heroine' of his book, either. No, I absolutely *will not* be accepting any apologies about that.

Not even if he begs me.

Which I'm secretly hoping he will, if we're being totally honest.

No, I'm just going to be polite but distant, and show absolutely no interest whatsoever in —

"Oh my God, look at this place!"

The words burst out of me as Elliot brings the car to a stop in front of a long, low building, which looks a lot like a box with windows. Even the *roof* is made of windows; it's one of those sloping ones that's made almost entirely of glass, and there's another wall of glass which takes up almost one whole wall of the single story building, allowing the light to flood in. Once we're inside the gigantic, open-plan living area, which has a dining table on one side and a sofa on the other, I see that the house looks out onto a snow-covered valley, all rolling hills and frosty treetops.

"Wow, look at this," I say, wandering over to a desk which has a laptop sitting open on top of it, and a row of black and white photos of the local area on the wall behind. "It's Bramblebury, years ago. And this one's..."

I stop in mid-sentence, realizing I'm looking at a photo of the village pond with its surface coated in thick ice. It must be from the same year Elliot and I skated on it; it has to be, in fact, because the pond hasn't iced over again since then. But here it is, frozen in time; maybe even on the same day I dropped my phone on its surface and Elliot told me he loved me.

But Elliot lied. The ice melted. Everything changed; which makes this particular ghost of Christmas past feel a bit like a slap to the face.

"Um, is this your new book" I ask, turning my attention to the laptop instead, to get the memory of that night out of my head.

"No," says Elliot, stepping up behind me and snapping it shut. "No, that's just some emails I need to answer. Do you want something to eat? Drink? There's a complicated-looking coffee machine in the kitchen. And something that looks like an old-fashioned stove."

"An Aga," I confirm, seeing the corner of it through the open door that leads out of the huge living area we're standing in. "I've always wanted one. Elliot, this place is amazing."

He shrugs modestly.

"It's not mine," he replies, smiling nevertheless. "I can't take any credit for it."

"No, but you can take credit for writing the book that paid for it, I guess," I say, thinking out loud. "My books don't even make enough to pay for the Aga."

"Your books?" Elliot replies, his forehead creasing in confusion. "I thought there was just one book? The one you're working on now?"

"Umm. About that," I begin, feeling guilty, but not really knowing why. It's not like I owe him an explanation of my life, after all. "I've been doing a bit of ghostwriting on the side. Quite a lot, actually. So I've written quite a few books. Just none you'd ever have heard of."

"Really?" He looks surprisingly interested in this. "What kind of books?"

"Non-fiction ones," I admit, not wanting to tell him any of the titles. "Except this current one. It's a novel. It's my first novel."

I feel absurdly proud saying this, even though I know it's not strictly true, because it'll technically be Vivienne's twenty-third novel — or whatever number she's up to now.

It's still *my* first, though; and I'm going to allow myself a brief moment of pride in it.

"It's my first *ghostwritten* novel," I clarify for Elliot's benefit. "It won't have my name on it, obviously, but it's my plot, and my characters. And my writing, obviously."

"That doesn't seem very fair, somehow," says Elliot. He puts Evie's box, which he's carried carefully in from the car, onto a glass topped coffee table near the window, then sits down on a long, L-shaped sofa. He gestures for me to come and join him, and it doesn't look like I'm going to be leaving here anytime soon, so I cross the room and take a seat at the opposite end of the 'L', as far away from Elliot as possible.

"It's a lot more common than you'd think," I tell him, sinking into the squashy cushions. "Ghostwriting. You'd be surprised how many authors have a bit of help from people like me. Well, I mean, *you* probably wouldn't be surprised, would you?"

Elliot's face instantly clouds over.

"I just meant you wouldn't be surprised because you're part of the industry, " I add quickly. "Not because ... because ..."

"Because my one and only book exists purely because of you?" he says, his voice ominously quiet. "Because you're the one who came up with the plot line that everyone loved? Because you helped me with those early chapters I showed you, when I was just fumbling along in the dark, not knowing where I was going with it? Because I took our relationship and turned it into a story? Is that what you were thinking?"

For the first time ever, I find myself wishing Levi was here, to jump in and take the focus away from me, like he always does. But there's just me and Elliot, which means it's up to me to answer him.

"No," I reply evenly. "That's *not* what I was thinking, actually. I really *did* just mean that you obviously know more about the publishing world than most people. But ... well, it *is* true, isn't it? You did do all of those things? Or am I wrong?"

I hold my breath, hoping he's going to tell me I am. Because, honestly, I'd *love* to be wrong about all of this; just like I'd love to wake up tomorrow morning and discover this was all a bad dream, and I'm 24 again, and in love with a man who loves me back.

Instead, Elliot gets up and starts pacing back and forth in front of the window. Actually *pacing*. Like Ebenezer Scrooge trying to figure out why all these ghosts are suddenly tormenting him.

"I know that's what it looks like," he says, turning to face me at last. "And I'm not going to tell you that you're wrong. But that's not what I was trying to do, Holly. It's not what I meant."

"So... it all just happened by accident?" I reply. "You just *accidentally* wrote the book, and it *completely by chance* ended up having a character in it who's almost exactly like me? Other than the thing with the doctor, obviously. And the bird. And, well, all the *shouting* she does. I'm not a shouter, Elliot. I hardly ever shout."

"You're ... kind of shouting now?" Elliot replies cautiously.

"You said you were going to make up a story for Evie and Luke, because we couldn't find out what the real one was," I point out. "But instead you just used *us*; you basically superimposed me onto Evie, and made me your story. Can you blame me for shouting?"

I attempt to sit up straighter on the sofa in a bid to assert myself, but the cushions are too soft for that, so I end up perching on the edge of it instead, like a budgie.

"I don't blame you," Elliot says in a new, harder tone. "But I'm not going to pretend I totally understand you, either. Not any more. Because, ever since I came back here, you've been acting like I did you some huge wrong, and all I did was write a book. That's it. Nothing more."

A dozen or more objections to this come rushing to my lips, each one jostling the others as it tries to get there first. Before I can pick a winner, though, Elliot jumps back in.

"You didn't ghostwrite my novel, Holly," he says wearily, "But you haunted it all the same. You haunted *me*. And you're there in every single page. Every last word. I owe it all to you. All of it. And I know you think I did it because I didn't care about your feelings, or because I was just using you or whatever, but I didn't. I swear to you. The book was never supposed to hurt you. It wasn't supposed to be an attack. It was supposed to be a love letter."

I teeter dangerously on the edge of my sofa-perch, feeling like all the air's been taken out of my lungs.

"A love letter? *The Snow Globe*?" I say, just to confirm we're talking about the same book here. "To *me*?"

"Yes, to you," Elliot replies, amused. "Who else would I have written a love letter to? Sandra at The Rose?"

"That would actually be slightly more believable than you writing one to me," I retort. "Especially one that wasn't true. And it wasn't, was it? The story you told wasn't even true."

My voice is starting to sound croaky now, which is a sure sign I'm about to cry; and I am *not* about to let Elliot Sinclair see me cry, so I jump up from the sofa — well, it's more like an odd kind of bounce, really, but hopefully he won't have noticed — and reach for my coat.

There's absolutely no plan in my head beyond getting out of this room before I burst into tears and embarrass myself even more than I already have. I have no idea how I'm going to get home in the middle of a blizzard. Or what I'm going to do once I get there. All I know is I don't want to be *here* anymore, so I pull on my coat and whirl around to face the door, ready for my big exit.

Only it doesn't quite work out like that.

Because the thick winter coat is both longer and *swishier* than I'd given it credit for. And, as I turn around in the space between the sofa and the coffee table, the hem whips out and hits something. Something fragile and old, which falls to the tiled floor with a sickening crash that seems to go on and on, even though it only takes a fraction of a second to fall; a fraction of second, in which Evie Snow's box hits the floor of a luxury Airbnb that she couldn't even have imagined existing, and breaks into a million pieces.

22

DECEMBER, 10 YEARS AGO

The next 24 hours are a blur of activity as we attempt to book me onto Elliot's flight back to the U.S., and sort out something called an ESTA, which is apparently necessary to get me into the country, and which I only *just* manage to apply for before it's too late for it to be approved in time.

For the most spontaneous thing I've ever done in my life, so far it's all been very ... admin-y so far. And with a lot more forms to fill in than I could ever have imagined. But finally it's done, and it's official: I'm going to America for Christmas.

I think I might be about to throw up.

I really hope it's from excitement rather than sheer terror, but I'll be honest: at this point it's impossible to tell the difference.

"Relax," Elliot says soothingly, throwing things into his open suitcase apparently at random as I sit on his bed at The Rose, watching him and thinking about how different this day would've been if I wasn't coming with him. "Everything's going to be fine. And I spoke to Mom earlier; she says they all can't wait to meet you. She's started baking already."

"That's great," I reply, trying and failing to imagine what Christmas will be like under the Florida sun, and whether Elliot's mother really will be as thrilled as she claims to be to welcome some random English women her son's known for three weeks into her home.

Well, I guess I'll find out soon enough.

"I have to go home and start packing," I say, getting up to give him a kiss goodbye. "I've just realized I have absolutely nothing to wear for this trip other than jeans and sweaters, and I'm not sure that's going to cut it, somehow."

"You'll look beautiful, whatever you wear," Elliot assures me, kissing me back. "You always look beautiful."

Nevertheless, I still end up spending the rest of the day pulling all of my clothes out of my wardrobe and then staring at them in despair. The plan is that I'll stay for Christmas and New Year, and fly back home on January 2nd — by which point Elliot should have told his family he won't be joining the firm, and we'll have a clearer idea of what the future looks like. That's just over a week I have to pack for, but, all the same, it turns out to be almost as difficult as that 1,000 piece jigsaw puzzle Dad insisted we try last year; and twice as frustrating.

The problem isn't just the change in temperature; it's also the fact that, from everything he's said about them, I get the feeling Elliot's family is just a *little* bit richer than we are. The fact that they own their own law firm, and a house on a golf course, kind of gave it away, really.

Elliot and I aren't just from different countries; we're from completely different worlds — and the fact that he's been able to fit fairly effortlessly into mine (A few minor 'dad issues' aside) doesn't leave me with any confidence at all that the same will be true in reverse.

Especially if I can't figure out something better to wear on Christmas day than the fleece dressing gown I'm currently wearing while I go through my closet, trying things on, before finally slamming the door shut, and telling myself I'll go shopping tomorrow and use the last of my savings to buy myself a whole new wardrobe, to go with this brand new impulsive personality I've suddenly adopted.

Goodbye, 'Sensible' Holly. Hello ... whoever it is I'm going to be next.

Seeing as Elliot and I are going to be spending all our time together once we're in the States, I'd told him I wanted to spend my last couple of evenings at home with Dad, so, once I've finished torturing myself by sorting through clothes that suddenly make me wonder what I was thinking when I bought them, I throw together some dinner for us both, and we eat it in front of the TV, as we usually do, both of us delivering Oscar-worthy performances as People Who Have Absolutely Nothing Unusual Going On Here.

I wake up the next morning in my own bed, feeling a strange mixture of nervous and excited. It's December 23rd, and I have just one day left in Bramblebury; which means I want to make the most of it. The first thing on my agenda is either getting my phone fixed or buying a new one (Which I'm really hoping I'm not going to have to do, on account of the 'whole new wardrobe' thing, which is item number two on the agenda...), so I get myself ready as quickly as I can, then head out into the still-snowy village, where I pick up some breakfast rolls at the bakers (Thanking my lucky stars that Martin isn't behind the counter this morning), then head over to Elliot's hotel.

Under different circumstances, of course, today would have been my last day with Elliot, and I can't stop thinking about that as I head straight up to his room, The Rose not exactly being the kind of establishment where they make visitors wait at reception.

"Elliot, are you in there?" I call when he doesn't answer my knock. "It's me. I need you to take me to get my phone sorted, remember?"

No answer.

"I've got breakfast," I add, wondering where he could've got to at this time of the morning.

Maybe he's just in a really deep sleep?

I bang on the door a little harder this time, hoping I'm not disturbing any of the other guests, but not seeing any other way to wake him if he is sleeping; my phone isn't working, and it's the only place I have his number saved, so without it I can't even call him from somewhere else.

"Elliot!" I call again, starting to get impatient. "Come on!"

But there's still no answer. Which can only mean he's not in his room.

"Are you looking for the American bloke?" says a voice from behind me.

Resisting the impulse to say that no, it's some *other* guy called Elliot whose name I'm shouting at a hotel room door, I turn around to find myself face to face with Sandra, who's carrying a pile of fresh bed linen and pretending not to recognize me, even though she's seen me here every day since Elliot and I met, *and* we were in the same year in high school.

"Hi, Sandra," I say with a friendly smile, wishing I had Elliot's easy way of instantly winning people over, rather than my own version of resting bitch face. "Yes, I'm looking for Elliot. Have you seen him?"

"Did he not tell you, then?" Sandra replies, a look of delight replacing her usual, vaguely hostile expression. "My, my, fancy that!"

"Tell me what? Has he gone out somewhere?" My stomach gives a tiny lurch, which I ignore, telling myself this is just Sandra's way of entertaining herself by messing with me.

"Well, you *could* say that," she replies with a chuckle. "You *could*."

"Okay, well, did he say where he was going?" I reply, still hoping I can coax the information out of her if I'm patient enough. "Was it The Brew? He sometimes goes there to write."

"The Brew! That's a good one." Sandra chuckles in a way that strongly reminds me of Gollum, when Bilbo's trying to persuade him to help him find his way out of the cave.

"Nah, he's gone to the airport, hasn't he?" she says, relenting at last. "Said he had a flight to catch. All stressed he was, poor love."

"The ... the airport? But ... no, that's not today. That's not until tomorrow. Surely..."

I pull my phone out of my pocket to check the date, suddenly convinced I've somehow managed to sleep through an entire day and miss my flight. But the broken screen of the phone remains frustratingly blank, and now I come to think of it, it's not particularly likely that would happen: either me sleeping for a full 24 hours without anyone noticing, or Elliot just getting up and leaving without me?

No. He would've come to wake me up. He wouldn't have just gone to the airport on his own.

So why is Sandra trying to tell me he has? And a day early, at that?

My stomach lurches again as Sandra pushes past me and inserts a key into Elliot's door.

"See?" she says, triumphantly pushing it open and letting me see inside. "I told you, didn't I?"

I step into the room, my legs suddenly feeling a lot like they did that time I decided to take a step class at the village hall, rendering myself unable to walk for 24 hours afterwards.

Sure enough, Elliot's room is empty. The bed has already been stripped; the covers piled untidily on top of a suspiciously stained mattress, the sight of which does nothing to settle my stomach. The wardrobe doors are wide open, clearly showing the empty interior, and the shabby little dressing table that Elliot used to use as a desk has been completely cleared of all the papers, notebooks, and other writing equipment that's usually piled up there.

He's gone.

Elliot has gone.

But ... no. No, he can't have. He can't have just *gone*. And especially not to the airport, of all places. I refuse to believe it.

I *won't* believe it.

"Do you have his number?" I ask Sandra desperately. "Elliot; did he give you a number when he checked in? Hotels take that kind of information, don't they?"

Sandra's eyes widen. She's thoroughly enjoying this, I can tell.

"Well, now, *hotels* might, I suppose," she says thoughtfully. "But The Rose is really a pub, you know? So no, we don't take down numbers. And I wouldn't tell you even if we did. Er, because of the data protection thingy," she adds quickly, realizing she's gone too far now. "We're not allowed."

"I need to go," I mumble, suddenly desperate to get out of here. "I have to go and find him."

"You okay? You're not going to be sick, are you?" Sandra says, sounding only mildly concerned as I brush past her. But I'm not listening. Instead, I'm stumbling my way downstairs and out into the street, my mind frantically scrabbling to make sense of what's happening, and how I can possibly figure it out.

But I can't. I can't think of a single person I know who'd have Elliot's phone number, other than me; and my phone's not working.

I stand there in the street in front of The Rose, frantically looking this way and that, as if I might spot him in the crowd, coming smiling towards me with the collar of his coat turned up against the wind, and his cheeks red from the cold.

Instead, all I see is Martin Baxter — whose cheeks are *also* red, as it happens, but who doesn't carry it off quite so well.

"Hello, Holly," he says cheerfully. "Mum said you'd popped in earlier. I must have missed you. Got yourself some bacon rolls, I see."

"Martin, you have a car, don't you?" I say, hope suddenly sparking in my chest. "You couldn't drive me to the airport, could you?"

Martin's china-blue eyes widen in surprise.

"The airport?" he says, sounding like he's only just heard of the concept. "I don't know, Holly. That's over an hour, even in good traffic. Mind you, if I took the motorway, I suppose that would shave off a few minutes. We'd have to come off at Hawkesbury, though; the junction after that's closed. Roadworks, apparently."

"Right," I reply, barely listening. "Please, Martin," I add, aware that I'm begging, but not really caring. "I wouldn't ask, but I'm desperate. I really need to get to the airport."

"Well—" Martin pauses, and I can tell he's torn between the need to feel important, and his reluctance at undertaking a journey by road without meticulously planning it first.

"You're my only hope," I say, remembering he's a big Star Wars fan, and this is something Princess Leia says in the movie. It works for her — at least, as far as I remember — and, to my knee-sagging relief, it works for me, too.

"Well, I suppose I'm not doing anything this morning," Martin replies, his chest puffed out with importance. "We'll have to stop to fill the car up, though. It's unwise to start a long journey without a full tank. And I should probably check the tire pressure, too."

"Sure, sure," I say quickly, grabbing his arm and starting to steer him towards the road, where I know he normally parks. "I'll pay for the fuel. And your time. I'll buy you new tires, even. Anything you like. You can have both of the bacon rolls. Just ... please, can we go? Right now?"

Martin nods, his cheeks turning even pinker at the sight of my hand on his arm.

"Anything to help a damsel in distress," he says gallantly. "To the airport we go."

And that's exactly what we do.

23

Okay, it's not quite a *million* pieces. It's more like three, really. But in the long moments that pass after the wooden snow globe box hits the floor, it seems to me that this is the kind of tragedy that can only be adequately summed up with the generous use of hyperbole; and, luckily, that's one of the things I'm good at.

"Oh my God, Elliot, I'm *so* sorry," I gasp, tears pricking dangerously at the back of my eyes as I kneel down to inspect the damage. "Seriously, I can't believe how clumsy I am. I'll ... I'll pay you for it, though, I promise. I know that's not going to make it any better, because it's basically irreplaceable, but ... Oh God, this is awful."

I sit back on my heels, looking at the broken pieces of Evie's work box. As luck would have it, the glass globe somehow landed on the sofa, so it miraculously survived the fall. And the little people, and other small pieces, are obviously okay too. But the lid of the box has come off, as has the base, and I reach for it now, wondering if there's some way it can be fixed.

"I really am sorry," I say again, glancing up at Elliot, who's suspiciously quiet for a man who's just watched the one thing he came all this way for, fall apart right before his eyes. "I'll take it to ... someone

... as soon as I get home, and see if it can be fixed. A carpenter, maybe. Or ... an antiques dealer, maybe?"

Elliot, however, doesn't answer. I'm not sure he's even *listening*, actually.

Maybe it's the shock? Maybe I should get him a glass of water? Or brandy, if he has it? Isn't that what people on TV always use for shock?

"What's that?" he says suddenly, breaking the silence.

"What's what?" I look around in confusion as he drops to the floor beside me, looking much more excited than I'd really have expected him to be about buying something only for his ex to instantly break it.

"Look, Holly. Look at this!"

Elliot reaches out and picks up the wooden base of the box, which I haven't dared touch yet, because I've been so busy trying to figure out how to reunite the lid with the sides. But now that I look at it properly, I see what's got his attention.

"Is that ...?"

I shuffle closer as Elliot turns the wooden base over in his hands, revealing a large gap at the bottom, through which something thin and papery can just be seen.

"There's a compartment in the bottom of this," he says, examining it. "Look."

I look. And he's right. What appeared to be the bottom of the box, is actually a kind of lid; one which Elliot carefully pries open with his fingertips.

"A secret compartment," I breathe, feeling like a little kid again, hiding in a corner of the bookstore with one of her favorite mystery stories. "I can't believe there's a secret compartment."

There is, though. And, all of a sudden, it springs open, spilling a bunch of folded paper onto the floor, all of it a distinctive pale blue color.

Letters.

The bottom of the box was stuffed with letters.

"Okay," I say, the smile on my face mirroring the one currently on Elliot's. "*Now* we're in a movie."

Outside the giant living room window, the sun is starting to make its way towards the horizon, turning the sky a soft pink which is reflected on the snow beneath it.

Elliot and I aren't looking at the view, though.

No, Elliot and I are sitting side by side on the sofa — in the middle this time, rather than at opposite ends — poring over the letters we found in the box, which are all dated from just after the war, and all written to Evie from Luke: Elliot's great-grandfather.

"He wasn't exactly a man of many words, was he?" says Elliot, once the initial excitement of finding the letters in the first place has worn off, and we've finally stopped repeating variations of the words, "I can't believe this! Can *you* believe this? Because I can't believe this!" over and over again.

"Well, these might not be *all* the letters he sent her," I reply. "There wasn't a huge amount of space in that box. These are probably just the only ones she kept."

"No, I just meant ... they're not exactly romantic, are they?"

I look down at the letter in my hand, in which Luke describes in detail a fishing trip he went on with his kid brother. It's one of only four letters Evie deemed worthy of The Secret Compartment, as we're calling it, and let's just say it's a good job it was Elliot who decided to write the greatest love story ever told (According to Levi, anyway...), because I'm not sure ol' Luke would've had it in him.

"Well, no," I admit, my eyes landing on a paragraph in which a tarpon puts up a particularly spirited fight. "But at least you know what happened to them now. You know there's no big mystery about why they didn't end up together. They just agreed not to. That's all there was to it."

And that is, it would seem, *all there was to it*. As far as we can tell from Luke's faded — and honestly kind of illegible — handwriting, Evie and Luke had themselves a bit of a fling while he was stationed in England, but they knew it was only temporary; that there really wasn't much prospect of them staying together after the war. And so they decided, by mutual agreement, to call it quits; although it looks like they did stick it out as pen-pals of sorts, for a few years at least.

They did what Elliot and I should have done when we met, in other words; they enjoyed each other's company, and then, when it was time, they went their separate ways.

YOLO, as Levi would say.

"I guess long-distant relationships weren't very common in those days," Elliot says thoughtfully.

"It would've been pretty difficult without email, at least," I agree, picking up one of the blue airmail envelopes. "Imagine how long it would've taken for this to make it across the Atlantic."

"And phone calls would've been expensive, too," adds Elliot. "I don't think Luke was particularly well-off."

"No. And it sounds like Evie had family here to think about, too. He mentions her baby sister a couple of times, and his little brother was only 10 when Luke enlisted. It would've been hard for either of them to leave their loved ones behind and just switch continents to be together."

Elliot doesn't comment on this, and I know he's thinking the same thing I am; which has nothing to do with Evie and Luke, and everything to do with me and him.

A love letter. He said his book was supposed to be a love letter. To me.

Now that I've had the chance to think about it, and take in what he said, I really want to ask him what he meant by that. It's all I can think about. But I can't seem to figure out a way to wrestle the conversation back to that moment before I tried to storm out of the room, and ended up changing everything.

*I really wish I hadn't done that now. Although, I suppose if I hadn't, we'd never have found the letters; which are now all **he** can think about.*

"Is it bad of me to admit I was hoping for something a bit more dramatic?" Elliot says, smiling ruefully. "Or at least some really solid reason why they couldn't stay together?"

"I think these *are* really solid reasons," I say firmly. "Family commitments, culture clashes, the difficulty of moving overseas ... Those things aren't nothing. I think it was very grown-up of them, actually; to realize it wasn't going to work and save themselves the heartache of trying to force it. Very sensible. Especially considering how young they were."

I'm still not sure I'm talking about Evie and Luke right now. And judging by the look on his face, Elliot isn't convinced either.

"Sensible, huh?" he says softly. "I guess that's one way to put it. Gotta keep yourself safe, don't you? Even if it means giving something up that could've been amazing."

He gets to his feet, running a hand through his dark hair in an agitated way that suggests I've hit a nerve.

"Not all stories have to have some kind of dramatic plot twist, Elliot," I say defensively. "Some of them are just ordinary. It doesn't make them any less magical, though. Ordinary things can still be beautiful."

I think of the photos he once showed me; the sheer joy radiating out of the couple's faces as they enjoyed their wartime fling. And I think of that first date, when we danced together in the town hall, and it felt like the start of something, even though it turned out to be just the beginning of the end. I think about a snowflake landing on the end of his nose. A glass globe containing two tiny people who looked just like us.

Ordinary things really can be beautiful.

Elliot looks at me for a long moment, his expression impossible to read.

"Do you want me to make us something to eat?" he says, abruptly changing the subject. "I don't think there's much chance of you getting home tonight; not in this."

I look at the window beside me, at first only seeing my own ghostly reflection in the glass, the light having faded even more in the time we've been talking. Once my eyes have adjusted to the darkness, however, I see the snow piled high outside, large flakes still drifting lazily down, although the blizzard has thankfully abated by now.

"Shit," I say, getting up and walking over to press my nose against the glass, as if moving closer will somehow change the view. "I haven't seen snow like this in forever. I have to get home, though, Elliot."

I turn to face him, suddenly panicky.

"Why?" he asks mildly. "Will Martin be wondering where you are? You could text him, if you want? I don't think snow affects cellphones."

"Martin?" I reply, gaping at him. "Why would I...? Oh. Right. You think me and Martin are still together? Well, we're not. Definitely not."

I attempt a lighthearted chuckle, just to underline how patently ridiculous this idea is, but I just end up sounding like Muttley, when Dastardly's latest scheme hadn't gone quite to plan.

"No? I must've got that wrong, then."

Elliot shrugs, as if he doesn't care either way. It makes me feel irrationally crushed.

"Yeah. You did," I tell him. "We haven't been together for a while now. But I still can't stay here, Elliot. I have ... I have ..."

I pause, trying to think of even one good reason why it would be impossible for me not to return to my lonely little cottage tonight, but there isn't one. Even Ed the Cat has chosen to stay with Paris in the flat, meaning there's literally no one to go home to.

"I have the book festival tomorrow," I say, trying not to dwell on the fact that I'm so lonely I can't even call myself a crazy cat lady any more. "We've got a table at it for the store. And I need to work on my book. I have a deadline."

"That's fine," says Elliot, turning and heading for the door that leads to the kitchen. "I'm going to the book festival too, so I can drive you. And you can borrow my laptop if you need to work."

I open and close my mouth like a goldfish in peril.

"There's a spare bedroom, if that's what you're worried about," he says over his shoulder. "And even if there wasn't, you don't have much of an option, I'm afraid. Look outside if you don't believe me."

He goes into the kitchen and I dash across the room to the front door, which I pull open, looking out at the other side of the house, just in case the snow isn't as bad there.

Surprisingly enough, though, it's exactly the same. On the driveway, Elliot's hire car looks like an iced Christmas cake, under its blanket of white. The narrow road which serves as a driveway looks completely impassable.

Elliot wasn't wrong. There's absolutely no way either of us is going to be leaving this house tonight; or not safely, anyway. And given that I value my life too much to go venturing out in a blizzard in just a wool coat and a pair of high-heeled boots, that leaves me with only one option: I'm stranded in a house in the middle of nowhere with the ex-boyfriend who broke my heart, and then wrote a book about it.

And there's absolutely nothing I can do about it.

24

DECEMBER, 10 YEARS AGO

I really wish I'd asked Dad to drive me to the airport. Or anyone else, other than Martin Baxter, who drives so slowly and methodically I'm pretty sure even Maisie Poole would have overtaken him if she'd had the misfortune to be stuck behind him on the winding country road he chooses to take us on.

"I thought you said it would be quicker to take the motorway," I say anxiously, almost squirming in my seat as Martin slows down to take a not-particularly tight corner. "It's going to take forever at this rate."

"More haste, less speed," replies Martin soothingly. "Slow and steady wins the race."

I grit my teeth in frustration, realizing that Martin's exactly the kind of person who repeats platitudes like "Everything happens for a reason," thinking they're being profound.

He's also, however, my only chance of finding Elliot right now — assuming Sandra wasn't lying, and he really did leave for the airport this morning — so I bite my tongue and try to focus on listing all the different scenarios in which Elliot would just up and leave the country on a different flight to the one we'd planned, and without bothering to tell me.

The problem is, there are none.

There are literally no scenarios in which Elliot — the man I was willing to change my entire life to be with — would fly back to America and leave me behind.

Are there?

"So, um, how well do you know this Elliot chap, then?" says Martin, awkwardly drumming his fingers on the steering wheel as we wait for a traffic light to change. "It's just been a couple of weeks, hasn't it?"

"Three," I mutter reluctantly, knowing where he's going with this, and not particularly wanting to hear it. "It's been three weeks. But it's ... it feels like longer, with Elliot. It feels like we've always known each other."

Just not well enough for him to tell me he was leaving, obviously.

The unspoken thought hangs in the air above us, and I stare at the road ahead of us, grateful that Martin's too polite to voice it either.

But the thought is there, all the same; desperate to be acknowledged. It whispers traitorously in my ear that three weeks is a pitifully short amount of time; not nearly long enough to really *know* someone, and certainly not long enough to love them.

And yet, Elliot did say he loved me. He said it first. He wouldn't have said it if he didn't mean it. Why would he say it if he didn't mean it?

The thoughts torture me all the way to the airport, getting progressively harder to ignore the closer we get. Just before we set off, I borrowed Martin's phone and looked up today's departures, so I know there's only one flight to the U.S. this morning, which Elliot could conceivably be on. It's going to New York, rather than to Florida, and it's due to take off in less than an hour, so if it's the one Elliot's planning to take, we don't have any time to lose. I have to get there before the flight takes off. I have to find out if he's on it. And if he is, well ... well, I guess I'll have to figure that out if it happens. Because, God knows, it's making absolutely no sense to me right now.

"Can't we go any faster?" I blurt out at last, my eyes on the speedometer of Martin's car, which is hovering just above 40mph. "Isn't this is a 60 zone?"

"The speed limit is a *limit*, Holly," says Martin pompously. "Not a target. Just because we *can* drive at 60, it doesn't mean it would be *safe*. And you want to stay safe, don't you?"

"I suppose," I reply reluctantly, thinking that just a little bit of danger wouldn't go amiss here. Not if it meant getting to the airport before Elliot can get onto that flight. But Martin Baxter would very obviously be the wrong person to voice that thought to, so there's nothing I can do but wait it out, as he drives agonizingly slowly the rest of the way there.

"I must say," he begins, clearing his throat importantly as we finally pull into the airport's giant car park. "I was surprised to hear you were going off to America, Holly. It's so unlike you."

"It's just for Christmas," I reply, barely listening to him as I press my foot to the floor of the car, willing it to go faster. "It's not a big deal. People go on trips all the time."

"Oh, I know," Martin agrees. "I know they do. *You* don't, though. I don't think I remember you ever taking in a trip, in all the time I've known you. You've always just been there, behind the counter at the bookstore. I always thought you were too sensible to go rushing off to the other side of the world."

He steals a quick look at me out of the corner of his eye; which is very daring of him, really, because he's talked a lot on the way here about the importance of keeping your eyes on the road.

"I really wish people would stop saying that about me," I say sharply. "Sorry, Martin," I add quickly, seeing the look on his face. "I didn't mean to snap. It's just frustrating, that's all: being constantly told what kind of person I am, and how 'sensible' I am. What if I don't *want* to be sensible? What if I want to take a risk now and then? What if I can't, because everyone's got me neatly pegged into this 'Sensible Holly' box, and it's impossible to break out of it?"

There's a silence as Martin tries to work out what to say to this; which is unsurprising, really, because I think this is possibly the longest conversation I've had with him in the entire time I've known him.

"Well, I think you're definitely breaking out of your box now," he says mildly. "I think this definitely counts as a risk. I just hope it works out for you, Holly. I really do."

"Thanks," I reply, reaching to unbuckle my seat belt, as the car finally comes to a stop outside the terminal. "I hope so too."

Then, before he can answer, I open the door and throw myself out and onto the pavement, almost falling over in my haste to get through the airport's revolving glass door.

"I'll just wait here for you, will I?" I hear Martin shout, as the door closes behind me. But it's too late to reply. Because now I'm pushing my way through the crowd of happy holiday makers until I find the information board, scanning it frantically until I find the New York flight.

NOW BOARDING, says the flashing sign next to it. *PROCEED TO GATE.*

But, of course, I *can't* proceed to the gate without a ticket. I can't even get *close* to the gate without passing through security first: an apt reminder that all of those scenes in movies where the guy chases the girl through the airport, finally catching up with her to declare his undying love just as she's about to board the plane, are a big, fat, lie.

There's no romantic reunion waiting for me and Elliot in this airport. There isn't even a satisfyingly dramatic scene in which I catch up to him and we have some tearful conversation about why he's leaving me behind; if, in fact, he even *is* leaving me behind, because I don't even know that yet. He might not even be on this flight. I could be doing all of this for nothing.

I hope he's not on this flight. I hope I'm doing all of this for nothing, and I'm going to go home and find him waiting for him, with some totally rational explanation for Sandra's insistence that he'd left for the airport this morning.

But this isn't a Hallmark movie, which means there's no guarantee of a happy ending. Instead, there's just a frantic dash through the Christmas holiday crowds, past shops and restaurants all blasting out cheerful holiday tunes, followed by a terse, and ultimately fruitless conversation with a stern-faced woman at security, who — somewhat predictably — explains that she can't let me through to the gate without a boarding pass.

Which I don't have; and *won't* have until tomorrow, when our actual flight was supposed to take off.

"You could buy a ticket," the security guard suggests, softening slightly when she realizes I'm about to burst into tears. "If you're really that desperate to get through."

"I can't," I reply, sniffing miserably. "I don't have my passport with me. And there's not enough time."

The woman shrugs, clearly wondering why she's the one who got landed with this wild-eyed, tangle-haired woman who seems to think she's in that episode of *Friends* where Ross gets to the airport just slightly too late. Later, it will occur to me that I could have asked her to send someone to find Elliot for me at the gate; or to put out an announcement over the loudspeaker. "*Would Mr. Elliot Sinclair, possibly traveling to New York, please return to the security gate, where his girlfriend is waiting to find out what the hell is going on here?*" Or something like that, anyway.

Right now, though, all I can do is walk back to the nearest information board, my shoulders slumped under the weight of my own misery.

DEPARTED, Elliot's flight now reads: one little word that has just casually changed my life and broken my heart into the bargain.

I stare at it for a little longer, as if the plane might suddenly change its mind and turn back, then, when it doesn't, I wander back over to the security gate, just in case Elliot changed *his* mind, and is, even now, pushing through the crowds, calling out my name.

That could happen, right?

Right?

But no. Of course it couldn't. Because the longer I stand there, watching people come and go, all of them having the absolute audacity to *not be him*, the clearer it becomes.

It's too late.

For reasons unknown, it's looking increasingly likely that the man who told me he loved me just two short days ago, has boarded a flight and flown to America, without so much as a backwards glance.

Elliot's gone.

And this has just become the *second* worst Christmas of my life.

25

I close the front door of the Airbnb, already shivering from the cold outside. From the kitchen, I hear the low murmur of Elliot's voice, and he emerges a few minutes later, holding his phone.

"I managed to get hold of the property manager for this place," he says. "She said the main road should be cleared by morning, so we should be fine for the book festival. We might have to dig the car out ourselves, though. There's a spade in one of the cupboards, apparently. I'll look for it later."

"Right," I say faintly, as he goes back into the kitchen without waiting for an answer. "I'll ... just have to wait it out then, I guess."

I go back over to the sofa and sit down, already worrying about what I'm going to look like tomorrow morning, once I've slept in my clothes; not to mention how I'm going to get through the next few hours with just me and Elliot, and absolutely no distractions.

*Unless we're counting that whole 'love letter' thing he said earlier, which is definitely proving to be one hell of a distraction for **me**...*

"Do you still like pasta?" Elliot calls from the kitchen. "I hope so, because that's all I've got."

"Um, sure. Whatever."

I've been so focused on everything else that's been happening today that I haven't even been thinking about food, but my stomach gives a loud rumble at the very mention of it, reminding me that I haven't eaten since breakfast.

"Feel free to switch the TV on if you like," he yells again. "This shouldn't take too long."

There's a moment of silence, then the radio comes on in the kitchen; a 70s rock band singing about how they wish it could be Christmas every day.

Yeah, right.

I take a quick look at the huge TV that's built into the wall above the fireplace, but the remote for it looks a bit like the control panel of the International Space Station, so I decide not to risk it, and set to work lighting the fire instead; which is harder than you might think, because it's one of those electric ones that are designed to look like real flames, and it, too, comes with a remote I'd need a degree to figure out. I manage it at last, but I somehow press a button that dims the living room lights at the same time, and it's only as I stand back to admire my handiwork, taking in the flickering logs and soft lighting, that I realize I've inadvertently managed to create quite a romantic little scene out here: a scene I'm still struggling to reverse a short while later, when Elliot appears in the kitchen doorway, holding two plates piled high with spaghetti, and looking completely taken aback by the changes in the room.

"I, uh, I was really cold," I say quickly. "I thought I'd switch the fire on, but then I did something to the lights as well. Sorry."

"Oh. Okay," Elliot says, carrying the plates over to the dining table and setting them carefully down. "D'you want some wine with this? There's a nice bottle of red in the kitchen."

Through the open door, *Jingle Bell Rock* comes to an end, and Ella Fitzgerald starts singing *Have Yourself a Merry Little Christmas* instead. I swallow hard, trying not to listen to the lyrics, which always make me cry.

"Fine. Sure," I say quickly, ignoring the fact that red wine always seems to stick to my teeth, making me look like Dracula's stressed-out sister. "Whatever you like."

I take a seat at the table and sit there silently as Elliot produces the wine and pours it into two crystal glasses. Ella's almost at the bit about how someday we'll all be together, and I'm dangerously close to tears now.

"Right," says Elliot, having finally run out of things to do rather than sit down opposite me. "Well, I guess we should ... hey. What's wrong?"

His 'man stoically about to face dinner with his ex' expression changes to one of concern as he catches sight of me sitting there, my bottom lip starting to tremble.

"It's nothing," I say firmly, determined not to let this get to me. "I'm fine. Seriously. I'm absolutely fine."

I pick up my fork and stick it into the pasta in a way that I hope demonstrates someone being 'absolutely fine'.

Elliot, however, knows me better than that.

"Holly," he says warningly, sitting down in the seat next to me, rather than the one at the opposite end of the long table, which I assumed he'd go for. "Out with it. Did something happen? Is it the pasta? I know I'm not the best cook in the world, but —"

"No. No, of course not. The pasta's fine. It's lovely," I tell him, forgetting that I haven't actually tasted it yet. "Look, it's just this song," I go on, seeing he isn't going to give up until I tell him the truth. "It always makes me sad. It's ... well, it's a difficult time of year. That's all."

Elliot listens carefully to the last few notes as they fade out.

"Is it your mom?" he asks, his face softening. "Does it make you think of her."

"Her and ... oh, just everything," I say, twirling my fork into the spaghetti. "It's one of those songs that tricks you into thinking it's lovely and festive, but when you really listen to it, you realize it's actually quite sad. It's about missing someone. About wishing things were different. God, I hate this time of year."

For just a second, I think he's about to reach out and hug me. For another second, I think I might quite like that. But then he appears to reconsider — or maybe I just imagined it — and picks up his cutlery instead.

"So you still hate Christmas, huh?" He takes a bite of his pasta, somehow managing to make it look easy, while I struggle to get mine to stay on my fork. "Even though you live in a town that seems to have become weirdly obsessed with it since I was last here?"

"Especially because of that," I reply vehemently. "It's like it's Christmas all year in Bramblebury now. Did you know we have two separate Christmas shops now? Only they're called 'shoppes' obviously, because that's what the tourists like."

"Sounds horrible," Elliot agrees gravely. "D'you want me to change the radio station? Or switch it off? I could put on some k-pop instead? Or, I don't know ... gangster rap? Death metal? That's probably as un-Christmassy as it gets."

"No, it's fine. We should be safe now that Ella Fitzgerald's done her bit," I reply, smiling in spite of myself. "If Joni Mitchell starts singing *River*, though, I won't be responsible for what it does to me."

"That one's my favorite," Elliot protests, grinning at me over the top of his wine glass in a way that takes me back ten years, to when he used to smile at me like that a lot, and it never failed to make my stomach flutter. It turns out it still does. This does not bode well.

"Oh, mine too," I reply, looking away. "It's a great song. But…"

"Sad?"

"Sad. Very, very sad."

I pick up my own glass and take a large gulp, wondering why so many Christmas songs are about people leaving places — or just *wishing* they could.

"This is really good," I say, gesturing to the pasta in a bid to change the subject. "I didn't realize you were such a good cook."

"Well, I didn't really get the chance last time I was over here," he replies. "But I'm a man of many talents. Cooking is just one of them."

He goes back to his food, and a silence descends, his reference to 'the last time' he was here serving as an unwelcome reminder that we're not just two old pals having a nice chat about our favorite music, and what kind of pasta we like.

"I still can't believe we found those letters," I say, grasping at the first topic that comes to mind when the silence gets too much to bear. "You couldn't make it up, could you?"

"No," agrees Elliot. "Well, you *could*, I suppose. It would make a great opener for a novel. I wouldn't have been able to resist the temptation to make their reason for not staying together something a lot more interesting, though."

"Zombie apocalypse?" I suggest, not particularly wanting to revisit our earlier conversation about whether or not Evie and Luke did the right thing. "Alien invasion?"

"I was thinking more along the lines of a deadly virus that sweeps the world," he deadpans. "But no. Just ... something other than them being *sensible*. I hate it when people are *sensible*. It's just so disappointing."

"I guess I can see why it would be a bit of an anticlimax for you, considering how invested you were in their story," I say pointedly. "You have to admit, it's realistic, though. That's how real life is, most of the time. I would know; my entire life has been an anticlimax."

It is, admittedly, a very weak attempt at a self-deprecating joke, but, judging by the look that crosses Elliot's face, he's taking it very seriously.

"Do you really think that?" he asks quietly. "That your life's been a disappointment?"

"Well, no, not *really*," I reply carefully, sensing that this conversation is about to take a turn I'm not entirely prepared for. "I mean, my life might not exactly be bursting with drama and excitement, but I have a house and a job. Two jobs, really. I have my health. So, you know, it could be worse."

I could be snowed into an Airbnb in the middle of nowhere with the ex who left me, for instance. Oh no, wait...

"'I have my health?'" says Elliot, the corners of his mouth twitching. "Oh, come on, Holly. It's okay to want more than that, you know. You're allowed to have dreams. Next you'll be telling me there are kids starving out there, so we have to count our blessings."

"There *are* kids starving out there," I mutter, stung. "And we *should* count our blessings. It's … well, it's what grown-ups do, Elliot. We're not kids anymore. And there comes a point when you have to accept that life isn't just all about doing whatever you want, without any consequences."

"We weren't 'kids' when we met," he points out. "We were in our twenties."

"Which is still *way* too young to be making any major life decisions," I retort. "That's why I think Luke and Evie did the right thing. It was … *sensible.*"

"Like you and Martin?" Elliot asks quietly. "Is that why you got together with him? Because he was 'sensible'? Because he was a 'grown up'."

"I did it because he was *safe*," I reply firmly. "And I knew he was never going to break my heart."

Like you did.

"I guess it doesn't get much safer than the boy next door," Elliot says, making the words 'boy next door' sounds like a particularly biting insult. "If that's what you're into."

He digs into his pasta in a way that suggests he might be imagining burying Martin in it.

"Right. And I guess you've been living some kind of wild, free-spirited life, filled with danger and excitement, have you?" I ask, rattled. "With someone much more interesting than the girl next door?"

This is such a transparent and clumsy attempt to try to find out if he's seeing anyone that I'm blushing even as I say it. But Elliot just reaches out and tops up both of our glasses again.

"The 'girl' who lives next door to me is 82," he says. "And I already told you I don't have a girlfriend. But you're right; my life's pretty boring, really. I think journalists even refer to me as a 'recluse' actually, whenever they have to write about me. So I'm sorry if I seemed like I was judging you. I don't have any right to."

I pick up my glass and take a sip of wine, feeling oddly wrong-footed.

"They do call you a recluse," I tell him at last. "And 'elusive'. I think they quite like it, though. It makes you seem mysterious and enigmatic. But ... why?"

"Why am I mysterious and enigmatic?" Elliot's eyes twinkle as he says it, and it triggers a memory of the first time we met; a memory which I quickly try to push to the side. "It just comes naturally, I guess. It's all part of my magnetism."

"You were never like that before, though," I point out, thinking out loud. "Reclusive, I mean. You were always so *open*. You had such a ... a zest for life, I guess. You wanted to see everything; do everything. You were going to see the world at one point. But now it seems like you just want to hide away from it. So, why?"

Elliot toys with the stem of his wine glass, watching the way the crystal catches the light.

"I did want to see the world," he says, still staring into the glass. "But I didn't want to do it alone, Holly. I wanted to share it with ... well, someone. But that's not how it worked out."

He looks up at me, and I'm suddenly very aware of how close he is. How painfully *familiar* he is. And, well, how unfairly attractive he is, too. Because, in spite of everything that's happened, Elliot Sinclair still makes my stomach flutter when he looks at me in that intense way of his; and I feel like that gives him a very unfair advantage over me in a conversation like this one.

In the kitchen, The Pogues start singing *Fairytale of New York*, almost as if whoever chose the set list for this radio show knew that we'd need to hear yet another song about missed opportunities and dreams that died, and we'd need to hear it right at this very second.

Ho ho ho.

"I haven't been 'hiding away', Holly, as you put it," he says simply. "I've just been lonely. Things were never really the same after ... after I left here. I thought writing about it would help; but it didn't. It didn't help. And now it seems it also just made you hate me, which ... let's just say that wasn't part of the plan, either."

He runs a hand through his hair, looking sadder than I've ever seen him. Every impulse in my body is screaming at me to comfort him — to just reach out and put my arms around him, and make everything okay — but I know I can't do it. Not until I know exactly what he's trying to say.

"You said the book was supposed to be a love letter earlier," I say carefully. "But I don't know what you mean by that?"

My heart flutters frantically in my chest, like a caged bird trying to get out. I've wanted to ask him this ever since he said it; but now I'm not sure I'm prepared for his reply.

"I meant exactly what I said," he shrugs. "I wrote it for you. To you. We hadn't figured out Evie and Luke's story by that point, so I used ours instead. Because even though it was over by then — and I know the ending wasn't a good one — it was still good while it lasted. Wasn't it?"

In the flickering firelight, his expression is a mixture of hope and resignation. And suddenly I think I know why he wrote us into his book.

"So it was a kind of goodbye, then?" I say softly. "A way to remember it?"

Elliot appears to consider this carefully for a moment.

"I suppose so," he agrees, nodding. "I guess you could call it that."

I watch as the light from his glass casts kaleidoscope images across the wall opposite me, and when I look back at him, I'm horrified to find that my eyes are filled with tears; and this time the radio's playing some strange disco version of *Rudolph the Red-Nosed Reindeer*, so it's definitely not because of the music.

Trust me to be having one of the most emotional moments of my life so far to the soundtrack of a novelty song about a reindeer.

"Hey," says Elliot, shuffling his chair closer until our knees are touching. "Hey, you're crying again. What's wrong? It's not still Ella, is it?"

I want to tell him that *everything* is wrong. Me. Him. The weather. Our relationship. This ridiculous song we're being forced to listen to. There are two things, however, that are much more 'wrong' than anything else; the main one being the small — but important — fact of me having just realized that I'm still in love with the man in front of me.

And the second being that the man in question has just confirmed that his book was an attempt to draw a line under our relationship; to say goodbye to us.

I want to tell him this, but now he's reaching out a hand and gently tucking a strand of hair out of my eyes. As he does it, his hand brushes my cheek, and it's all I can do not to lean into his touch; or, better still, to slide onto his lap, wrap my arms around him, and let him hold me, the way he used to before he decided we needed an 85,000 word 'goodbye' to our relationship.

"Holly," Elliot whispers, his lips dangerously close to mine as he leans towards me. "Tell me what's wrong. Is it the book, still? Is it what I said about it? Because I wasn't trying to hurt you, I swear."

"I know," I reply, somehow managing to get the words past the lump that's formed in my throat. "I know you weren't. But I just ... I just wish you'd found some other way to say 'goodbye', if that's what you had to do. A normal way. Like to my face, say. I think ... I think that would've been better."

"I could never have done that," Elliot replies, his eyes dark with some unspoken emotion. "I couldn't have said goodbye to you, Holly."

He's even closer now. So close that when he reaches up and cups my face in my hand, it feels almost like the logical thing to happen next. My body reflexively responds to his touch, as if it's triggered some kind of muscle memory that's just waking up, like Cinderella after Prince Charming's kiss.

He's going to kiss me.

I want him to kiss me.

I want it more than anything I've ever wanted in my life. Even more than that rare first edition of *Pride and Prejudice* that Dad keeps saying he'll buy for the shop one day, but never has. So much, in fact, that I find myself almost subconsciously leaning towards him, willing his lips towards mine.

Maybe just one last time? For old time's sake? Maybe it wouldn't even hurt.

But, of course, it would hurt. It would hurt a lot. And I know that beyond doubt, because I've been here before. I've taken the risk. I've kissed the guy. And I've ended up broken-hearted, and promising myself I'd never let it happen again.

Which means I need to urgently hit the stop button on this scene that seems to be writing itself, taking its cues from some long-forgotten script, and do the one thing I know he hates more than anything: I have to be sensible. Because it's the only way to keep myself safe from him.

"Well, it's getting late," I announce, standing up so abruptly I narrowly miss bashing heads with him and knocking us both out; which I guess would be one way to bring this ... whatever this is ... to an end. "I think I'll turn in."

I have no idea where the spare bedroom Elliot mentioned is, and there's approximately zero chance of me getting any sleep tonight. But as I walk on shaky legs towards the door I hope will lead to somewhere I can be alone with the tears I know are coming, I can't help but want to pat myself on the back.

Because I did it.

I walked away from Elliot Sinclair, and the danger he represents to me. I did the right thing, even though it hurts.

Maybe I'm more like Evie than I thought I was.

26

My intention when I walked away from Elliot was to stage a dignified, classy kind of exit that, once all of this was over, would allow him to remember me as the strong, capable woman I am. Or that I will be, anyway, once I've completely changed everything about myself — which is the very next thing on my agenda, I promise.

Instead, I first of all walk into a bathroom, and then into a cupboard filled with cleaning products and other random household items.

On the plus side, at least I found the spade I'll be needing to dig myself out of the snow first thing tomorrow morning.

On the minus side, however, I still have to dig myself out of the mess I've made of the last few hours; the memory of which makes me cringe all the way to my toes as I think about everything from the broken snow globe box to the way I almost started crying over a Christmas song. And, as if that wasn't enough, once I find my way to the spare bedroom I then realize I'm going to have to go right back out again to use the bathroom before bed.

As exits go, then, it's not a *great* one. Then, when I return to the room after my bathroom trip, I find one of Elliot's sweaters lying neatly folded on the bed; I guess he must have left it there for me to sleep in. It has a Miami Dolphins logo on the front and is so over-sized on me it reaches my thighs, but it smells like Elliot and makes me sob uncontrollably for a few minutes, before falling into a surprisingly deep sleep, from which I wake the next morning with a pounding headache, and a furry feeling on my teeth.

So much for classy and dignified.

In a rare moment of good luck, however, it seems the snow has thawed slightly overnight, and by the time I emerge from the bathroom, having attempted to brush my teeth with my finger, I find that Elliot's already cleared the driveway, and is waiting for me, looking like he's had a solid 12 hours' sleep, and is about to star in one of those aftershave commercials, where a square-jawed man does rugged, manly things, ideally while accompanied by a wolf.

"Ready to go?"

He's standing by the door, and is in the process of pulling his sweater on over the long-sleeve t-shirt he's wearing underneath, having presumably removed the top layer while he shoveled the snow. As he raises his arms above his head, the t-shirt rides up slightly, revealing a sliver of skin that makes me wish I'd gotten up earlier to watch him at work. He might look kind of bookish and intense when you first see him, but it looks like Elliot Sinclair is no stranger to the gym these days, either: a realization that does absolutely nothing to ease the confusion I've been feeling since all of last night's mixed signals.

"Sure. I've, uh, got your sweater in my bag," I tell him, patting the bag in question to prove it. "I'll wash it and give it back to you."

"Don't worry about it," he replies, picking up a set of car keys from the table next to the door. "It's an old one anyway, and I'm going home tomorrow, so I won't need it. Just keep it — or throw it away, or whatever."

He turns away to open the front door, and my heart gives a lurch of disappointment, which is either from the thought of him leaving, or the offhand way he's speaking to me, as if we *didn't* almost kiss last night.

Or as if it doesn't actually matter to him either way.

I know it's stupid to feel like this. I'm the one who walked away last night; and if I hadn't, he'd only have hurt me again, anyway. I did the right thing. I know that. So I don't say anything else as I follow him out of the house and into the car; and the silence continues all the way back to Bramblebury, where he drops me off at my house, then drives off, almost before I have time to get out of the car.

Right. Cool. So I guess we're back to being strangers again.
Talk about confusing.

My emotions are still completely scrambled after everything that happened yesterday. All I want now is a long, hot bath, an indecently strong coffee, and maybe a rummage around the bookstore for some kind of 'How to Get Over the Ex Who Wrote a Book About You' self-help guide. But I promised both Lorraine and Dad that I'd be there to help out at the book festival, so, even though it's the last thing I feel like doing, I have to settle for a quick shower and a cup of instant, before I pull my coat back on and make my way cautiously down the still-slippery hill that leads to the village hall, which has a huge banner strung over the door declaring it to be 'The birthplace of *The Snow Globe*!'.

I have a feeling this is going to be a very long day.

As soon as I walk in, I'm ambushed by Levi, who hauls me over to our stall, where Dad is presiding importantly over the stacks of books, with Paris sitting behind him, looking bored. Annoyingly, Martin is standing beside her, looking awkward and out of place — so, just the same as always, really — but still steadfastly keeping his position, his eyes lighting up as he sees me coming towards them all.

"Morning, Holly," he says brightly, almost knocking Paris off her seat as he takes a step towards me. He reaches out as if he's going to hug me, but I step out of the way at the last minute, so he ends up just standing there with his arms out like a wooden soldier; a sight that makes me feel even worse than I did already.

Why can't you just be nice to him, Holly? He's not the one who abandoned you at the airport, remember?

"Er, you didn't answer any of my messages about your ankle," Martin says, recovering. "So I thought I'd just pop in and see how you're doing?"

"My ankle? Oh. Um, yes; yes, it's fine. Thanks, Martin," I reply, going to stand beside Dad, who gives my arm a quick squeeze of solidarity. "All better."

It feels like weeks ago now since I sprained my ankle. I'd almost completely forgotten about it. Trust Martin to not only remember, but to use it as an excuse to see me again, even though he knows perfectly well that it's over between us.

Looks like making that message even clearer is going to have to be yet another item on my 'once all of this stuff with Elliot is over' agenda. Maybe I should buy myself a notebook, so I can keep track of all of this?

The room is already thronged with people, all chattering excitedly about their Christmas plans as they wander from stall to stall, but my eyes keep wandering over the largest stall, right at the very front of the room, which has the Saturday Lane logo plastered all over it, and copies of *The Snow Globe* piled high. The woman I saw with Elliot at the book signing is standing in front of it, talking to a man in a suit, who looks like he might be someone important. The stall itself is right in front of the little stage, which is normally used for the annual panto the village school put on every year. Today, there's a couple of seats up there, with a microphone between them, making it look like the set of a 70s talk show.

I guess that's for Elliot, and the announcement his publishers are supposedly planning to make about his next book; the one he asked me to help him write.

The memory makes me feel suddenly nauseous. Or maybe it's just the thought of seeing Elliot himself again. He doesn't seem to be here yet, though. At least that gives me a bit longer to prepare myself.

"Holly! Oh my God, Holly, I love it! I just love it. I can't tell you how much I enjoyed it."

Aunt Lorraine comes bustling up to our stall, carrying a clipboard, and looking like she's about to burst with excitement.

"Huh? Did I miss something? I thought this thing had only just got started?" I reply, checking the time on my phone.

"I'm not talking about the festival; I'm talking about your book, silly." She punches me playfully on the arm. "Well, what I've read of it so far. I can't wait for the rest, though; honestly, Holly, it's so good. I think Vivienne Faulkner will be so happy with it."

She beams at me, and I grab her arm, quickly towing her out of earshot before Paris or Levi can overhear us.

"Shhhh!" I say warningly. "You know I wasn't supposed to tell you who I was writing it for. I've signed an NDA. Did you really like it, though? Really?"

I hold my breath as I wait for her reply. I have to admit, I haven't even been thinking about my ghostwriting job lately, and I'd almost forgotten I'd sent Lorraine those first few pages to read. But suddenly it occurs to me that this is the thing I should be focusing on; not ex boyfriends and the books they write — or might write in the future — but *my* book, and the opportunity it represents to start doing something I really love. The present, not the past.

"Holly, it's fantastic," Lorraine says, patting me on the arm. "And you know me; I'd tell you if it wasn't. But I'm loving it. Write more. Do it soon. Okay?"

"Okay," I agree, my cheeks hot from the unaccustomed praise. "I will. I really need to get on with it, anyway. I've been neglecting it since ... oh."

Across the room, Elliot has finally appeared, and is talking to his publicist, who's wearing a cream-colored dress today, confirming my suspicion that she's the kind of woman who's never spilled anything in her life, and thus doesn't have to worry about the same things as the rest of us mortals. Her shiny hair is slicked back in a low bun, and her arm is on Elliot's, as she turns him around to show him something on the book table. Elliot looks in the direction she's pointing, then glances back up, his eyes sweeping the room, until they find mine. He holds the glance for a second, making my heart flutter traitorously until he gives me a terse nod, then turns away. Interaction over.

Well, that was definitely different from the last time we were in this particular room together.

Heart still pounding, I give myself a quick shake, before following Lorraine back over to the Hart Books table, where Dad's busy serving customers, while Paris and Levi appear to have put their differences aside for once to join forces in gossiping about Elliot, and what his 'big announcement' is going to be.

"I really hope it is going to be the *Snow Globe* sequel," Levi says dreamily, his chin resting on his hands as he sits behind the stall, completely ignoring the line of customers. "I don't think I can go on living without knowing what happened to Evie and Luke after she stood him up at the village Christmas tree"

"She didn't stand him up," I snap, before I can stop myself. "She would never have done that. It was him. It was all him."

Paris and Levi exchange looks.

"Breathe, bestie," says Paris, eyebrows raised. "It's not that deep."

"Don't listen to her," interrupts Levi, looking excited. "It's *totally* that deep. Tell us everything you know. Because you *do* know, don't you, Holly? You know how it ends? You *must* do. Because it's *you*. It's *him*. So come on, I'm begging you. Take pity on a poor boy who just wants a happy ever after."

I roll my eyes. "There's nothing to tell, Levi," I say firmly. "And if I never hear another word about Evie and Luke, it'll be too soon. Trust me."

"So, I'm assuming you *didn't* leave him waiting in the village square, like she does in the book," he goes on, as if I haven't spoken. "Because that's, like, right next to the shop, so he'd just have come in and found you rather than standing there like an abandoned puppy. So, where did you do it? And how long did he wait, do you think?"

"I *didn't* do it," I reply, my voice rising in frustration at the unfairness of this. "I didn't do anything, Levi. *He* did it. Elliot did it. He was the one who left *me*. And I'll never, ever forgive him for it."

The last words come out into complete silence; or near enough, anyway. There's still some noise from the people at the front of the hall, next to the stage, but everyone around us has stopped what they're doing to look on with interest as I deliver this little speech, the words tumbling out of me as if they've been waiting a long time to do it.

Which I suppose they have.

It's only as I open my mouth again to try to explain myself — not that it worked particularly well the first time — that it occurs to me that the eyes of the people around me aren't actually on *me* at all. No, they're all staring at something directly behind me; which is a relief, until I turn around and realize what it is.

Or *who* it is, rather.

Elliot is standing at my shoulder, having presumably walked over at some point either before or during my little outburst. His face is pinched and white with shock — or anger, or some other emotion which I don't have to be a psychologist to know is most likely a sign that yes, he definitely *did* hear everything I just said.

Looks like I was right then. This is definitely going to be a very long day.

"Holly. Can I have a word, please?"

It's phrased as a request, but there's absolutely no way I can refuse it without turning this into even more of a scene than it already is, so I decide to take the path of least resistance and turn to follow Elliot meekly toward the nearest exit, feeling countless sets of curious eyes — and quite a few phone cameras — on us both as we go.

This may not be the show they came for, but it's definitely the one they all wanted. "Care to explain what that was about back there?"

Elliot whirls around to face me as soon as we're in the corridor outside the main hall, his eyes flashing dangerously, and his voice a little louder than is wise, given that Levi probably has his ear pressed to the other side of the door we're standing in front of.

"I *left* you?" he goes on, before I have time to answer. "I *left* you, Holly?" Is that what you just said?"

"Um, well, yeah," I reply, shifting awkwardly from foot to foot, and feeling a bit like a naughty schoolgirl who's been called to the headmaster's office for a telling off. "Look, I probably shouldn't have said it right there. I get that. It was ... unprofessional. Or something. But ... well, it was also true, so..."

I trail off, not knowing what else there is to say.

Elliot stares at me in astonishment.

"It's true that *I* left *you*?" he repeats, as if he's determined to keep on repeating the words until they somehow make sense. "Shouldn't that be the other way around?"

Now it's my turn to do the staring-in-astonishment thing.

"I didn't leave you, Holly," Elliot says firmly, crossing his arms in front of his chest in the manner of a man who's utterly convinced he's right. "I think you'll find you were the one who left me."

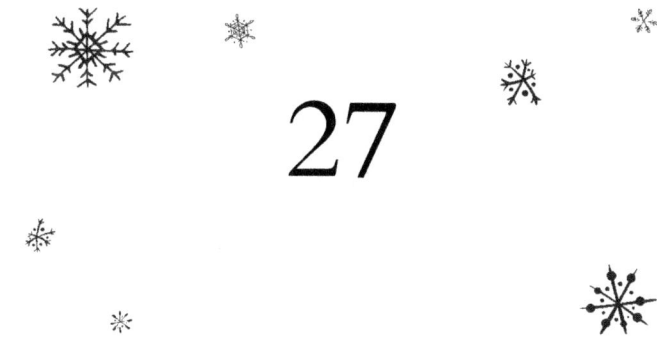

27

"Um, no, Elliot," I tell him, shaking my head until it hurts. "Uh-uh. You're not doing that. You're not getting to rewrite the past by saying I'm the one who ended it. I know that's what you did in your book — that whole thing with him waiting for her at the Christmas tree, and she never shows up? But that didn't happen, did it?"

I prop my shoulder against the wall, and cross my own arms just as tightly, convinced I've made my point, and made it well. There's no chance of him wriggling out of this one.

"Yes, it did," Elliot says, speaking quietly but firmly. "And, no, not at the tree; that was a bit of artistic license. I waited for you at the airport, though. For as long as I possibly could. I waited until the flight had finished boarding and they told me if I didn't get on it, it would leave without me. I waited and waited, Holly. But you didn't show up."

"I *did* show up!" I blurt out, incensed. "Of course I did. *I* waited at the airport! But you seem to be forgetting that you left on the wrong day, Elliot. We were supposed to leave on Christmas Eve, but you went the day before. Didn't you?"

I glare at him, daring him to challenge me on this. Because I know I'm not wrong here. I know because I checked the ticket a million times; both as soon as I got back from the airport that day, and on all the days after it, until I finally accepted that I hadn't made a mistake. My flight was definitely booked for December 24th. His was too. Which means this is still failing to make any sense at all to me.

"Well, yeah," Elliot replies, frowning. "Yeah, I had to get an earlier flight home. But you knew that. I left messages for you. Tons of them. I told you to meet me there, and we'd try to change the ticket. There was no time to do it before that; it was all such a rush."

"A rush?" I reach up and massage my temples, where a headache's starting to form. "Well, yeah; I mean, I know it was a bit of a rush trying to get everything sorted in time. That doesn't explain why you suddenly decided to change your flight and leave early, though. We still had a whole day to get everything done."

Elliot just stares at me for several long seconds.

"My dad," he says at last. "My dad had a heart attack the day before we were supposed to leave. They didn't think he was going to make it. When my mom called, she said ... she said I needed to get there right away. But you know this. Surely you know this? I sent you so many messages."

I shake my head, silently trying to process all of this.

"I didn't get any messages from you," I tell him quietly. "I couldn't have. My phone was broken, remember?"

"Yeah, I know. That's why I couldn't call you. Or message you. But I came round to tell you myself, Holly. It was the middle of the night, but I knew I had to let you know what was going on; and not just for your sake, but for mine, too. I needed you with me, Holly. God knows, I didn't want to have to do it alone."

He's looking me right in the eye. He sounds so sincere that it's impossible to think he could be lying about this. And yet...

"So, why didn't you?" I ask desperately. "Why didn't you tell me, Elliot? I was right there. If you were coming to tell me, then why didn't you? I'm not *that* deep a sleeper. I'm pretty sure you could've woken me up."

Elliot rakes a hand through his hair, exasperated.

"I was on my way to your place," he says, "When my mom called again to say she'd booked me onto the next flight out. She was freaking out, Holly. Like, completely hysterical. And the flight she'd booked was leaving almost right away. It was so tight. Honestly, I'd never have made it if I hadn't walked right into your neighbor. Well, your boyfriend, I guess. Or whatever he is. Martin."

He pulls a face which suggests that whatever Martin is, it's not to Elliot's liking.

"You met *Martin*? But what does he have to do with any of this?"

Elliot looks at me as if he can't quite believe he's having to tell me this.

"He heard me on the phone," he says slowly. "Asked if there was anything he could do to help. And when I told him what was going on — because I was kinda freaking out myself at that point — he said not to worry, he'd go and get you, while I went back to the hotel to grab my stuff. He said he'd explain what was going on, and bring you to meet me, so we could go to the airport together. And my mom was still panicking on the other end of the phone, so I took him at his word."

"Well, you shouldn't have." My entire body has gone cold at the implications of what he's just told me. "Because he *didn't* come and get me. He didn't even *tell* me. This is ... this is the first time I've heard any of this."

I'm really glad I'm leaning against this wall, because my legs have suddenly started to shake, as if they're doubting their ability to hold me up.

"Are you absolutely *sure* it was Martin you met?" I ask suddenly. "You only really met him that one time at the bookstore. And it would've been dark. Maybe it wasn't him? Maybe it was ... um, someone who looked a bit like him?"

*Maybe it was a demon? Or one of those Japanese spirits that can change shape? Because either of those options would be significantly more believable than it having been **Martin**.*

*I mean, **seriously**.*

Elliot, however, just looks at me skeptically.

"Holly, Martin drove me to the airport," he says calmly. "I spent almost an hour in the car with him. So I'm pretty sure it was him."

"But ... Martin drove *me* to the airport," I shriek, feeling like I've slipped into an alternative reality. "Don't you think he'd have mentioned taking *you* there too?"

A flicker of doubt crossed Elliot's handsome face.

"He took you to the airport? But .... when? Because when he came to the hotel to pick me up, he told me he'd gone to the flat to wake you up, but you wouldn't come. He said you point-blank refused, actually. And when I tried to come and see you myself, he said there wasn't time, and he was right. I had to get to airport or I would miss my flight. He promised that he would speak to you and try to persuade you to come the next day."

I gape at him incredulously.

"Elliot, absolutely none of that happened," I say shakily. "None of it. I woke up in the morning and went to your hotel room, like we'd planned, but you weren't there. It was Sandra who told me you'd gone to the airport, not Martin. Martin didn't say a word. Not a single word."

My voice is wobbling dangerously by the time I get to the end of this, but Elliot just shakes his head.

"He *must* have," he insists. "He told me he did. And not just that night, but afterwards, too. He texted me when I got back to the States: said you'd asked him to get in touch and tell me to stop messaging you, because you didn't want to hear from me. I'd sent you so many messages at that point; so many emails. I ... well, I guess it took a while for it to sink in that you just didn't want to hear from me."

He swallows, as if this was a hard thing for him to get out, and now he wants to get rid of the taste of it. Possibly because, as far as I can tell, he appears to be speaking a completely different language; and it's not one I'm even remotely fluent in.

"But I *did* want to hear from you!" I wail, feeling like stamping my foot in frustration. "I got a new phone as soon as the shops opened after Christmas. Martin helped me set it up. All the numbers on the SIM card were lost, so I couldn't call you, but I kept the same number in case *you* called *me*. But you didn't. You definitely didn't, Elliot. I think I would remember."

I'm *sure* I would remember. I definitely remember all the sleepless nights I spent endlessly checking my phone for messages, then the laptop for emails. Going back and forth between the two, and always ending up disappointed.

"Martin helped you?" Elliot says slowly. "And he told you all the contacts were missing?"

"Yeah. He said all the data had been wiped when the phone fell. And it *was* lost. The numbers weren't there. I checked about a hundred times."

Actually, it was more like a thousand times, if I remember rightly; and I'm pretty sure I do. I take a deep breath as more memories of that time come flooding back to me; most of them involving me wandering around in my dressing gown, with puffy eyes and chocolate ice cream dribbled down my front.

"It was a cracked screen, Holly," Elliot points out. "And I'm no expert, but I'd be surprised if what happened to the phone was bad enough to destroy the SIM card."

I'm about to point out that there isn't much point in us debating the finer points of technology from a decade ago — he's actually starting to sound a bit like Martin himself with his insistence on focusing on this — but then another memory hits me.

Martin, standing at the shop counter, with the laptop I shared with Dad at the time open in front of him. The look on his face when he heard Dad and I talk about my plans to go to the States with Elliot.

My headache suddenly intensifies.

"Martin had access to my email, too," I say, an idea starting to take shape in the back of my mind. "Dad asked him to come round to fix his, but Martin said he'd have to take the computer away to look at it. He had it for a couple of days. I didn't think anything of it at the time..."

... but I do now.

And, judging by the look on his face, so does Elliot.

"Martin did this," he says, as matter-of-factly as if we're discussing the weather. "He didn't give you my message, then he lied and told me he did. And I guess he did something to block me from contacting you after that. What was it you used to call him? A nerd?"

"A geek," I reply, my voice croaky. "Because he always said there was nothing he didn't know about tech. And, well, also because he loves *Star Wars* so much."

"There's nothing wrong with loving *Star Wars*," comes Levi's voice from the other side of the door. "Enough with the geek-shaming."

For once, though, I don't have the energy to resent the intrusion; or even to tell him off for eavesdropping. I'm too busy watching Elliot's expression change from the guarded mistrust he started this conversation with, through the dawning realization that we've been played: and by Martin Baxter, of all people.

Finally, we're on the same page.

Elliot didn't rewrite our story when he used it in his book. There were just two sides of it all along; and now we're finally getting to read both of them — just a little too late.

My heart does a weird little duh-DUM that feels a bit like a jump scare.

"Elliot? Oh, there you are."

With the worst possible timing, the door into the hall opens to reveal Elliot's publicist, plus a sheepish-looking Levi, who starts backing away slowly as soon as I make eye contact with him.

"Everyone's waiting for you," the publicist says, looking from Elliot to me and then back again. "If you're ready?"

No, I want to tell her. No, he's not ready. Because he's in the middle of a very important conversation — one it's taken us an entire decade to get around to — and interrupting it now would feel like deciding to leave the theater right before the end of the movie, and before you get to find out whodunnit. (Although, in this case, I think we all know whodunnit; and he's currently standing at the Hart Books table, wearing an 'ironic' Christmas jumper, and a self-satisfied expression which I'm planning to remove as soon as I get the chance...)

"I can't stall the crowd much longer," Publicist Woman adds, as if she's read my mind. "They're all so excited for your big announcement."

Elliot hesitates, his eyes flickering over to me as if he's trying to make his mind up about something.

"I'm sorry," he says softly. "I have to do this."

"Sure. I understand," I reply quickly. Then I remember something.

"Elliot," I call, as he turns to follow the woman into the hall. "Your dad. I wanted to ask. Did he ...?"

The ghost of a smile flickers around the corners of his lips as he pauses in the doorway, Levi hovering excitedly behind him with his eyes like saucers.

"He pulled through," he says. "Eventually. But it was touch and go for a while there. We were basically living in the hospital. It's all a bit of a blur, to be honest. Sorry, Harper," he adds, looking over his shoulder. "I'm just coming."

He gives a small, apologetic shrug, before walking away, and I frown to myself thoughtfully as I watch him go.

Harper? His publicist has the same name as the one I've been assigned to at the ghostwriting agency? What are the odds of that?

I shake off the thought as Levi comes bounding over to grab my hand and tow me back into the hall, babbling something about Martin, and how romantic it is that he would go to such lengths to see off his rival and win the hand of the woman he loves.

It's obvious that Levi and I have very different ideas about 'romance'.

The room in front of me is now at least twice as busy as it was when I left it, with people crammed into every available space, all of them facing the stage, where the man I saw earlier, talking to Elliot's publicist — *Harper* — is sitting on one of the chairs in front of the microphone. Levi and I squeeze our way through the crowd and back to the Hart Books stall, where I notice Martin has made himself at home in my absence, and is sitting next to Dad, chatting away like they're old pals.

Well, we'll see about that.

I grit my teeth as I approach them, my head pounding with rage as I think about what Martin did — what I'm absolutely *sure* he did — to split up me and Elliot ten years ago. Before I can confront him, though, and create my second scene of the day, there's a shrill screech of feedback from the microphone, and I look around to see Elliot standing next to it, looking handsome and self-possessed, with absolutely no trace of the fact that he's had his world rocked by the knowledge that his ex-girlfriend's neighbor-turned-boyfriend deliberately sabotaged their relationship.

From the other side of the stall, Martin grins across at me, and it takes every ounce of strength I have not to reach over and shake him.

I'll have to save that for later.

At the microphone, the woman Elliot addressed as Harper starts talking to the crowd, introducing Elliot — as if he needs introducing in this town — and explaining that he'll make a brief announcement, before going into a question-and-answer session with the man in the suit, who's now accompanied by a cameraman, and someone carrying one of those huge furry microphones. At the front of the stage, a small crowd of photographers jostle for space, while, just behind them, the people in the front row all hold their phones in the air, ready to hit record, as if they're at a rock concert rather than a book festival. Levi gives me an apologetic look before rushing off to join them. After a second, Paris goes too, only without the apology.

Now it's just me, Dad, Martin, and my burning sense of outrage, which is now so huge I imagine it taking physical shape and floating in the air above me, like a demon. Oh, and a few hundred other people in the audience, who are the only reason I'm not letting that rage-demon loose.

At least, not yet.

"Please welcome the award-winning author of *The Snow Globe*: Elliot Sinclair," says Publicist Woman, forcing me to look back up at the stage, where Elliot is stepping in front of the microphone, raising his hand to acknowledge the thunderous applause from the crowd.

He hasn't said a word, and he's already a hit.

"Thank you," he says, his eyes roving across the rows of heads in front of him. "Thank you all for coming."

"Thank *you*," yells someone who I'm pretty sure is Levi. Elliot smiles, looking totally at ease.

"My publishers asked me to come here this morning to talk to you about the sequel to my book," he says, to another flurry of applause. "But I'm not going to do that."

The crowd falls instantly silent. From his position in the front row, Levi twists his head around and shoots me an accusing look.

"Instead," says Elliot calmly, "I'd like to tell you a story, if I may. I'd like to tell you the true story of *The Snow Globe*."

28

I'm not sure the Bramblebury Village Hall has ever been as silent as it is now. It's as if the entire village is collectively holding its breath.

On stage, Elliot's publicist exchanges worried looks with the journalist who's waiting to conduct the interview after what was supposed to be Elliot's big announcement.

But the announcement hasn't come.

Instead, Elliot stands at the microphone, and starts to speak.

"Ten years ago," he says, in a low voice which is nevertheless carried easily all the way to the back of the hall, "I came here to Bramblebury to research a non-fiction book I'd been planning for a while; a biography of my grandfather, Luke Sinclair. You might recognize his first name from the pages of *The Snow Globe*."

There's a murmur of excitement from the audience.

"Luke also came to Bramblebury," Elliot goes on. "Many years before me. During the Second World War, in fact. And while he was here, Luke met a woman called Evie."

The crowd rustles again, excitedly aware that they're hearing the story that directly inspired the book they all love so much.

"Luke and Evie fell in love. And so did I. With the town itself, but also with a local woman I met while I was here." All around me, the heads of the villagers who know about me and Elliot turn to stare at me curiously. This part of the story, at least, is one many of them already know; Bramblebury's worst-kept secret. Nevertheless, a small forest of cellphones is suddenly pointing at me. I can almost sense Levi regretting his decision to leave my side and go to the front of the stage; it's making him miss out on a share of the limelight.

I take a step back, desperately fighting the impulse to crawl beneath the table of books and hide. Who knew that a village book festival could be so completely terrifying?

"Ahem."

Elliot clears his throat in a bid to regain the attention of the audience, who turn reluctantly back to him.

"I only spent three weeks in Bramblebury," he says. "But they were some of the happiest weeks of my life."

A collective 'awww' goes up from the audience.

"But my stay was cut short."

The 'awww' turns to an 'ooooh'.

"I was called home urgently because of a family emergency. I lost touch with the love of my life. I thought that was her choice. I thought she hated me. I thought I'd never see her again. I went from being the happiest I'd ever been to total and utter despair. Honestly, if you'd seen me, you'd have wanted to either slap me or hug me; it was all very dramatic. Even my mother struggled to put up with me."

He gives a wry smile, and the audience gazes up at him, every one of them very clearly in the 'hug him' camp.

A few rows in front of me, a woman I recognize as Sandra, landlady at The Rose, turns and gives me a hostile look which suggests she'd happily hug Elliot, but might be waiting outside later to slap *me*. My legs instantly start trembling again.

"I've recently found out that I was wrong," Elliot says quietly. "That the woman I loved didn't choose to cut contact with me. It was ... not a misunderstanding, exactly. That's the wrong word. It was something that wasn't her fault, though. I know that now. But that's a story that isn't mine to tell."

The audience sends up a murmur of disappointment. Out of the corner of my eye, I see Martin tugging at the collar of his sweater; a nervous tick of his that he always does when he's stressed. I turn my head just enough to allow me to glare at him, while still keeping one eye on Elliot; a piece of multi-tasking which would be quite impressive if I hadn't also broken into a cold sweat at the same time.

"I couldn't live out my own love story," Elliot goes on. "So I decided to write it instead. I used my story — our story — as the basis for the one that became Luke and Evie's in *The Snow Globe*. I hoped she'd see it. That she'd read it, and she'd know how much I loved her. Because I really, truly loved her. More than anything in the world."

Okay, I actually think I might die now; I might just fall to the floor and die. I'm not sure whether it's going to be from the words he's saying, and the way they're twisting painfully around my heart, or from the sheer embarrassment of all these people staring from me to Elliot and then back again, as if they're spectators at a particularly enthralling tennis match, but, either way, death feels like the only option right now, and I will welcome it with open arms.

"I wrote our story because I thought that by doing it I could somehow change the ending," Elliot says from the front of the room, where he's blissfully unaware of the effect he's having on me. "That she would read it, and she'd find some way to get in touch. But instead, it did the opposite. *The Snow Globe* reached all of these people — hundreds of thousands of them — but not the one person I wanted to reach. Not her. So she didn't come looking for me."

"For shame," I hear someone mutter in a stage whisper. I think it might be Maisie Poole, actually.

"Heartless," adds Elsie, not to be outdone. "Martin was right when he said she was frigid."

"Holly isn't frigid," says Paris loudly. "Or, at least, not as far as I know."

From beside me, there's a scraping sound as Dad pushes his chair back. At first I think he's about to challenge Martin to a duel for calling his daughter 'frigid', but instead he just takes my arm and makes me sit down in the chair he's just vacated. Which I guess is a much more sensible reaction, really.

"But what happened next?" someone yells. "Please tell us you didn't just give up?"

There's a sudden flurry of movement as Martin rushes past me, en route to the exit. I get quickly to my feet again, wondering if I should follow him. It's not like I need to hear the rest, after all. I already *know* what happens next: and it's *nothing*. Elliot *did* give up. So did I, for that matter.

I have a feeling this audience is about to be really disappointed in the end of this story.

"Oh, I didn't give up," Elliot replies, making me sit back down abruptly. "There was no real way for me to speak to her; or not when I was so certain she didn't want me to. So I started writing to her, instead."

There's a muffled gasp of surprise at this. What's even more surprising is that it comes from me.

This isn't right. Elliot didn't write to me. Or, if he did, I didn't get his letters: or emails, or texts, or whatever it is he's trying to say he did.

*What **is** he trying to say he did, though?*

"This is something I've never told anyone. I'm probably going to get myself into a bit of trouble over it, actually."

For the first time since he took the mic, Elliot looks unsure of himself. He glances at his publicist, then runs a hand nervously across his chin, looking exactly like the bashful 26-year-old who walked into the bookstore that day, and handed me a snow globe.

"This will probably surprise any of you who've been following my career in any detail." He grins ruefully. "But *The Snow Globe* isn't my only published novel. I've written a few more since then. Well, quite a lot more, actually."

In the silence that follows this statement, you can literally hear the intake of breath from the assembled crowd, before Levi's voice rings out across the hall.

"What the actual fuck?" he yells, almost dropping his phone. "How did we not know this? Paris, how did we not know this?"

He glares accusingly at his colleague, who glares back at him, fighting mode engaged.

"I'm going to assume most of you know what a pen name is?" Elliot interrupts them.

I lean forward in my seat, along with everyone else in the room. On the stage, Publicist Woman is frantically stabbing at her phone, a look of panic on her face. The journalist is beckoning frantically to his cameraman to keep filming. Levi appears to be about to explode.

For once, I relate.

"A pen name is a fake name an author adopts when they want to keep their real identity private, for whatever reason," Elliot explains. "And there are lots of reasons authors do that. Some of them just do it because they want to try out a genre their audience isn't used to, for instance. Others do it because they want to write smut and they'd rather not have to discuss it with their mom."

He grins again, and there's a ripple of laughter from the audience, plus an audible sigh from Sandra, who appears to be quite taken with the idea of Elliot writing smut.

"In my case, I used a pen name because the type of books I started writing were a little different from *The Snow Globe*," Elliot says. His cheeks are starting to turn red now, and he's looking more and more like the younger version of himself who would never have believed he'd one day stand in front of a crowded room and ... admit to secretly writing smut? Is that what he's doing here?

"Not *totally* different," he goes on, ignoring his publicist, who's now abandoned her phone to hover anxiously by his shoulder instead. "They're still about relationships. But while *The Snow Globe* was a love story, my other books are very much *romance*."

The emphasis on the word *romance* is one that only the kind of people Paris describes as "book people" will understand. But I know what he means. Love stories don't have to have happy endings. Romance books do. Which means Elliot's been writing...

"Billionaires," he blurts out from the stage. "Enemies to lovers. Fake dating. All that kind of stuff."

The crowd murmurs, not really knowing how to react to this. Well, with the obvious exception of Levi, who appears to have expired, and is being fanned with a book festival brochure by Paris, who isn't even looking at him as she does it.

"Well, well," says Dad quietly from beside me. "Who would've thought it?"

I grip the edge of my seat tightly, feeling like I'm in the middle of some kind of weird fever dream as I wait for Elliot to finish.

"They're not the kind of books that tend to win prizes," Elliot says quietly, once the hubbub dies down. "But they're the books my girl ... that Holly used to love. Because every single one of them has a happy ending."

His eyes somehow find me, all the way at the back of the room, but I'm finding it hard to focus on him because it would appear mine are somehow swimming with tears.

"I wrote all of my books for you, Holly," he says. "You're the heroine of every story; not just *The Snow Globe*. And I never knew if you'd read them or not, but I hoped you would. And I hoped they'd bring you some of the happiness I obviously couldn't."

"God, he's good," sighs a woman standing near me.

"I'll buy every single one of his books," agrees her friend. "I don't care what name he writes them under."

Everyone in the room is now staring at me; I mean, if I thought all the stuff about me being the inspiration for *The Snow Globe* was bad, it's going to be absolutely nothing compared to this little bombshell. I will *never* live this down. I'll probably have to change my name and move town. And, honestly, I don't even care, because it's embarrassing, and it's awkward, and when I look back at the footage from today that's inevitably going to end up on TikTok I'm going to really wish

I'd taken the time to style my hair properly before leaving the house tomorrow.

But it's also kind of wonderful, really. Because the man I've loved for a decade now is standing on a *literal* stage, telling the entire village that he loves me; and that he's been trying to tell me that in dozens of different ways for years now.

At least, I *think* that's what Elliot's saying.

And, if he is, that would definitely explain all of these tears that are suddenly running down my face.

"What's the pen name, though?" shouts someone from the middle of the crowd. "You have to tell us the pen name! Don't leave us hanging here!"

I'm not remotely surprised to find the question is Levi's. I'm slightly more surprised, though, when I look over to see him standing next to Paris, both of them squeezed together on the bronze 'first kiss' plaque in a way that suggests they've picked this spot on purpose.

If it was anyone else but them, they'd look quite romantic, really.

"Yes," shouts Aunt Lorraine, who's materialized beside me at some point during all of this. "Tell us so I can buy every single one of those books."

The room falls silent.

Everyone looks at Elliot.

Elliot looks at his publicist.

His publicist looks at her phone, then back up at the audience, as if she's trying to decide whether allowing Elliot to reveal his secret pen name has the potential to be the kind of news that will sell thousands more books, or the kind that will completely ruin his career.

For a full 30 seconds, those two possibilities compete with each other. Then the woman turns to Elliot and gives a tiny nod, before turning and abruptly leaving the stage, as if she's washing her hands of whatever's about to happen next.

Even from where I'm sitting at the back of the room, I can see the indecision on Elliot's face. It's evident in every movement; from the way he reaches up to adjust his non-existent glasses, to the way he swallows uneasily before speaking.

I get quickly to my feet, torn between the need to let him know he doesn't have to tell us if he doesn't want to, and the equally pressing desire to know what his pen name is, and whether I've read any of his books.

Elliot clears his throat.

"My pen name is one I think quite a few of you will know, actually," he says, with a nervous laugh. "It's Vivienne Faulkner."

29

Outside the village hall, it's started to snow again; tiny, silver-edges flakes which land on the branches of the giant Christmas tree and glitter there like jewels.

Not that I notice any of that.

Well, it's hard to think about the scenery, really, when you've just found out that the ex who may-or-may-not still be in love with you is also the person you're supposed to be ghostwriting a book for, and now you're making a run for it; dashing out of the room like Lizzie Bennet after she turns down Darcy's proposal.

As always, Elliot is the twist in every plot.

"Holly, wait."

I've just passed the Christmas tree and am headed for the inflatable snow globe when Elliot appears at the door of the village hall, with a small crowd of people — including the guy with the giant furry microphone — behind him.

That's when I start running.

"Would you just back off?" I hear Elliot yell at the photographers and other curious onlookers as he sets off in pursuit. "Give a guy a minute, would you? Holly, wait!"

But I do not wait. I am very much done waiting, actually. Instead, I run all the way to the bookstore — okay, it's just a few meters, but still — rummaging in my pocket as I go, and almost sobbing with relief when my fingers close around the keys to the shop, which Past Me somehow had the sense to pick up before she left the house. The store is closed today, because everyone's been at the book festival, but at least it'll be somewhere to hide until all of this has blown over.

So, about the next hundred years or so, then.

That should just about do it.

The same keys that will allow me to escape the prying eyes of the entire village, however, are also the ones that lose me a precious few seconds as I fumble them into the lock. Those seconds are all it takes for Elliot to catch up with me, and, before I know what's happening, I'm opening the bookshop door, and we're somehow going through it together, Elliot slamming it firmly closed behind us.

"Look, I can explain," he says, holding his hands up as he turns to face me. "I get that this is a shock, and I promise, I can explain, but ... just give me the keys first, will you? I'd rather do this in private, if it's all the same with you."

No sooner has he spoken than Levi and Paris appear, their faces distorted against the glass as they peer through the shop door. Now it's like a scene from *The Walking Dead*.

This day cannot end soon enough for me.

"Holly, let us in," yells Levi, who's clearly living in even more of an alternative reality than I thought he was if he thinks he's getting to film this for his Booktok channel.

I step forward and pull down the blind, hiding them both from view, while Elliot locks the door.

"We do work here, you know," comes Paris's voice from the other side. "You can't keep us out. We have contracts."

"I'll pay you double-time if you go home and leave me alone," I yell back.

There's a short silence as they debate this, then their shadowy forms disappear from behind the door, leaving Elliot and I alone at last; something I'd have welcomed just a few minutes ago, when he was being all cute and eloquent, and referring to me as 'the love of my life', but which is now about as welcome The Grinch on Christmas morning.

I'm about to tell him this, but then I remember how he said he could explain, and, actually, that's something I'd *love* to hear around about now.

"Go on, then," I say, leaning against one of the bookshelves and giving him what I hope is an appropriately forbidding look. "Explain."

Elliot reaches up and once again tries to adjust the glasses he no longer wears.

"Um. I just need a second," he mutters, making me sigh in exasperation. "It's ... complicated."

"Which bit?" I ask, unimpressed. "The bit where you revealed yourself to be Vivienne Faulkner, or the bit where you booked me to ghostwrite a book for you? Because that was you, right? I'm not imagining this? There's not two Vivienne Faulkners out there, both writing romance books, is there?"

"No, that was me," Elliot admits, shamefacedly. "Well, it was Harper, really. She's the one who found you on the ghostwriting site and got in touch. But I asked her to do it, obviously."

"Harper." I nod, thinking about how wrong I was when I'd pictured shiny-haired, well-dressed Harper Grant as some kind of jolly old cat lady. "Right. But how did you even know to look for me there? How did you know I was ghostwriting? I only told you about it a few days ago, but I'd already been booked by 'Vivienne' before that. Or … wait. Did you use ghostwriters for *all* of your books as Vivienne? Is that what you're saying?"

I cross the room to one of the sofas and let myself sink into it as I consider this horrible possibility.

"No! No, of course not!"

Elliot tries to sit next to me, but changes his mind when he sees the look on my face, and takes a seat opposite, instead.

"I wrote every word of those books myself," he tells me, firmly. "And I didn't hire you for the latest one because I didn't think I could write it myself. I did it because I wanted to help you."

"To *help* me?" My eyes are so wide the air is hurting them. "Why would you think you needed to *help* me? And you haven't answered my question about how you knew I was a ghostwriter in the first place?"

Elliot stares at his feet.

"I found out completely by chance," he says. "Honestly. I have a lot of contacts in the publishing industry, that's all. One of them had become a pretty good friend, and he recognized your name from some work you did for his publishing house. He told me because … well, I guess I'd mentioned you a few times. More than a few times, really. Okay, a lot. I mentioned you a lot. And you have quite a memorable name, so…"

"That's totally unethical," I interrupt. "All of my ghostwriting was supposed to be confidential. This is a complete abuse of trust."

"I know," Elliot says miserably. "And I'm sorry. Really. But once I knew you were writing, Holly, I had to know more. It was the first thing I'd heard about you in years, and I just ... I just grabbed it."

"I can't believe you let me sit there and tell you all about my amazing new career last night when you already knew about it," I go on. "Why didn't you say something then?"

"I wanted to let you tell me in your own time," he says, looking uncomfortable. "I wanted to tell you — really, I did — but I felt like it should come from you. And, I mean, it's a hard thing to just blurt out, isn't it? Especially when we were having such a nice time. Well, *I* thought it was nice, anyway. I thought we were starting to get somewhere, and I didn't want to ruin it by suddenly revealing I was Vivienne. I figured it might be a bit of a mood killer."

"You don't say," I reply sarcastically.

"I was planning to tell you, though, Holly," he says earnestly. "It's just ... last night I felt like you were finally starting to open up to me again, and I didn't want to ruin that by telling you I'd read all of your books."

"Oh, God." I put my head in my hands. Not even Aunt Lorraine has read all of my books. And Dad says they're 'not quite his thing'. But now Elliot's read them, which is all kinds of mortifying, really, until I remember that this is the man who apparently wrote *Dancing With a Daydreamer* and *Passport to Passion*, and I feel a bit better.

"Don't be embarrassed," he says, chuckling. "I really liked them."

"Really?" I peer at him through my fingers.

"Really. *Boss Babe 101* is my favorite. It's like a road map for your soul."

"That's a line from the blurb."

"I know."

He smiles again, and I have to bite the inside of my cheek to stop myself from smiling back at him.

I wish he didn't have this effect on me. Especially when I still don't understand even half of what's going on here.

"I'm not lying when I say I liked the books, Holly," Elliot says, seriously. "You're a great writer. I've always known that. But I also know this isn't the kind of thing you want to write. Self-help. Non-fiction. You were born to write stories. And that's why I got Harper to invent a book for you to write. I thought if I just gave you that nudge you needed, then maybe..."

"Do you have any idea how patronizing that sounds?" I object. "Seriously? The big shot, published author, coming riding to the rescue of poor little Holly, who can't come up with a plot on her own? And you were going to *pay* me to do it? Like I'm some kind of charity case? I just ... I'm sorry, I still can't believe this is happening."

My cheeks are burning with shame as the full weight of what he's telling me finally hits me.

I was absolutely fine with not being credited for my work when I thought it was someone other than my ex-boyfriend who was paying me for it. But the thought of *Elliot* doing it fills me with the kind of fury that makes me pop up from the sofa like a rocket about to launch.

"Holly, no," Elliot insists, jumping up too, and grabbing me by the arms. "It wasn't charity. It was a fair wage for the work."

"The work that *you* were going to take credit for?" I hiss, shaking him off. "Like when you used my ideas in *The Snow Globe*?"

Elliot lets go of my arms, his face ashen.

"I was never planning to publish your writing under my name ... um, my pen name, I mean," he says quietly. "I wouldn't have done that. I was going to tell you who I was. I was going to persuade you to publish it under your own name. I swear to you, Holly; that's what I was trying to do. It was about you, not about me. And as for *The Snow Globe* ... well, I've already tried to explain that to you. I don't know what else to say except that I'm sorry. I messed up. I really, really messed up."

He sits back down and puts his face in his hands. I stand there next to him, anger slowly fading as it occurs to me that there's much more to this story that I still haven't heard.

"Wait," I say, going over to one of the display tables and picking up a copy of Vivienne Faulkner's newest release. "There's something I still don't understand."

I thrust the book under his nose, forcing him to look at the photo of 'Vivienne' on the back cover.

"Who's this?" I demand. "And why did I spend a bunch of my time feeling sorry for her, what with the mystery illness that was apparently stopping her from writing her book?"

Elliot takes the book and turns it over in his hands, as if he's never seen it before.

"Look, Holly, I never intended for anyone to find out about this," he sighs at last. "I've probably just destroyed my reputation by talking about it now, in fact. That was never part of the plan. I've already got at least a dozen missed calls from my publisher on my phone. So believe me when I tell you that I didn't set out to purposefully deceive anyone with .... this."

He places the book on the coffee table in front of him, and I perch on the edge of the sofa, interested in spite of myself.

"So, what did you set out to do?" I ask softly. "And who is she?"

"She's a model," he replies, shrugging. "She posed for the author photos. We made up a fake biography for her to make it seem real. I did it because I had no intention of ever being associated with those books. I mean, me? A romcom writer?" He laughs without humor. "My family accepted *The Snow Globe* ... eventually ... but I'd never had lived down this kind of thing." He taps the cover of the book in front of him. "Never. Not in a million."

"But you wrote them anyway?"

"Yeah. Because I enjoyed it. And because I knew you liked romance books. It made me like them too. You're not the only one who appreciates a happy ending, you know."

I take the book back and flick through it silently.

"I do like romance books," I admit at last. "I like yours. Vivienne's. Whatever. I've read them all."

"Really? Even *S'More Than Friends*? I was never really sure about that title."

"Yup. All of them. Even this latest one. I read it as soon as it arrived. I really enjoyed it. I just can't believe *you* wrote it."

From the cover of the book, 'Vivienne Faulkner' beams up at me. It's strange to think she isn't real; or isn't who she seems to be, at least.

Just another thing that turned out to be fake around here.

"I can't believe I wrote it either," says Elliot, rubbing his chin. "I can't believe I wrote any of them. My family doesn't even know it's me. Shit. I expect they will now."

He looks up at me, eyes wide as he realizes exactly what he's done by deciding to unmask himself on the stage earlier.

"Um, yeah. I'd say so. Levi will have it on TikTok already. It's probably gone viral by now. No, don't look," I add quickly, seeing Elliot reach for his phone. "It's best not to read the comments. Trust me, I've been working with Levi and Paris for long enough to know that you never read the comments when something goes viral."

"Right. Well, I guess I have a lot to learn."

"I think we both do."

We look at each other, suddenly shy. So much has happened over the last 24 hours that it's almost impossible to process it all.

Elliot is Vivienne.

Martin is a dirty, rotten liar.

Harper Grant isn't a matronly looking cat lady.

I'm ... confused. I'm just very, very confused.

"Come here," says Elliot in a soft voice. He pats the sofa cushion next to him, indicating for me to sit down. "Come and talk to me, Holly. Properly, I mean. I think we owe each other that much, at least. Don't you?"

I swallow nervously, then nod.

"Okay," I say, allowing myself to slide from my position on the armrest down to the seat next to him. "Let's do it. Let's talk."

30

Sitting this close to Elliot feels both comfortingly familiar and excitingly dangerous.

Especially with his thigh pressed up against mine, and our hands almost close enough to touch.

"Why did you stay here?" he asks suddenly, reminding me that I'm supposed to be thinking about talking, not touching. "At the bookstore, I mean? I know you didn't want to leave your dad when he was struggling. But then, once things started to pick up? Once it got to the point he was able to take on more staff? Why did you stay then? I've been wondering. I've been wondering a lot, actually."

"It wasn't that simple," I reply, sighing. "Nothing's ever as simple as you like to pretend it is, Elliot."

"Okay, so tell me about it, then," he returns, folding his arms across his chest and leaning back in his seat. "I've got plenty of time. My flight home doesn't leave until tomorrow afternoon."

My heart does another jump-scare thud at the thought of him leaving again. I really wish it would stop doing that.

"Force of habit, I suppose," I say. "At first I told myself I was just staying to help out until things settled down a bit, and Dad got used to it being so much busier. But then ... I don't know. I guess there just wasn't a good enough reason for me to leave by then. You were gone. I didn't expect to ever see you again. And I was with …"

"Martin," Elliot finishes for me, his expression stony.

"Yup. Him." I can't even bring myself to say his name right now. "I … well, I obviously had no idea what he was really like. What he'd done. And he'd been kind to me after you left, so I suppose I felt grateful to him. God, I feel so stupid now I know the truth."

I hide my face with my hands again, and while my eyes are closed, I feel the sofa underneath me shift slightly as Elliot takes the seat next to me.

"Don't feel stupid, Holly," he says softly. "It's not your fault. He lied. He lied to us both. That's all on him."

Through my fingers, I see his hand sneak out, as if he's going to take mine, or maybe put his arm around me. But before he can reach me, I remember that he lied too — he lied about being 'Vivienne', and even though he claims his intentions were good, I'm still not sure I can get past that particular revelation in the space of a few minutes, so I shift slightly away from him.

"It's not just that he lied about you," I tell him, taking my hands away from my eyes. "He lied about everything. He made me feel like there was no point in trying to do anything with my life other than just sticking around here." I make a gesture with my hands that's supposed to encompass both the store itself, and Bramblebury in general. Hell, maybe even all of England.

"He kept telling me how great it would be; him with the bakery, me with the bookstore. Both of our families close by. A whole, tight-knit little community to look after us. He made it sound amazing. I mean, who wouldn't want all of that? It's perfect. Like a Christmas romance novel. I think 'Vivienne Faulkner's' written quite a few like that, hasn't she? Haven't *you*, I mean? Wow, it's going to take a long time for this to stop being weird."

"'Vivienne' has written a few Christmas romances," Elliot agrees. "But they're no more real than she is, Holly. They're fun to read — at least, I hope they are — but they're not a reflection of real life. You know that. I know you do. It's just a story. It's wish-fulfillment, for the most part."

I nod, miserably.

"It was never *my* wish, though," I say. "Martin really made me think I'd be stupid not to believe in it, though. He made me feel guilty for wanting something different. Ungrateful. Like I'd be turning my back on something most people would give anything to have. It's like everyone else wants to be the girl in the picture-perfect small town, who marries the wholesome boy next door and lives happily ever after, with, like, a couple of kids, and, I don't know, *chickens* or something. But not me. No, *I* have to go and want the Christmas romance in reverse, don't I? I'm the girl who wants to *leave* the small town and go and live in the city with a guy who has the potential to break my heart and totally destroy me. And I don't even *like* chickens."

The last words come out in a strangled kind of sob, which I do my best to turn into a laugh. But Elliot isn't fooled.

"Is that really what you want, though?" he asks cautiously. "Still?"

"Well, yeah," I reply. "It's just ... I still want the happily ever after bit, too, though. And I'm not sure I can have both. I'm not sure I can have the danger, and the excitement, and the ... the *passion* ... without the risk that comes with it. You know?"

"I do know," he says seriously. "And I think you're right. I think you have to take the risk if you want to have the rest. I think that's how it works."

"And there's the problem," I say in a small voice. "I don't like taking risks."

"You did once. Or maybe you didn't *like* it, exactly, but you were prepared to do it. Weren't you?"

I look up and into his eyes. He's sitting very close to me; so close that I can see the flecks of gray in his deep blue eyes. So close that it's going to be very, very hard to pull myself away from him again.

"I was," I say in a whisper. "But then it all went wrong. And it was *awful*, Elliot. It was so, so awful. I don't think I could go through that again."

"Maybe you don't have to," he says instantly. "You know now that I'd never hurt you, Holly. You do know that, don't you? You know I still love you? Please don't tell me I made that speech back there on the stage for nothing. It was embarrassing enough as it was."

He makes an attempt at a smile, his eyes filled with hope. And this time, when his hand makes a move towards mine, I reach out and meet it halfway.

"It wasn't embarrassing," I assure him. "Well, not for you, anyway. Or it shouldn't have been. You weren't embarrassing. You were actually kind of adorable."

The blue eyes crinkle around the edges.

"Adorable, huh? I can definitely work with that," he says. "I meant everything I said, though. I never got over you, Holly. No one ever came close to making me feel the way you did. And I want that again. All of it. The whole reverse-fairytale, or whatever it was you called it.

I don't care. I just want *you*. And I know I just said you have to take the risk to have the rest, but I'm not a risk to you. I'm not going to break your heart. I'm not going to leave you. And I definitely won't ever make you get chickens, because I'm not sure I'm particularly keen on them either, to be honest."

I think about how perfect this moment is, with the only light in the room coming from the Christmas tree lights, and the man of my dreams sitting next to me telling me I really can have it all. I think about how much I want to believe him when he says that, and then I don't think of much at all, really, because suddenly his lips are on mine, and he's kissing me; soft and hesitant at first, as if he's not quite sure if this is real either, then his hands come up to cup my face, pulling me closer as the hesitation melts away, along with all the reasons we shouldn't be doing this.

His hands are in my hair now, his lips urgent but soft. He still tastes vaguely like peppermint. He still feels like home. He still kisses me as if there's never, in the history of the world, been anything more important than this moment, and I still respond to him as if I fully agree.

We could have spent the last ten years kissing like this. I would feel resentful that we haven't, but I'm too busy making up for it, my arms reaching up to loop themselves around his neck as if they have a mind of their own, and pulling him closer still. His tongue dances against mine, and I moan softly as I remember all the things that come next: the late nights, the early mornings, the way everything feels different when we're together. I remember it all; and now it's right there — once again within my grasp.

"Come back to the States with me," Elliot says, his eyes shining as we finally pull apart. "It might be too late to get you a visa by tomorrow — it probably will be, in fact — but that's okay ... I'll change my flight. I'll take a later one. It doesn't matter. As long as I know you're going to be with me this time."

He kisses me again, and I kiss him back, both of us falling easily back into the familiar rhythm of shared breaths and soft touches; neither one of us wanting to stop. But as Elliot's arms find their way to my waist, and I fall back against the soft cushions of the sofa, I start to remember other things, too. The airport on Christmas Eve. The empty hotel room, with the sheets piled high on the stained mattress, and the dust motes swirling in the air. The mascara on my cheeks in the rear-view mirror when I finally got back into Martin's car, and the sympathetic look he gave me, which convinced me he was the good guy, and Elliot the enemy.

This is all so very familiar; all of it — from the taste of his lips, right down to the flight that leaves on Christmas Eve, and the mad rush to fill in the appropriate paperwork. And we both know what comes after that.

"Elliot, stop," I say hoarsely, struggling reluctantly out of his arms. "Stop. This is crazy. It's completely crazy."

The light goes abruptly out of his eyes.

"What do you mean?" he asks calmly. "Look, if it's too soon, that's fine. I get it. There's no rush. You can come later. You can come whenever you like, really. Just ... you will come, won't you? At some point? We can do all the things we said we'd do last time. Disney. The beach. And we can start writing together again. Because I meant it when I told you I wanted you to write the sequel to *The Snow Globe* with me. Full credit, obviously. Your name on the cover, next to mine. Assuming the publisher still wants it, of course. What do you say? Will you help me? Will you come to America with me?"

I look at him sadly.

"I can't," I say in a whisper. "I'm really sorry, but I can't come with you, and I can't help you write your sequel. I love you too, Elliot — I really, really do. But we've been here before, haven't we? Making the same plans, saying the same things. And it didn't work."

"It didn't work because Martin made sure it didn't," Elliot bursts out, getting to his feet angrily. "If he hadn't lied to us both, you'd have got on that plane with me. We'd have gone home together. It would've worked. *We* would've worked."

"We don't know that, though, do we?" I reply. "We don't know what would've happened if Martin hadn't gotten in the way. Because we didn't think that would happen either, did we? I didn't think I'd have to spend the rest of my life without you. You knew how scared I was of that. You knew I'd already lost Mum. You knew I couldn't go through that again. And I know it's not your fault that I did — I know that was down to Martin. But it still terrifies me. And I'm not sure I can get past that fear."

"You can. Of course you can." Elliot strides over and crouches down until he's almost kneeling in front of me. "I'll help you," he says, taking my hands in his. "We'll figure it out together."

For a moment, two possible futures swim in front of me: one of them bright and dangerous, the other duller, but safe. I look around the store, at the piles of books, the gleaming wood surfaces, the shiny new coffee bar we could only afford because of Elliot and his book. The shelf closest to me is has all the books arranged by color: I know

Paris or Dad will probably roll their eyes and change them all back as soon as they come into work tomorrow, but for now it looks perfect to me; organized and calm, in a way that soothes my soul.

"I can't do it, Elliot," I tell him, my eyes filled with tears as I look back up at him. "I can't go with you."

"Is this how it's going to be, then?" he says, getting to his feet. "Both of us loving each other, but not ever allowing ourselves to be together, in case we get hurt? And we're going to do that forever? Am I getting that right? That's really what you want, Holly? You want to one day be lying there on your deathbed, thinking, 'Thank God I didn't try to make a go of it with Elliot, because I could've got hurt? Remind me how this works again?" he goes on, his tone somewhere between anger and hurt. "When does the 'not getting hurt' bit start? Because I sure feel hurt right now."

I mean, when he puts it like that...

"I don't ... I can't ... I ...."

I have no idea what I'm trying to say. I try my best, but the words don't come out. It's like one of those nightmares, where you're trying to scream, but no one can hear you. Not that I know what I'd say even if they could.

"Look," Elliot says, his shoulders sagging as the anger drains out of him. "My flight leaves at 3 o'clock tomorrow. If you change your mind, you know where to find me."

It's quite possibly the worst thing he could have said to me, instantly triggering an avalanche of memories; the infuriatingly slow drive to the airport; the argument with the security officer; the crushing realization that it was all too late.

"I won't," I reply, somehow finding my voice at last. "I won't risk the same thing happening again, Elliot. I'm sorry. I love you, but I can't."

Elliot just stands there, his expression shifting from the anger of a moment ago to something that could be either hurt or acceptance.

Then he gives a single, terse nod, before turning and walking away; across the room, and right out of my life.

Again.

31

Martin is waiting for me when I turn up at his doorstep the next morning.

I say 'doorstep'. When we broke up, Martin was forced to move back in with his parents for a bit, because the house belonged to me, and there was nowhere else for him to go. Six months later, he's still there, living back in the flat above the baker's, and next door to the bookshop; which means I have to spend an awkward few minutes talking to his mum about our respective Christmas plans, before she lets me go through the shop and upstairs to find him.

"I know why you're here," he says, as soon as he opens the door. His face is pale and waxy, and he looks like he hasn't slept; which could just mean he's been up all night gaming as usual, of course, but which I secretly hope is a sign that he's been tortured with guilt.

"Yeah, I expect you do," I comment, following him into the living room, which looks out onto the village square, just like our old flat next door. From where I'm standing, I have a perfect view of both the Christmas tree and the snow globe; neither of which does much to improve my mood.

It's Christmas Eve, and I could not possibly feel less festive.

"Why did you do it?" I ask bluntly, not bothering to sit down. "Why didn't you tell me Elliot was looking for me that night? And why did you tell him I didn't want to see him? Don't bother denying you did it; I *know* you did it. I just want to know why, that's all."

Martin opens his eyes very wide, in a way that makes me think he's probably been practicing what he thinks is an 'innocent' look in the mirror, in preparation for this.

"Isn't it obvious?" he says, holding his hands out like a man begging for his life. He's obviously been practicing that too. "I did it for you, Holly. I did it for *love*."

Aaaand it looks like he's been listening to some particularly cheesy love songs, too. I think I might throw up if this continues.

"You know I've always loved you, Holly," he says earnestly, trying to take my hand and failing. "Ever since we were at school together. Remember how we used to sit together at lunch? And how we'd always pick each other when we had to pair up for something in class?"

"I sat next to Fern Clark at lunch," I tell him. "And the teacher always paired people up. I think I remember being put with you once? Maybe?"

"Oh, come on, Holly," Martin says beseechingly. "We were made for each other. Living next door, both of us the children of entrepreneurs..."

"Martin, none of this is even remotely relevant," I snap, already exhausted by him. "You don't hack someone's email just because they lived next door when you were kids and once shared a packet of Quavers at break time. And if we were destined to be together, you wouldn't have had to lie to make it happen."

I see hope spark behind his eyes at the mention of the Quavers — that was a mistake on my part — so I move quickly on.

"You did do that, didn't you?" I ask. "You hacked my email? And you did something to my phone to block Elliot from calling me?"

"I didn't *hack* it," he says, pouting. "Your dad *gave* me the laptop. And you gave me the phone. So I didn't have to *hack* anything, I just..."

"Oh my God, stop being so pedantic!" I slap my forehead in frustration. "It doesn't matter what the technical term is for whatever you did; you did *something*. And you outright lied to Elliot when you told him I didn't want to hear from him."

Martin stares at his feet. He's wearing a pair of very sensible slippers that make him look cozy and benign, when, in fact, I now know him to be an arch-manipluator, and expert gas lighter.

I can't believe how wrong I was about him. "He wasn't good for you," he says at last. "Elliot. He changed you. You weren't the same person after you met him. And you weren't thinking straight. Anyone could see that. I could see that. And okay, maybe I shouldn't have intervened in the way I did. I know it was wrong. But I swear to you, Holly, I was acting in your best interests. I might have done the wrong thing, but I did it for the right reasons. You were being reckless; making decisions that would ruin your life. You're still doing it now; breaking up with me, taking this silly ghostwriting job. It's not you, Holly. And I'm just trying to help you. That's all I want."

I glare at him through narrowed eyes, trying to figure out which TV show or superhero movie he's blatantly stolen the 'wrong thing, right reasons' line from. I know it's not his. Martin doesn't have a single original thought in his head. He's not like...

But anyway.

"Elliot didn't change me, Martin," I say slowly. "I've always been like this. You just didn't know me well enough to see it."

But *he* did. Elliot did. Elliot saw me. And he didn't turn me into someone I wasn't; he just helped me see the person who was there all along. And now that I've been reminded of who she is, I think it's maybe time I started getting to know her again.

"There are no right reasons for what you did, Martin," I tell him firmly, pleased to see that my voice is only shaking a little bit. "None. You barely even knew me back then. We weren't friends. And even if we had been, my life is my own, to ruin as I see fit. It wasn't your place to decide that for me. It wasn't your place to decide *anything* for me; and it never will be, because I never want to see or hear from you again, okay? I'm blocking your number. I'm changing my Netflix password. And if I ever see you in the street, I will cross to the other side, and pretend I didn't. Is that clear?"

Martin nods miserably, looking like a schoolboy who's just been given detention.

I straighten my shoulders, proud of myself. The old Holly would never have stood up to him like that. She would never have asserted herself. But I did it. And the new Holly may technically have been lying when she said she'd change her Netflix password, because she's not totally sure how to do that, but still: she'll figure it out, just like she'll figure out everything else.

We'll figure it out together.

That's what Elliot said last night; right before he said that thing about how I'd feel on my deathbed, when I realized I'd spent my entire life without him, just to avoid getting hurt.

But I'm already hurt. I can see that now. I've been hurting for ten years now, and if you give me another ten, I'm pretty sure I'll be hurting still.

When does the 'not getting hurt' bit start?

I could be wrong, but I'm pretty sure 'never' is the answer to that question.

Seeing Martin today has made that abundantly clear; because I thought he was the safe option, and he turned out to be the dangerous one. Because nothing he ever did made me stop missing Elliot; and I don't think anything ever will.

Which means I know exactly what I have to do next: for once in my life, I have to become the main character. And that's exactly what I'm going to do.

I have to get to the airport. And there's absolutely no way in hell I'm going to ask Martin to take me this time, which means I need to get there myself.

Like, *now*.

Just as I'm about to leave, though, something large and white drifts past the window, making me turn and look out. It's snowing again. And either I'm imagining things, or there's a man who looks a lot like Elliot standing in front of the village Christmas tree, looking up at it.

I move quickly closer, pressing my forehead against the glass as I try to get a closer look.

In the square below me, the man turns slightly, looking over at the snow globe, with its usual line of people waiting to be photographed in it. He has dark hair, and is carrying a rucksack, as if he's getting ready to go somewhere.

It's definitely him. It's definitely Elliot.

He's not at the airport; or, at least, not yet.

He's right here, outside the shop.

"I need to go," I tell Martin, turning around so fast I make myself dizzy. "Don't contact me again, okay?"

Then I run for the door, my mind made up.

On the first night I met him, Elliot told me he'd always remember me. But I don't want to be someone he just remembers. I don't want our relationship to be just a story with an unhappy ending. And now I just have to hope he still feels the same after everything I said to him to contradict that yesterday.

Ignoring Martin's confused questions, I race down the stairs and into the baker's shop below, which is filled with customers buying last-minute mince pies and Christmas cookies. Flying past them all, I fling myself out into the street, skidding on the snow that's still covering the ground.

He's still there. Elliot's still there, standing looking up at the huge Christmas tree, with its hundreds of tiny snow globes dangling from the branches.

I don't go to him, though.

Instead I turn and pull open the door to the bookstore, hurrying inside to where Dad and Levi are both busy serving customers, while Paris stands on a ladder, rearranging that shelf of books I arranged by color, when I was trying to calm my anxious thoughts by bringing order to chaos.

But that was fake too, wasn't it? All of those pretty, colored spines just gave the illusion of order; underneath, it made it impossible to find anything, and I feel like this is an important realization for me, somehow. Maybe all this time I've spent telling myself I'm in control,

I've just been secretly creating more chaos. And maybe it's time to stop kidding myself that I'm not.

"Great work, Paris," I yell as I race past her towards the office. "Keep it up!"

Paris stares at me, nonplussed, but I've no time to stop and explain myself. I have to get to my office, where I pull open the bottom drawer of my desk, and rummage around inside it until I find the thing I'm looking for. And then I'm off again, sprinting through the store and back out into the street, before you can say *ho ho ho*.

Please let him still be there.

Please let him still be there.

It takes me less than a minute to reach the part of the square that houses the Christmas tree and the globe; the area I saw Elliot in from the upstairs window.

He's still there.

Just.

I reach out and grab him by the sleeve of his coat, just as he's about to turn and walk away.

"Holly! What are you doing?"

Elliot's eyes are slightly red, and his face is paler than usual. But he still smiles when he sees me, and it's all I can do not to throw myself into his arms, without another word.

But there's something I have to do first.

"I got you something," I tell him, holding out the snow globe. "A Christmas gift. Well, you got it for me. But it's always been yours, really."

Elliot takes it from me silently, holding it up to the sky. Inside, the little people stand steadfastly holding onto each other while the snow whirls violently around them, stirred up by the shaking of the glass as I ran here with it in my hand.

Outside the glass, it's snowing too; heavier now. All around us, people start walking faster, and stallholders begin packing up their wares, not wanting to stay out in this weather.

Elliot, however, just stands there, looking at the glass globe in his hand.

"How funny," he says at last, his eyes locking onto mine. "I got something for you, too. I came here to give it to you, actually. I'm sorry I didn't have time to wrap it."

He reaches into his coat pocket and pulls out something small and round, which he hands to me silently. I look down.

It's a glass snow globe, with two tiny people inside; her in a red dress, him with dark, floppy hair. Instead of a snow-covered village behind them, though, there's a row of palm trees; and, as I look closer, I see that the flakes floating around them look more like glitter than snow.

"It's a glitter globe," he says. "For people who don't like the snow."

As if on cue, the flakes around us get thicker. The people waiting in line for their snow globe photo have gone now, and the photographer is taking down his sign and starting to pack away his camera. No one wants to stay out in a blizzard.

"I've started to think it's not so bad, actually," I say, smiling up at him. "The snow. The town. But I have to admit, I'd love to see some palm trees like these ones."

I hold the new globe up against the old one, noticing how similar they are, despite the changes that have been made to the scenery.

The same, but different.

"Well, now you have the best of both worlds," says Elliot, returning my smile. "If you're sure that's what you want?"

"Oh, it is," I assure him. "What I said yesterday, Elliot ... I didn't mean it. I was just scared. I still am, really, but you were right. I can't stop myself from being hurt by not being with you. It's too late for that. And I know it's too late to get on that flight with you now, too, but ... maybe after Christmas? And we can stay in touch this time; properly, I mean. I'll write your number on a piece of paper, instead of just saving it on my phone. I'll write it everywhere. Anything to make sure we don't lose each other again once you're back in the States."

The snow is falling so fast now that I can barely see him through it, but I *can* see his smile; and I can see that it's the same one he gave me when we stood in this same spot just over a decade ago, with the same snow globe in our hands.

"I'm not going to the States," he says, his grin getting even wider. "I canceled my flight. I still have three months left on my visa, and I'm going to spend it here, in Bramblebury. I'd already decided that before .... before this." He holds up the snow globe I gave him with a laugh. "I told you I wouldn't leave you again, Holly, and I won't. I didn't fight for you the last time. I'm not going to make the same mistake again."

My cheeks are suddenly wet, and I'm not sure if it's from tears or just the melting snow, which is soaking into my clothes and making me shiver.

"Come on," says Elliot, taking my hand and pulling me in the direction of the plastic globe, which now stands empty, everyone but us having gotten out of the blizzard. Hand in hand, we run towards it, ducking through the plastic flap that serves as a door and letting it fall shut behind us.

Inside the transparent walls, the snowflakes still float past our heads, but the rest of the world seems to melt away, the sounds of the street outside muffled by the globe, and the lights above the square shimmering softly all around us.

I always thought all of this stuff was fake; just a manufactured attempt to make Christmas feel magical. Right now, though, the magic feels very, very real; and, for the first time in years, I think I might be starting to understand just why people love this time of year so much.

"Are you absolutely sure about this?" Elliot asks, taking me in his arms.

I nod once, and then he kisses me; his lips warm against my cold skin, his arms tight around my waist, holding me safe from the storm outside. He kisses me, and I allow myself to melt into him, everything else fading into the background, until all that's left is me, him, and whatever happens next. It is very much what I think Elsie Poole would call a 'main character moment'. And, as it turns out, I really quite like it.

"I want to write the sequel to your book together," I tell Elliot breathlessly, when we pause for breath at last. "I want to figure out how it ends; even if it's messy and imperfect, and even if some bits of it go wrong and we have to start again."

Elliot smiles, then kisses me again.

"Then that's exactly what we'll do," he says. "We'll figure it out together."

He pulls me in for another kiss, and as I kiss him back, I think about the first time, in the town hall under the mistletoe, and how I thought that these kisses were finite in number; each one just counting down to the last, which was always hovering on the horizon. I thought I needed to protect myself against the moment when they finally ran out, and that if I could just figure out how to do that, I'd never get hurt.

But now I know it doesn't work like that.

And, even if it did, it's a moot point, because I have a feeling these kisses are never going to run out.

This one in particular.

Finally, though, we're forced to pull reluctantly apart, and, when we do, Elliot brushes the hair gently out of my eyes, and we grin stupidly up at each other, laughing at the sheer miracle of us having found our way back to each other again; which, when you really think about it, is the kind of thing that only really happens in stories.

Which I guess is appropriate for us.

Now we just have to figure out what happens next. As we step back outside the snow globe, though, and into a full-blown blizzard, Elliot stops and tilts my face up to his, ignoring the snowstorm as he leans down to drop another kiss on the very tip of my nose.

"It's you," he says, grinning down at me through the falling snow. "It's always been you."

32

It's my first real Christmas in ten years.

It's not *completely* perfect.

I don't have a Christmas tree here at the house, for one thing. There's no food to eat, or crackers to pull, and I never did get around to that last-minute Christmas shopping I kept meaning to do either. So, as Christmases go, I don't think this one would win any prizes.

But this morning I woke up with Elliot for the first time in a decade. The snow that started on Christmas Eve continued throughout the night, which meant we opened the blinds to what I think fully signed-up Christmas people would probably describe as 'a winter wonderland', and which even I have to admit is quite pretty, really.

If you like that kind of thing.

"Happy Christmas," says Elliot, handing me a steaming mug of coffee as I lie in bed, looking out at the snow.

"Happy Christmas."

We clink mugs in a toast, then he climbs back into bed and puts his arm around me as we lie there together, enjoying the tranquility of the scene in front of us. Later, we'll walk over to Dad's place on the other side of the village, where he's announced that we'll be abandoning our now traditional takeaway in favor of a small turkey, cooking instructions for which he claims to have looked up on 'the Google'.

Fortunately, I've got the takeaway's number on speed dial, just in case.

"This is cause for celebration," he said when I called him first thing this morning to ask if I could bring Elliot with me when I called around for dinner later. "I'm making the turkey and opening the good champagne. First, though, I have to call Levi and let him know he owes me £10: he bet me you two would never get your act together."

"I didn't think we would either, to be fair," I laughed. "But here we are. It's a Christmas miracle."

And it honestly feels like it is.

"Seeing as we're bringing partners this year," says Dad, sounding uncharacteristically shy. "I, er, don't suppose you'd mind if I invited Elsie Poole, would you? Not that she's my partner, you understand, I just ... well, I thought she might be lonely, that's all, because Maisie's spending the day with her daughter and —"

"It's fine, Dad," I interrupt, not quite knowing whether to laugh or cry at this news. "Invite her. I'll see you later, okay? Oh, and happy Christmas!"

I put down the phone and sit staring at Elliot with my mouth open.

"I think my dad might be 'courting' Elsie Poole," I manage at last. "And we're going to be having dinner with her."

"Wow. That's one I didn't see coming," says Elliot, his eyebrows raised. "But, I mean, good for him, I guess. At least Elsie will be able to help cushion the blow if we decide to base ourselves in the States."

"Don't." I wince at the thought of Elsie Poole 'cushioning' anything. "This is going to take a bit of getting used to. Quick, say something to distract me. Anything."

"We could split our time between here and Florida," says Elliot, continuing a conversation that started last night, and has continued intermittently ever since. "I know the paperwork would probably be a bit of a pain, but it's not like either of us has a boss to answer to. We're writers. We can work from anywhere we like."

"I think the commute between England and America might be a bit much, don't you?" I reply, snuggling into him and still trying not to think about Dad and Elsie. "Not to mention the visas we'd need. Is it even legal for me to work in America? Or for you to work here?"

"No idea," he says, cheerfully. "We'll add it to the list."

He reaches over and picks up a notebook from the nightstand. Because, like he said, we're writers: of *course* there's an actual list — one we started last night, when we realized we had too many questions to be able to keep track of them all. We've called the list 'Things We Need to Figure Out', and item number one is where we're going to live after Elliot's visa runs out and we have to decide what happens next.

(Item number two is what we should name the dog we're planning to get as soon as we've decided: so far we're thinking Bark Twain for a boy and Virginia Woof for a girl, but we're open to suggestions...)

(Oh, and item # 3 is what the title of the *Snow Globe* sequel should be. We're not going to be starting on that until I've finished writing the book I started as a ghostwriter, but will be finishing under my own name, though: my first real novel. And hopefully not the last.)

But there's plenty of time for all of that.

For now, we have to get dressed and head out into the snow. We have Christmas dinner to eat, Dad's 'good' champagne to drink, and a long conversation to be had with him about the fact that I'm probably not going to be working at the books store any more; although I somehow think that particular bit's going to be a lot easier than it was the first time, considering that he was planning to call Paris as soon as he was done with Levi, to offer her my job.

It would be fair to say that a lot has changed since the last time Elliot and I were together.

It would also be fair to say that there are even more changes to come; some of them exciting, but some of them low key petrifying, as Paris would say.

"I never thought I'd say it," I tell Elliot as we wrap ourselves up in coats and scarves, ready to brave the walk to Dad's place. "But I think I would miss it here if I left for good. I know that's all I've ever talked about since I was young, but, I don't know. It's like, I still want to see the world, but…"

"But this will always be home?" Elliot finishes for me. "That makes sense. It's a pretty cool place. I loved it too, from the moment I got here. But I guess that's the beauty of having a job that doesn't tie you to a particular place. You can move around. Try out different places for size. And you can do it knowing you can always come home if you want to. It'll always be here for you."

"The best of both worlds," I reply, thinking of the two snow globes, which are currently sitting side by side on the mantelpiece in my living room. "I like the sound of that."

I take his hand, and we step out together into the snow.

"Oh, I forgot to mention," I tell him, breathing in the sharp, December air. "When I was talking to Dad earlier he said he'd been speaking to Martin's mum, and she told him Martin's leaving town after Christmas. It was a very sudden decision, apparently. She didn't know quite what to make of it."

"Um, I think I might know something about that," Elliot replies, his cheeks reddening slightly. "I, er, might have popped in to see him yesterday morning. Not long before you did, in fact."

"Really? What did you say to him?"

I glance up at him curiously, trying to imagine mild-mannered Elliot confronting Martin, and running him out of town. It doesn't seem possible. And yet...

"Well, let's just say I'm not surprised he decided to leave," says Elliot grimly. "I can be rather ... persuasive ... when I want to be."

"Right. Well, whatever you said, it obviously did the trick," I say, impressed by this new, commanding version of the man who was once too scared to tell his dad he didn't want to join the family business. "At least we won't have to worry about bumping into him around town now."

"Exactly."

Elliot squeezes my hand, and we make our way cautiously down the hill.

"We're definitely getting a Christmas tree next year," I say as the village square comes into view, the decorated tree rising up in the middle of it.

"Not a sad little raggedy one like last time, though?" replies Elliot, with a grin.

"Oh, definitely a sad little raggedy one. I'm going to get the most unloved tree on the farm. And then I'm going to decorate it to the nines, and cover it with lights, until it's the happiest little Christmas tree in all the land."

"That's quite the turnaround," laughs Elliot. "Maybe we'll make a Christmas person of you yet."

"Maybe we will," I reply, grinning as I stand on my tiptoes to kiss him in front of the once-hated plastic snow globe that now deserves its very own brass plaque declaring it the spot of Holly and Elliot's *second* first kiss. "I really think I'm starting to like it. I have to admit, it's pretty romantic, really."

"They certainly seem to think so," says Elliot, nodding in the direction of a young couple who've just appeared from the direction of the bookstore. As we watch, the man reaches out to take his partner's hand, and ...

"Oh my God."

"Isn't that ...?"

Elliot and I watch in astonishment as Levi and Paris go strolling off together, pausing only so that Levi can aim a quick kick at the wheel of Martin's parked car as he walks past it.

"Okay, now *that's* a Christmas miracle," I say, once I've regained the power of speech. "And here was I thinking Dad and Elsie would be the biggest plot twist of the day. Or of my *life*, really."

"It's a real enemies-to-lovers arc," agrees Elliot. "We should make a note of it for the book after the Snow Globe sequel."

"I've been thinking about that, actually," I tell him as we resume our walk towards the house Dad bought when he moved out of the flat and rented it to Paris. (And also Levi, it would now appear. No,

I'm definitely going to need a *lot* more time to get used to this...) "The next book. I was thinking I'd like to write about Mum. I don't know what, yet, but she was a bookworm, like me. She would have loved the idea of being part of a story."

Elliot looks down at me, his eyes soft.

"I never got to meet your mom," he says. "But I think she would be so proud of you, Holly. I really do. The bookstore, your writing ... *you*. I mean, *I'm* proud of you, so I reckon she'd be about fit to burst if she could see you now."

"Especially if she knew I'd worn this red sweater because it's the closest thing I have to a Christmas jumper," I reply, somehow managing not to start crying at this, even though I *really* want to. "She'd have loved that, for sure."

"Next year we'll buy you a real one," Elliot says, wrapping his arm tightly around me. "One with, like, an elf on it. Or a snowman."

"And we'll put fairy lights around the house," I add. "Wherever it ends up being."

"We'll drink eggnog."

"And watch *It's a Wonderful Life*."

We smile up at each other. Next year, everything will be different. For now, though, we've reached the end of Dad's street, which is quiet and sleepy, with just a handful of people outside — kids playing with the new toys they got for Christmas, and adults out for a walk. As we walk, I think about all of the people that came before them, and all of the other Christmases they've celebrated. Evie and Luke, crunching their way through the snow on their way to a dance at the town hall. Mum, laughing as she pulls me up the hill on a sledge, just so she can watch me slide right back down, before asking if I can do it again.

All of the ghosts of Christmas past.

But now it's time to take them all with us into some yet to be written future. All the people we've lost: their laughter, their smiles, and all of the weird, wonderful, and totally random things they did. I hold all of their stories inside me; and when I write them down, they'll no longer feel like ghosts.

THE END

If you liked the book can I ask you kindly to leave me a rating on Amazon? As a self published author this would mean so much to me.

Also if you turn the page you can read the first chapter of my next book for free.

Chapter 1

Everyone has a theme song.

Oh, come on; don't try to tell me you don't know what I'm talking about. Don't pretend you haven't danced around your bedroom with a hairbrush for a mic, singing like no one's watching. Or run for the bus in the rain, secretly imagining you're in the opening scenes of a movie; your wet hair cascading dramatically down your back while the music plays and the credits roll. In that moment, you're not just some random woman who's going to be a few minutes late to her boring admin job if she misses that bus; you're the Main Character — and you have your very own theme song to prove it.

And so do I. Except, in my case, the song in question doesn't just play *in my head*; it plays everywhere I go.

And I *hate* it.

"Hey, Lana! Listen to this!"

As if to prove the point, my friend Angelina reaches over the top of the bar and cranks up the volume on the radio that's playing there.

"It's your song," she beams, as the opening bars of *Bikini* boom out across the little taverna, and I slap my hands quickly over my ears as if I can block it out that way, even though I know from bitter experience that I can't. And trust me — I've tried.

Just like everyone else, I have a theme song.

Unlike everyone else I know, though, *my* theme song is a song I wrote thirteen years ago ... and which was stolen from me by the man I hate more than anyone else in the world; the same man who went on to become famous from it, while I just ended up feeling like I'm being *stalked* by it.

Sometimes life *really* isn't fair.

"It's not *my* song, Angel," I remind her, wrinkling my nose in protest as the voice of Leo Wilde fills the night air, making people pause their conversations and look up from their moussaka. Leo tends to have that kind of effect on people.

He would.

"It's *not* my song," I repeat, as Angel turns the volume up another notch, taking advantage of her status as the owner's granddaughter to do whatever she likes, as usual. "I hate this song, remember? And I've heard it at least twenty times today already."

I pout, looking out over the terrace to where the sea is lapping gently against the shore, the normally soothing rhythm of the waves completely drowned out by the sound of the Brit-pop boy band floating down from the taverna.

Okay, *twenty times* is possibly an exaggeration; but only a very slight one.

Bikini was the song that woke me up this morning, blasting out of the old-fashioned radio alarm I'd set as a backup, just in case my phone died in the night and I missed my flight. It was playing in the taxi on the way to Edinburgh airport, and then again over the speaker in the departure lounge. It was the first thing I heard when I boarded the plane — and that made it the *last* thing I heard before I put on my noise-canceling headphones in a bid to block it out.

(Pro tip for anyone else who finds themselves in the oddly specific situation of being stalked by a song they wrote years ago, but didn't get the credit for; *yes*, it's worth splashing out on the expensive headphones...)

It's almost as if I'm being *haunted* by it, really.

"D'you think you can be haunted by a song?" I ask Angel, accepting the glass of ouzo she hands me, even though the stuff makes my eyes water. Well, when in Greece, and all that.

"Like an ear worm, you mean?"

"No, more like a stalker. A really, really determined one. The kind that stands outside your front door for hours so they can give you a picture they made of you from their toenail clippings."

"*Bikini* isn't *stalking* you, Lana," Angel says, downing her own drink in one. "And that's a really disgusting visual, by the way. It's just super-popular, that's all. You're going to have to get used to hearing it, *agapi mou*. Especially here."

I sip my drink and give an involuntary grimace. Angel's right. If there's anywhere I should expect to hear *Bikini* — or any of the other songs from The Wilde Boys' debut album — it would be right here on the island, wouldn't it?

This *is* the place I wrote it, after all ... and the place Leo stole it from me.

Not that Angel knows *that* bit, of course.

No, the only person who knows that a vaguely uptight teacher from Edinburgh wrote one of the biggest hits of the last decade is *me* — and, of course, Leo Wilde himself.

And, in the absence of any proof to the contrary, that's how it's going to stay.

Unfortunately for me.

Angel goes to serve a customer, and I treat myself to a sneaky spin on my bar stool, just like I used to do when I came here as a kid.

The taverna's had at least one lick of paint in the decade or more since I last saw it, and someone's strung fairy lights up over the wooden terrace that forms the outdoor seating area, to make it a bit more Instagrammable, but it's otherwise unchanged. I can even see a photo of me and Angel, aged about 12 or 13 (She's got her tongue out and I've got both eyes closed: standard...), pinned up on the wall behind the bar, surrounded by dozens of other snapshots, all depicting happy holiday-makers in various states of inebriation.

I look quickly away before I can see the one of Leo Wilde and his band mates that I know's up there somewhere, too. It's bad enough that I have to hear his voice everywhere I go; I don't want to have to *see* the guy, too — which makes me quite possibly the only single, straight woman in the world who *doesn't*.

Get out of my head, Leo Wilde. You definitely don't belong there.

"Okay, okay," Angel huffs, seeing the look on my face as the final chorus of *Bikini* kicks in. "I'll put on something else if it'll stop you making that face at me."

She ducks behind the bar and starts fiddling with the radio, which is almost as old as she is, and which spits out a bunch of static, before finally finding a new station.

Which is *also* playing *Bikini*.

Of *course* it is.

"Okay, that's it," I say, throwing my hands up in a way I know is overly-dramatic, but which feels like the only fitting response to being haunted by your own song. "I'm out. I'm going to head back to the beach house to unpack."

"Oh, come *on*, Lana," Angelina says, pouting. "You just got here. I haven't seen you for *years*. You can't run off again before Yiayia even has the chance to feed you. You know how seriously she takes food."

"I know."

I smile at my friend. I haven't seen Angel since we were teenagers, but, before that, we spent every summer together, right here on the island she grew up on, and which my parents first visited on their honeymoon, and then almost every year since; to the point that they ended up buying their very own beach house here, rather than wasting money on hotels.

Well, what can I tell you? I guess we Lawsons are creatures of habit; or, as my sister Eden would have it, "Really freaking boring."

"Look, it's not because of the song," I lie, knowing perfectly well that it's *totally* because of the song. "I'm just tired. It's been a long day.

And I need to call Mum and Dad and give them a status report on the house. They'll be waiting to hear from me."

"I can't believe they're actually selling it," Angel replies, her brow creasing under her heavy fringe. (At some point in the years since I last saw her, it seems Angel has grown her hair and started wearing makeup. It suits her, but it's taking a bit of getting used to, given that the last time I saw her she had a short bob and was occasionally mistaken for her twin brother, Atlas; and, on one occasion, her uncle, Costas. I'm pretty sure the woman who said that was just being mean, though.)

"I know," I say again, quickly arranging my face into what I hope is an appropriately mournful expression. "It's... well, it's *sad*."

"It's more than just 'sad', Lana," Angel says, eyes widening in protest at the inadequacy of the word. "Think of all the summers you've spent here. The Easter breaks. That Christmas when you cried because you were expecting it to be as hot as it was in August. Think of the *memories*."

She gestures to the photo wall behind her, and, of course, her waving hand just so happens to land right on the one photo I've been trying to avoid, forcing me to look at it, in the same way my so-called theme-song demands to be listened to. Repeatedly. Until I want to cry.

It's just as silly to be scared of a photo as it is to be haunted by a song, though, and I am nothing if not sensible (Or, again, *boring,* according to Eden...), so I flex my shoulders, like an aging boxer limbering up for his last big fight, and stare right at it, just to prove I can; to rob it of its power, if you like.

And there they are. The Wilde Boys, all lined up in front of the taverna, the summer they became famous.

The summer Leo Wilde casually ruined my life.

My shoulders drop in defeat.

Round one to Leo; already looking like the golden boy he became in his photo, even though I know perfectly well that his soul's as black as the center of the volcano this island sprung from.

"I didn't think they'd ever sell it either," I reply, realizing Angel's still waiting for a response. I twist around in my seat so The Wilde Boys are no longer in my line of sight. "But Eden's baby's due any day now, and you know what Eden's like; she's got absolutely nothing ready for it. Mum and Dad are going to need all the money they can get to help her out."

"I can't believe Eden's old enough to have a baby," Angel replies, attempting to pour herself some more ouzo and spilling most of it on the bar. "Isn't she, like, 12, or something?"

"She's 28," I reply, my fingers tightening around my glass. "It's ... well, it's been a while, hasn't it?"

A wave of nausea hits me; jet lag, or nostalgia, or something else I can't quite name, but which I know is somehow connected to the song, and the photo, and being back here on the island after all this time.

"Sorry, Angel," I say, feigning a yawn, "But I really am knackered. Rain check?"

"Rain check," she confirms, her hug as warm as ever, although I can tell by her eyes that she's worried about me.

I'm used to people worrying about me, though. And coming back here was supposed to be a way to escape that; a fresh start, of sorts, even though I can't help feeling like I'm going backwards to go forwards. So I plaster on my brightest, fakest smile, and tell Angel I'll definitely get drunk with her tomorrow, before wandering the short distance across the soft white sand to where the beach house sits waiting for me, a single light shining out from one of the windows, as if it's beckoning me home.

Although the front of the house faces onto the street, the back door — which is the one we always used — opens straight onto the beach, with just a little wooden deck separating the house from the sand. Unlike the taverna, the villa *hasn't* had much in the way of TLC over the last few years, but the white-painted exterior and blue shutters are comfortingly familiar, and the spray of purple bougainvillea trailing down from the upstairs balcony brings an unexpected lump to my throat; as does the 'for sale' board sticking out of the sand.

(At least, I'm *assuming* that's what the Greek words on the board say: it was Angel's Uncle Costas who put it there, though, so there's every chance it *actually* says something like 'Bite me' or 'Your Mom', or whatever English/American insult is Costas's current favorite. Note to self: double-check that tomorrow…)

Inside, my suitcase sits in the middle of the living room, where I left it when I arrived, and the house still has its distinctive scent of salt air and sunscreen. I know in a couple of days I'll stop noticing the smell, but for now it turns the house into a time-capsule, transporting me back through the years until I'm ten years old, stepping through the door for the first time; then 19, and leaving for what I was sure would be the last.

But now I'm back.

Which feels all kinds of strange, really, even without all of the *memories*, as Angel would have it. It's weird being here on my own, when I've only ever stayed here with Mum, Dad, and Eden. I don't like feeling like *I'm* the responsible adult in this situation, when, in my head, I'm still only about 14, and up past my bedtime.

I distract myself from that thought by dragging my suitcase up to the bedroom that used to be mine, which is at the front of the house, with white painted walls and a colorful patchwork quilt on the little single bed. We only used to come here in the school holidays, so there are no posters on the walls or clothes draped around to make me feel like I'm sleeping in my childhood bedroom again. All the same, though, I still find myself glancing over my shoulder, almost as if the ghost of my younger self is about to come marching in to throw herself on the bed and complain about how *mean* everyone is to her.

Which, to be honest, I still feel like doing sometimes.

I move around the room, methodically unpacking my stuff, and doing my best to ignore the painful little pangs of memory that keep poking me in the chest every time I find something from Back Then. Like the pile of books on the bedside table, which I quickly flick through, part of me hoping my song book will be among them — that I somehow just left it behind, as opposed to having it snatched out of my fingers and carried off before my eyes — or the little carved wooden statue of Eros I bought from Costas's short-lived market stall one year, and which makes the God of Love look a lot like Jabba the Hut.

Right at the back of one of the drawers, though, my fingers close around something soft and slippery, and I pull it out to reveal a tiny red bikini, which I drop as if I've been stung by it.

*Not just **a** bikini: **the** bikini — the one I was wearing that last day.*
*But I'm not going to think about **that**, am I?*
Well, not any more than I have been almost every second since I got here, anyway.

I stuff the offending swimwear back into the drawer, then finally, with nothing else left to do, I pour myself a glass of wine to calm the nerves that started jangling at the sight of that triangle top and side-tie bottoms, and wander out onto the balcony, where the soft breeze lifts my long hair off my neck, and the sound of an acoustic guitar floats through the air from the direction of the house next door, making me cross my fingers and hope I'm not going to be forced to listen to *Bikini* again.

For the love of Eros, anything but that...

The house in question is the one Leo and his band mates stayed in, that last summer, before anyone knew how big they were about to become. It was the island's main claim to fame, actually; there was even some talk of erecting a plaque outside, declaring it to be the birthplace of *Bikini* at one point, but then, a few years ago, someone bought it, and knocked the whole place down, before putting up a glossy, glass-fronted cube in the place where the traditional, stone-built cottage used to stand.

Take that, Leo Wilde and your stupid plaque.

The guitarist is still strumming away, and I sip my wine, allowing my soul to be soothed by the sound. Then he switches to a different tune, and it's like that moment when the needle scratches on a record.

No.

Please let me be imagining this. Please let me have fallen asleep on the plane, and be dreaming right now.

*Or... or **dead**, maybe? Because being dead would be preferable to this, too.*

It's not *Bikini*, but I know this song, too. Pretty damn well, in fact. I know this song because I *wrote* this song; or a fragment of it, at least.

It was one of the many little tunes I'd scribbled down in my notebook, having painstakingly picked out the notes on my piano back home, going over them again and again, until the melody was more or less imprinted on my brain.

I wrote this song.

I know I did. I remember it as clearly as if it just happened; as if I've only just closed the book and placed it on top of the piano, pen carefully tucked inside it, ready for the next time inspiration hit; which, in this case, it never did. So the melody was incomplete (as most of them were, back then) ... but it was *mine*.

And now here it is, being played by some random rich guy with a big house and a guitar.

This can't be happening.

Not **again**.

It must be the ouzo. Or the jet-lag. Yes, that'll be it; I just need some sleep to make all of this go away.

But as the notes of the song come floating through the still-warm air of the Mediterranean night, louder now, as the singer gains confidence, I know that not even Angel's extra-strong ouzo has the power to make me think some stranger on a beach can be playing *my* song.

Which means there's only one person in the world this so-called 'stranger' can be — and he's the very last man I expected to see here.

It's Leo Wilde.

Find out what happens on Amazon

https://www.amazon.com/dp/B0FBJXDHMV/

Hi, I'm Amber Eve! I write romantic comedies filled with heart, humor, and happily-ever-afters. My stories are all about relatable women, unexpected love, and the messy, magical journey to finding your person—usually with a few laughs (and mishaps) along the way. I live in Scotland, which is where most of my small-town romances are set. If you love feel-good stories with warmth, wit, and a big dose of romance, I hope you'll enjoy spending time in my imaginary worlds.

You can keep up to date with my life and novels here: foreveramber.co.uk

Printed in Dunstable, United Kingdom